CARTILAGE AND SKIN

CARTILAGE AND SKIN

A novel by

Michael James Rizza

Starcherone Books   Buffalo, NY

ISBN: 978-1-938603-18-1
e-book ISBN 978-1-938603-19-8

General Editor: Ted Pelton
Cover Designer: Julian Montague
Cover Photograph: Mark Hillringhouse
Book Designer: Rebecca Maslen
Proofreaders: Jason Pontillo and Sarah Kinne

The first chapter of *Cartilage and Skin* was performed at
Playwrights Theatre in Madison, New Jersey. An excerpt also
appeared in Atticus Books Online.

State of the Arts

NYSCA

This book is made possible with public
funds from the New York State Council
for the Arts, a state agency. Starcherone
Books thanks the Council and New York
State taxpayers for this support.

Table of Contents

For My Brothers

Carmen, Joe, and Dave

"But the infant had survived, by nursing from her corpse."

—Thomas Pynchon, *Gravity's Rainbow*

PART ONE:

CARTILAGE AND SKIN

I was coming down the hall behind him, when my landlord paused before a door and rapped two times, hard, with the butt of his palm.

"Claudia," he called, leaning his head near the door. "Claudia."

Then he turned toward me and smiled. He was a short, balding man with tiny black eyes, like a rodent's.

"She never gets her mail, so now the guy just leaves it on the floor."

He walked a little farther and held up a set of keys, which I took out of his hand.

"If you're bringing in your things, don't prop the main door open," he said. "Also, I saw you give money to that kid outside. It's not a good idea."

"This is all I got for now."

Looking down at my suitcase, he smiled again.

I watched him as he started down the hall. When he came to Claudia's door, he knocked once more and looked back at me, still with that smile on his face.

"A gross woman," he said. "It's hard for me to even look at her."

"Thank you," I said, and he nodded.

It wasn't long before I had the little boy, "that kid outside," fetching me coffee each morning from a store around the corner. I'd give him two dollars, and he'd pocket the change of course. Poverty had affected him in its natural way, turning him into a selfish thing that would grab at whatever it could, a quiet and secretive miscreant who would no more trust you with his name than show you the contents of his pockets. I had little concern for him because I was sure that he'd already rooted through and made his home out of the darkest and deepest city hole. It wasn't his youth, but rather something quirky in his gestures and sharp in his hazel eyes, that made me suspect he was unlike other boys who would hang out in bathrooms and on doorsteps, waiting for some nameless man to come along and buy their sex. A man warped enough to take that little boy to bed probably wouldn't have returned him too readily or in a condition too recognizable or whole. My landlord began to hate me on account of the boy.

I came into the hallway and stood my dripping umbrella against the wall, so I could look through my mail. Since I had fallen into the routine of picking up Claudia Jones's mail and slipping it under her door, the mailman began putting her mail into my box. Her most regular correspondent was somebody named W. McTeal, who never gave a return address. The day my landlord confronted me about the boy, McTeal had sent a manila envelope, marked "Photos. Do Not Bend." I was holding the envelope up to the light, when my landlord appeared on the staircase.

"Dr. Parker," he said as he leaned his stomach against the banister. "I need a favor of you."

"What's that?"

"I need you to stop encouraging that boy. He lingers around the building all day, and I don't want it. I'm sure you know what I'm talking about."

I nodded.

"I don't want that kind of element on my front steps," he said.

"He gets me coffee."

"I don't care what he does for you."

"That's what he does."

"Be that as it may—"

"No," I said, taking up my umbrella. "I don't like what you're implying."

"Understand my position, Dr. Parker. I don't want that element."

"I understand." I stepped forward and tapped my umbrella on the floor, to underscore my words. "Now understand me. I don't care for your position."

I turned my back to him and started down the hall.

"Dr. Parker," he said, but I continued forward. "I thought you had some morals."

Without a word, I casually opened my door, taking my time, all the while aware that his rodent eyes were on me. My mail, along with Claudia's, was tucked under my arm.

"Dr. Parker," he said, with something imploring and warm in his voice, which I didn't trust.

Although I had enough troubles not to worry about my landlord, I couldn't let the issue rest, so I began to hire the boy for other odd tasks. I would let him go to the convenience store for me and buy something, whether I needed the item or not. One time, on another rainy day, I came out of the front doors of the building and before I was ten paces into my errand, the boy was walking beside me, his dark hair matted to his wet head.

"I don't need you," I said.

"Where you going?"

"To the library."

"Give me a dollar." He held out his hand.

"I don't need you."

"Give me a dollar."

"No." I stopped and held the umbrella over his head.

"What book do you want?"

"No."

"Come on," he said, still holding out his hand.

I made the mistake of giving the boy a dollar he didn't earn, just so I could say, "Now get out of here." Somehow, at that moment, although I didn't recognize it then, a new dynamic entered into our relationship; the power roles shifted just a bit. When the boy began knocking on my living room window, instead of waiting on the front steps of the building or across the street, I only saw his need for my generosity. Without realizing that he was overstepping his bounds, I'd hand him money through the open window. I even started to think that it was convenient that I didn't have to leave my apartment, but simply raise the blinds and open the window.

There was an alley outside my window, where some tenants hung their clothes on a pair of drooping lines. For the three months since I'd first rented the apartment, I would only see an overweight, middle-aged woman with a weathered face and bright red fingernails. If I opened my window, I was able to hear her humming Christmas carols, though the season was far off. I would watch her through the blinds as she lifted each garment out of her basket and gave it a brisk snap, before putting it on the line. *This must be Claudia Jones*, I thought. She had dark eyes, set deep into her face, and a fat tongue that rested continually on her bottom lip. I remembered that my landlord had called Claudia "a gross woman," and this woman surely looked idiotic, if not gross. Watching her, I soon came to believe that it was out of stupidity, and not indifference, that her mail went so neglected.

The manila envelope from McTeal was the first of several pieces of Claudia's mail that I began piling on the corner of my desk. As I have hinted, I took the first piece by accident because my landlord had distracted me. I would like to say that I began collecting more of her mail simply as a sort of ransom, maybe as something that might have called her out of her apartment and made her acknowledge the living.

The truth, however, is that I found a strange pleasure in the theft, the kind of pleasure found in vandalism: Sin for sin's sake, perhaps, where nothing is gained but a little sense of power, of the standing beyond good and evil. Interestingly, this petty violation of Claudia paralleled the boy's intrusion into my life. In fact, the day the boy first knocked on my window was the same day I picked up the manila envelope, which had sat untouched on my desk for several weeks, and opened it.

W. McTeal was a hairy man with a pocked face and thin wire frame glasses that sat at the very tip of his aquiline nose. He had a tuft of hair on the small of his back and a rotund stomach that seemed to be as hard as bone. He gave me the impression—whenever he leaned back against the headboard and planted his feet flat on the mattress, with his knees apart and his penis sleeping lifelessly on his thigh—that he was trying to give birth to something. His most absurd posture was apparently his favorite: He would get on his hands and knees, and point his ass toward you, always with his face between his thighs, peeping past his stomach, looking puzzled for some reason. The only part of his home that I knew was a sliver of his bedroom, simply a straight-on view of his bed and the wall behind it. The wall was barren, a plain off-white that told me nothing about the man. Because he was always naked, I wasn't able to make any judgment from his clothing. He had two sets of bed sheets, one aquamarine and the other light brown, which he would change about once a week. As bizarre as it might sound, he obsessed me for a while; I looked forward to getting the mail, just to see what new pictures he'd sent to Claudia.

I began an elaborate character study of him, although he offered me no more to build upon than silly poses of himself. Obviously, the ruling question, the key to the man, was why would he send these pictures to the idiot woman, who didn't seem to care about them at all. His skin tone, facial features, and the shape of his head suggested to me that "W. McTeal" was surely not Irish, but probably Mediterranean.

Possessed as I was, I ignored my work for a while and spent my time trying to discover a clue in his pseudonym. The fact that a teal is a short-necked wild duck helped me in no way, so I played with anagrams. Considering the pictures, I found something in "cwt. meal," namely that the man regarded himself as a hundred pounds of meat. This failed on a literal level because the man was clearly over a hundred pounds and cannibalism didn't seem likely—but in all probability he was speaking figuratively, as well as hyperbolically, about his penis, his hundred pound meal. Although it was fascinating to consider what kind of person would have such an exaggerated perspective, I ended up dismissing this anagram because he seemed more interested in his ass than in his sleepy penis, fellatio precluded. I arranged and rearranged the letters, and the only idea that made sense in the end was "wet clam." I don't need to say what thoughts followed this discovery, what threads of speculation dressed the man.

The central question still remained: Why the idiot woman?

It was early July when I opened my window a crack to listen to her hum. She was bovine to the bone, moving slowly, stooping over her basket—then with sudden deftness—snapping out this or that garment and putting it on the line. When she finished, she stayed with her clothes to watch them dry and presumably to guard them from thieves. She sat on a turned-over milkcrate and hummed "What Child Is This?" Because she stared blankly toward the street, I saw no reason to continue watching her.

I went back to my desk and booted up my computer, figuring that I should get some work done. I had enough personal troubles and didn't need to worry about my neighbors. After a while, Claudia's humming became a soft noise in the background. I was reworking a paragraph in my manuscript and suspected that I had misquoted a source. The book was on the nightstand beside my bed, so I left my desk to get it. When I came back, the humming was stopped and the blinds were scraping back and forth over the windowsill. I was terrified for a moment, standing dumbly, feeling inexplicably vulnerable and powerless. Then I was at the window. The alley was empty; the bovine idiot and her clothes were gone.

I shut the window and locked it. My apartment seemed foreign to me as I turned and scanned it, although nothing looked out of place. Claudia's mail was still on the desk, my wallet still on top of the television. Soon I was giving my apartment a thorough search, thinking that maybe the boy had snuck in; lately he had been asking if he could watch my television and use my bathroom. But I was alone; nothing vile was coiled up in some dark corner; no monster crouched in the closet. The feeling of unease, though subsiding, didn't completely leave me. That night I lay in bed, feeling a bit displaced, wondering what had moved the blinds. I was certain that someone would have been in my home, standing among my belongings, violating my valuables with lustful looks and grubby fingers, if I hadn't been there.

The rest of the summer was a difficult period for me. Through a series of small misfortunes and an instance of bad timing, my social life began a slow decay, with every cherished piece turning color and falling off like a leprous appendage. As a result, my manuscript suffered. My home, however—where the boy would run up and down the street with a few other kids; my landlord would barely give me a passing nod in the hallway; my bloated-tongued neighbor, with or without laundry on the line, would sit on the milkcrate in the alley and hum; and the mystery man, though now with a unexpected welt on his ass cheek, would still look confusedly though his spread legs—entered into a holding period, a welcomed block of banality.

Sometime in late August, on a muggy evening when the sewers smelled a little more pungent than usual, I decided to take action, to force the moment to its crisis, to shake off a kind of prufrockian paralysis. I had just finished a long distance call to my mother, who had encouraged me to try to regain my social standing. I splashed water on my face and then looked at myself for a long time in the bathroom mirror. My face seemed so waxen that I thought if I pressed my thumbs into my flesh, they'd leave imprints. A recent bout with insomnia was rending my nerves. Although I was resolved to phone a man named Morris, I procrastinated by practicing what I would say, needing to get my tone, as well as my words, correct. But the actual sound of his voice asking, "What can I do for you?" with a flat, distant calmness, as if he were talking to a lamppost or a chew-toy for a dog, made me start to babble. I needed someone to understand my perspective, and Morris—with his thoughtful nod and his lazy gaze like a dream-struck lover—hadn't completely turned on me. He was an empathetic man, well-respected in my circle of friends and colleagues. In fact, it was the sage Morris who had recommended that I get my own apartment, so I'd have the time and peace not only to devote to my manuscript but also to give the sore spots in my life a chance to heal. But mine was a chronic and leprous condition. I'm certain that as I talked to him on the phone, he smelled the festering rot; he knew that I needed him. I was pathetic; I pleaded, agreeing with him at every turn. He had helped me once before, yes, found me an apartment, yes, stuck by me when I was ousted, yes, my only friend, yes. In the end, he conceded to meet me for coffee, perhaps just to see what I had become or if anything left in me was worth saving. Before he hung up the phone, almost as an afterthought, he told me to bring the manuscript. He knew that a man's labor was an unbearable burden if it had no purpose and no one even cared to glance at it. Such a simple comment made my heart swell with hope.

Even so, on this muggy night, in sewer reek and subway steam rising though grates to the sidewalk, I abruptly stopped walking and disregarded Morris. Suddenly, I didn't care that he was waiting for me in a coffee shop. I couldn't care. I was willing to lose my last connection to society. Perhaps my soul swooned, my poordjeli jouissanced, all at the sight of a young woman bending over to tie her sneaker. The elegance of her spine, the curve of her haunches, the liquid ease of her fingers among the laces, and the smooth outline, in the lamplight, of crease and crevice beneath her khaki shorts, was its own promise of life, of regeneration, of a hope that didn't depend upon my degradation and another's grace.

My Lord, may Morris rot in pieces.

Although I knew the street was otherwise empty, I gave a quick look around to make sure no one saw me staring so conspicuously at the woman. For my pleasure, when she made her nice little bow, she shifted her weight, put her other foot forward, untied and then re-tied that sneaker. Because I am more of a tactilian than a voyeur, I found myself stepping closer, wanting to get on my knees, on a dog's level, and breathe her in. She straightened up and looked back at me. I nodded and walked past her, as if I had been walking all along and had just approached her at that moment.

I listened to her footfalls behind me, thinking that even her face was pretty, though in truth it looked haggard, with hollow cheeks and bleary eyes. I slowed my pace, until she was walking closer. Then, when it sounded as if she were right on my heels, ready to pass by me, I stopped. Her fingers brushed my back, her form slipped around me, and she continued on. Her words were gritty, as if her voice were scarred and scratched: "Excuse me."

I dropped my manuscript.

"Watch it," I snapped.

She paused and looked back at the manuscript at my feet. Then she lifted her gaze to my face. She appeared as if she were looking at some grotesque deformity, a glistening knot of cartilage and skin.

"You watch it," she said.

I was hoping that she would have apologized and maybe even have picked up the manuscript, but she gave me one last snarl and briskly started walking away.

"Bitch," I called.

The word stopped her. She turned back around and pointed one of her lovely fingers at me.

"What did you say?" she asked. "What did you say to me?"

I stood dumbstruck for an instant, fearing this delicate girl with her raspy voice and gaunt face.

"Bitch," I said, a little more sheepishly than I would have liked.

When she leapt at me like a lunatic feline with lithe limbs and a pair of claws, I flinched, covering my head with my arms. She hit me in the chest with both hands, pushing me off the curb and into the street. After an instant of cowering, I realized the assault was over, and watched the woman walk away. A car with a rash of rust came sickly down the street; one of its back wheels was in miniature, like an atrophied limb. The woman glanced at the car when it passed her, heading toward Walnut Street, only a few blocks away. I felt a little defeated, not because the woman had struck me, but because she was leaving. I was about to call out "Bitch!" sort of as a final effort to make contact again, but an unexpected sight buoyed my spirit; the woman had my manuscript tucked under her arm. Of course, I chased after her.

Given my long legs and lanky stride, I assumed I could have caught the woman easily and resumed our little struggle. But she glanced back at me and began to run as if overtaken by frantic and dire urgency, her elegant form completely abandoned to spastic motion. I ran, shouting out "Whore!" and "Bitch!" thinking that I would catch her soon, and then what? Wrestle her to the sidewalk? Grapple in the street? Yet the distance between us grew. The little thing was out-running me. Panting, I lost sight of her somewhere around Walnut and Broad Street. I sat on the curb to relax for a moment. The sultry August air coated my skin.

That night I wandered around the city for a couple of hours in hope of seeing the young woman again. I played our entire encounter over in my head, and I realized that her bizarre behavior made sense if she had known that I had been gawking at her from behind. Only when I walked past the coffee shop, did I remember that I had ignored Morris. I was amused by the idea that he had waited for me and gotten more frustrated by the moment. Most likely, he'd suspected that I had intentionally snubbed him, given one last insult, some spit in the eye. I happily accepted the role of bastard and artificer. There were more groups of people in the world than the one that had rejected me. Let them rot. My new feeling of liberation, of unconcern, of I-will-no-longer-be-fixed-sprawling-on-a-pin-like-a-lifeless-bug, was mildly subdued by the fact that the woman had stolen my manuscript: two years of work tucked irreverently under her arm.

At home, in bed, I lay on my stomach, my forearms on my pillow, and read a freshly printed copy of my manuscript. The thing was so recondite, each page laden with erudite jargon and convoluted with tortuous syntax, that I doubted the woman with her wasted countenance that hinted at mental anguish or physical addiction, did anything more than glance at the first page, find it abstruse, flip to the center, find that frustrating, and then in a final vindication of her self-esteem against my leering eyes that had reduced her to mindless meat, to the juice in my jouissance, she closed my manuscript, and with too much indifference to take the time to set it aflame or tear it to confetti, she simply dropped it into a garbage can or pushed it off into some corner to collect dust.

By September, the young woman had fully seeped into my fantasies. She was the skirt-clad student in the front row, who crossed and re-crossed her spindle-legs, with a flash of auburn floss. She caught my eye and gave me an insidious smile that unraveled my thoughts. Then after class, when everyone else had filed out the door, she was leaning across my desk, pointing to a page in the book she needed explained. No sooner had I begun to talk than her little hand with its chewed back fingernails made a furtive disappearance under the desk. *You like that, Professor?* She was also the neighbor bending over her laundry basket. When she had all her sheets hanging from the line, forming a thin curtain, I glanced back at the busy street, before stepping through the sheets. I approached her from behind and cupped my hands over her small, nubile breasts. She rubbed up against me as she squirmed to free herself. Then yielding to lust, she was bending over her basket, and I was getting onto my knees. She was also the miscreant spread out in a heap of rags on a doorstep. I gathered her into my arms and carried her tired body home, where I bathed her, kissed her bruises, and nursed her soul. One evening I found her framed in my bedroom doorway. She was backlit and dressed in nothing but a white button-down shirt that she'd borrowed from my closet. Without a word, she took a hesitant step forward as I propped myself up on one elbow to squint at her. Then, like a scared child, she scrambled into my bed, to be held throughout the purple hours of the evening.

In late September, this last fantasy somehow coincided with—either slightly prior to or after—my discovery of the boy, my little hazel-eyed errand-runner, hugging his knees on the front steps of my building. It was dusk and rush hour. Because of road construction somewhere in the tight city grid, every car with wheels was rerouted down my narrow road. They crept along, windows open, each playing its own song on the radio. I felt as though I were on display and that everyone was driving past my building to watch me act out the scene with the boy. Both of his knees were a tender red, and his eyes, usually alert and agile, now looked as if they'd been smudged by grimy thumbs. The pallor of his face told me that he hadn't slept for days or that he was very sick.

"What's the matter?" I asked.

"What?" He lifted his head and looked at me.

"Are you sick?"

"My stomach. I got to throw-up."

"Are you faking it?"

"I got to throw-up."

I glanced back at the busy road as I mounted the steps and opened the front door.

"You better not be faking it," I said.

The boy watched me holding the door open for a moment, before he realized what I intended, and got to his feet. He walked before me in the corridor. It was a lumbering shuffle, which saddened me a little. He moved as if all his bones were soft and bending beneath the weight of his flesh. Then he did something that disconcerted me: When I let him into my apartment, he walked directly to the bathroom with his head down, apparently already familiar with the inside of my home. I leaned against the wall beside the bathroom door, with my arms crossed, and listened to him vomit. Evening was settling down, filling my home with dark pools and shadows, but still I listened and waited. The toilet flushed once; then after a while, it flushed again. There was silence for a long time. I left my post and went into the kitchen to make myself a cup of hot tea. I drank it at the table as I looked at my mail. Although W. McTeal had sent nothing, between my phone bill and a coupon for a health club was a little envelope with tight, neat script, a letter from Teresa Morris. She was a clean, polished woman, who orchestrated her days around the Sunday church service and other holy functions. Her letter read something like this:

Dear Dr. Parker:

My brother is a kind man, perhaps too kind. I'm aware that he went out of his way to help you, and that you have made no effort to repay him. He says that it was an investment in a brilliant mind. Knowing him, I'm sure that the sum he confesses to, is only a fraction of what you truly owe him. I appeal to your heart. Say nothing of my intervention into your affairs, and please make some kind of effort, no matter how small, to repay my brother. He has a family of his own to support.

I responded promptly, not with a check to Morris the man, but with a little note to Morris the sister. I enjoyed adopting her method of corresponding by mail because I imagined that this petite, religious woman felt it was more sly and secretive than a phone call. Perhaps she believed she was letting herself get involved in an intrigue that was unseemly but darkly pleasurable. Perhaps, between the lines, she had written, *Burn this letter when you've finished reading it. Burn it now.* Yet I wrote very formally, explaining that Morris and I were no longer on speaking terms and that he was probably too proud to accept my money. If sister would like to accept the money on his behalf, then meet me at such and such a coffee shop at a particular time and date. *I look forward to meeting you, so I can finally have this matter resolved. I appreciate your tact and understanding.* I set the meeting for the first Friday in October, hinting that I hoped that sister could repair the rift between Morris and myself. *Your brother is a generous man.*

"What are you doing?" the boy asked, standing beside my chair.

"Are you done being sick?"

"I'm okay."

Biting his bottom lip, he leaned forward to look at the letter on the table. Then he pulled out a chair and sat at the table. I was hoping to see him look around, but he sat as if he had been used to sitting there his entire life.

"Do you want me to mail your stuff?" he asked.

"No," I said. "I want you to go home. It's getting late."

He nodded at me and slipped from the chair to his feet. He stood with his hips slightly cocked and his thumbs tucked into the pockets of his cut-off shorts.

"Can I have a dollar?"

"Go home." I turned my gaze back to the letter, as if to dismiss the boy. I sensed him lingering, but I refused to look at him. He began to shuffle away, his little body wasted down to threads. I listened for my door to open and shut, and it did. Strangely, I slightly regretted that the boy had left so easily. I got up from the table and searched my apartment, thinking that the boy might have tried to trick me and that he was now hiding somewhere. I didn't find him.

A little while later, when I was sitting at my computer and pointing at the screen with a pen, there was a knock on my door. I buttoned up my shirt as I walked over to the door. I was about to throw it open, when I heard my landlord's voice.

"Dr. Parker."

"What?" I asked, with the door between us.

"I need to talk to you."

"Talk."

"Can you open the door?"

"What do you want?"

"I can't allow you to bring that boy inside the building. Did you know that last week he was caught stealing a carton of cigarettes. I was talking to the clerk."

"I don't care."

He knocked again.

"Dr. Parker."

"Leave me alone," I said and went back to my desk. I couldn't resume my work because he continued to knock and call my name. Although he went away after a while, I was too annoyed to concentrate. I hated the thin wisps of hair on his bald head. I wanted to do something to him that for the rest of his days would grate up and down the knots of his spine whenever he remembered me. I wanted to haunt his mind with trauma and disease.

In bed, with the covers pulled over my head, I was on the edge of sleep, imagining the young woman reclining against me on my couch, her fingertips casually moving in circles on my thigh, my fingers in her hair, my lips at her ear. I heard a faint tapping and sat up in bed. I drew my robe around me, cinched it at the waist, and followed the sound of the tapping into the living room. The boy was at the window. I opened it and looked down at him shivering. Without a word, he reached up and grabbed onto the windowsill. He started to pull himself up, as if he wanted to climb through the window, but I put my hand on his forehead and pushed him down. He stepped back into the center of the alley, where he stood and quietly inspected me.

Leaning slightly out the window, I saw that he was alone. We watched each other for a moment; then the boy came forward and grabbed onto the windowsill again. I pushed his head. His feet scrambled against the wall, and a strange gurgle escaped from his throat. He dropped back into the alley. He stared at me, as if I were somehow confusing him.

"Go home," I said.

Watching me, he stepped up to the window. This time when he started to climb in, I retreated into the room. He slipped in headfirst, his legs following in serpentine motion. He dropped fully to the floor, as if issued into my home, a thing without bones that slivered along the dimly lit floor and found its way to my couch. He scrambled up and curled himself in a tight ball.

I shut the window and locked it. For a little while, I sat on the coffee table and watched the boy sleep. When I went back to my bedroom, I shut the door and locked it. I had a difficult time trying to fall asleep. Although I had left the boy in the other room, the image of his small, motionless frame and the sound of his breathing were smeared against the back wall of my mind.

I would like to skip the details.

Let the saints and martyrs talk about the long, dark night of the soul, and how something inside of them twists around and around until they feel their bodies contorting in painful knots. Let them sweat drops of blood. Let them pray. I'm past anguish now, though there was a time in my life when my body would buckle beneath a sudden flash of guilt. Words and images swarmed my mind, each one with a little stinger, pricking me into raw pulp. Somewhere in my crippled form my heart beat like mad. *Where are your accusers now? Who condemns you?* I wanted to be dragged out into the street and kicked. I wanted someone to clench my neck from behind, press a gun to the back of my head, and turn my brain into a mist. But I curled up under my bed covers and searched for a place inside of myself that wasn't touched, smudged, or soiled. Not finding that place, feeling incapable of being happy just for an instant, was another burden. It was a loss of control, a loss of agency and self. The swarm of words and images made me wonder into how many pieces my mind was fractured. Rubbing my palms against my eyes, holding my head in my hands, I was certain that I was crazy. I was also certain that I was dying. I imagined tumors and worms. Strangely, this comforted me a little as I lay in bed, wishing my organs would rot more quickly, feeling my heart slowing down at last.

The night the boy slept on my couch, with his knees drawn up to his chin and the fingertips of one hand lightly touching his lips, I was so alone in my own repugnance that it was a long time before I fell asleep. Because such nights are rare and not indicative of my character, I don't like confessing to them. I would like to say that the boy had a peaceful night, but in the morning, after I unlocked my bedroom door and came out of my room, I learned that the boy had his own plague to deal with. I would like to say that after I discovered the couch empty—though with a dark, pungent stain on it—I also discovered my home empty, and that the boy had left sometime in the early hours before dawn. I would like to say that a warm little nook opened up somewhere in the fabric of the city, and the boy slipped himself in, as if somewhere in the total mechanism of inhumane humanity a single cog broke loose and in that flaw, that immeasurable lapse in design, the world created a warm little nook for the boy. I would like to say that all the monsters had their claws removed and that the hearth fire burned at a steady even glow all year round and the biscuits were always cooked to perfection by some maternal old aunt with a ready kiss and smile. But innocence presupposes decadence, and in all likelihood, neither one exists—just shadow and act, and the meat, sinew, and bone of neither saint nor sinner, under a firmament that is neither sacred nor profane, spinning toward an end, which is just an end. In the meantime, lions don't lie down with lambs; they chew them up into bloody flaps of flesh. And little boys don't escape; they curl up on bathroom floors, with their shirts splattered and their shorts soiled.

I lightly poked his ribs with the toe of my slippered foot. The boy made a soft noise, and his body attempted to straighten but then curled itself up again, more tightly than before. A sour stench filled the room. The faucet ran at a trickle. I had an impulse to leave him, as if I could efface him from the world by simply closing the bathroom door. But I kneeled down on the tile and lifted his head. I remember that I kept speaking, saying things like "Come on now. Get up," hoping to bring his limp body to life. He was a wet, disgusting thing. Apparently, sometime during the night, as I'd sweated and tossed in bed, everything inside of the boy had tried to evacuate itself through every orifice it could find.

After the ambulance ride and the long hours in an orange plastic chair in the hospital waiting room; after the policeman with broad shoulders and a thin, lipless mouth; after the plump woman from Dyfus with her slow, soothing voice and her dark eyes that never left my face during the entirety of our discourse—which she called our appointments—all the while my refrain sounding again and again: *I don't know the boy or what has happened to him*; after a thorough inquiry was made and even the boy himself was by then well enough to be questioned, and my life was raked down to the roots, so all that could be seen was seen, and I felt as though I had been pumped dry by a chafed hand; after all that and so much more which I'm happy to pass over and never preserve with words—what finally exculpated me, what finally saved me despite my landlord's slanders, was that out of the three different traces of semen collected from the boy's body, none was mine.

PART TWO:

MOTHERS AND WHORES

Even though I was eventually able to wash my hands of the boy and leave him to his lunacy, to howl and slobber and writhe within the walls of some white ward, where all the staff, mostly women, was trained to smile mechanically and speak in warm soothing tones— my brief encounter with my errand-runner continued to influence my life. I felt that I was constantly under surveillance and that I would continue to be a suspect despite my apparent freedom. From the cashier at the checkout line in the grocery store to the chubby, pimply boy where I rented movies, everyone seemed to watch me. I no longer bought the food I usually bought or rented the kind of movies I liked to watch. Everywhere was a monitor, which made me a bit irascible and curt. I couldn't even find the humor in the little prank I played on Morris the sister. After we'd arranged our meeting by letter, she went and sat alone in the coffee shop and waited for me; in the little drama she undoubtedly cooked in her little brain, I was to play Parker the penitent, while she was Mother Morris the sister. Yet the day came and went. I sensed that something was special about the day, but I couldn't remember what I was missing, what holiday, feast, or national day of observance. Perhaps it was the anniversary of my father's death. The exact date had slipped my mind years back, and I'd refused to ask my mother because I feared fixing it in memory or being tempted to mark it down, once and for all, on the calendar or the wall. I preferred ignorance over commemoration. Just knowing the month was enough. He had once written me a brief letter, in which he apologized for making fun of me. I kept it hidden behind the cardboard backing of a picture frame; a print of the poem "Footprints," in neat curvy calligraphy, faced the glass. I had no reason to lift it from the wall and dismantle the frame because I knew what the letter contained: *I feel bad about saying your hair is a filthy rat's nest.* Of course, this was an easy apology to accept, given that my first knowledge of this particular insult had come through the letter itself. Still, I didn't like thinking about any of this, for a vague, pestilent cloud of dread hovered within my mind—when, instead, I should have been laughing at the sister, who wished to reconcile me with my lackadaisical benefactor, but who simply sat with the collection plate in her lap, waiting for my tithe and my penance. The joke was wasted, the day just another unpleasant day.

What's more or, rather, what's worse was that my fear of surveillance compelled me to destroy my character study of W. McTeal. At first, immediately after I had returned home from the hospital to await the diagnosis of the boy, I had simply hid the pictures and the profile. I'd pulled off the back panel of the nightstand beside my bed and slipped the packet in a slight crevice between the drawers. Convinced that the hiding place would never be discovered, I prided myself on being clever, but I couldn't help feeling vulnerable. The cloud of dread lingered, as though forgetting the exact day of my father's death somehow allowed me to wallow in it for a full month. Eventually, the boy was placed under the state's care, to be pimped out with pills and probed with inquiries by interns taking turns on him, and I was thanked for my efforts and patience during the investigation. Apparently, the boy agitated the plump woman from Dyfus. Beyond what I ever could have expected, his mind was diseased, his attitude vile, and his story filled with gaps and puffed up with nonsense. The woman's equanimity and control amazed me at first; her demeanor appeared so studied and exact that I suspected that such training was a standard part of the curriculum of a social worker. One afternoon, however, I noticed something strange while she sat at the table with her usual mug of coffee. Despite her apparent calmness, she continued to put the mug to her lips and take sips, even though it was empty. She looked about thirty years old; she had no ring on her finger, and her body, as shapely as a tree trunk, seemed to contain no sap of sexuality. She had spent so much time studying psychology and urban malaise that she'd forgotten about her own needs, such as companionship, desire, and love. She had smooth skin and a scent like baby powder. In truth, however, all I really knew about her was that she possessed a fierce intelligence. Whether she went home every night to spoon-feed and sponge-clean some aged father, or leapt headfirst into an orgiastic feast of bloated and disgruntled lesbian flesh, or simply watched television with a bowl of ice cream in her lap, I do not know. In fact, I had no time even to wonder or care. I was at stake, the boy was at stake, and she was the faceless and anonymous mouthpiece of our fate. Watching her drink sips of phantom coffee from the mug, I gathered that the boy made her job difficult. She didn't seem to know how to reconstruct his story from what he said—a task that I have taken upon myself; it is the saddest story I have ever heard. At first, my intention was to wait for enough time to pass—giving me a safe distance from the horrid events—and then send my fuller reconstruction of the boy's story to the social worker, to alleviate her confusion. But now I know that she is a deceptive, cruel monster who deserves no kindness from me. At the appropriate moment, I will relay her treachery and the boy's defilement.

After the initial police investigation, I was left alone. Yet the tentacles of their inquiry had wormed deeply into my life—how many calls to my mother, my colleagues, and my neighbors? I didn't know.

More than ashamed, I was terrified. I doubted that the investigation could just stop cold. Behind the sudden silence and peace, some massive onslaught seemed to be gathering strength and getting ready to crash over me at any second. The waiting drove me mad, so one night I pulled off the panel backing, took out the manila envelope, and carried it to the kitchen. Save for the flickering light cast by the gas burner, the room was dark. I put the stopper in the sink and turned on the faucet. First, I made ribbons out of each picture, one by one, with a pair of scissors, and then I picked up each piece with a set of metal salad tongs and watched the sliver of photograph dissolve and burn black in the blue flame of the stove. Each time, I held the burning strip above the sink as it curled and burned down, dropping ashes into the water. When I destroyed the last piece of evidence and thus, in a sense, dismembered and incinerated the freaky, naked man, I let the water out of the sink—but the ashes didn't swirl away as I'd expected; instead, they coated the sink with gray scum, which, because of the darkness, I didn't notice until the next morning.

Even though this scum was the least incriminating trace of my case study, I became scared the instant I saw the residue: I had left myself vulnerable and exposed all night long. I went mad with panic. My heart leapt to life in my chest, as if it were a wild rodent suddenly tossed into a sack. However, while I was frantically scrubbing the sink, something peculiar happened to me. I seemed to step outside of myself for a moment and watch this tall, lanky man with pale arms, in his white tee-shirt and underwear, leaning into his sink. From this perspective, he looked absurd. What had made him so confused? What exactly had violated him to the breaking point? What had driven him to treat his own humanity as just a tangle of flayed skin that he used to cloak himself whenever he encountered another person? I began to see myself more clearly. The dark cloud of dread lifted a bit as a strange, new calm descended upon me. I understood that the most unsettling violation of my freedom was my fear that the authorities would never stop investigating and invading the life of their suspect, Parker the pervert. Yet where was my hiding place and from whom was I hiding? The spastic thing inside my chest began to settle down. I began to breathe again. *Where are your accusers now? Who condemns you?* I sensed that on this morning I had experienced my last bout with anxiety that I would have in my life. The demons had fled; the ugly swine had drowned themselves. Since puberty, I'd suffered random and unexplainable panic attacks. Then all at once, at my kitchen sink, something deep in my brain realigned, and I knew that the attacks were gone.

Nevertheless, I waited for the fiendish swine to return. I was dimly aware that my anticipation itself could have reopened the door and ushered the demons back in: Anticipation could have given way to brooding, and then brooding to repossession. Yet I was saved by another force, sort of distracted by a desire to revel in myself, to open up and unleash myself, but I couldn't decide what I wanted to do or how to go about doing it. Apparently, there were more demons inside of me than a phantom father and a hyper-refined sense of chastity.

After all, a person who lives in his mind has trouble living in his body. It becomes an absurdity to him because he doesn't know what to do with it. There is even the chance that it can become grotesque. He knows that it is located in the world, that it moves in time and space, and that it is, at least, a receptacle for his mind, to say nothing of his soul. The body is at the mercy of innumerable necessities, from water and food to atmospheric pressure and the exact degree of tilt to the earth's axis. The irony is that while the body is the most empirically known part of man—because it bruises easily, tastes fruit, and has orgasms—it is the lesser part. Given a universe of necessities, the body remains helplessly outside of a person's actual control. Perhaps it is for this reason that the collective unconscious of the human race has invented the soul—that part of us that slips beyond the reach of the world. We have no idea what a soul is or how it is contained in a body. This ignorance is essential because the moment we locate the soul is the moment we lose it, as well as our humanity. Like Diogenes the Cynic, we can take our business outside and crap in the street. All the old verities and truths of the heart won't even be around for "when the last dingdong of doom has clanged and faded from the last worthless rock hanging tideless in the last red and dying evening," because man will neither endure nor prevail; his insides—that which makes him man—have been sucked out and thrown away. Of course, if we are going to have a soul, why not say that it is made up of stuff that is impervious to the world, and while we are at it, why not add that its true home is beyond the world? In the meantime, we can abhor our bodies like good Neo-Platonists or squat like heavy rocks in a Giotto painting, as we wait to get to our eternal home, back to the real and true ground of our being. Or like good Americans, we can apprehend our souls just enough to give us a sense of hope and a cozy feeling in our hearts. Unfortunately, in this sense, those of us without a soul are homeless. At best, our body becomes a piece of equipment, and whatever we do with it has no consequence on any soul. After a while, we may wonder why do anything with the body at all, as all the delights of sensation begin to lose their thrill—why should a magician keep repeating the same old trick once it's been figured out? And it is a trick, isn't it, a gross trick played on us by nature, that we should be so dependent upon and mingled with such a helpless and futile thing as flesh? Once a person begins to retreat into his mind, he might find that it is a mansion with many rooms, and like any good homeowner, he will want to warm them all and turn on all the lights, one by one, until his mind has far outgrown the confines of his gelatinous brain and bony skull.

But there is something else he might find. Worse than the

possibility that the content of his thoughts has no partner in reality, he might find that his mind is all potentiality, like a pantheistic deity. The normal mind is only aware of its trinity of subject, agent, and object, such as when a man says *I know myself.* This is obviously a little different from saying *I walk the dog* because in the former the self is divided into three parts: the subject *I* who has the power or agency to *know* the object *myself.* Of course, Saint Augustine used this minor trinity as an analogy of a Triune God, and the saint's presumption—once again, of course—was divine arrogance in microcosm. Following him, this spirit of confidence began to fester in the western world, and it spread into every appendage, until even the dirty, toothless peasant boys were professing that man was the center of the universe. It was a pandemic disease. The Cartesians, persisting under the same delusion, convinced themselves that *I think* was a sturdy foundation for certainty. We remained solid and certain for centuries, so we powdered our white wigs and swallowed the keys to the locked boxes of our maidens' crotches. That was all splendid until our arrogance slowly began to crumble, and the body—which had been suppressed by our arrogance—began to figure as the main factor in our thinking. But we weren't quite sure what to do with it. Diogenes re-lit his lantern. Philosophers started carrying hammers into the marketplace. The psychologists then came along with their scalpels and cut up the subject *I* into little bits, and they replaced the soul with a void. The first premise *I*—let alone the *know* and the *myself*—was all mutilated.

Now, we have the soulless man living in a fractured mind.

We can't ask the soulless man who he is, nor categorize him by characteristics and qualities. Once possibility becomes as real as actuality, man is nothing definite but everything potentially. In man, the order of being has been reserved. At one time, Aristotle would've had us think that prime matter was at the lowest echelon, as some type of gob without form, just waiting to be shaped—while at the highest echelon was the wholly actualized and definite, pondering its own perfection. But now, in man, the definite has become the limited, boxed in, and stifled, though still pondering itself under the delusion that it is a whole. Yet the soulless man is as polymorphic as prime matter; he is always becoming but never being, and though he is becoming, he becomes toward no end—

Or better yet, just forgive me now. Just ignore me. My god, my god, my god. Like any normal man, or even like a twelve-year-old boy, I should be able to speak clearly, without all this rambling. Yes, I confess, I was horny. After my anxiety had left me, I languished alone in my apartment, feeling the tug of desire. All my babbling has come to this little head: I was desperately and wickedly horny. But for my body, my body, my body. Hungry and obsessed with food, I starved myself, and all my rationalizations and reveries fail to explain such desiccation.

Some women have beautiful mouths, and some women rise out of chairs, and they sit down in chairs, and some women tilt their heads, and their skirts sway with the movement of their hips, and some women yield a power in their eyes, which is soft and kind and warm, and more alluring than a siren's song. All the while, their limbs exude sexuality like a sticky scent. They move among us, in the office, on the college campus, at the checkout line in the grocery store. These women have become their bodies. Most women, however, reserved from moment to moment, become their bodies more fully when the lights are low; against the drowsy backdrop of night, against the rhythm of a beating heart, something inside of them begins to hum and glow. But meanwhile, in a sad city apartment, a tall, awkward, pale man leaned over his sink, conscious of his own absurdity. His sexuality wasn't so much a lure, an enticement, as it was an offense.

Although this thought bothered me for long stretches of time, I had moments when my mind turned toward other subjects. It was at these moments—when through some gradual circumlocution of ideas—my mind slid along, back to the oppressive thought, approaching it from an unexpected angle. For example, one evening I was sitting at my computer, working on my manuscript, when I paused for a second and tried to remember if I was supposed to put out the blue recycling container this Tuesday or the next. I got up and went to the kitchen to check the calender magneted to the refrigerator door. All the while, my mind was slowly sliding along a seemingly innocuous track of thought, and when I returned to my desk chair, I began to wonder if I had made a mistake by snubbing Morris the sister. This woman was in my mind, and against my will, she crept upon me as a sexual prospect. Another time, I woke up in the night to use the bathroom, and as I leaned over the toilet, urinating, in a mild, groggy daze, I suddenly realized that I was thinking about Claudia Jones, what child is this, sitting on her milkcrate and humming her song. Her plump, milky flesh—mute and stupid and heavy—somehow struck me as appealing and comfortable.

Other, more conscious moments, I tried to remember my waif, the young woman who had run off with my manuscript, but she had abandoned my fantasy life. Because I had played with her too much in my mind, she seemed to lose her flesh. Ironically, she ceased to be a real person, and thus being a fantasy, she was evicted from my fantasies. At last, I wanted something I could actually touch. Unfortunately, my social circle was so small that scarcely anyone dwelled within my range. The woman from Dyfus was just as unreal as my skinny thief; besides, the woman represented a force and a threat. I was less likely to give her a kiss than to stand upon a train track, open my arms, and take a full-bodied, locomotive kiss. Most men—perhaps driven by instinct to preserve the species—erect their whole persona upon this basic pursuit. They comb their hair, buy their cars, and build their houses the same way that a spider weaves its web. All their energy, under a thin disguise, goes toward the conquest. Like other men, as well as every pubescent boy, I was finally willing to take part in the struggle. I had discounted myself for my whole life. But now I was caught between the extremes of male sexuality, lusting after the two ends of the spectrum. They just happened to be my most obvious prospects. On one end, just one space left of the Whore, was the bovine idiot, as thick as flesh and fetish. And on the other, a little right of the Mother, was that sacred lady, layer upon layer of ivory and porcelain.

I knew that if I were to make a concerted effort upon the playing field of men, I ought to have as many fronts as possible, and thus work upon both women at the same time. For Claudia Jones, because I was a complete stranger to her, I had the bridge of apathy to cross. Of course, I could have made myself known to her; that would have been as easy as throwing a stone at her. The real task was to make her want to know me, to make her interested. I didn't bother to consider the next step, namely how to convert docile bovinity into desire. I figured that once I was near to her, I could simply move myself upon her body, while she would put less ardor into her lovemaking than she put into her eating; all my sweaty effort could provoke no greater reaction out of her than that vague, listless indifference with which a grazing cow lifts its head for a moment, continues to chew, and then, still chewing, turns its face back toward the ground. For Morris the sister, because I had offended her, I had the citadel of animosity to raze to the ground. For all intents and purposes, I had already whacked her with a stone. I hoped that she was of that religious type who not only expected pain and suffering from the world but also wore her battle scars as proof of her faith. I wrote her a letter explaining that I fully understood why she'd snubbed me and left me sitting alone in the coffee shop. I deserved to be treated severely. As a side note, I added that on that fateful Sunday afternoon I finally realized how awful I must have been for such a kind woman to treat me so cruelly. I licked and mailed the missive. I had nothing to lose. Undoubtedly, finding the letter in her mailbox, she would first feel a bit shocked, and then reading it, she would become confused—until, of course, her eyes lighted upon the word "Sunday," which wasn't the day we had arranged to meet on. If she were as trusting as I hoped, she would assume that I had made an error or, perhaps, that she'd made the error. I could still be saved.

My first front mobilized, I had only to wait for the response, and if I heard nothing for a week, I'd make another advance. I didn't know what this would be, but I knew that if it also failed, I'd try again. With persistence, I planned to worm my way into the heart of that little peach. Although all my past experience told me that women are unfathomable, distant, and closed, I recognized that the history of man was a history of seduction. Of course, I wasn't made like a mighty son of Priam, who could take a woman by force and lock her up in his bed chamber. Nor like a young, handy, rutting scholar, could I have been bold enough to saunter up beside her, grab hold of her by the quim, and swear my death was imminent without her loving. Yet, Homer and Chaucer aside, perhaps I was able to act like a cousin to the sweet maiden, drive her around and around until her fatigue and my constancy wore her down, and then, at that moment, work my puny, insidious magic charm. Unfortunately, Victorian modesty prevented Thomas Hardy from fleshing out the details of such a young girl's seduction, and so my manual was lacking. Even though I didn't know how the "cousin" actually un-frocked and de-bloomered the maiden, I knew that he pestered and wooed her until she finally gave in. If Hardy proved anything about the female race, it was that a woman is simply seething passion all bundled up and straining against the seams of her corset, waiting for the slightest tug upon the slightest thread, so she may burst forth and unravel upon her man. With hope, Morris the sister, my own pretty "Tess," may have unraveled upon me.

On the other front, undoing Claudia Jones's knot, pulling her string, required the same sort of machination, though on a more stupefied level. I could have been a slobbering idiot who pursued her from pasture to pasture, then down across a foreign field, the both of us lumbering on, until I had her trapped in some ravine. There, in the thick purple hours of twilight, we would meld together, not just our flesh or the noise of our bellows and moans, but also the mild confusion, the indifference, and the languid passion that belongs to all the over-ripe, simple beasts.

II

The second week of autumn brought with it a spell of dismal weather that had apparently chased Claudia indoors. A gray drizzle seemed to be in a constant state of fading, of tapering into a mist, but after a few days of these vague diminutions, the gloomy weather didn't seem as if it would ever break. I set myself before the window and watched the alley. As puddles formed, the oil and grime rose off the pavement to the surface of the water in twisted hues of purple and yellow and green. A few stray clothespins hung from the line, and the milkcrate was turned over on its side against the wall. I had a book, written by one of my colleagues, opened facedown upon my thigh. She was a short, intense, over-wound woman, whose voice—when I was forced to hear it in an elevator, hallway, or meeting—always metamorphosed in my mind into the violent yappings of a small dog. I was reading her book because of an unwritten rule among the faculty: We all read each other's work, not so much to honor the writer or ever really to mention the text in detail, but simply to consume the person. I tried to play my part in this sober, pedantic game. Now, however, as I watched the alley, I had trouble concentrating; I couldn't sink my teeth into the puppy. I was half-expecting to see the boy trot up to my window in his little cut-off shorts and a flimsy tee-shirt. I was also half-waiting for Claudia Jones, though I knew I'd do better stationed in the hallway outside her door. If there was something self-defeating and repressive in my method, I didn't realize it at the time, for I imagined myself sitting there with the patience of a baited trap. Sometime during the second day, I decided to read only the first and last paragraph of each chapter of the book. Everything I read, however, sat so disconnected in my mind that I finally found myself reading the introduction, hoping this would join together the jumble of ideas. The city outside seemed moribund, as if the air were contaminated and everyone were diseased and quarantined. It wasn't so much the gray weather or my sporadic sleeping, as it was my low, gray shiftless mood that seemed to blend the boundaries of day and night, so I didn't know exactly at what moments I picked up the book or put it down, but eventually I came upon a moment when I opened the book and discovered that there were no more pages left to read. This act of completion roused me a little, making me realize that although all the world appeared to be overcast by a desultory haze, I alone was suspended. Elsewhere, life was being lived: Plans were enacted, lusts consummated, and bodies splayed on both sheets and spikes. Perhaps, right at that very moment, W. McTeal was on all fours, still baffled, and looking past his thigh at a propped camera; meanwhile, on a stark corner cot in a white ward, the boy was trying to gnaw through his restraints (this was how I always imagined him for some reason); quiet and faceless, in a damp, windowless chamber in a cellar, in the gloom of a single light bulb dangling from a wire, the social worker was selecting her leatherwear and whip; and perhaps somewhere in West Virginia, a young, goofy-looking man was furtively leading his favorite goat behind the barn and unwittingly preparing himself to usher in the Apocalypse, by siring Satan. Although it was difficult for me to imagine that terrible cosmic drama, in which the human race was not only the prize but also the playing field, I felt a small prompting in my heart, and whether for the light or for the darkness, I abandoned my post at the window and stood in the middle of the room. I slowly turned my head, my eyes passing over everything, as if all the objects that surrounded me, which in fact defined me, from the bookshelves to the microwave, belonged to no one, least of all to me. The clock read 1:14, sometime in the afternoon or the night. In this drunken, fog-bound mood, I left my apartment and entered the hallway. I had a vague notion of walking up to Claudia's door and rapping hard upon it. After all, despite her idiocy, she must have known that I existed, because who else had been sliding her mail under her door? I stood before her apartment and tried to peer in the peephole, but I merely saw the reflection of my own eye. I leaned back for a second and then, by impulse, rapped two times, hard, with the butt of my palm, just as I had seen my landlord do on the day I'd first moved into my apartment. I looked at my eye again in the little circle, and as I stared at my eye, I sensed that the tiny window was the only thing separating me from Claudia Jones, we were eye to eye, and both of us were looking at the same thing: my eye. I was thrilled by the proximity, by my boldness, and of course, by the sudden realization— not that I was on the threshold of making an absurd gesture—but that never once did I ever see the bloated woman in the hallway; I had no reason to assume that the woman in the alley was in fact my neighbor Claudia Jones. This new idea nearly prompted me to scramble away from the door like a startled rodent. Yet my world suddenly seemed larger than I'd originally imagined; I had more prospects than the alley-woman and Tess. I had the unknown, and maybe she was waiting for me behind some closed door, in an art gallery, or in a used clothing store. Somewhere in the city. Leaning against the door, still trying to stare through my own reflection, I hoped that the real Claudia Jones would be a new discovery. If she were "a gross woman," and not actually an imbecile, I was curious about what kind of disfigurement plagued her body or marred her soul. Knowing my landlord, I safely guessed that he simply meant that she was a dissolute creature.

Then I heard a noise: A body moved on the other side of the door as the floorboards creaked. I didn't pull away or look up and down the hallway. We waited in silence for a long a time, until I was able to make out the muffled sound of her breathing, and I knew for certain that she was there, inches away from me. I began to wonder why she didn't respond to my knock. Perhaps she'd looked through her peephole and had seen only my eyeball, and she was afraid. I took a step back and knocked again, softly this time. Off to my left, someone entered the building and started up the staircase, but I didn't turn to see who it was. Trapped in the moment, I faced the door and smiled vaguely.

"Just slip them under." The real Claudia had spoken at last. Her voice was thick, as though she had a wad of phlegm at the back of her throat.

"I'm your neighbor," I said. "I thought it would be nice—"

"Just slip them under."

"—it would be nice to say hi."

"What do you want?"

"I thought it would nice."

Silence filled the pause.

"Oh now," she said, and I heard her stepping back. "Fuck it to hell. Keep them all." Her voiced lowered, as if she were speaking to herself.

"If you want to say hi sometime, I'm right down the hall." I tried to sound pleasant. I imagined that if she opened the door and gave me the chance, I could have been mildly charming.

She didn't say anything else. The floorboards creaked; she was walking away.

I waited for a few seconds, hoping she would come back, then thinking that I should knock again. I didn't quite realize at the moment that standing before her door, at some odd hour, in a white tee-shirt and a pair of shorts, was a lanky, disheveled man who hadn't showered, shaved, or even brushed his teeth in several days. I was too obsessed with the situation to see myself clearly. I started back toward my apartment. As far she knew, I still had her mail. At first, she'd figured that I'd come to return it, but then she'd suspected that I intended to use W. McTeal to draw her out of her apartment. This fact seemed so obvious that I supposed that she saw through me: I—like all other men and pubescent boys—was an individual with a dimly concealed ulterior motive. And what was wrong with this? Pleased with myself, though somewhat blank and benumbed, I returned to my apartment, burrowed beneath my blankets, and slept the kind of sleep that could have been minutes or days long.

When I woke up, I felt rejuvenated, and though the bleak weather continued, I was certain that it was morning. I didn't immediately consider my encounter with Claudia Jones—not until I stepped barefooted on the chilly white tile in the bathroom and began to urinate; then, all at once, I was struck by the weight of the episode. I was a grotesque absurdity, a lumbering monstrosity who attempted to function smoothly in society—and now my disguise had been torn from me, the brown sack pulled off my horny, bulbous head, by the simple gesture of knocking on a stranger's door in desperation. Yet a part of me knew that life required risk, a person must put himself on the forefront and leave himself vulnerable; this was the essential factor to all relationships. To a faint degree, I felt excited and engaged— but even so, to a larger degree, I was mortified. I didn't understand enough about people to trust that they usually expect another person to be slightly goofy, weak, and flawed. This tender spot, this openness, connects friends, family, and lovers, and enables them to say that they truly know or love someone else. While I urinated, however, I assumed that the real Claudia Jones thought I was a nut, and I surely gave myself too much credit—in all likelihood, I was no more than a passing thought in that woman's mind, or if she did think of me, it wasn't with the violence and vehemence that I imagined.

Nevertheless, a barrier had been crossed, and though I stumbled awkwardly forward, there was no reason to retreat now. I planned to knock on her door again.

III

The possibility of the unknown motivated me to clean myself up and leave my apartment. In my charcoal overcoat, and with a paperback novel tucked in the side pocket, I picked up my umbrella and headed down the hall. I walked past Claudia's door without giving it any notice. Mail was piled on the landing, but I didn't bother with it; nor did I check my own mailbox, though I was waiting for Morris the sister's reply. I descended the cement stairs, where once the boy had sat and waited for me. The air was cool and wet, but I kept my umbrella closed, since it could do nothing against a fine mist. Although I had no definite location in mind, I wanted to go some place where people gathered, such as Market or Broad Street, and milled about in front of stores. The weather apparently dissuaded most pedestrians, and the few that ventured out moved slowly and silently, bundled up, with their faces turned downward. I tried to look at everyone. I imagined that a hint of something composed and dignified colored my expression. Yet luckily no one returned my gaze, for the person would've seen—not the cultured man, the refined intellectual who brimmed with social graces and little knowing grins—but rather some eager-eyed, hysterical loon. There was nothing charming about me at all. Despite my self-deception, or perhaps because of it, I felt determined. I was uncertain what I was searching for, but I was going out to find it or maybe to let it find me. Fortunately for the world, it was spared of me for a while longer because the mist began to dampen me too, weighing me down. I came to the corner and paused. The crossroad seemed barren in both directions, with nothing inviting me forward. When I looked back down the direction I'd just come from, I saw a few people on either side of the road, walking close to the buildings in an attempt to stay dry. One figure, however, didn't move at all. He simply stood under the stone arch of a doorway, at a distance too far for me to distinguish his features. He was wearing a dark green baseball cap and a corduroy jacket that came down to his knees. He faced the road, as if waiting for a ride to pull up or for something else to happen. I didn't remember passing him, so he must have been walking behind me and only recently stopped for shelter. I noticed this all in a glance, but it didn't hold my interest because in the same sweep of my eyes, I discovered a bus stop beside me. I stepped inside the thing, which offered poor protection from the weather. If a bus came, I was ready to get on it and let that movable contraption take me wherever it would. I would let chance have her way with me. Yet, while I stood there, I felt a pressure inside my chest, and I knew the sensation; it always forewarned me of a terrible wave of sadness. The pressure would get thicker, with a dull, steady squeeze. Despite the chilly air, I could already feel the perspiration beneath my collar and the heaviness in my head. There was nothing the matter with me, I told myself, just a general fatigue of the soul. After all, on the very day I'd gone out to encounter the world, "to force the moment to its crisis," there was no moment to be found. I felt concealed in the bus stop because the three glass walls were covered completely over with bulletins, most of which posted by college students looking for roommates, trying to sell used books, or announcing a silly event. The walls seemed to bear testimony to life, if for no other reason than the freedom and nonchalance with which these people displayed their phone numbers. A bright pink sheet stated "Female Models Wanted," specified the desired dimensions, and provided a row of tabs to be torn off; if a model wanted to call the artist, she needed to "ask for fred," as the bulletin informed. Two tabs were already taken. Was it that easy? Could I simply plaster my number on a wall? I plucked a pink tab from the sheet and slipped it into my pocket beside the paperback book. I didn't know why I took fred's number, but it calmed my nerves a little. Then I noticed something on the wall that actually interested me. That coming Saturday, on the second floor of one of the poorman's galleries, a doctor Barnett—a gentleman to whom I'd actually nodded once or twice in the hallway, a little, graying, wizened thing who always wore a brown felt hat—was giving a free lecture. Of course, it was the kind of lecture that offered wine and crackers to bribe people to come, and those who showed up undoubtedly would be the doctor's own pliable, obsequious, sycophantic graduate students; the old Bohemian dilettantes who wore scarves and frequented all the coffee shops, galleries, and poetry readings; and the true scholar or two, just to make an appearance and nod approvingly at Dr. Barnett. I knew nothing of the man's training or background, but his lecture had an appealing title: "Iago as Id." Unfortunately, the bulletin probably had been made and posted by one of the doctor's hopeful protégés, who'd neglected to put tabs on the bottom, so I had to remember the date and location, in case I decided to attend. Inspired by the bus stop walls, I stepped back out into the mist and continued walking. Although I hadn't drank alcohol in a long time—simply because there were several periods in my life when it unfailingly exacerbated the very problems I'd wanted it to help me escape—I headed for one of the local pubs. A beer wouldn't hurt me, and I could've used a plate of french fries. Occasionally, cars crawled by, their tires hissing on the wet pavement. The only vehicle that caught my attention, however, erupted loud and violent upon the somber scene. A motorcycle sped down the center of the road; the rider was a helmet-less black man, with hair as seemingly round and solid as a ridiculously oversized helmet. The front tire skimmed and skipped across the surface of the road, in perfect time with his gunning of the throttle. At first, I had an impression that the man had a maniacal appearance, with glaring white eyes and teeth protruding from a face as otherwise broad, black, and expressionless as a balloon. Then, after he disappeared and the sound of his bike faded, I realized something even more disturbing about the man; I had seen him all wrong. He was in fact as calm and sober as some stuffy, contemplative Englishman. This man, perhaps, was the real Dr. Barnett. Rather than question my initial racist impulse, I marveled at his mixture of repose and insane bravado, at once civilized and brutishly free. I became a witness to the grand endeavor of the Enlightened, western white man insouciantly epitomized by a man and a machine. I felt a wave of intimidation and realized that I was more closely aligned to James Baldwin's oppressor than I ever suspected. I felt a bit overwhelmed, something close to mute awe, as I began to consider the possibility of violence and sexuality getting all mixed together when the body isn't allowed a regular discharge, when the history of convention and custom, of edifice and enterprise, is erected, from tea cups to towers, in a revulsion to cartilage and skin, to juice and joussiance, and manifests itself in our desire to powder our white wigs, brush up on our book of manners, and spread our nobility into the heart of darkness, to plunder with Christ on our lips and civilize with swords in our hands, or, as in bald, black Baldwinian terms, to lynch and castrate on Saturday night, go to church on Sunday morning, and by midweek once again feel ashamed by our own pale flaccidity.

Meanwhile, a tall, lanky man in a charcoal overcoat was suddenly arrested in mid-stride, in front of a large window that was fancifully frosted around its edges.

I peered through the window at a painting hanging on the wall. I was utterly stunned, for it bore the title of one my private thoughts. I needed to see the painting more clearly. When I opened the door, I heard a single muffled chime from a more distant room, and this colored my immediate impression of the place—not the sickly redolence of wood polish mixed with a lower, softer scent of potpourri; not the odd shadows cast by track lighting filtering through make-shift partitions draped in lace or else shining straight down upon a series of twisted metal objects and a pair of large disfigured human heads sculpted out of wood; not the vibrantly colored tapestries on the far wall nor the paintings and sketches on either side of me. Although the sound of the bell died instantly, it seemed to reverberate, to hang suspended in the air, mildly foreboding, as if by opening the door, I had not exactly triggered a trap but merely signaled my own presence. Now, no more than three paces into the gallery, I had to put on my social disguise and smile at whatever creature I'd awoken in the back room. I heard chair legs slide across the wooden floor. The thing was coming near, and I had yet to inspect the painting that I'd seen through the window. I was looking at it, moving toward it, when I heard behind me the rattle of beads and a male voice say, "Hello." I glanced at him, nodded once to be polite, and hoped he would leave me alone. All the while I stood in front of the painting and stared silently, still not certain what it was supposed to be, I felt disturbed by the man. I sensed him behind me. I looked at the painting as though I were gazing at a printed page but not registering the meaning of the words. Most certainly, the man, who had parted a curtain of beads with his stubby body, was now quietly watching me, as the swaying and rattling beads began to settle. I could envision him behind me in his gray suit, his face and neck covered in a closely trimmed gray beard, his eyes seemingly magnified by his glasses. I knew he was waiting to speak again; all I had to do was make some gesture, and he would take the opportunity. I still wasn't seeing the painting, though by now the man probably assumed that I was enraptured by it, caught in a state of mystical and static apprehension, simultaneously pulled by fear and tugged by pity.

"She's a local artist," the man said.

I glanced at him. He was beside a table, trying to separate coffee filters. I looked at the painting again and nodded, as if his brief explanation suddenly made the whole thing clear to me.

Despite the lace, the lighting, the beads, and the cloyed scent, the man had a robust voice, coming from deep inside his barrel body, effacing the femininity that his surroundings seemed to thrust upon him. He wasn't so much a bull in a china shop—because a bull would have been markedly displaced—but rather some androgynous and tortured globule with no definite identity, shape, or place within the world. Perhaps I intuitively imagined this about the man because all the artwork in the gallery possessed a twisted ugliness. The community of art aficionados and the man himself probably would've offered some label or another, such as "abstract art," to explain or justify this collective perversity—as if the artist were abstracting ideals or concepts out of the concrete world or else attempting to reshape the world against the normal flow of perception, traveling from subject to object as if it were possible for a person not to be defined from without, not to be born and tossed into a ready-made world, but rather to make it out of himself, without any objective, sensual reference point. Yet I didn't buy into their delusions. I knew that the world in fact formed them; its tools were sorrow, pain, and death; and the enormity of the thing shriveled their spirits and gave them the official stamp of insignificance. Of course, I had to give the artist more credit than the man-in-the-street, who tacitly accepted a single composite image of himself. The artist, receptive and sponge-like, tried to define himself according to as many facets of the universe as he could, but the parts were so disconnected that when the artist looked inside of himself at what he'd gathered up, he saw no harmony or meaning. In depression, angst, and loneliness, he fought back, and believing that he was forcing his puny self upon the world, he made his twisted, ugly art.

The man was saying something, and I looked back and nodded assent to whatever was coming out of his mouth. I wanted him to leave, and he did, carrying an empty coffeepot through the curtain of beads, into the back room. At last, I had a moment alone with the painting near the front window, though it wasn't the painting itself that had first attracted me, but rather its title, printed on a card beside it and affixed to the lavender window moulding: *Material: Perverse, Polymorphed, and Primed,* and beneath this was the artist's name, Celeste Wilcox. I was dumbfounded. Here, in a little, goofy gallery was the exact subtitle to the third chapter of my manuscript. Either I had to believe in a remarkable, celestine coincidence and that Ms. Wilcox and I had kindred minds, or else somehow among the vast multitude of people in the city, I once again encountered the girl of my fantasies—the skinny, haggard waif who had stopped to tie her shoelaces and thus, by bending over, had severed me once and for all from my professional and social circle. When I had chased her, I never imagined she was stealing my manuscript to this extent. Seeing my ideas in this new context, barely a yard away from a pair of bloated wooden heads, I was suddenly disgusted with my whole project. I had only one option: to burn my manuscript in the sink and flush it down the same drain that had swallowed up W. McTeal.

The fat man was making a soft guttural sound as he breathed.

"This is sort of wonderful," I said at last, and he took this as an invitation to step closer to me. He looked thoughtfully at the painting, which was about the size of a folded newspaper.

"Yes," he said. "It's a wonderful piece."

Although an instant ago he had appeared anxious to talk, he now seemed to settle back in contemplation, to join in my rhapsody. He no longer needed to persuade me toward the sale but simply to approve of my choice. On a little card, in the bottom corner of the frame, read the price in tight, quaint calligraphy: $975. I knew what he wanted from me, the customer, and I knew what I wanted from him—namely, every detail, large and small, from the shoe size to the mother's maiden name of my skinny, urban nymph.

"Yes," he said again, as if to himself.

"Do you have anything else by—" I began to say, but paused to look at the name card, as if needing to refresh my memory, and then I continued, pronouncing the name slowly, sounding out each syllable with the same care a person gives to a foreign language— "by Celeste Wilcox?" She felt nice in my mouth, on my tongue. "Celeste Wilcox," I repeated, getting comfortable with the two words.

"One other piece, but it isn't framed yet. I have it in back."

"Can I see that too?"

"Sure, sure. He started away. "Help yourself to a cup of coffee. There's only powdered milk, though." He smiled apologetically. "It keeps better." He disappeared through the curtain.

Although the coffee smelt tempting, I didn't take a cup. I still had an urge for beer and french fries.

The painting was a loathsome thing. Out of a dark background, objects and figures took shape, passing along the color scheme of a bruise, as they twisted toward the foreground; but rather than peak at yellow, they reached the red heat of raw skin, before morphing back into the darkness. What was worse was not that a rocky landscape grew out of the blackness, but that the landscape turned into manmade structures, which themselves turned into figures, neither quite male nor female, adult nor child, and then the figures, stretching closer to the foreground, became body parts, some of which cracked open, split against the strain, and out of these wounds, bloomed strange, fresh organs lined with blue veins. Despite all this, the softness, the intimate flesh tones, and the curves of the shapes lent to the painting a subtly provocative and sensuous feeling.

$975, I thought, curious what determined the last dollar. Why not $974?

The fat man bustled out with another painting. At first, he held it out toward me. Then he set it on the ground, leaning it against one of the wooden partitions. We took a step back together, in order to appreciate the piece. Through some wild stroke of genius, Ms. Wilcox had managed to produce something even more disgusting.

Inexplicably, my voice somewhat excited, I said, "I love it."

"It's striking."

"I like the whole equipage." This comment made no sense, but the fat man agreed.

"Yes," he said.

"And the self-reflexive motif."

"It's very smart."

"And the autoeroticism."

The fat man agreed again, as though all my absurd observations were plainly obvious. I was beginning to like him very much.

"It's extremely—" I paused for an instant, searching for some outlandish word.

"Carnival," the man said, filling the void.

"Yes." I lowered my voice, feeling the force of the man's precision. I was surprised how quickly he'd earned my respect. "Carnival," I said. There was no better word. The painting suddenly fell into place and began to brim with significance.

"What's it called?" I asked.

"*Carnival*," the fat man answered, and I realized that it wasn't him at all whom I was beginning to respect and like. It was Celeste Wilcox, for she'd undoubtedly named the painting.

After a few more minutes, I began to detest the man. In a very pleasant manner, he continually put me off; he refused to tell me anything useful about Ms. Wilcox. When I casually asked whether she was a student and where she studied, he told me that her method was apparently Baroque. When I asked if she was exhibited elsewhere and if she ever personally visited the gallery to promote her work, "to chitchat over wine and crackers," the man responded by saying, "Sure, sure," but added that she had nothing scheduled. I understood his tact;

he was the middleman, the one getting the commission, and he didn't want me trying to approach Ms. Wilcox directly and thus to cut him out. The more I ventured to elicit information, the more he began to sense that I didn't want to give him my money. As we talked, I became conscious of a steady, annoying tapping sound, and then I realized that it was me, that by some nervous reflex, I was tapping the metal tip of my umbrella on the hardwood floor. Even so, I continued to make the sound.

"Then tell me," I said suddenly, "does she do portraits, say, of my wife or little daughter?"

"I'm not certain."

"Could we possibly arrange something, ask something. I mean, you could ask her, right?"

"Sure, sure," the man said.

We weren't looking at each other, but at *Material: Perverse, Polymorphed, and Primed.*

"Yes," I said, just to emit some sound. If in a single move I could turn myself into a husband and a father, then why not into a rich man too. Glancing back at the painting on the floor, I asked, "Of course, you'd frame that if I wanted it."

"Of course." The man nodded his round head.

"Could I get matching frames?"

"I don't see why not."

We were silent for a moment, looking back and forth between the paintings, avoiding each other's eyes. I was simultaneously frustrated, agitated, and amused. Indeed, what a loving man I must have been, to have wanted the precious image of my wife or daughter rendered by the hand of that tortured artist!

"And those heads." I gestured to the hewn blocks of wood. "Do they come as a set?"

"Sure, or separately," the man said.

"They'd—" I started to say that they'd go perfect in the baby's room, but I stopped myself.

"Is it possible," I continued, "for me to give you my name and address, and if Ms. Wilcox is interested in doing a portrait, then you can give me a call?"

"Of course."

The man produced two business cards and a pen from the inner pocket of his suit. When he handed me the cards, I read his name: Lyle Tartles. I wrote my information on the back of one card and slipped the other into my pocket with the novel and fred's number.

"Mr. Tartles," I said, smiling. "This is an impressive place."

"Thank you," he said. "There's a lot of talent in our city."

I surveyed the gallery slowly, nodding my head.

"You'd understand, Mr. Tartles, if I returned with my wife. I'm not free to spend a single dime on my own. You understand."

"Sure." The man smiled too.

He was so agreeable and pleasant that it was difficult for me to get an accurate read on him. Was he just humoring me, following business protocol, or actually believing my spiel?

"You couldn't possibly hold these pieces?" I asked.

"Sure," he said. "If you want to leave a—"

"No." I cut him off. "I shouldn't commit to anything yet. My wife would see red. Take my head off."

The man smiled.

"Mr. Tartles." I abruptly grabbed his meaty paw and pumped it once. "Thank you."

I wanted to add some finishing touches, to convince him thoroughly of my sincerity.

"I'll see you again," I said.

"Sure."

On my way toward the door, I paused to inspect the pair of

grotesque heads. I considered them in a reverential way, as if trying to take in the full impact of their beauty or truth. I even touched my chin and nodded thoughtfully at the sculptures. When I turned to leave, I looked back at Mr. Tartles, to see if he'd witnessed my little show. There was a strange grin on his face that suddenly unnerved me. I couldn't tell whether he had seen through my charade, only that he was apparently amused by me. This misshapen, unfortunate globule was amused by me, as though I had been a pubescent boy casually browsing through a car lot and expecting the salesman to show me the respect due to a man. The only thing I could do was smile, nod, and rush out the door. As I hurried away, heading along the sidewalk in the gray mist, I began to feel even worse, more exposed, like a pubescent boy caught in the middle of algebra class, trying, like a dirty fiend, to sneak the porno-stroke under his desk. I lurched forward with my head down. Before the shame could fully overwhelm me, the man on the motorcycle—the real Dr. Barnett—exploded out of a side street, turned the corner, and whizzed past me. He jolted me out of my self-affliction. His mixture of ease and insanity made him my hero. Even though he was just some guy joyriding on a dreary Sunday afternoon, he managed to deflate the fat man and imbue me with a bit of strength.

Now as my mind swarmed with thoughts, with urgency, and with a single drop of borrowed potency, I found myself walking faster. A strange compulsion drove me forward, though I didn't exactly know what I was running toward or away from. The black man reminded me that I was supposed to be on the playing field of men, which meant that I was no longer going to bother erecting a world of massive monuments with vaulted ceilings and endless corridors and chambers stretching as deep as my tiny, gray brain could imagine. I was going to assert myself using my body. With a little spasm, a momentary shudder, and a drop of potency, if a person was not quite born into manhood, then he was at least allowed into the arena and given a chance to test his mettle.

As I hurried forward, I became aware of the buildings looming up around me, of every bit of earth covered up with concrete and tar, and of the air saturated less with the natural elements than with waves and signals and blathering voices too numerous to fathom. It all seemed significant and portentous, as though the grimy fingerprints of man could not only be seen on everything but also were intimately and mysteriously connected to the secret places of my own heart. I wasn't quite certain what this meant for me or what I actually needed to do.

IV

Before I had the time to contemplate these ideas further and drift into a new reverie, I found myself beneath the muddy green awning of a pub, which I promptly entered. The interior was deep and narrow. The bar was on the left; every stool was taken, and behind the seated patrons, more were standing. Along the opposite wall ran a thin counter that people used to abandon their empty glasses and bottles, or, by reaching backwards, to retrieve a drink, tap ashes, or snuff a cigarette. Nobody turned to look at me as I stood by the front door, wet with sweat and mist. I took off my overcoat and folded it over my forearm. I was surprised to find the place so busy at this hour. Beyond the bar area, elevated a single step, were two rows of tables. I made my way through the crowd of mostly young men and headed toward the dining area. Even though I squeezed between people, fixed my eyes upon their faces, and uttered, "Excuse me," no one seemed to acknowledge my presence. A space cleared, providing me a sudden opportunity to belly up to the bar and order a drink. Hugging my overcoat and umbrella against my body, I was about to step forward. Yet I felt someone move behind me. In fact, just beneath the hem of my jacket, gliding across one cheek and then the other cheek of my ass, might have been either the back of a hand or the soft corner of a woman's handbag, but I feared that this casual, accidental touch was something worse. My body tensed, and I squirmed away, not turning around to see which body and face belonged to that sausage and sack. I reached the end of the bar, where a large speaker bracketed to the wall emitted a lot of noise. Several tables were vacant. When I ascended the single stair, I turned and faced the bar again, and looking across the tops of their heads, I was intrigued that people preferred to pack together, rather than step back into the empty floor space.

"You eating?" someone asked me, shouting above the music.

"Yes," I said.

He was a wiry young man with raven black hair, which seemed to be greased or wet. He raised his arm toward the tables and limply waved two fingers, as if to shoo me away. A squiggly black line twisted down his forearm. He said something I couldn't hear, but I knew he was telling me to take a seat.

I found a table that had been robbed of all its chairs but one. I set my umbrella on the floor beside the chair and sat down with my overcoat in my lap. Some laminated menus were propped between the salt and pepper shakers and a napkin dispenser. I read a menu, though I already knew what I wanted. When the waiter finally came over and took my order, a look of annoyance came over his face.

"What kind of beer?" he asked.

"Oh, what do you have on tap?"

He drew a breath and began to rattle off a list of words, a jumble of sounds. I cocked my head, as if I were interested.

"What was that last one?" I asked, but before he even got out the name, I said, "That sounds good."

He disregarded me at once and walked away.

Even though I knew I was overdressed, too old, and solitary, I resisted the urge to feel displaced. I tried to act at ease, so I took my damp overcoat from my lap, bundled it up, and put it on the table.

Then I wiggled out of my jacket, hung it from the back of the chair, and unbuttoned the cuffs of my shirt. Years ago, in my silly and benumbing baccalaureate days, I used to attempt to give myself a dab of charm and grace by pretending to be a dashing ivy-league man. I often wanted to impersonate F. Scott Fitzgerald, but because I knew very little about the writer himself, I had to settle for such characters as Jay Gatsby and Dick Diver. Now, sitting at the table, waiting for my order, this old desire to emulate someone else returned to me. I remembered the scene when Dick Diver was sitting in a bar surrounded by his cronies. He had just secretly performed a handstand in his room, to give a little color to his face, and now he was leaning back with a drink in his hand, while his company paid him homage; they were scanning the establishment, looking to see if anyone in the whole room had as much repose as Dick, but no one there could match his elegance. As I looked about the bar, at all the goofy, eager, boisterous young men, I realized that not one of them had the romantic equanimity of a cultured lover, and furthermore, none of them cared to have it. They didn't bother with refined manners and tastes, and perhaps most young men never did, even in Fitzgerald's time. Why make such an elaborate show when they could expose their desires as plainly as a pack of rutting dogs slobber and howl?

The waiter brought me a plastic basket of french fries and a glass of something thick and black. When I looked up at him, to question what was in the glass, I noticed that the tattoo that wound up his arm and disappeared under his shirtsleeve, apparently spread over the rest of his body in some mysterious fashion and peeped up around the edges of his shirt collar. Not saying a word, I simply looked at his shiny, black eyes, but still he seemed to become very annoyed with me. He waited a second and then stepped away. Whether he acted like a bitter, ugly thing to all the patrons or just to me didn't matter; I decided not to leave a tip unless he showed a glimmer of warmth the next time he came to my table.

I sipped my beer and found it tolerable. The french fries were thick-cut, salty, and soggy. Even so, I ate and drank and watched the people seated in the dining area, since my back was toward the bar. The couple sitting in front of me appeared to have only recently met because the young man was interrogating the girl, who looked like a delicate creature, with soft bare shoulders and auburn hair. His words were abrupt and quick, swarming all over the girl. Unfortunately, rather than a frontal view of her, I had one of his cherubic face, which was round, pink-cheeked, and coated with a closely trimmed beard.

Through his questioning, I learned that she was the youngest of three girls and, because of the decade or so separating her from her sisters, she was a "change of life baby" or, as her dopey date interjected, "an accident." I couldn't see her expression, but a slight, telling pause in her voice preceded her correction: she was "definitely planned." In fact, she was lucky to have been born later because by then, her parents were already established in life. While her sisters had "to play with pots and pans and to make toys out of sticks and mud," she got everything she wanted. Just as I was beginning to appreciate the young woman's wit, the bearded boy felt compelled to interrupt.

"A spoiled little girl."

He grinned stupidly and babbled on. He used his fork to punctuate his sentences in the air, and although she started to say that even in childhood she'd "never really cared for material things," he began another line of questioning. He wanted to know what she intended to do with a degree in English. He asked this in a roundabout way, not only implying her impracticality but also alluding to the spoiled little girl theme. Beneath the flourish of his words and the humor in his tone, he in essence accused her of having the comfort of getting a useless degree because she planned on being supported by a happy husband. It took him a while to get to the point because he somehow connected it to, or rather veiled it within, an anecdote about his cousin's ex-fiancé. She let him finish, before simply calling her education "a pleasant stepping stone" to law school. She had wanted to be a lawyer ever since she'd read about Atticus Finch and Sol Stein's magician in ninth grade.

The inflection in her voice suggested that this subject thrilled her. She clearly wanted to continue talking about her plans, such as what law schools interested her and also what branch of law. Yet the buffoon swallowed whatever was in his mouth, set down his fork, and looked seriously at the girl.

"Promise me this," he said. "As soon as you finish all this schooling and you start raking in the cash, if you're still looking for a husband, well—" He broke off with a smile.

"You'll be the first guy I call."

"It's a deal."

He held up his glass of beer, and they toasted.

By now, my own beer, as well as the fries, was finished. I looked around for the waiter, and seeing him going from table to table, I wondered if he was intentionally avoiding me. At the same moment that I was trying to get the waiter's attention, the young man held up his hand, as though hailing a taxi, and called to the waiter as he skirted past our tables.

"Another round," the young man said.

The waiter nodded once and continued walking. His little black eyes met mine, but he kept going without a word.

My interest in the prospective lawyer and her suitor was momentarily diverted because two young women sitting across the aisle had just rejected their first round of libidinal advances. They were both pretty blonde-haired girls dressed in black. When the set of guys approached them, sat down at the table, and exuded a profusion of arrogance and idiocy, I at first assumed that they were the girls' dates, boyfriends, or lovers. Defeated, they eventually got up and headed back to the bar.

The girls set their empty martini glasses at the edge of the table, and the wiry waiter exchanged them for fresh drinks. Shortly afterwards, a second round of rutting young men advanced. They stood above the table, drinks in hand, and talked to the girls, who gazed up thoughtfully. This pair of young men was less bold, or perhaps more sensible, than the first one because they didn't plop themselves down uninvited. The girls nodded and responded, apparently willing to give the rutting boys a chance to make their appeal, put on their show, or do whatever kind of trick needed to woo the girls. Because of the music, I could only discern random fragments of their conversation. These two weren't actually rejected because the spokesman had the foresight to take his leave before he ran out of things to say or was unequivocally dismissed.

"I tell you what," he said. "I'm going to have your waiter bring you your next drinks on me, and while you are—"

"Don't bother," one of the girls said and slid two empty, turned-over shot glasses to the edge of the table.

"Better yet," he said, smiling.

"I think they're from that guy." The girl pointed toward the crowded bar area.

"Better yet. While you're drinking that guy's drinks, let us know if we can join you, just for the drink."

"We'll let you know," the girl said.

His eyes lingered on her face as he first turned his body and then his gaze, in slow motion, away from her. Suavely, he started away, his sidekick following.

The waiter dropped off the drinks that the young man with the beard had ordered, and although I held up my hand and said, "Excuse me," the waiter turned his back to me and faced the blonde-haired girls. He said something that made them laugh.

"Excuse me," I repeated, but to no avail. He was gone.

The bearded boy was watching me, but I looked down at the empty plastic basket and then pushed it and the glass to the edge of the table, as I'd seen the girls do. The waiter was so obviously snubbing me that I wondered what I had done to him, if not recently, then perhaps long ago—but I couldn't recall ever seeing him before; I'd have remembered his tattoo, let alone his effeminate cheekbones and his fierce little eyes. I absently scanned the room, which was decorated with pictures of lighthouses and seascapes and craggy shores, as though I couldn't hear the bearded boy softly explaining to the girl that the "waiter was being a prick." Out of the corner of my eye, I noticed that the girl with the lovely smooth shoulders turned in her chair to steal a glance at me. She then said something in a hushed tone, at which her cherubic companion chuckled, saying, "Poor bastard." If the girl returned his laugh, I would have felt wounded and pathetic. Instead, the girl got up from her seat and walked past me toward the bar. I followed her with my eyes and, from behind, saw that the lower part of her was also sweetly shaped. When I turned back around, her date had his eyes fixed on me. He apparently didn't notice or care that I had just been ogling her.

"What'd you do to him?" he asked.

"I didn't do anything."

"Well, Miriam, that girl, went to get you a drink." The slight smirk on his face suggested that he found the situation entertaining.

"I'm okay," I said quickly.

"Well, she's got it in her head now. No stopping her."

"I wish she didn't."

He shrugged, and I shifted my attention back to the waves crashing against jagged rocks in the picture above my table.

When the waiter returned, he wordlessly set down a fresh glass of the thick, black brew and cleared away the things I'd dirtied. Of course, I had planned on ordering a different kind of beer, but I didn't say anything. I was curious on whose tab was this drink and thus to what extent I was obligated to thank Miriam. I started to lower my mouth down to the glass, but then suddenly conscious that this movement lacked elegance, I sat back, lifted the glass in my hand, and took a sip. Watching me, the bearded boy grinned.

Miriam came back and slipped herself onto the chair. Looking over the rim of my glass, I watched her as she began to turn around in her seat, my eyes lighting first upon the gentle curve of her breast and then briefly upon her forearm that was placed on my table, before moving up to her smile and beholding the face that belonged to that tantalizing figure. Her shrunken chin sloped radically toward her neck, and her raised upper lip revealed an expanse of pink gum, and her eyes, unfortunately, were set too close to the bridge of her nose, which, by the way, was dimpled at the tip. All the desire she had aroused in me an instant ago was abruptly shocked by her ugliness. As I felt my blasted passion begin to shrivel beneath the radiance of her beaming countenance, I returned her good humor the best I could; I imagined that I smiled back at her or at least did something semi-civil with the corners of my mouth. She apparently didn't notice my disgust because she said, "Don't mind that bastard," then held out her glass to me, and added, "Cheers."

I clinked my glass against hers. Slowly sipping my drink, I vaguely listened to her speak, transfixed by her mouth shaping the words. Evidently, her upper gums were always exposed, even when she wasn't smiling. My beer, she said, was on Stephen's bill.

"Wait a second." The bearded boy laughed. "It's nice of you to be generous with someone else's money."

"You don't have to—" I started to say.

"I didn't—"

"Don't you be a bastard now too." Miriam cut him off.

They both seemed very happy.

"Really," I said, looking at him now because it was easier. "I'll pay for my own drink."

"No, no." He waved his hand. "It's my one act of charity in this life. Don't take that from me."

"Thanks then," I said.

"Besides, now I won't have to spend so much time in purgatory."

The girl began to turn around and settle back in her seat.

"Let me treat you two next then," I said.

"I don't know," he said. "I would like my drink today, if you know what I mean. By the time you get service—" He ended this sentence with a chuckle.

"I have no idea why he's snubbing me."

"Oh, I know," the girl said, with her back to me again. "I asked him." She fell silent, as if to tease me.

I waited a moment and then asked, "Why? What'd he say?"

Before she would answer, she wanted me to join them at their table. Gathering up my umbrella and overcoat, and switching my sports coat to the back of a different chair, I sat next to the girl; I couldn't imagine sitting across from her. The waiter had given her a very brief explanation, and she wanted the rest of the details from me. The girl said that I had insulted the waiter's mother.

At this, Stephen perked up in his seat and started to laugh. "What, ho?" he exclaimed.

"I don't know him or his mother," I said.

"Out with it, Walter," he said.

"I have no idea."

I also had no idea why he suddenly called me Walter.

By the way the two of them had welcomed me, I sensed that I was acting for them as a reprieve from each other. My presence afforded them a break from the inane inquisition.

"I suppose we can get the waiter's version," the girl said. Although she sounded as if she were attempting to taunt me, I readily agreed.

"Get his version."

At once, the girl rose from her chair and sprung away with a tiny, happy bounce in her step. Both Stephen and I watched her go; then Stephen made an audible sigh. All the joy on his face dissolved into an exaggerated pout.

"Shame, isn't it?" he asked.

"What?"

"I have no luck at all." He shook his head, but suddenly his grin returned, as if he'd just realized something. He leaned over the table and whispered: "You know why they really call it doggy style, don't you?" He nodded knowingly, sat back, and sipped his drink.

Realizing that I wasn't going to respond, in fact didn't know how to respond, he leaned forward again.

"When you're doing her from behind," he whispered, "you don't have to look at the mutt's face."

He erupted with laughter, and his cheeks grew even rosier.

"I have no luck at all," he repeated.

He was still laughing when Miriam returned. Seeing him so pleasant and jovial, she lit up with a smile.

"It was in a doctor's office. That's all he would say."

I tried to think, but I was certain that the bastard, the prick, was mistaken; I didn't know him.

"A doctor's office?"

"That's what he said." The girl sat down with her foot under her, elevating her a little.

Besides the optician and the dentist, I hadn't been to a doctor in many years, even though I was at an age when I should get regular checkups. I wasn't enthused by the prospect of having some doctor's lubed finger wiggle its way toward my prostate. Like most men, I decided to wait until I pissed blood or couldn't pee at all.

"No, the prick's mistaken," I said.

Amused, the bearded boy pretended to be stunned by my profanity.

I suspected that all his expressions were not only exaggerated but also mock expressions. While such jovial affectation seemed to give him a bit of charisma, it also suggested that any relationship with him would be carefree and involve scarcely any emotional investment, both easily established and easily broken.

Despite having no story to tell, I remained at their table and listened to them. I treated them to the next round of drinks. On a plate in front of Stephen was a half-eaten baked potato, a dollop of sour cream speckled with parsley flakes, and a few sliced mushrooms sitting in a thick brown pool. The waiter twice tried to take the plate away, and each time Stephen picked up his fork and said, "Hold up, my friend." Then once again, the plate sat untouched.

Miriam began a story of her own, to which the bearded boy silently grinned like a culprit to some petty, ludicrous crime. I learned that over the past month or so, Miriam and Stephen had gotten to know one another pretty well by way of email. They had met in a chat room for Jewish singles, and because neither of them was actually Jewish, they were drawn together. At this point, Stephen interrupted to say that he was surprised to discover that, like him, Miriam leaned toward Mardukianism. Miriam humored him with a flash of her gums and said they were having trouble finding a church. Anyhow, after they'd typed their way into each other's heart, it was her idea that they arrange a meeting, face-to-face.

"That's sweet," I said.

Interestingly, their conversation was more fluid and natural when they had me as their medium. They weren't so much concerned with finding out about my life as they were with using me to reveal each other. After a while, however, even this became stale, and Stephen decided that we all needed a shot.

"Why are you still holding that stuff in your lap?" Miriam asked me. Before I answered, she picked up my overcoat and umbrella, her fingertips brushing along my thighs, and handed the bundle across the table to Stephen, saying, "Put this on that chair."

When the shots came—some viscous liquid the color of urine—I reminded myself that not only was I a lousy drunk but also I was supposed to be Dick Diver.

"Pick them up, boys," Stephen said.

"What is it?" Miriam asked.

"No questions," he said, raising his glass. The girl looked doubtfully at the shot, but then picked it up. I felt obliged to follow.

"What are we toasting?" she asked.

"Alcohol."

"No. How about to happiness?" she suggested.

"Sound good, Walter?"

"No," I said, feeling self-conscious and silly, as I held up a shot glass with two strangers.

"What, ho?" Stephen exclaimed.

"To stupidity," I declared, but before I could drink my shot, Miriam grabbed my wrist.

"That's no good at all."

"I like it," Stephen said.

Because she was holding my wrist, I switched the shot to my other hand.

"Then let's toast to love," I said quickly and gulped down the putrefaction in one swallow.

Stephen followed first, then Miriam.

"That was a better toast," she said.

"It was the same thing," he said.

"Don't be a brute."

Maybe to some degree it was the alcohol, yet this was the first thing that Stephen had said that struck me as genuinely funny; in fact, it was the first thing I'd heard in a long time that made me laugh, and once I started laughing, it seemed to erupt out of me in great waves of mirth that came from deep within.

"What, ho?" Stephen started laughing too, apparently pleased with himself for affecting me.

"A pair of brutes," Miriam criticized, but her gums were all exposed in a frightening smile.

Any semblance I had to a cultured lover soon evaporated as I continued to laugh, not because I'd completely collapsed in a hysterical fit, but rather I doubted that such a charming man would have regurgitated his drink and allowed a few burning drops of alcohol to bubble out of his nose. I held a napkin over my mouth and began to cough.

"Watch it," Stephen said. "That's the end of my potato." He pushed his plate away.

Miriam was patting me on the back. When my coughs subsided and I wiped the tears from my eyes, I noticed that Stephen was steadily grinning at me as if I, too, were a culprit.

"If you're going to waste a shot like that, you're going to have to pay for your own next time," he said.

Even though I regained my composure, Miriam kept her hand on my back. Strangely, as the puerile talk resumed, I was less conscious of the soft pressure on my shoulder blade than I was of the cool, lingering prints that her fingers had left on my wrist. Meanwhile, they were playfully arguing over whether Stephen really intended to eat the potato and the congealing sauce or if he was just being "a goof ball." She said something that gave me the excuse to turn my head, smile, and look her full in the face. I wondered if I could eventually get used to it.

When she got up to go to the bathroom, Stephen leaned across the table again and whispered.

"What am I going to do?"

"She's a real sweet girl," I said.

"Yeah." He leaned back and seemed to consider the situation seriously. "I ought to at least fuck her one time."

"I don't know."

"Not for me." He smiled. "For her sake."

Wanting to defend Miriam, who, after all, really was a sweet girl, I found the bearded boy loathsome. Yet I couldn't help admiring him. Something about his attitude seemed more than honest; it seemed right.

"Here's the question though, Walter: Do I tell her first or afterwards? You know what I'm saying? It's a risk. 'I'm sorry, Miriam; I don't think you're the right person for me, but if you want to have a little sex, no strings attached, I'd be into that.' She might think I'm an animal." He was now pointing the fork at me. "But believe it or not, Walter, that's what a gentleman would say. Most guys would take her out to dinner a couple of times, and once they'd fucked her from behind, they would find a way to get away from her. You know I'm right." He jabbed the fork in the air, as if to keep me from possibly springing upon him.

"Why have sex with her at all?" I asked, but he didn't seem to hear me.

"Once a guy puts some time in with a girl and spends a few bucks, he figures he ought to at least try to close the deal. He treats her like a whore. You know why, don't you?" He leaned forward again and grinned mischievously. "It's because they put women on a pedestal, or they're afraid of them or something. They turn them into whores because they can't be honest. But I'm honest with women; I know they get horny too."

He sat back and dropped his fork on the plate. He was talking rapidly, getting caught up in the flow of his own words, though there was nothing terribly profound in what he was saying.

"I'll put it in email though. Maybe. I haven't decided. But who knows? She might be into a little carefree sex. She seems to like me."

He looked at me now as if he wanted an answer. I wondered if this was normal guy talk, if he needed me to support him, to help convince him that his plan was valid. There seemed to be something noble about him.

"Why have sex with her at all?" I repeated.

He smiled at me, as though he assumed I was pretending to be naïve.

"Maybe I won't. Nothing's certain. Here she comes." He sat upright and looked serenely pleasant, and although I didn't turn around to watch her approach the table, I knew by his expression that they were both looking at each other.

"The great irony," he said, with his eyes still on her, "is that whores don't get horny. I bet your mom gets more worked up than any whore."

Behind me, Miriam began to laugh, and sitting down in the chair, she said, "What in the world are you talking about?"

"Walter's mom. Who wants another shot?"

"Only if I get to choose," she said.

Stephen put his elbow on the table and held up his forearm, apparently readying himself to hail the waiter. We were all silent for a moment. I glanced over at the two blonde-haired girls because a fresh set of young men was lured to their table. One of them squatted as he talked.

"I feel like I missed something," Miriam said, and she looked at me to fill her in.

"Walter was just telling me that whores aren't really into sex," Stephen said. "I guess I agree with him. He's got some crack-pot theory."

Miriam laughed and said, "That's what they say about nymphomaniacs."

My mind, a little fuzzy from the alcohol, began to teem with bleak thoughts. I wanted to leave the happy couple, go home, finally check my mail, and then burn my manuscript in the sink. Celeste Wilcox, I thought, in a blur of contempt and lust.

Stephen began to play with his potato, pushing it around on the plate and poking it with the fork. "I heard the same thing," he said. "But I suppose it doesn't matter if they like it or not. As long as they pretend." With this, he plunged his fork into the potato and started waving to the waiter.

"You're a brute," Miriam said.

"Pick the shots. Nothing too girly."

Miriam perked up in her seat and made a jittery, excited swaying motion more appropriate to an anxious child than to a prospective law student. When the waiter came over, his venom was now replaced by a black indifference. Miriam tugged his arm, brought her mouth close to the side of his face, and whispered.

"What?" he asked, slightly recoiling from her proximity.

She pulled him again and restated her order.

Before stepping away, the waiter considered Stephen's plate, hesitated to venture picking it up, and then apparently abandoned the thought.

Miriam sat bristling with joy. She wanted to entice Stephen with the secret of the drinks, but he didn't seem like he cared to play with her anymore. She made some lilting sound that vaguely resembled a giggle. The drinks were getting to her. We all became silent, and at that moment, I became aware that I was not the only one who felt uncomfortable and out of place. I wanted to leave.

When the waiter returned and set down the three small glasses, Stephen leaned forward and sniffed his.

"What is it?" She challenged.

As an answer, he picked up his glass to toast. "To Red Death," he said and instantly threw back his shot.

"To Red Death," I said, and was surprised that despite its name, the drink was less putrid, if not almost tasty.

"To Red Death," Miriam said, and then, as she wiped the corner of her mouth with the back of her hand, she gave Stephen a sly look, as if to say he was a clever boy for guessing correctly.

Once again, he didn't reciprocate her playfulness. I started to feel sorry for her—as the pleasant young man whom she'd come to know via the Internet was now cooling off before her. During the next few minutes, it was a sad spectacle to witness her flitting about, dimly confused and nervous, and all the while trying even harder to lure Stephen back into the happy game.

I looked for the waiter, so I could settle my tab. I was so anxious to leave that I swore to myself that if he snubbed me this time, I'd pelt him with the potato, to get his attention.

Breaking an awkward, silent moment, Miriam took her cell phone out of her purse and said that she needed to make a call.

"I can't in here," she said. "The music and all. I'm going to try outside."

When she stood up, she placed her hand gently on my shoulder and gave me a wan smile. Although her eyes were close-set and unattractive, they now conveyed a hint of sorrow, the dull ache of remorse, or possibly some deeper pain that she'd been carrying with her for her whole life. She took her purse from the back of her chair and slipped it onto her shoulder. Because she hadn't taken her purse on her earlier trips to the bathroom, I knew by this gesture that she was saying goodbye to me.

"I won't be able to hear in here," she said.

I wanted Stephen to say something, but he simply assented with a nod of his head.

As soon as she reached the bar area and descended the single step into the throng of people, Stephen pushed away from the table, causing the glasses to wobble slightly.

"You know what that means?" he asked.

"She's leaving." I had a sudden impulse to lash out at him, which was checked and vaguely tempered by a slight feeling of admiration.

He shook his head.

"Not yet," he said. "She'll wait a while on the sidewalk or by the front door. She wants me to chase after her. But I'll give her a few minutes." He looked at his watch.

We sat together in silence. He glanced at his watch once and smiled.

"A minute and fourteen seconds left." He drank his beer with complete repose, as if he couldn't be any more composed and in control.

I glared at him, hoping to convey something with my eyes—but my conscious expressions, no matter how intense, always came across a bit blurry and ineffectual.

"All right, my friend," he said at last, standing up. "I'll be right back. Don't vanish on me yet."

When Stephen stepped past me, I noticed that not only was his head round but also that the area from his midriff to his thighs ballooned as though he were a woman, like a pear or a bag of milk. Somehow, the shape of his body seemed to eradicate any claim he had to manliness. All his supposed knowledge of women, all his boyish charm, faded with the loose jiggling of his ass. I doubted the bearded boy had as much confidence with women as he'd led me to believe, even though I'd heard many times that it is precisely this assuredness, and not so much a man's physical appeal, that mostly attracts women. It makes them respect him and feel secure and protected in his strength. This theory, of course, lacked relevance to me.

While I waited to get my bill, I was curious why Stephen didn't want me to leave. Perhaps he wanted to come back from his sordid outside adventure and tell me what had transpired. He wanted to relish the details with his fellow man, so we could bask and gloat in the aura of our own testosterone.

I twisted in my chair, craning my body in an attempt to find the greasy, absurd creature who had accused me of insulting his mother. By now, I was hoping that I had truly degraded the woman, and I longed to repeat the offense—whatever it was—and maybe hurl a few more obscenities her way. At the very moment that I was contorted in my seat, with my body leaning into the aisle and my eyes full of frustrated savagery, I noticed the two blonde-haired girls smiling at me, as though I were a poodle performing a cute trick.

Rather than regain myself and say something funny and captivating, I recoiled as if they'd just spit at me. Then I casually began to inspect the waves and the rocks hanging on the wall, not only as if the girls were un-noteworthy and incidental but also as if my spastic response to their momentary attention hadn't actually happened. I was tempted to glance at them; instead, I peered into my glass and swirled around the residue of beer.

"You need another?" The waiter was beside me.

"Just the tab, thanks."

"And what about them?" He pointed to Stephen's plate with a pen.

"He'll be back."

Although his sharp black eyes were fixed on me, he seemed vacant of any emotion, as though I were no longer the person who had offended his mother but rather a shoehorn or a doorknob. He discarded me again to fetch my bill.

V

Sitting there alone, I felt strangely captive. When I had originally stepped out of my cramped apartment, I had been anticipating my release; I had wanted to explore broader options. But now among the noise, the permeating cigarette smoke, and the diverse people, I sensed that the vast world—with all its petty dramas, its sincere flashes of emotion against a general backdrop of apathy, and its countless personal anguishes not only borne in silence but also veiled beneath the all-important cloak of code and custom—offered no freedom at all, but only drove the individual deeper into himself. I wanted to creep back to the tiny, stuffy refuge of my rented home.

Eventually, Stephen returned, and on his way to his seat, he drummed his fingers on the table of the blonde-haired girls and, in passing, said something to them, which I didn't hear. When he sat down, he started telling me that the rain was coming down hard now outside and it was already as dark as night. Although I informed him that I'd requested my bill, he blathered on with several innocuous observations about bars on Sundays during football season. He occasionally glanced at the table across the aisle, as if he, too, weren't interested in what he was saying to me. He then leaned forward and paused for a second, apparently ready to whisper something. Finally, I thought, he was going to tell me about Miriam and how his plan to close the deal had worked on her. Instead, he said, "Are you with me, my friend?"

Although I didn't respond, he assumed I knew what he was talking about.

"Follow me." He got up from his seat and, holding an empty glass, stood before the girls' table. They both tilted their heads to look up at him, at his face. I imagined that with his female hips and broad ass, he would soon return to his chair, but once he started talking, the words flowed out of him, and the girls, first one and then the other, had fresh smiles on their faces.

Although I couldn't make out all that he was saying, I heard him say my name, but no, it wasn't actually my name. He was still calling me Walter, and now it seemed too late to correct him. One of the girls glanced at me. Her hair was pulled back in a ponytail, yet a few loose locks fell along the sides of her face. Whatever he was saying somehow motivated her to slide over into the next seat, making room for him to sit down. After a moment, he turned to me.

"Right, Walter?" he said. A barely perceptible message flashed in his eyes, but I wasn't certain what his message was meant to convey.

I nodded my head, still without the nerve to "follow" him.

They continued to talk, and conscious not to stare at them like some geeky boy at a school dance who gawked at all his classmates having fun and romancing one another on the dance floor, I only peeked occasionally at the trio. The girl with the ponytail had a beautiful but serious face, which gave her a haughty, intolerant appearance that I found intimidating. The other girl, despite her beauty, seemed more approachable; even the way her hair curved softly around the sides of her face and rested gently on her shoulders suggested that she was warm and kind.

"Walter," Stephen called across the aisle. "What are you doing?"

"What?" I asked, still trying to keep up my charade of casual indifference.

"Come tell us a story," he said to me; then turning back to the girls, he added, "This guy has got some of the best stories I've ever heard."

The girl in the ponytail looked at me, as if daring me to move. "Come on, Walter," she said. Her eyes were the color of emeralds, bloodshot, and glazed with drunkenness.

I got up and sat across from her at the table. Like Stephen, I'd carried my empty glass with me, realizing that there was a certain comfort in having my hands occupied.

Stephen introduced the girls. In response, the girl with the ponytail briefly nibbled her bottom lip, slowly blinked her emerald eyes, and nodded; her name was Ann. The other, softer girl turned in her chair to shake my hand. Her hand was warm, but for some reason, it was also wet. She was called Bruni because her actual Russian name was long, unpronounceable, and filled with y's and v's.

Although she was drinking a martini and smoking a thin menthol cigarette, she wasn't so much sexy as hopelessly cute.

As the three of them talked, I fell silent.

The waiter returned with my bill and set it on the vacant table where I'd left my things. Despite our empty glasses, he walked away without saying a word to us or even seizing the opportunity to take Stephen's plate.

"Fucking bastard," Stephen said, when he noticed that the waiter had ignored us

Ann laughed and looked around, curious about what had provoked Stephen.

"Excuse my language, ladies." He placed his hand on his chest like an old, stuffy, white-wigged gentleman. "But I was raised by a French whore."

"Hey!" Ann slapped his arm, laughing. "My mother's a French whore!"

"Look at that, Walter," he said. "We're in good company."

"Damn right," Ann said, and the two girls clinked glasses across the table.

No sooner than Bruni snuffed her cigarette, she picked up the pack and offered each of us a cigarette. Because everyone decided to smoke, I felt strangely obligated to participate, in order not to be left out of the mix, which would have surely continued to swirl around just as well without me. I now understood that sometime before Miriam had left us, Stephen had been planning to approach these girls, and this was why he'd told me not to vanish. Even so, I questioned why he wanted to attach himself to me. Were we supposed to pair off in couples? Was I supposed to make him look good? Did he need to feed off me to keep the conversation lively?

Then there was a slight break, a pause in the conversation, and Bruni, as though she'd been waiting for such a moment, turned to me, and with her breath held, with her lungs filled with smoke, she said, "All right, shy guy. Tell us one of your stories."

"I don't have any stories."

"Come on, Walter," Stephen said. "Don't hold out on the ladies." In a more flat and serious tone, he added, "We need to get him stoned. He's nonstop when he's stoned."

"For now, get him another drink," Ann said.

"I'd like to, but we're being snubbed." Stephen pointed his cigarette at me. "He insulted the waiter."

This seemed to pique the girls' interest; they both looked at me.

"That's not true," I said coolly. "I insulted his mother."

"He's a crazy fuck," Stephen said, and the girls laughed, apparently indifferent to his cursing.

"Go apologize. I want another drink." Ann held up her martini glass, pinching the stem between her thumb and ring finger. "What's up with you two? You both have a thing for insulting a person's mother?"

"It comes natural to us," Stephen answered.

"Come on, shy guy. Where's your famous story?" Bruni tapped her ashes. "You get no more cigarettes if you're going to let it burn down like that."

"Sorry." I picked up the cigarette and took a drag; it was nearly down to the filter.

"I want a drink," Ann said, now standing up. "When I come back, I want to see a drink on the table."

She started away, and without a word between them, Bruni also stood up.

Instinctively, I looked at her as she moved past me. She was wearing a pair of gray, soft slacks that clung so smoothly to her, without a single wrinkle or crease, that apparently the girl was wearing either a thong or no underwear at all.

"My God," Stephen said to me. "I'd burrow my face in that for hours." He laughed. "It's the bit of Italian blood in me. I hear it's common to all the sons of matriarchy."

"I have no idea what you're talking about," I said, with a sudden desire to destroy the silly look of glee on his round face.

Disregarding my comment, he kept talking.

"These girls seem to like us," he said. "They're partiers. They're looking to have fun. They were sitting at the table, off by themselves, all dolled up, drinking vodka drinks. You can't pass that up, Walter. You've got to make a move. But remember, my friend, always wait until the girl is on her second or third drink. That's a good rule. These girls were primed for us. All the other guys in here left them disenchanted. Sometimes that makes them more desperate to have fun."

"They're as primed as goats," I said sarcastically.

But Stephen eagerly started to look around.

"As hot as monkeys," I said.

"Where's that fucking bastard?" He suddenly stood up. With a jiggle of his ass, he strode toward the bar and left me sitting alone.

Adorning the girls' table hung a picture of a calm, aquamarine sea and a crystal sky, but in the upper right-hand corner, a dark ominous cloud threatened to creep upon the peaceful scene with violence and devastation. Apparently, either Ann or Bruni didn't like the green olives because a small collection of them soaked a square bar napkin on the table. They had been dissected, possibly out of boredom, "disenchantment," or even "desperation": On one side of the napkin were pitted olives and, on the other, a red, glistening pile of pimento. I briefly imagined that it was for the sake of this very operation that the girl had not requested her drink without olives—everyone has quirks.

Stephen came back right away, stood beside table, and pointed at me. He appeared to be standing with his feet wide apart, but that, again, was just his thighs.

"Wake up, monkey-boy," he said. "You can't leave just yet; you've got another drink coming."

"Monkey-boy?" I asked.

"Talk a little. I hyped you up. Just don't blow anything out of your nose again."

"I was going to leave."

"I don't see a ring on your finger." He sat down and started gathering together the empty glasses. "You've got no place to go. You'd rather go home and jerk off? Relax a little. Just don't blow your nose on these girls."

"My name's not Walter."

"They don't know that." He smiled again, as though we were in cahoots.

"I'm too old—" I started to say.

"That's your advantage," he blurted. "Everyone else here was popping pimples a few years ago. They don't know how to talk or even think yet, except what they've learned from stupid sitcoms and MTV. What's more," he paused for effect, propping his elbow on the table and pointing his finger straight at my chin, "you're established."

"I'm established?"

"Yeah. No one else here has a pot to piss in, let alone any W2 worth bragging about, unless their daddy is helping them out. I hate those trust-fund babies. Fucking twits."

"I don't have any money," I said, and before I could explain that I'd spent a decade as a bookworm, acquiring debt and student loans, he waved his hand in my face.

"They don't know that either. Right now, shy guy, they're in the bathroom, sizing us up. They're saying that I'm a tad dumpy and you're a tad dull. But every girl will take dumpy over dull any day. Wake up, Walter. Here come our drinks."

Stephen studied the waiter intently as he set down our order and cleared away the empty glasses. He seemed too occupied or uninterested to notice Stephen.

Silent now, Stephen began to tap his finger against the side of his beer.

After a while, I began to think that the girls had run away from us.

"Maybe they had to shit," Stephen said so calmly, so matter-of-factly, that I couldn't help but smile.

Seeing my amusement, he warned me again: "Watch that nose of yours."

Eventually, the girls returned. Ann had her arm over Bruni's shoulders and was speaking into her ear. Ann detached herself to pat the top of my head.

"You apologized." She picked up the martini and took a sip. Apparently, she didn't care about toasting.

I then learned a few things about Bruni: It was she who disliked and dissected olives, and her hand had been wet because she'd used her fingers to fish the olives out of her glass. She gave me a brief, sweet smile that seemed to confess that her petty eccentricity, along with whatever else she might do, was hopelessly cute. However, when she casually put a wet finger into her mouth, to clean the drink off, I had a sudden realization that Stephen was right: I needed to wake up.

According to Stephen, although the actual details of my occupation were unclear, I was an expert in suicide. Somehow, I worked for the police department, but not quite officially as a detective, a doctor, or even a forensic scientist: I simply specialized in suicide. I would have liked to have been involved in the psychological end of this particular field, to have worked with troubled individuals in a preventative and recuperative way, and to have expounded for the girls a theory of mental anguish that leads to self-annihilation—but Stephen deftly foreclosed this option for me and placed me straight down within the gritty physical aspect of my clients' last farewell.

The girls seemed to become intrigued by my expertise, but they couldn't possibly be enticed by it. Rather than visit clinics in Yalta or upon the Swiss Alps, I squatted beside corpses in garages, basements, and lonely apartments. With this current invention, though creative,

Stephen seemed to have faltered a little—unless, of course, his machinations surpassed any concern for me in order to work somehow solely in favor of his own penis. For the sake of entertainment, he had committed me to telling a story, and he'd apparently assumed that if I were left on my own, without his assistance, I would flounder.

Bruni asked what was the worst way to kill yourself.

"It's hard to choose," I found myself saying; the alcohol was making me more adventurous. Despite my desire to see her smile or laugh, I adopted a false, serious tone. "Do you mean in terms of mess or in terms of pain?"

"I don't know."

"In terms of mess, people are very innovative. I don't like to talk about it."

She had light brown eyes, which now looked at me with a tinge of pity, searching my face. I felt obliged to keep talking, though I didn't like this charade at all.

"I suppose the worst I've ever seen, in terms of pain, was with a small caliber gun. Before people shoot themselves, they often have a wrong idea about what is going to happen."

At this point, Stephen chimed in, and the heavy sluggishness of his tongue made me realize that he was noticeably drunk. "Sometimes, if they get the angle wrong, when they put the barrel in their mouth, they blow off their cheek or the back of the neck." As he spoke, he tapped his finger against his cheek and then the back of his neck. "But most often, it's the roof of the mouth and the nose."

"Oh, God," Ann said.

"And they have to keep on living with that wound. Tell 'em, Walter."

"No," I said. "They don't want to hear the gory stuff. Within a year, I'm going to be working more on the psychological end. This now is just a sort of internship. There is a position opening up in a clinic in Yalta, a very prestigious place, but they demand several years of fieldwork before they even consider you." I sipped my beer, self-conscious of being the center of attention. "You can actually learn a lot about a person by the way he kills, or tries to kill, himself. The act correlates intimately to his self-image."

Bruni briefly touched the back of my hand with her finger. She seemed very sad. She moved her head and eyes slowly, in a mixture of drunkenness, sorrow, and sensuality.

"What about the small caliber gun?" she asked, the tone of her voice convincing me for a moment that I was, indeed, a suicide specialist.

"In the terms of anguish, it's the worst I'd ever seen. People think it will make a clean hole through the other side of the head or maybe even burst out. What happens sometimes, however, when the caliber is too small, is that the bullet has enough power to enter through the bone but not enough to exit. The bullet ricochets around inside the skull, like a bean rattling in a jar. This one man had a wife and a kid, but he left them because they made him miserable. They were a yoke he could not bear. Yet, after a week or so of living on his own, he sliced up his brain pretty good. He stayed alive in his apartment for at least a day or two, walking around, shitting and pissing himself. We found him dead in the hall closet. He had chewed his fingernails down until they'd bled horribly."

By the time I finished speaking, a silent sobriety crept over my audience. Even Stephen, the inventor of my occupation, now seemed struck by my story; he'd apparently forgotten himself and become caught up in my words, as though I possessed the bewitching capacity to speak my new identity into the existence. Feeling Bruni's fingers on my hand and her soul reaching out to me in sympathy, I had an urge to abandon my vocation, but I couldn't; I felt trapped in the moment. It was too late to unweave my words. Beyond my bleak theme, what had truly disturbed everyone must have been my delivery, for my voice had gradually become strained and quivery, as if I were struggling against a terrible burden within myself, which had grown heavier and heavier with each word, until I'd wrapped the whole table in the gloom of a funeral. If I wanted to take back the entire episode, it wasn't because I'd lied, but because I had revealed too much of the truth. When my father had put a bullet in his brain, it might not have ricocheted around in the way that I'd described, but it had certainly reduced a perfectly fine man into a state of retarded infancy, but not one marked by silly giggles or the senseless gaze of the lobotomized. Rather, his curled body had seemed to shrivel and twitch in response to some secret and paralyzing terror, as if the bullet had increased the very torment it'd been intended to relieve. Strangely, when I had started explaining my expertise to the girls, I had no idea that I was going to incorporate any personal information, let alone this. If not the alcohol, then surely Bruni's hand and eyes had unsettled my dormant demons.

"Excuse me," I said. It was my turn to use the bathroom.

When I started walking away from the table, I had a feeling that I wasn't going to return. Although it would cost me my umbrella, overcoat, and sports jacket, not to mention a paperback, fred's number, and Lyle Tartles's card—I would be free. I edged my way through the mass of people in the bar area and followed a yellow arrow pointing into a narrow corridor. The bathroom doors were marked "Lads" and "Lasses," and seemed to offer little privacy, not simply because they were louvered doors on spring hinges, but also because they were too small to fill their doorframes, stopping far too short of the floor and also the top of the frame. When I swung the lad's door open, a girl was pulling up the zipper of her jeans, which were apparently a little tight on her. She glanced up at me, and before I could apologize for the intrusion, she informed me that the toilet for the lasses was clogged. I stepped back into the hallway and waited. Somebody came up behind me and asked if I was in line. I half-turned, nodded, and mumbled something. When the girl finally came out, possibly after many adjustments before the mirror or another bout upon the bowl, the young man playfully asked her if she'd remembered to "strike a match in there." She told him to "fuck off," which he seemed to interpret as flirtation because, smiling, he told her that she was "cuter than a button hole." As soon as I entered the bathroom again, I heard the young man start talking to someone else who had just joined the line. I had my choice between a toilet and a urinal that were barely separated by a low partition bracketed to the wall. I chose the toilet. Before I even began to urinate, I recognized that the conversation behind me was about the accommodations in the restroom; then, as if to satisfy their curiosity, the young men crowded into the room. While one lingered directly behind me at the sink, the other hobbled forward and leaned over the urinal. He sighed the moment he began to relieve himself. I stood there with nothing happening. He flushed the urinal before he finished peeing, and when he at last finished, he flushed a second time. Laughing, he advised me not to try so hard. I continued to stand over the toilet, and in the reflection of the water I could see both my face and my genitals. I listened to the second young man urinate and then spend an agonizing amount of time primping himself in front of the mirror, before finally leaving. When I was alone, a few drops squeezed out of me and disrupted my reflection; then relief came in a steady flow. With the thought of returning home, my neighbor Claudia Jones entered my mind. I imagined she was a perverse woman who was somehow dispassionately associated with the ambiguous and naked W. McTeal. She appeared veiled in a dark mist of sensuality. Behind the door of her apartment—indifferently clothed in thin, delicate garments—she moved with gaudy ennui, from shadow to purple shadow. Somebody then burst into the bathroom. As the door clapped back and forth on its spring hinges, the person released in fits and starts a series of farts that he'd most likely been holding in; he grumbled, as if angry or annoyed, and then quickly departed, setting the door into furious motion again. The disturbance halted both of my streams: that of urine and fantasy. By the time I washed my hands and reentered the hallway, I began to think how foolish it would be to abandon two pretty, drunken girls sitting at a table. Thus far, my life was a collection of botched moments and missed opportunities, and rather than alter this pattern, I was ready to perform another act of stupidity that I would one day probably regret. The image of Bruni's wet finger gliding into her mouth and then, licked clean, glistening with her saliva—enticed me back to the table. As I approached, however, I saw that the table was vacant, save for Stephen, who was holding up a slip of paper, apparently calculating his tab. He looked at me and smiled, but he wagged his finger at me, as though reprimanding a child.

"Welcome back, monkey-boy." He shook his head in feigned disappointment. "My bad luck charm."

The girls were gone. They'd taken the cigarettes but left the drinks.

"We shouldn't have lied," I said. "What a stupid lie."

"Oh, that was beautiful. But it was my fault. I can't blame you."

He started to compare us to baseball players, saying, "If you bat .300 in the big leagues, you're a fucking professional. That means most of the time, you're going to fail. It's the law of averages."

As I stood beside the table, looking down at him and listening, I fought an urge to slap his happy, cherubic face. I imagined him saying something ludicrous or crude to Bruni and Ann to scare them off. In his drunkenness, his boyish charm must have cracked, revealing beneath that superficial veneer, the bone and pulp of his naked and grotesque desire.

"What did you say?" I asked abruptly.

"Nothing at all." He pointed his finger at me again. "What, ho?"

Despite Stephen's age and his ability to grow a beard, he wasn't too different from the stupid, rutting high school boys of my youth—whose casual behavior, conspicuous sexuality, and easy friendships provided a vivid contrast to my social ineptitude, frustrated lusts, and sense of alienation. I suddenly realized that Stephen reminded me of a melon-headed boy whose cheerful jesting often used to incite me to rage. I felt the old beat of my adolescent heart. Somehow Stephen managed to stir up some distant association in my memory and inadvertently to finger and poke at the dormant emotions of my slow, painful pubescence. Despite my agitation, he didn't seem to notice. He was too amused.

"Sit down. Sit down, Mr. Parker," he said and started to lean across the table, as if he intended to whisper to me again. Captivated by the sudden use of my name, I sat down and listened to him tell his story. As he recreated the scene, I was able to picture him inclining his round head close to Ann and saying that because she was so pretty, she was able to do him a favor: She could coax the waiter into explaining how Walter had insulted his mother. Stephen hadn't actually been as interested in the waiter's gripe as he'd been in finding a way to slip in a compliment to Ann. As a side note, he advised me that it was sometimes smart to present your lust casually as a foregone conclusion, rather than to fawn and blatantly announce that the girl "turns you on." He then imitated a dim-witted farm boy who began and ended his profession of lust with the word "shucks." I resented Stephen's assumption that, regardless of my superiority of age and education, I was someone who needed sexual advice from him. The more he spoke and prolonged his story, the more anxiously I wanted to hear how the soft young Slavic woman with the wet fingers would play a role. Instead, Stephen emphasized the effects of his flirtation upon Ann. The particulars of the waiter's grievance, however, must have genuinely interested Bruni because in the end, she was the one who had flagged the wiry, greasy, tattooed thing to the table. Because Stephen was calling me Mister, and not Doctor, I now had a timeframe; if the waiter remembered me as Mr. Parker, then he must have been a child when I insulted his mother. Listening to how the two girls had beguiled the story out of the waiter, I felt a sudden pang of terror. All at once, I knew exactly what doctor's office it had been and why I had overlooked it, mistaking it for a dentist's or optometrist's. With a little sneer, I had always refused to give my therapist the reverential title of doctor. The forgotten episode came back to me now. Perhaps somewhere in the waiting room, among the maroon cushioned sofa, the potted plants, and the magazines on the coffee table—while the room seemed to pulsate because, turn by turn, each slow-spinning blade of a ceiling fan passed over a recessed light; while the music piped in from some other room sounded less like easy listening than like the sustained moans of an afflicted soul; and while a pale, lanky man sat waiting and consuming himself with the idea that the whole universe was cleanly divided into categories of me and not me—a young, quiet boy must have sat dead still in his seat. At first, I used to arrive to therapy early, primarily because of the bus schedule. A woman was always in session with the doctor prior to me. She seemed to be a picture of decorum—a polished woman who went to the beauty salon at least once a week—but sometimes through the closed door I could hear her screaming. After a while, I purposely began to come early, just to listen to whatever I could. I would lean forward in my seat and strain my ears to hear. I imagined that she was weak and that her mind was a tattered rag. Even though she always emerged from the office composed and erect, and walked past me with complete indifference, I lusted for her fiercely. I created little fantasies. I longed to be her therapist, so I could draw out her secret tremors and poke my fingers around in her wounds. In the end, I never said a word to her, and in the pitch of my excitement, I never fully realized that she might have been a mother whose young son silently waited in the same room with me. Twice a week, he must have watched me writhing in my seat over his luscious mother. The poor traumatized child. I'd imprinted myself so darkly upon his mind that perhaps over the span of time I was the secret cause of at least some of his tattoos, a nest of black coils and barbs etched upon his skin.

More or less, this was the story that the girls had used their feminine graces to get out of the waiter. Add to this the idea that I'd made a career out of analyzing corpses, and then it was no wonder that the girls had picked up their cigarettes, shunned the drinks, and politely fled.

"They said, 'See you next Tuesday.'" Stephen laughed. "They weren't too keen on you cursing in front of a kid. But it's my fault. You didn't want to tell the story, but I had the girls ask him anyhow."

I didn't remember cursing or even saying anything at all; but then again, I didn't remember any kid either.

"See you next Tuesday?" I asked.

"You've got a foul mouth, Walter."

Because Stephen appeared as happy as before, I began to appreciate that not only did I fail to revolt him; I was entertaining in a quirky way. His theory of the law of averages, as well as his conviction of persevering in the quest for women, somehow cleared me of blame. We talked for a little longer. I was conscious that he refrained from asking me about my therapy. In return, I didn't mention Miriam. If he wanted me to know her response to his plan, he would have told me. I sensed that he didn't like hurting her feelings.

"I warned them that you're a crazy fuck," he said.

When I was leaving, he told me to send him a postcard from Yalta.

Back outside, hunched under my umbrella as the rain sounded loud upon the pavement and the parked cars, I didn't regret that Stephen and I had ended up as culprits in a petty crime after all: We had put our heads together and conspired not to tip the waiter. I undoubtedly ruined my option of ever returning to this particular bar, not because of the fear of stepping into an awkward and embarrassing scene with the tattooed boy, but because of the fear of sabotage. Even if I avoided ordering any food that he could spit on, and even if I cautiously stuck to beverages, I still ran the risk of the slighted waiter stealthily dipping his greasy, wiry penis into my beer. I would have been naïve not to know that such acts of revenge—which were exactly this puerile, furtive, and perverse—were as ubiquitous as disgruntled teenage boys working in kitchens and cleaning dirty plates off dirty tables. They were angry at the world, and whosoever wanted to substitute mashed potatoes for french fries or complained the meat was a bit undercooked or asked if the air conditioning could be turned down just a smidgen, was not only accountable for the miserable world but also susceptible to consuming unknowingly all manner of mucus and grime.

VI

All the while I walked, the rain refused to ease up. It was cooler and darker, and although I tried to avoid puddles, I couldn't keep my socks from turning into wet mush inside of my shoes. The weather had the effect of driving out of my mind the recent episode in the bar. I needed to get home. I increased my pace. My sense of urgency gradually closed around me until I was nearly running, blinded as much by the water on my face as by my singular focus. Anybody watching me would have assumed that I was making a mad dash for shelter, not that I was on the brim of some unexpected and hysterical frenzy—on the brim, barely restrained—as some dark effusion was getting ready to rise, bubble, and seethe. I didn't know what had brought about this change in my emotions; a sudden sense of guilt stirred inside of me. I'd done nothing wrong, yet my incrimination started to rise to the surface of my skin. I consoled myself with the thought that the demons had fled, that the ugly swine had drowned themselves. Yes, I was merely on the edge of panic, feeling just a general uneasiness, like a harmless, slimy film upon the skin that needed to be desperately washed off. I had broken my routine, that was all, revealed myself as both a social and sensual animal. To a very small degree, I had taken the risk of exposing myself in ways I neither controlled nor expected. That was all.

As I hurried forward, I became conscious that I was envisioning myself from the perspective of a stranger. Anyone watching me, I thought, but then, why should anyone be watching me? Of course, not long ago, a young boy had curled up on my bathroom floor, and despite the cogency of my explanation, I could never escape my connection to that horrible scene. Surely, the investigation would persist. When all the possible leads were worn down to nothing or bluntly stopped by a dead end, then the officers assigned to the case would start afresh, and my life would have to endure another session of scrutiny. I try to reason with myself that the city street showed me nothing more than its blank, indifferent face, with no malicious intent lurking behind the windows or around corners, no probing eyes tracing my every foot fall along the wet concrete. Even so, I slowed down to a brisk walk in order not to appear guilty. I was thankful for one of my peculiar habits. Ever since my long ago days in therapy, I'd conducted almost all of my affairs in cash, renouncing receipts and any paper or electronic connection to even the most banal aspects of life. What had begun as my embarrassment over needing psychological relief had eventually turned into a mild phobia of there being any record of me as a social animal. If I'd ever previously upbraided myself for living a life of constant and trivial caution, then at last, on this Sunday night, my long observance of my particular paranoia seemed worth the effort. It gave me some comfort. Try as they might, investigators would only discover a quiet, unobtrusive, reclusive man who contented himself with the pleasure of books. All my reasoning, however, failed to alleviate my sense of being under surveillance. I didn't know what exactly on the street had triggered my suspicions, but, in retrospect, I see now that I was undoubtedly a little misguided. Rather than fear that some legitimate investigator wanted to drag me out of hiding and expose me to the light of truth, I would have been closer to reality if I'd imagined a stranger crouched in a doorway, ready to spring on me and cut my throat or, better yet, bludgeon my head with a hammer.

By the time I reached my apartment building, I was cold and wet, but my nerves were no longer agitated. The lingering traces of alcohol left me drowsy and dull. Several days' worth of mail, for both Claudia Jones and myself, was stuffed in my mailbox. In the hallway, I leaned my umbrella against the wall and shuffled through the mail. Although Teresa Morris hadn't replied yet, W. McTeal had sent something to my neighbor, but not the usual manila envelope with its stamped warning against bending the pictures inside. Now, it was a simple white envelope, which seemed to contain, when held against the light, a handwritten letter. Because of my recent encounter with the real Claudia Jones, I no longer felt at liberty to tear open her correspondences. The rest of the mail, both mine and hers, was junk. Someone's footsteps sounded on the landing at the top of the stairs, and I instinctively wished to avoid meeting my landlord, who would leer at me with his rodent-like eyes, silently accuse me of being intoxicated, and thus claim another reason to consider me loathsome. I gathered up my umbrella and headed down the hall in a hurry, even though I heard the person vanish down the second floor corridor, rather than descend the stairs. When I squatted before Claudia Jones's door and began to slip her mail under, one piece at a time, a sudden compulsion to knock took hold of me. If my landlord could do it loudly and without reserve, then nothing should have prevented me. But I didn't knock. I stood motionlessly. My senses seemed to be keenly tuned. I could smell the dull odor in the hallway as the caked dust on the radiator slowly smoldered. The air was heavy with moisture, and outside—as faint as an indefinable mood—the rain pounded the narrow city street. I felt sensitive to the tiniest movement and sound, but everything was still and silent. Drops of water fell from the hem of my overcoat. After a moment, I placed my hand on the doorknob and strained to discern any possible warning. I remained frozen for a long time, my eyes fixed on a section of the door's molding. What if the latch jiggles and she hears me? I thought. What if the knob turns quietly and the door pushes open without the slightest creak of its hinges? Something vaguely palpable, which seemed darkly sweet and illuminated by thick purple light, tempted me. My breaths, going in and out, were like the mild ebbing of my hazy mood.

"Claudia Jones," I said, and then hearing the sound of my own timid voice, I repeated more loudly, "Claudia Jones." I knocked two times, hard, with the butt of my palm.

I waited for a response. When none came, I believed that somehow by knocking and calling her name, I'd earned the right to try the doorknob.

The mechanism moved, the latch slipped clean, and a wild fluttering possessed my heart. The gradual inward progress of the door, however, was abruptly arrested as a thin chain pulled taut across the sliver of the opening. I tried to look through the gap, but the interior was too dark for me to see clearly. I could make out the side of a couch and, beyond it, the framed opaque darkness of a windowpane. If Claudia Jones were in the room, she would have certainly been aware of me because I was letting the light from the hallway into her apartment. I searched for her among the shadows.

"Claudia," I said through the crack. "I've got your mail," I added, though I'd already slipped her mail under the door.

"Claudia. I just want to say hi."

I obviously had no good excuse for opening her door, and even less of one for lingering there.

"All right then. I'll talk to you later."

Pulling the door closed, I stepped to the side, out of range of the peephole, and waited, hoping that Claudia Jones might think I'd walked away. I listened for a long while, but I didn't hear anything stir within her apartment.

Now that I was returning home with nothing but my own mail, the phone numbers of two men, fred and Lyle Tartles, and the same articles I'd left with originally, I began to regret giving away the letter from W. McTeal. I'd spent so much mental energy trying to piece together a character study of the freaky man that I now appeared to have squandered a substantial clue. For the first time, I'd had his own words in my hand, and a possible explanation of his connection to Claudia Jones. The central question still remained: Why did he send pictures of himself to my neighbor?

Back in my apartment, I stripped out of my wet clothes, took a hot shower, and dressed myself in my robe. It was a light blue cotton garment that I'd purchased on a whim. Though a simple and common piece of clothing, it allowed me to imagine myself as luxuriating with the extravagance of a great poet. However, lacking a sweet-smelling pipe, laurels, and talent, not to mention an innate sense of ease, I probably more closely resembled a lonely housewife. After all, the robe had come from the women's department of the Macy's in Center City.

I made myself a cup of hot tea and sat at the kitchen table with my manuscript. As I was reading, my own words felt alien to me, both insincere and inane. I didn't like that they were supposed to represent me and that, through them, Celeste Wilcox had formed judgments about me. My ideas had passed through her mind, which had sifted and measured me out. Even so, I couldn't bring myself to destroy my work. It was enough for me simply to abandon my project and leave my computer files indefinitely closed. Anyway, my boring, pedantic exercise seemed to be no more than a formality at the college. Certain officious types were unquestionably bent on seeing me go through the customary motions. They had granted me leave, under the auspices of personal academic development and with the expectation of a final product—but, in return, I intended to give them nothing. I couldn't have found a more effective way to jeopardize my position. Whenever I picked up my tea to take a sip, I absently set it back down upon the title page of my book, but always on a different spot, until the whole sheet was covered with rings from the cup. I figured I had several options open to me. The least likely was to confess that I didn't satisfy my end of the agreement: There would be no book. Also, I could have stalled everyone, Morris included, and gone on pretending to be hard at work. Another possibility was to write something entirely different, although I doubted this would have appeased anyone, especially considering the rough ideas I had in mind. Discomfited by my situation, I started to feel a bit rash and vindictive. On the backside of a sheet from my manuscript, I briefly sketched the outline of a new book. Either the third or fourth chapter would focus on the power structures within a liberal arts education. Once again, as in my previous book, I would use a Hegelian model, arguing that power proper is empty of all meaning save for the sound of its own senseless fiat. Obviously, all the vacuous jibberings of the collective mass of supremely esoteric and distended specialists ultimately amounted to nothing, and the real position is not the ideas espoused by any particular modern day "-ism," but the position of power. Of course, some people, professors in particular, think they've got something to say, and so they delude themselves and never quite realize (or confess) that they are merely props in a much larger play. Meanwhile, fresh "-isms" splinter off of older splinters, and a new specialist is created out of the very emptiness of his thinking because he has merely decided to become more specific and his investigation is not an expansion, but a fraction of a regress that is potentially infinite. He bounds himself in smaller and smaller shells and then counts himself a king of infinite space by virtue of the continual division and re-division of his domain. Thus, the entire schema—descending from Deans and theorists, to earnest teachers and students, and finally down to the un(formally)educated—would have four positions in relation to power: pure command without meaning; the delusion of having meaning; the quest for that meaning; and the ignorance, indifference, or resentment toward being outside the institution. Knowing all of this, I nonetheless remained an ostensible part of the institution—while, in actuality, I hovered outside the total schema, paring my fingernails.

Before I even finished my outline, I discarded the whole thing; it was too derivative and uninspired. I needed to think of another book, maybe even something creative. I could dig up my youthful passions and try to write a collection of poems, which was so far from what people expected of me that I would have been accused of full-blown lunacy. Regardless, I no longer cherished my obligations or my connections to the people who supposedly made up my professional and social circle. I was on my own. If I failed as a poet, then I would simply reweigh my options. Besides, other opportunities surely existed outside of my field. Considering my recent experiences with the boy, I imagined that there might have been a public interest in an exposé of the underground world of pedophilia. A man's descent into that world was undoubtedly marked by a complete range of troubling emotions—as well as a series of risks and encounters, of fits and starts—that lowered him deeper and deeper. After all, how does a person go about finding partners in that particular crime? I suspected that most pedophilia rings weren't a secret society; they were formed impromptu as the coveted object got passed from one man to another. What would be the code of conduct among such men? In all likelihood, the group would be organic, protean, perhaps centered upon a ringleader, perhaps raising up leaders out of chance, compromise, and the fluid travails of shifting circumstance. The difficulty in writing such a book would've been collecting information; the fullest report would've required the author himself to become a shade of the underground, a chronicler of his own descent. With this thought in mind, I gathered up the pages of my manuscript and dropped them in the trashcan. I washed my teacup in the sink and decided to try my hand at poetry.

VII

As the days grew colder with the onset of the winter months, I found myself frequenting coffee shops and bookstores. Squirreled away at a corner table, hunched over a marble-covered notebook, and drinking cup after cup of coffee, I went through various stages of self-revelation. My heart was more encrusted with pretense and guile than I ever expected. As I scraped away layers of calcified knots and nubs, I began to fear that beneath it all, there might not have been any core of purity to discover, any underground truth to express. But even if I didn't doubt its existence, I knew that it would always resist exposure, for in the very act of trying to unearth it and drag it into the open, I would mar the delicate thing and smear it with my grimy fingers; all the while, in a process of its own, it would react to the violation by secreting cloudy juices, coating itself over again, adopting new, false labels. I had to settle for pretense and guile because there was nothing else. As I scribbled lines of doggerel in my notebook, I was mildly thrilled by my petty plunge into the realm of art, precisely because it came at the cost of defiance and spite. By rebelling against my peers and fellow pedants, I began to nurture a secret pleasure, such as a poacher must feel, squatting at the edge of his campfire light, chewing on stolen meat. Like him, I had for my tools silence, exile, and cunning. Unfortunately, I lacked talent.

I spent so much time in one particular bookstore that I started to suspect that the staff of high school students—who put more energy into flirting with one another than into making sure the tables were clean—began to regard me as a serious writer. I overheard a squat, happy girl say, "J. C. is in his corner again."

Keeping my head down, I pretended to disregard the comment. I was curious how I'd acquired the nickname and when had they started calling me J. C. It seemed to be an implicit compliment; whether they regarded me as inspired and prophetic as Jesus Christ or perhaps as deranged and solipsistic as a false messiah, the students nonetheless saw that I possessed a glimmer of poetic lucidity—sacred or insane. From then on, every time I visited the counter for a free refill, I gave a slight smile to the girl or to whomever else was working. I felt a bit lofty. Despite never really talking to anyone, I felt a connection to the staff. I was friendly. One day when I got up to use the bathroom, I asked the squat girl if she could watch my books and my coat at the table.

"No problem," she said. Her round head swiveled forward as she nodded.

As I headed toward the restroom, I heard her whisper to her co-worker. They both giggled. Of course, it was at my expense, but they were just silly girls. I remained patronly.

Standing before the urinal, I began to think about Claudia Jones. I had fallen into the habit of knocking on her door at least once a day. I would slip her mail under, knock, and call out in a pleasant, neighborly voice, "Claudia, your mail's in." It had been several weeks since I'd opened her door and scanned the dark contents of her home. In that time, I had also received a short message on my answering machine; the gallery owner wanted to inform me that Celeste Wilcox lived "some distance away" and only came to the city about once a month. However, she was "represented," and Mr. Tartles had passed my request along. I suspected that Mr. Tartles was dismissing me with a lie, which was a nice courtesy, given that he could have kept me waiting indefinitely. Feeling somewhat defeated at least put me in the mood to generate one or two of my poems.

On my return from the bathroom, I heard the girls giggle again. I became a little self-conscious, and once seated at the table, I slyly checked my zipper. I then inspected my shoes to make sure no toilet paper was attached to my heel.

Every Tuesday and Thursday afternoon, a young boy with a

scrappy goatee worked the counter. He seemed to derive a peculiar joy whenever someone ordered a latte; it excited him, at least by all appearances, to froth milk and listen to the machine whir. Many teenagers had this kind of innocuous, giddy quirk when they were among their peers and away from the haven of their home. I supposed it substituted for an actual personality, at a time when the character of the boy was still undefined. Whenever milk needed to be frothed or coffee beans needed to be ground, the boy's co-workers would happily call him over for the task—and his ego was thus shaped around this artificial eccentricity. Also, he would remove his apron with great theatrics and flare, toss it beneath the counter, and announce that he needed to make "a head call." It was his signature gesture for going to the bathroom. During one of these performances, the squat, giggly girl mockingly said, "Have fun, J. C."

He pretended to be offended, and she giggled.

Later, as I walked home in the gloom of a cold twilight, I found myself replaying in my mind the little scene in the bookstore. Initially, I'd disregarded it, thinking that the girl must have called everyone J.C.—but this idea didn't feel right because I was J. C. A slow, lingering snowfall throughout the day had polluted the sidewalks and streets with gray slush. I tried to walk in the footsteps of other people. I was hurrying home because I felt the coffee straining my bladder to the bursting point. Every store I passed along the way was closed. If a public restroom didn't appear shortly, or if the internal pressure didn't subside, I was prepared to huddle up to a building, find some sort of crevice or enclosure, and relieve myself. At least, the gray slush would conceal the evidence. I cursed myself for drinking too much coffee. How and where I eventually resolved the small problem of my bladder isn't as important as the sudden realization it disclosed to me: The nickname J. C. had nothing to do with divine inspiration or the lucidity of the mad. It somehow referred to going to the bathroom. All my coffee drinking had me running to the men's room an inordinate number of times, and apparently the young staff had noticed. My mystique of being a serious writer evaporated under this new image of myself: I was the strange man who peed a lot. By the time I arrived home and mounted the stairs of my apartment building, I was convinced that I'd correctly guessed what the initials stood for: John Crapper, the erroneously famed inventor of the toilet.

All these thoughts, however, abruptly fled my mind the instant I discovered in my mailbox the long-awaited response from Morris the sister. Excitedly, I opened the letter in the hallway. She understood the "miscommunication" regarding the date on which we had arranged to meet each other in the coffee shop. Her point, however, was that she didn't see why any of that was necessary. I'd written her several letters, and in none of them did I enclose a check for her brother. She didn't understand why we needed any other interchange beyond a monetary one. Despite her evident, though polite, dismissal of me, the quiet inclusion of her email address seemed very suggestive to me.

The moment I entered my apartment, I booted up my computer, signed onto the Internet, and responded to the woman. I began by saying how much I appreciated having her as an intermediary. I indicated my sincere affection for Morris the man as well as my bewilderment over how this rift arose between us silly boys. We were both obstinate and proud, and left to our own devices, neither of us would ever take a step toward reconciliation. I needed to meet her in the same coffee shop as before, but no mistakes this time. I set the date for the third Tuesday in December and signed the email "your devoted friend."

I began to fear that if I were going to make progress with Morris the sister, I would have to pay back her brother. I needed to be tactful; I would have to feel her out, and only if I received a clear indication of hope, would I then give up the money. If I dangled the money to lure her near me, then I might have to pay up, in order to "close the deal," as Stephen would say. My prospects seemed dim, but I knew that I ought to explore them.

Throughout the evening, I periodically, though fruitlessly, checked my email for her reply.

VIII

In bed, reading the paperback novel that I'd been regularly carrying around in the pocket of my overcoat, I was struck by a sudden realization: The letter from Teresa Morris had made me so anxious that I'd rushed into my apartment without sorting out the mail that belonged to Claudia Jones. Using the pink slip with fred's number on it as a bookmark, I closed the novel and got out of bed. In my slippers and with my blue robe cinched about my waist, I first went into the kitchen, and not finding the mail on the table or counter, I then shuffled into the living room, which was dimly lit, blue, and chilly. According to the small VCR clock, it was just past midnight. The mail sat on the corner of my computer desk. I clicked on the desk lamp, so I could read. A flyer for replacement windows—a $75 coupon and a picture of an extremely happy woman standing in front of glinting windows—was the only mail addressed to Claudia Jones. I doubted that my neighbor needed new windows and, given that she rented, even had the right to change one. Yet I carried the flyer out of my apartment and down the hallway. In front of Claudia's apartment, I squatted with my knees together, like a woman in an evening gown, and slipped her mail under the door. My senses were attuned to something both mildly enticing and foreboding. Perhaps because I had stood there before—as an odd disheveled man at a strange hour and with no apparent intent, trying to peer into the peephole—I felt more accustomed to the situation. The lights overhead filled the hallway with a pale, shadowless stillness.

I was cold and at least partly aware that the most sensible thing was to go quietly back to my bedroom and curl up beneath my blanket. Instead, I lightly tapped on the door. I imagined that I was possibly on the cusp of some great, romantic intrigue, displaying the passion of a chivalric hero, and not simply violating the rules of etiquette and normalcy.

"Claudia," I whispered, as though gently rousing her from sleep. "Claudia."

I tapped again, feeling a faint, tremulous connection between myself and the unknown woman beyond the door. I sensed that the show that was being played out on the surface of our daily lives—comprised of my warm entreaties and her continual coquettish refusals—now exposed itself as a façade, blown softly away; and our true passions, which we'd both tacitly understood from the beginning, were finally being embraced, with no more game playing.

"Claudia," I whispered.

What would I do, I thought, if trying the handle, I found that it turned and that the door, moving inward, opened without impediment, so that I was at last standing upon the threshold of her dark apartment, which except for a different arrangement of furniture, replicated mine, room for room and wall for wall? As the thrill of this prospect took hold of me, I gently seized the door handle, but it didn't turn.

I stood outside her door for a long time, feeling the mild ebbing, the cozy somnambulism, and the haze of my swooning soul. I whispered her name: "Claudia."

Finally forlorn, I turned to leave. Yet, as I headed back toward my room, having taken no more than three or four steps, I was stopped by a sound behind me. I looked back to see Claudia Jones emerge from her apartment. The woman wore beige sweatpants, hiked up high and stretched over her bloated stomach; a thin white tee-shirt loose at the collar, as though she habitually pulled on it; and a long flannel shirt, which would have been more effective in concealing her bulk had it been buttoned up. Her face was weathered, and her mouth partly open, as though her bottom lip had been anesthetized. To my dismay, here stood the woman from the alley, but now only worse, because she was up close.

"Why don't you leave me alone?" she asked.

"I'm sorry."

She inspected me with slow, dull eyes, yet I sensed that beneath the drooping stupidity lived something that calculated and devoured.

"I'm sorry," I said again.

"Fuck it all, yes." She took a step forward. Her tongue poked itself out briefly, like the head of a turtle. "Don't apologize to me. I'm not interested. So, you're a fan of mine. Is that it?"

She looked at me, waiting for an answer, but I didn't know what to say. My prepared excuse came out.

"I just thought it would be nice to say hi."

She nodded her head.

"Because we're neighbors," I added.

"So, how's your little friend?" Her tone seemed insinuating. The fading traces of my warm and softly pattering feelings, which had moved me only a moment earlier, lead me to imagine that her words were suggestively sexual.

"My little friend?" I asked.

"Is he still sick?"

"No," I said. "He's never been sick."

She looked at me, and the ensuing silence seemed to indicate that she was measuring me in her mind.

"You're crazy through and through," she said at last.

"Maybe."

She scratched her chest with one of her long red fingernails.

"You're stealing my mail," she said.

"No."

"Of course, you are."

"No," I repeated. I'd never really regarded it as stealing because her mail had been as neglected as trash and I'd been under the impression that she was no smarter than a cow.

"Another crazy fan. Fuck it all. One is enough." Her tongue poked out of her mouth. She tilted her head, and her eyes, still focused on me, appeared to be settling sleepily in their sockets.

"Are you jerking off to my mail?" she asked.

"No," I blurted. "I didn't even mean to take it."

She inspected me with disbelief.

"Keep it all," she said. "Have fun. But he's more crazy than you. He loves me."

"McTeal?"

"Jerk off all you want. I'm not interested. But watch out for him. It's like you're stealing his love letters to me. At first, he didn't know, but now he does."

"I burned them," I exclaimed.

She continued to scratch her chest. Ignoring my assertion, she turned toward her open door, as if I were too absurd to warrant further conversation. I sensed that as soon as she shut herself back in her apartment, she would never allow herself to be drawn out by me again.

"I'm not a fan," I said quickly, desperately, not even certain what this meant.

"Well, he is," she said. Then, as if to herself, she added, "But I don't think he'd hurt me."

With that, she disappeared, leaving me standing alone in the hallway and listening to her bolt her door and slide the little chain in the slot. But I didn't hear her walk away. She most likely stationed herself at the peephole, to make sure I left.

"Claudia," I said, but I knew she wouldn't respond.

Her departing comment disturbed me. Did she mean that, unlike McTeal, I was someone whom she feared might hurt her? If this were the case, I had no idea how to proceed with my seduction. Of course, by now, I was less attracted to her than I was to a mound of peat moss. Even so, by some peculiar spark of the brain, the momentum of my first intention still carried me forward. Rather than relinquish all I'd invested in her, I was absurdly curious how to salvage the refuse. I continued to stand in the hallway and to listen for her footsteps retreating into her shadowy home, as she undoubtedly waited to hear me move away, my lingering presence causing her additional fear. When I started back toward my apartment, crossed the threshold, and turned around to lock my door, I considered another possible meaning of her words. Maybe they were a warning. Although her crazy fan might not hurt her, this didn't preclude him from hurting me. As I stood in the dark, looking at the tiny blue glow of the VCR clock, I began to realize the dimensions of my terrible situation. Somewhere in the city, a freaky man not only obsessed over my bovine neighbor but also believed that I had intercepted his pictures, "his love letters," as she called them. From his perspective, I was a wild absurdity, something unexpected, a random annoyance that appeared one day out of a cloudy gray sky. How would he react if he realized, though incorrectly, that all this time I'd been masturbating to pictures of him; or worse yet, what would he think if he'd ever learned the truth? For reasons unfathomable to him, I'd shredded his professions of love, held each burning sliver with salad tongs, and then rinsed the ashes into the sewer. I dreaded the possible conclusions he might concoct in his malformed brain. Perhaps he would see me as a contender for Claudia's love, and now, with all the strange weapons that lunacy could devise, the time for battle was at hand.

I desperately reasoned that I was deluding myself, and I happily welcomed my original interpretation of Claudia's words: She was afraid of me. This was a pleasant idea compared to the threatening alternative. But what if, I thought with new alarm, McTeal took it upon himself to defend the helpless damsel from her deranged, onanistic neighbor?

No matter how I played the situation in my mind, I found myself in the losing position. A monster was at large.

IX

The following morning I woke up early. Unrested and with a headache, I took a long, cold shower, which failed to revive me. A sense of dread pervaded my bones. Undoubtedly, from then on, I was going to avoid Claudia Jones, even if I had to climb over a pile of mail every time I came in and out of my apartment building, even if she lost a hundred and forty-four pounds and personally sought me out for a casual, sweaty tryst. I couldn't shrug off the urgency of my situation. I needed to respond to the threat of McTeal, but it was difficult to imagine what I could do, save run away.

It snowed again, piling up on my window ledge, clinging to the roughly parged wall opposite me, and coating the floor of the alley. The tracks of a small animal, perhaps a cat or a sewer rat, made several circuitous routes that all vanished or began at a window-well to the basement across the way. Claudia Jones's milkcrate was an indistinguishable shape beneath the white blanket. Not long ago, my neighbor had been a regular feature of the scene, along with the boy, whose countenance became increasingly vague to me. Normally, I had a precise memory, but after my recent bout of languor and lethargy, my mind felt as though it had been steeping a long time in milky water. The alley seemed vacant and desolate. It made me dimly remorseful because at one point—when I'd first moved into my apartment, back when Claudia Jones hummed carols and the boy ran my errands—the alley had been my primary access to a larger world. But these were stupid, idle memories. I didn't really understand what I was feeling. Perhaps my home had simply lost the freshness of its original appeal; the more accustomed I became to my surroundings, the drabber they appeared.

Sitting in my desk chair, looking out the window, I sank into a mild, dismal reverie, the sort that usually provided me material for a new poem. However, I eventually turned on the computer and checked my email. There was nothing from Teresa Morris. I took this as a matter of course; after all, my discovery of the real Claudia Jones, not to mention the dead prospect of the supposedly distant Celeste Wilcox, seemed to thwart all my hopes. My efforts upon the playing field of men and pubescent boys alike had proved futile. The drop of potency that I had borrowed from Dr. Barnett, that joy-riding hero of urban streets, had dried up into flecks of white crud. Even though it was only morning, I wanted to drink myself into oblivion. Yet I had taken that route before, and I knew where it would lead me. Instead, I gave myself the screen name, the alias, Marduk and spent an hour in a chatroom for Jewish singles.

Later, I was once again under the delusion that I knew "noble accents and lucid, inescapable rhythms," so I took up my marble notebook and decided to go to the bookstore, drink coffee, and write. I would be John Crapper for the afternoon. In the hallway, I hurried past Claudia's apartment as silently as I could, but before I made it to the exit, a sudden compulsion took hold of me, and I found myself ascending the staircase to the second floor. With a mixture of trepidation and stealth, I headed down the corridor, eyeing the doors and occasionally looking back at the way I'd come. I felt something similar to what a middle-class family man might've felt as he approached the side door of a whorehouse in his hometown for the first time. However, unlike him, I wasn't at the risk of losing my picturesque life, exposing myself to possible shame or expulsion, or even contracting a raw, sour-smelling disease. I merely needed to ask my landlord about Claudia Jones: Why was she gross and why did she have fans? Of course, the rodent-eyed man would meet my interest with suspicion, and if he one day mentioned my inquiry to Claudia, then she would be further confirmed in her belief that I was obsessive and crazed. I stood before apartment 2F and knocked. I waited and knocked again. Laminated signs were posted beside his door, giving instructions about smoke alarms, pets, blown fuses, lost keys, and other petty concerns, all presumably to circumvent any tedious tenant from making contact with him. After a minute outside his door, I suspected he wasn't home.

I scrawled a brief note on a clean page in my notebook, asking him to come and talk to me. I ripped out the sheet, folded it in half, and using a tack from one of the laminated signs, affixed my request to the doorframe.

A moment later, however, I found my landlord outside, in front of the apartment building, at the bottom of the steps. When I came out of the door, he looked up at me with an expression of undiluted scorn, which he surely must have been wearing prior to my appearance before him. He was hunched over, bundled against the cold in a puffy jacket, and gripping a shovel by the middle of its handle, as if he'd just recently been choking it. His hat was pulled down over his brow, giving him an added touch of savagery. Amid faintly falling snow, alone in the blue-gray, somber cold, my landlord struck me as the last figure in a wasted world, with the narrow road behind him rendered inoperable and the buried vehicles not merely abandoned but left over from a livelier civilization.

"Careful," he said.

At first, I assumed he was warning me about the slick steps, but I glanced down and saw a bag of salt at my feet.

"Thanks," I said.

As I didn't descend the steps, he continued to look up at me, relaxing his hold on the shovel.

"I was just looking for you," I said.

"Oh. What about?"

"I wrote you a note."

"You wrote me a note?"

"Yes. I wanted to ask you a question."

"Where's the note?" He watched me, expectantly, as if I might have the note upon me.

"I don't have it. I put it on your door."

"Okay," he said. He made a gesture with the shovel, which seemed to imply that he was busy right now and he would read my note a little later.

"It's nothing," I said.

"Oh," he said again and then started to shovel the snow off the bottom step. I knew the man didn't like or trust me. I was an object of suspicion to him, a pet annoyance. I always suspected that he secretly enjoyed grumbling bitterly and stewing in his own rancor; he was the kind of person who needed to complain. After all, it was an easy way to deal with life: to nurture social barriers and thus protect himself. By turning away from me to clean the step, he was presupposing that a conversational gap existed between us and that my silly little note acted as our intermediary.

"I just have a question to ask," I said.

Stooped over, he paused for a second and turned his head to fix me in his gaze.

"Claudia Jones," I began to say, and he straightened up, his eyes more intense. I added, "I was just curious about what she does."

"Are you still bothering her?"

"No. I just want to know about her work. You called her gross before."

"Yes," he said. "And, Dr. Parker, that's perhaps a good reason to leave her alone. Stop bothering her."

"Did she say that?"

"I know she likes to keep to herself."

"But she told you that?"

"She doesn't have to tell me."

"I'm not bothering her. Listen—"

"No, you listen," he retorted. He seemed anxious to argue with me, as if his insides were seething with contempt. He knitted his brows, pursed his bluish lips, and then repeated, "You listen." He was angry and commanding. "You hear me. You listen."

But he didn't say anything else. He simply glared at me with incipient rage.

After a moment, I asked, "What?"

"Stick to yourself. That's all."

"I do," I said quickly, pitifully aware of the enormity of this truth: I was always alone. Sometimes, after several days, I would suddenly realize that I hadn't heard the sound of my own voice because there was no one to talk to, even though all around me a whole city heaved and sighed.

"Should I remind you—?" he began to ask.

"No."

"Dr. Parker."

"Don't remind me. Whatever it is."

"Whatever it is," he echoed, aghast. "Whatever it is. I had—"

"I know. I know."

But he desperately wanted to remind me.

Yes, he had paramedics carting a little boy on a gurney through the hallway and down the front steps of his apartment building, and he had the police asking him questions, and in the aftermath, he had all the nosey people in the vicinity of his home whispering to one another as well as annoying him with questions daily.

"Don't," I said.

"Then listen to me. Stick to yourself."

"I just wanted to ask a simple question."

"Keep it to yourself."

"You called her gross."

"Yes." He was holding the shovel with one hand, and he was

becoming so agitated that he actually shook it at me.

"Tell me," I said, unwilling to cower or back down.

"You've got a computer. Go see for yourself."

"What?"

He was bristling. He wanted to tell me. He was aching to tell me.

"What?" I repeated, my voice louder, sterner.

"Her website."

"What is it?"

"I wouldn't bother to remember," he said, his words tinged with contempt. It must have been something lurid, something pornographic.

I opened my notebook and fished a pen out of the inner pocket of my overcoat.

"Come on now. What is it?" I had my pen poised, ready to write down the web address.

"I don't remember it," he responded curtly, as if defending himself against a charge of outlandish perversity.

"Well, can you get it for me later then?" I asked, with a sly suggestion in my tone, as if I knew that he had the address memorized and, moreover, I understood the reason for his denial. "Just get it for me later," I said, aware that I was provoking him.

I wanted to end this conversation. I felt amazingly calm and somewhat amused.

"Dr. Parker," he snarled, brandishing the shovel.

Ready to leave, I no sooner closed the notebook and returned the pen to my pocket than I found myself suddenly tumbling spastically over the side railing and landing on the sidewalk. Sprawled face down on the cold, wet concrete, I felt as though my head was shattered. I tasted blood in my mouth, and I knew that it was welling up in my eyes. Terrified, I tried to push myself up, and supporting myself on one forearm, I looked at the dizzying ground several inches before my face, where a crimson spot swirled in a patch of snow. My entire head throbbed with blood, as I started to sink back to the ground, which was now heaving beneath me, as if I were floating on the surface of rough waters, swirling away toward some dismal void. Before the darkness completely swallowed me up, I was frightfully convinced that splinters of bone were piercing the gray pulp of my brain, and what was worse was that I needed to get away, but I couldn't. I was losing consciousness. Fading and throbbing, I was anxious for the petty, bitter little man—straddled above me in a posture of outraged morality—to bring his shovel down upon my head for a second, a third, and then a final time.

PART THREE:

BOYS AND MEN

The boy's story came out of him in pieces. I learned most of it secondhand and a little bit directly. The elapsed years have granted me the objective distance needed to consider his story calmly. I have rounded it out, given it flesh, and filled its darkest places with my imagination. I have labored under the aegis of past masters, in search of an appropriate prose style, and discovered that maybe "this is the saddest story I ever heard." It belongs to "the record of humanity," which, indeed, "is a record of sorrows." But how can I begin to put these people on paper, when, in elegant English, one of my masters inquires, "Who in this world knows anything of any other heart— or of his own?" In fluid French, another one remarks that "our social personality is a creation of the thoughts of other people... We pack the physical outline of the person we see with all the notions we have already formed about him..., that each time we see the face or hear the voice it is these notions which we recognize and to which we listen." Even so, perhaps out of a repudiation of the tree-shaped social worker, I seem to be primarily influenced by a concise, imperative German voice. "Never again psychology." In search of a style, I have "packed" myself with voices, and for the boy's story I would like to choose one that is fair and calm, as indifferent as the night sky, into which I now gracefully fade, so the boy may increase all the more, which is a Johannine doctrine, appropriate for a love story.

Suppose for a moment that a tall man, bundled against the cold, began to fill his car with boxes of books. Or, better yet, a different man stirred sleepily in his bed and reached over for his wife who was no longer there. But wait. Perhaps it's better to begin with a picture of the boy. But no, wait a moment: not the boy, but a boy. Yes. Now suppose the cold again. Now the picture; it begins to take shape. It is all picture, all image. It is, yes. Suppose this:

I

It was a high country, as cold as iron, still and gray. The road was lined with sheer black rock on one side, and overlooked a pitched landscape, blanketed with snow and cluttered with evergreens, on the other. A silver colored sedan appeared out of the dawn. In the backseat, a boy leaned his head against the window, staring out at the rock or maybe at the streams of ice that clung to its face, as though flowing water had been caught by surprise by the cold, even though the cold seemed as if it had always been there, and it would always be there, so there never could have been water in the first place, only ice.

The car's tires made a steady, whispering sound.

A thin girl sat cross-legged in the front seat, with her long fingers laced between her naked toes. She had directed all the heater vents toward herself. She was biting her bottom lip and slightly bobbing her head; she was in control of the radio. Every once in a while, she turned around in the seat and watched a baby who seemed to be not only sedated but also strapped and bound in a car seat. The girl leaned forward and rested the tip of her finger on the baby's lips, but the baby didn't respond. The girl grinned as if the child had just communicated something that only she understood.

"Why are you always trying to upset her?" the mother asked. She had both of her hands on the steering wheel and the seat so forward that she appeared cramped.

"I'm not," the girl said. She lightly ran her finger down the bridge of the sleeping baby's nose, then turned around, and gave her attention back to the radio. She adjusted the volume but left the station alone.

The boy watched the road whispering beneath them. Mildly entranced by the endless stretch of guardrail, he looked as though he were ready to fall asleep. He had dark pupils and long lashes. His cheekbones and jaw would have been sharp and angular if not softened by his smooth, almost feminine skin. His thick, red lips were somewhat ludicrous for a young boy, making him appear at once oddly sensual and apathetic. Although his face hinted that he would one day possess an exotic beauty, now he seemed to be in a constant state of pouting and languishing.

When it began to snow, the mother pulled herself up in the seat. An elastic band held her hair back from her face. Without makeup, her face looked blotched, worn, and tired. She was dressed in dark blue sweat-clothes and a pair of sneakers. At first, the snow vanished as soon it hit the windshield, but eventually she had to put on the wipers. Despite the radio and the gentle sound of the tires, everything was hushed: the baby sleeping, the boy gazing out the window, and the girl in the front seat abstractedly occupying herself with her own fingers and toes.

The road wound downward; its surface gleamed black and wet, with an occasional dirty patch of churned snow. From the right, a river came out of the mountains and began to follow the road for a while. Thick ice lined its banks, and the water seemed as motionless as the road itself. Farther ahead, as if at the very base of the desolate landscape, the road and the river crossed and went their separate ways at a stout, dull green, metal bridge. It was here that the car abandoned the road and seemed to ease itself into the water without making a sound. The car submerged, and bubbles burst to the surface as air rushed out of the vehicle.

Then everything was very quiet and undisturbed.

Inside the car, however, it became darker and darker as it sank, sealing within itself a wild, savage flutter of limbs and bodies that beat at the windows and tore at the seats, hysterical voices mingled with cries—a convoluted mess of fear, panic, and desperation—until the rising waters seeped in and drowned it all, first with silence, then with darkness.

About fifty yards from the bridge, an object, as dark and indistinct as a piece of driftwood, broke the surface of the water. It floated with the slow current, dragged against the icy bank for a ways, and was finally caught in a tangle of pale, yellow weeds. The flowing water made a trickling sound as it passed the body. Only a clump of wet hair was visible, like that of a lifeless beaver or rat washed ashore. Then maybe because of the steady force of the current or an abrupt weakest in the yellow weeds, the body rolled over and a sliver of face appeared in the open air. In time, the falling snow would have covered it, but all of a sudden, as if startled from a violent dream, the head and torso rose upright. Without looking around, with a strange, silent calmness, the boy turned over and crawled up the bank. He crawled until he came to the road; then he got to his feet and walked along the black pavement. He limped because one sneaker was missing. He seemed to be heading toward the bridge, but then he crossed the road and sat down with his back against the guardrail. He drew his knees up to his chest, wrapped his arms around his shins, and stared forward, neither at the falling snow nor at the nearest mountainside. He stared blankly, calmly, with an attitude as detached as a corpse's. After a while, he let his chin rest on his knee, and his head sunk so forward that in all appearances he was probably dead.

II

A barebacked man stood in front of a full-length mirror on a closet door. He was middle-aged, with a big build that was covered with a layer of soft flesh. His hair was still wet from a shower, still uncombed. He stared at himself intently, almost as if he were waiting for, or perhaps daring, his own image to make a quick, unexpected gesture. He let his eyes inspect his body. He lowered his underwear down to his ankles and continued to stare at himself. After a moment, his piercing gaze and his rigid expression—as if his face had been carelessly hewn from wood—began to slacken, and his eyes became glazed, perhaps from staring too hard for too long. He touched himself, running his fingers gently across the spot where his testicles should have been. He exhaled audibly and, with abrupt deftness, pulled up his underwear and walked away from the mirror.

He dressed himself in a pair of black dungarees and a matching shirt and jacket; it was a uniform for a commercial refrigeration company. He seemed oblivious to his surroundings, moving by blind routine. The room was bright and clean, with knickknacks displayed on the dresser and pictures hung on the walls; his family smiled inside their frames. The man straightened the bedcovers and paused for a moment in the center of the hardwood floor. He seemed to be shutting down, turning into wood, his face drained of expression. This wasn't struggle, but surrender and defeat. But then, as suddenly as a switch thrown on inside of him, he came alive again; he stuffed his hat into his back pocket and turned toward the door. However, instead of leaving, he strode over to a mahogany crib against the wall. He picked up a small blanket, unfolded it, refolded it, and then draped it over the side of the crib. He lifted his head and looked around as if he were only now realizing where he was. When he left the room, he had a faint smile on his face.

III

The clouds gathered thicker, darker, sustaining the mood of a bleak dawn for a while longer into the morning as the snow came down sideways, slanted by the wind, and as the wind whistled across the high, jagged terrain, stirring the evergreens and moving thin ripples across the surface of the river, which was nearly as unperturbed and implacable as the road, while the road itself now began to vanish under a fine coat of snow, as if nature not only conspired to blot out any indication of human handiwork but also to make the whole landscape so unwelcoming as to keep people away—but, nevertheless, a battered station-wagon drove slowly across the stout, dull green bridge and then stopped, with the snow glinting in the beams of its headlights and with one windshield wiper slapping furiously, in double-time to compensate for its partner, a useless blade that rested perpendicularly on the windshield, not moving at all. The car door swung open, and music, just a heavy, throbbing bass, spilled out of the car. A man emerged, with his chin pressed against his chest and his coat collar pulled high over his ears. He walked in front of the car, took hold of the dead windshield wiper with a gloveless hand, and began yanking on it, as if he wanted to rip it off or perhaps believed that this was how to make it work again. The other wiper slapped back and forth. The man cupped his hands before his face and blew on them. He had long fingers, and his face seemed as though his skin had been pulled tight over his skull. He had a small, crooked vein at his temple; high, hard cheekbones; and thin, bloodless lips. He was a tall man, dressed in a black pea coat and a pair of jeans. He cleared the snow off the windshield with his forearm. Muttering and visibly annoyed, he stared at the car. He walked back toward the open door and got in, shutting in the music as abruptly as he had released it. Although idling loudly, the station-wagon didn't move, except for its single, furious wiper; snow already began to gather on the quiet side of the glass. The boy, as slight and absurd as a famished monkey, was standing in front of the car. When the car door opened a second time, the boy took a hesitant step backwards. He cautiously watched the vehicle, and as soon as the man made a gesture to get out, the boy turned and ran, limping because of the one missing sneaker. Running down the center of the road, he seemed crazy enough to try to outrun the car, as if he'd just challenged it to catch him and he didn't think that it could. But the car made no attempt to pursue the boy. The man merely pulled the door shut and watched the boy through his windshield. About fifty yards ahead, the boy suddenly stopped running, walked over to the side of the road, and sat down with his back against the guardrail. Then the car began to inch itself forward, slowly, possibly afraid of startling the boy into fleeing again. When the car was beside the boy, the door opened and the man got out. The boy was hugging his knees, staring blankly at the man and the station-wagon. The man squatted and began to inspect the boy, the way he might inspect something he intended to buy, like a used lawnmower. He didn't speak. Apparently satisfied, he raised the boy by the arms and helped him to the car, supporting him as though he were drunk or drugged.

IV

By afternoon, the snowstorm had traveled southward, and although most of its force was already spent, it had managed to foul up the roadways. On a suburban street, two boys trotted through one front yard and then the next, wandered onto the road, then through someone else's yard. They talked loudly, having the calm, silent road all to themselves. At last, they stood before a yellow house whose lawn was cluttered with low, snow-covered shrubbery and scrappy trees. The boys walked up to the front door and rang the bell. They waited and rang again. After a while, they left the house, ducking under a fence and continuing on through peoples' lawns. Their voices faded, soft and indistinct.

The snow fell faintly, lingering on, and by dusk, it was over. Because the road wasn't plowed, cars had worn a single lane down the center of the road. A navy blue van, bearing the logo of a refrigeration company, approached the yellow house and pulled into its driveway. The man in the dungarees got out, slapped his hat against his thigh, and put it on his head. He walked down the driveway, his boots sinking into the snow, just above the ankle, with each step. The man took the mail out of the mailbox, and then started back toward the house. When he came to the front door, he paused for a moment with his keys in his hand; he was looking at the tracks the two boys had left in his yard.

A little while after the man had gone inside the house, the two boys returned, this time with shovels. They rang the bell, and the front light came on. The man opened the door. He was now wearing only the pants and a white tee-shirt. No sooner than he looked at the boys, he started closing the door.

"No thanks," he said.

"What about Nathan?" one of the boys asked.

The man held the door still for a moment, so just his face was revealed.

"He's not home."

"When's he coming back?"

"He's away for the weekend, visiting his aunt."

"Tell him Ray was looking for him," the boy said. "He knows me from school; I'm a grade ahead of him." Ray was wearing a florescent pink headband over his ears, which gathered his hair in a loose bunch at the top of his head. "Nathan's not here," Ray said to the other boy, even though he was standing there and listening himself. Without a word to the man, the two boys hoisted the shovels onto their shoulders and turned to leave.

"I'll give you fifteen dollars," the man said.

"We'll do it for twenty," Ray said.

"But you have to do the front walk also."

For an answer, the boys merely lowered their shovels and started to clear the walkway.

The man went back inside. A floodlight came on and shone on the driveway. Ray paused for a moment, leaning on the shovel, looking at the light. The air was redolent with the odor of chimney smoke. He began to work again, as steady and composed as a full-grown man. The boys separated and shoveled each end of the driveway, both working toward the light. This gave them extra time. Before they finished, the sky became completely dark. The man stood in the doorway, watching them; he might have been watching them all along. His face seemed less harsh now, as if he'd had some time to relax, maybe with a few glasses of wine or something harder, for he stepped out into the cold in his tee-shirt and came a few paces down the front walk in nothing but his socks.

Ray gave the other boy his shovel and walked toward the man.

"Does it look okay?" Ray asked.

"It's real nice," the man said, but he didn't seem to notice the driveway at all. He handed Ray some money.

"Are you sure you want to give me this much?" Ray asked, already putting the bills into his pocket.

The man nodded.

"Thanks. That's more than double." Ray looked down at the man's feet; then he took his headband off and stuffed it into his coat pocket.

"Apparently, he's not visiting his aunt, after all. I just called there," the man said. "I don't know where he is." He smiled and nodded again. His voice was flat, without urgency. "I don't know where she took him. And my baby and my daughter. But I knew she would. I can't blame her."

"Sure," Ray said, moving away. "Thanks again."

"A woman needs a man, you know."

"Of course."

"She needs to be fucked."

Ray nodded now. He turned and left the man standing on the walkway. When he reached the other boy, he took back the shovel and rested it on his shoulder. The two of them started down the driveway, out of the range of the floodlight and into the darkness, their voices vanishing first, and then their figures. Even so, the man remained outside on the walkway, looking after them.

Sometime past midnight, all the fires were most likely extinguished because not a trace of chimney smoke remained in the air. The neighborhood had shut itself down for sleep, except for the man's house. Although it sat silently, the windows were lit up; every light was on in every room. The man was in the kitchen. He was sitting on the counter, slumped forward with his hands dangling between his legs. The tiny blanket that had been in the crib was now draped over the back of a kitchen chair. The hood exhaust whirred loudly, apparently in an effort to suck out of the room the odor of vomit. There was vomit in the sink. The man sat for a long time; then he slipped off of the counter and staggered to the table. He picked up a cordless phone. He began talking before he even dialed or held the phone up to his face. With his voice steady and flat, he continued talking as the phone rang. He was in midsentence when someone answered.

"—everything here in the house," he was saying.

"Kyle," a woman said.

"She's just got to come for it. Everything is here for her."

"Get some rest now. I've called the police. They're searching the roads."

"If she's there," the man said, "tell her I don't blame her, and everything is here waiting for her. Everything I've ever made, every cent I ever earned, is hers. I want none of it."

"Kyle, go to sleep now," the woman said. "Please go to sleep. You can't keep calling me."

"I can go away. I can leave instead of her. It's easier that way because of the kids and all."

"Believe me." The woman was crying now. "She's not here. She never showed up."

"Tell her—" he began, but he stumbled, and the phone fell from his hand.

V

In a room dimly lit by a tall, freestanding lamp, the man, no longer in the pea coat but still in his boots, stood with his back against the wall and seemed to be quietly inspecting his surroundings. He might have been waiting for something to happen, for something to move, but the room was still. It was a meagerly furnished apartment, with a kitchen sectioned off by a counter and with a narrow bathroom behind a narrow door. The only thing that might have moved was the boy, but he appeared as good as lifeless on the bed. It was pushed up against an empty bookshelf and an old-style cast-iron radiator, though not long before, in all likelihood, the bed had been beneath the single window, where the floor appeared conspicuously bare. The blinds were closed, and a dark bath towel was tacked to the window molding. The man stepped into the center of the room, as if he were about to do something but suddenly checked himself. He appeared to be waiting to move. After a while, however, he went to the bed and raised the blanket. The boy was on his back under a white sheet. The man covered him again with the blanket, so just the boy's face was exposed. The man gathered his coat from the floor, shut off the tall lamp, and left the apartment.

He was gone for a long time. At one point, a commotion occurred in the hallway, angry screaming and a woman crying, but the boy slept through it. The room was so dark—filled with the same stale, thick, eternal darkness of a cave or a tomb—that if not for the sound of a random cockroach scuttling across the wooden floor, the stillness would have been thorough and unbroken. When the man finally returned, nothing at all had changed, so it might have been that time itself hadn't moved either, as if in one motion the man had merely walked out of the room and then back into it. He took a brown bag out from beneath his coat and set it on the corner of the bed. He threw his coat against the wall, walked back to the door, and jiggled its locked handle. He moved slowly, setting a metal folding chair beside the bed, then making several trips to the kitchen, carrying only one thing at a time, though the items were small: a dish towel, a wooden cutting board, a plastic grocery bag. He finally sat down on the chair, at the foot of bed. All the while he didn't speak, and he didn't look at the boy's face. He tore open the paper bag, which contained a hammer and a pair of chisels. He held a chisel in one hand and the cutting board in the other, as if he intended to carve something out of the piece of wood. Yet he set the board on the bed. He then fished under the covers and drew out the boy's foot, which looked like dead meat, completely drained of blood. The man stood up again and made another trip to the kitchen. He turned on one of the stove's burners and rested the chisel's blade in the small, blue flame. He came back with a few more dishtowels and half a bottle of vodka. The other half might have been in the man already or maybe in the torpid boy. Without sitting down, the man picked up the tools and then froze for a moment, as if listening to something far away. For the first time since he'd returned to the apartment, he seemed like he had no idea what he was doing. He placed the cutting board on the chair and studied it as though he doubted it belonged on the chair. He took a pack of cigarettes out of his breast pocket and emptied two cigarettes and a lighter onto the mattress. Squatting beside the bed now, the man tried to place the boy's foot flat on the cutting board, and rather than move the chair closer, he pulled the boy by the ankle. The boy's toes were as white as bone, expect for a rich purple spot beneath the big toe, which was already beginning to rot, and the purple seemed to promise that it would turn black and that the black would spread. The man still didn't say anything or look at the boy's face, and the boy still didn't respond. The man took a swig of vodka and returned the bottle to the floor. As he positioned the chisel straight up from the base of the boy's big toe, he seemed confused, sucking in his thin bottom lip, holding the upraised hammer, suspended and motionless, above his head. Then he moved the chisel to the smallest toe, while the arm with the hammer remained frozen. He didn't look like he was trying to work up the courage, but genuinely confused. He spun the chisel halfway around, as if all along he'd been calculating whether it was better to have the flat or the beveled edge of the chisel at the base of the toe. He chose the flat edge and brought the hammer down with a solid thud, severing the tiny extremity and at the same time cracking the cutting board down the middle. He quickly dropped the tools. The boy still didn't move, even as the man began to burn the wound with the lighter. Apparently, it was a bad idea because the raw flesh continued to bleed and the lighter extinguished and it wouldn't re-light because of the blood. Maybe the man was simply experimenting with the lighter, or maybe he'd forgotten about the other chisel a few paces away in the kitchen, but at last he retrieved the chisel off of the burner, hastily wiped the wound with a dishtowel, and pressed the hot blade against the stump, holding it there for a little while longer after the sizzling had stopped. The man did all this calmly, in control. With the lighter now cast away, he repeated the process more swiftly with the next toes, working his way up to the larger ones, realizing, apparently, that there was no reason to raise the hammer so high. When one half of the broken cutting board became greased with blood, he replaced it with the clean second half, as if he'd planned beforehand to have it on reserve. He took a swig of alcohol between each operation, giving the chisel time to reheat in the fire. When only the big toe remained, he sat back on his heels. Four little, bloody nubs were in the plastic bag, along with several bloody dishtowels. Maybe it was the blood or the stench of roasted meat or even the vodka that caused the man to get up and stagger away from the scene. Kneeling on the bathroom floor, he gripped the sides of the toilet and heaved several times. Nothing came out. He sat back, breathing heavily, his face strained and red. Although he seemed as though he were composing himself, he suddenly leaned forward and vomited. He vomited several times, with a long pause, a sort of fake composure, between each spasm, and then after the bottom of his stomach came out—just a mouthful of something black and rancid—the man merely started to dry-heave again. Exhausted, he slumped against the wall. His hazel eyes were bleary, his mouth open in an idiot's gape, as though his lips were numb. He flushed the toilet, rinsed his mouth in the sink, and continued to slump against the wall. Then he closed his eyes and didn't move for a long time. When he finally woke up, once again nothing seemed to have changed, so as far as time was concerned, the man might have just closed and opened his eyes, without sleep or anything else occurring in the interval. He pushed himself up and crept back into the other room, approaching the bed slowly, with his head slightly cocked to one side, looking at the chair, the tools, and the blood, as if the entire scene itself were something that would wake up if he made too much noise. He squatted beside the bed again. The boy's foot was beneath the covers now, so the boy must have moved. The man reached under and drew out the boy's foot. Although he had seared the wounds, they had continued to bleed a little. The man took another swig of vodka. He picked up a cigarette from the bed and lit the cigarette with the stove's burner, which had been left on the whole time, its heat cracking the wooden handle of the chisel. He needed to use a dishtowel to pick up the tool; he inspected it and then set it back in the flame. He moved without haste and smoked his cigarette down to the filter. His face looked waxen, his eyes tired, almost sorrowful. When he kneeled beside the chair again, he stared at the boy's mutilated foot. The rest of the boy didn't seem to matter to him, as if the boy's mortality was never in question; or perhaps the man had already resolved that issue because he might have known that the boy was not almost dead but certainly drunk or drugged, or maybe because he believed that the boy's life or death was no longer controllable and in meantime, just in case, the man would cure what he could, namely the boy's foot. He picked up the chisel and the hammer, and readied himself to amputate the remaining toe. He positioned the blade on the knuckle, finding the weakest point, the cartilage beneath the skin. However, this time, motionless and suspended, his arm didn't seem to be arrested by confusion, but by a lack of courage. He began to breathe faster and harder, and all of a sudden, he completely ceased to breathe at all as his arm swung fast and hard, not only severing the toe and splitting the piece of cutting board but also driving the chisel into the thin metal of the chair. Calm and without haste again, he finished the rest of the operation; he cauterized the wound, smeared some ointment on the entire mess, and lightly dressed it with gauze.

He didn't clean up the scene right away. Instead, he pulled the chisel out of the chair and then sat down at the counter with the bottle of vodka. He smoked his last cigarette and drank. He actually looked composed, relaxed. Strangely, it was only now that he noticed that while he had been sleeping in the bathroom, the boy had been walking around the apartment. A trail of small, bloody footprints led in and out of the kitchen, up to the bathroom door, and in fact, all over the room. This didn't startle the man. He reclined at ease, smoking his cigarette and drinking his vodka, as if he had anticipated everything beforehand.

VI

The man named Kyle was no longer drunk as he sat at his kitchen table, which at noontime was bathed in sunlight shining through the bay window, forcing—with its blinding glare—the two men who watched Kyle from across the table to sit nearer to one another than they probably would've liked to sit, so even while the sunlight seemed to delineate obvious sides—two men pitted against one—the two appeared a little silly, sitting uncomfortably close and squinting all the same, their faces somewhat grave, somewhat inquisitive, sipping coffee, talking in turns with careful, measured phrases, and evidently preferring to endure the glare than to draw attention to it or anything else that might not have been on their agenda or in accord with their little notepad on the table, as if these men were conducting themselves not exactly in the moment but rather for the moment's future significance, so even before the conversation had begun, it'd already been deemed officially significant, and everything was going on record for later use, except, of course, for pointless gestures, such as when Kyle—somewhat sleepy and somewhat intense, like a man aware that he is in the middle of a serious situation that has nothing at all to do with him—reached over to the bay window and lowered the shade, almost as an afterthought, because he was already rising and already saying, "Let me get you guys some more coffee."

The smaller, balder man slid his chair over, and when Kyle's back was turned, the man stared intently at him. The man lightly tapped a pen against the side of his head.

"Mr. Douglas," the man said. "Are you sure your wife had no reserve cash, nothing stashed away, no college fund for the kids or anything?"

"I don't think so."

"She had about two, maybe three, hundred dollars on her, and she hasn't used any of her credit cards or written any checks. I'm sure you understand what I'm saying. She's been missing for ten days now, and somehow she's been supporting all four of them, for ten days, on just that little bit of money."

"I understand. Sure," Kyle said. He came back to the table with the coffeepot and refilled the mugs. "I thought about everything."

"You know what I was thinking?" the second man asked. He was stirring milk into his coffee and looking down at it. "I was wondering that maybe she knows somebody you don't know."

"You mean a boyfriend," Kyle said quickly. "I thought that too. In fact, that's what I think about the most because I told her one time (I was upset when I told her, but I did say it) that she should get herself a lover. Only, I said, don't tell me about him and don't fall in love with him. Just those two things."

"Did she?" the man asked.

"I don't think so."

The smaller, balder man now tapped the notepad with his pen.

"Then why do you think about it the most?" he asked, his tone slightly accusatory.

"I don't know," Kyle said, sitting down again. "Maybe I hope for it. I want him to be a good man, though, as long as I don't have to know what he looks like or what his name is. Does that make sense?" He smiled faintly, and his voice had a dreamy quality.

"Mr. Douglas," the man said abruptly, as if he were calling him back from afar, maybe out of a mild rhapsody, or just waking him up. "Tell me now," the man said, and he asked Mr. Douglas why he'd been "upset," latching onto the word as if it were the key to everything. He was less pleasant than the other man, and his caustic attitude seemed to be as intimately involved in his identity as his stature and his baldness.

"I'm sorry," Kyle said. "What were you saying?"

VII

Two women stood facing one another in front of a fireplace, in the middle of a party. One was holding a drink in her hand, and the other—a big woman dressed in an oversized black gown that attempted to conceal her bulk—placed her drink on the mantel after each sip.

"My, that's strong," she said and smiled. She had a pretty smile; in fact, her whole face was pretty. "I'm glad Ralph is going to drive home tonight." She laughed.

"Don't forget to ask him about next weekend," the other woman said.

"Oh, we'll go. He loved your stuffed grape leaves last time. That's all he could talk about for days." She sipped her drink. "Oh," she said, smiling. "And Ed's wine." She leaned closer to the other woman, as if to impart a secret. "That's the key to have a good time every time: a husband who's a connoisseur of wine. Ralph was impressed. He thinks high of Ed; he told me so. He said, 'Ed knows his wine better than any man I know.'"

"So you're coming," the other woman said. "Now that makes me glad. Seven o'clock sharp. Just bring yourselves."

"I might bring a bell." The fat woman laughed. "Oh," she said. "I think I need to put some more ice in this." She held up her glass, though it was nearly empty. She began to step away. "Besides, I ought to check Ralph before he begins to miss me."

"I'll catch up with you later. Don't leave without saying goodbye."

"Of course," the fat woman said, then leaned nearer, and spoke covertly behind her hand. "I forgot my bell tonight. I believe at least one person should wear bells at every party."

The other woman smiled weakly, which was the only response she offered.

The fat woman nodded and started away. She walked through the living room with her head up and her eyes beaming, ready to make contact with whoever glanced at her. Inviting and amiable, she smiled at everyone. Most of the men wore sport coats, although a few were in sweaters; and almost all of the women, like the men, were dressed in dark clothes, so if not for the smiles, laughter, and abundant food and beverages, the occasion would've appeared as somber as a funeral. Compared to the fat woman, everyone seemed to be imbued with a rigidity that was passing itself off as etiquette. They noticed the woman and let their eyes linger long enough to remember, to keep a tally. It was an impersonal look. They probably didn't have anything in particular against the woman; they simply might have needed to have something against someone, to be allied and bound in even the most trivial and fleeting pact. The woman had begun her tour of the party with easy gestures and a ready smile. At the bar, she skipped the ice and refilled her drink. By the time she entered the foyer, passing under an arched doorway and into a long room with ice-blue ceramic tiling and murals of waterfalls on either side, the woman seemed heavier, lumbering, and tired. A small group of men were gathered at the archway to the great room. They stood erect and composed, with an air of confidence; yet something artificial tinged their postures, as if they had groomed themselves for a long time for the sole purpose of standing among one another, properly. The tallest man in the group had his back to the woman as she approached. She delicately placed a hand on his shoulder. He turned and smiled and brought his face near to hers.

"What is it?" he whispered.

"This place is cold," she said.

"It's business."

She looked at him doubtfully.

"This is my boss's house, remember." He kissed her cheek. "Be patient, okay. Why don't you get yourself another drink?"

"That's a good idea. Would you like one?"

He shook his head, and as he looked at her, his hazel eyes had a quality that was soft and tender, glazed with something like compassion or possibly love, which began to fade the moment she turned and moved away from him. He watched after her. She visibly drew a deep breath, as if gathering strength, and exited the foyer without glancing back. The man turned his attention to the group of men again, who had continued their conversation as if the man had never left it or had never been a participant in the first place. He appeared to possess a singular charm, even though he wasn't handsome. His face was all bone, his skin as thin as paper, revealing his veins at his temple. The other men laughed when he spoke. They undoubtedly had no idea that not long ago their colleague had taken the toes off of a young boy's foot. When the conversation drifted toward money, the man watched the others with an amused grin.

"Ralph's awfully quiet," one of them said.

"He guards his portfolio like it's the keys to heaven."

"I just don't say anything," he said.

"We know."

"Give me your money then," Ralph said. "I'll invest it for you."

The men chuckled.

"Sure, then you can give up your moonlighting and start investing in a new car or a boat for yourself."

"I'll skip the boat," Ralph said. "I'm not a fan of the water."

"Hey," one of the men said softly, leaning into the center of the circle. "What's this about moonlighting?"

"Ralph's into sales," another man whispered, as if Ralph weren't present and they were gossiping about him.

"Really?" A man nodded knowingly.

"Religious propaganda."

"What religion?"

"Christian."

The men continued to throw glances at Ralph, as if he were on the other side of the room.

"As long as he doesn't try to peddle that voodoo crap around the office."

"No problem," Ralph said at last, still grinning, still composed. "But I'll remember that the next time you try to peddle your daughter's Girl Scout cookies at work."

The group chuckled again.

"It's a little book route I do once or twice a month," Ralph explained. "I had it for years. I just never let it go because it's a peaceful drive. It's nice. It keeps me sane. Other men golf on the weekend."

"And other men fish."

"Other men fish," Ralph agreed.

"But you're afraid of the water, right?"

"I wouldn't say 'afraid,'" Ralph said. Then he slowly passed his eyes over each man in turn. "And some men take Prozac."

He could have been bluffing, yet he seemed to know something about one or all of the men. Even so, nobody stepped forward, to contradict him or to confess. Someone laughed, and the group disbanded with smiles.

Above the general bustle and the murmur of voices, the sound of music from a piano flowed out of the great room. With his hands in his pockets, Ralph walked casually and let his gaze roam with a bit of detached interest, going beyond familiarity and ease—disclosing an attitude, not of a guest, but more like the owner of the large house, someone who had emerged out of a secluded, quiet room, just to make a brief appearance and then depart again, wordless, unobtrusive, and seemingly indifferent, as if the house merely belonged to him by accident and the whole thing could vanish as easily as the final, dying note of a song. In addition to the squat, black piano and the thin, tuxedo-clad man who played it, the great room was decorated in leather, mahogany, and brass. There was a pair of rich, maroon rugs, and at every few paces along the walls hung a painting illuminated from above by a brass lamp. People drifted back and forth, from listening to the music to inspecting the paintings, possessed of the same milling gait and mute reverence found in an art gallery. The paintings seemed to take on value, or reach a higher level of art because of their elegant surroundings. They were mostly still-lifes of trivial objects: a basket of knitting supplies, a place setting, a postcard leaning against a coffee mug, all painted in a childlike imitation of Matisse. There was, however, a single portrait of a middle-aged woman attempting to be refined in her dazzling jewelry and by her lofty expression, but who was nonetheless vandalized by the artist's hand, possibly the clumsy, twisted paw of a crippled child. Even so, Ralph's gaze seemed to give as much attention to any one of the paintings as to the wall from which it hung.

"I think this one is the best," a woman said.

"Yes," he answered, looking at her face, bright and smooth and young, before he even bothered to look at the painting. "It's interesting how," he began to say—his eyes now focusing beyond her, but only lighting for an instant upon the painting before returning to her again, as if a cursory glance sufficed—and so he continued without pause, saying, "such a delicate subject can have such harsh and brutal contours."

The woman turned toward the artwork and appeared to be reassessing it according to Ralph's comment. Composed only in three stark colors—navy blue, dirty yellow, and brown—a part of a doorway, or maybe an open window, revealed the edge of a chair in the background.

"A delicate subject?" the woman asked. "I guess it can make you feel small and lonely, or just common."

"That might explain the crude style," he said, still looking at the woman. She was dressed in a black gown, scooped low in the front, her naked throat more delicate and enticing for its lack of jewelry.

"You can overanalyze anything," she said; then with a trace of amusement on her face, she leaned closer, as if to confide in him. "I was just thinking that it's the only piece that doesn't make me want to leave the room."

"It's all repulsive." He sounded definitive, as though this were the best way to appraise the artwork.

"His father-in-law painted them all, so he's probably forced to hang this stuff under the threat of death or at least divorce."

"Probably," Ralph said. "So, you know his wife?"

"I heard of her, that she's shrewd. She runs the business behind the scene."

The piano ceased, and the people began to move away, no longer held by the spell of the music or by some tacit, respectful obligation to listen. Voices grew louder, and a few people began to exit the room.

"You must be one of the new consultants," Ralph said.

"You're the first person not to assume that I'm somebody's girlfriend."

People shuffled past them now, like a departing audience, and Ralph stepped back from the woman, as if he were at risk of getting caught in the flow of people.

"Stick your head into my office sometime," he said. "I'm on the third floor."

She smiled again. Her hand rose slightly and then returned to her side; perhaps she stopped herself from giving him a small, silly wave goodbye.

"There's no reason you should feel like an outsider in the company," he said.

"You're Ralph Banks, right?" she asked, and before he could respond, she told him that her name was Amanda.

"Of course," he said.

Bemused, she looked at him for an instant; then a faint smile crept on her face as he too smiled. "Of course," she echoed.

Later—proud, amused, and detached—he stood before the fireplace and inspected everyone, as if he were a director of a play and the men and women, dressed up in their business attire and ruled by decorum, were his actors, a group of children on a school stage, the players at a community theatre. The fat woman was sitting in a high-back chair before a bay window. Although she appeared a bit listless and sleepy, the man glanced at her from time to time, apparently more intrigued by her performance than by anyone else's. She kept looking at the doorway, probably waiting for Ralph to come rescue her; she never turned around in the chair to see him standing just a few feet behind her. She dipped her finger in her drink and then placed the tip of her finger on her tongue. Then again, she poked the floating ice cube to the bottom of the glass and licked her finger as the cube bobbed back to the surface. Crossing and re-crossing her thick legs, she continually looked at the door. When she finished her drink, Ralph came up behind her.

"You almost ready?" he asked and placed his hand on her shoulder.

"If you're ready." She set the empty glass on an end table and slowly rose to her feet, pushing herself up from the chair, like an old, brittle woman. With his hand on the small of her back, he ushered her out of the room, into the foyer. He brought his mouth close to the side of her face.

"How do you feel?"

"Tired."

He left her in the foyer, where she stood looking down at the tile floor, almost entranced, the entire mass of her body delicately balanced upon two weak ankles, like an egg on its end. Ralph returned shortly with their coats over his arm. He touched her back again, steadying her. When they came to the front door, she hesitated.

"I promised Susan I say goodbye. She invited us to dinner."

"I spent the whole evening saying hello and goodbye. Give her a call tomorrow."

He opened the door and led her out into the night, which was charged—tinted with a veil of thin blue—as if the clear, cold stillness were somehow electrical. They walked down the wide driveway, lined on one side with cars and a low fieldstone wall topped with yellow lanterns, the sickly glare of which seemed frozen, like golden halos painted upon the dark backdrop of night. The couple walked with their heads down, their breath floating in gray puffs before their mouths. Once inside their car, a metallic silver Volvo, he reached over and placed his hand on her leg, and driving off, away from the party and the enormous house, she seemed to settle into the seat, as if her bones grew pliant and bent beneath the weight of her own flesh, while her fingers untangled themselves from the fabric of her dress that she'd been clutching, and her hand, relaxed now, crept over and covered his hand, her fingers slipping between his fingers, curling into a single fist, his hand and her hand, on her thick leg. She settled further into the seat and allowed her head to loll. He stared blankly out at the road before him and continued to hold her hand even after she fell asleep. Their house was a little ranch, set far back from the road, at the end of a packed gravel driveway. He pulled beside the parked station-wagon. She lifted her head and looked about dreamily, finally retrieving her hand from his, to scratch at white crust at the corner of her mouth. He walked around the car, opened the door for her, and stooped a little to slip his arm around her back. She leaned against him as they headed up the slate walkway. Upon the cement steps, he fumbled out his house keys, her head on his shoulder, his arms around her.

"Are you going to be sick?" he asked, but she didn't answer.

The inside of the house was warm, and a faint sour odor permeated the rooms. He was already undressing her as she pressed into him more fully, leaning now with no more effort to stand on her own. He let her coat fall to the floor, and brushed it to the baseboard with an awkward swipe of his foot. They lumbered as a single body down the hallway, her hands dangling limply as his hands tugged at her zipper, exposing her broad, white back. He had to lean away from her to allow her black gown to slip down to her feet, and the gown, now gathered about her ankles, was shuffled and dragged along the hardwood floor; she made no attempt to lift her feet free until she came to the edge of the bed. There, with a little push, he deposited her. He squatted beside the edge of the bed, balled up her dress, and tossed it beneath an ironing board standing in the corner. He took off her shoes and, by some apparent whim, threw one into the bathroom and the other out into the hall. Then, with a soft moan, he slid up her body, tracing his chin along her thigh and resting it just beneath her breasts. He watched her lips move with her heavy breathing. Shutting his eyes and turning his head, he kissed her pale skin, his hands now gliding up her arms, his fingers slipping under her bra straps and easing them off her shoulders, all the while his body moving further up, until his temple rested upon the V of her collarbone and the whole weight of his body was atop her. He nestled and stirred, as if settling into plush couch cushions, burrowing into her flesh. The light was on, but he didn't bother to get up and shut it. They remained motionless for a long time. He would have appeared to be sleeping if not for the occasional moment when he pressed his lips to her shoulder, not so much to kiss her skin as to taste it. The first sign of dawn revealed itself through the window as the daylight spread deeper into the room, vanquishing the odd shadows cast by the dim electric light. When he finally rolled off of her and lay on his back, she also moved. She mumbled. Her arm rose of its own accord, her big hand groping for him; she was uneasy and restless, until she found his belt and held onto it. He slipped his hand over hers, and again they slept. She breathed audibly, her mouth partly agape. Suddenly but slowly, he sat up, peeled her fingers from his belt, and eased himself off the bed. He went into the bathroom, came out again, and saw that she was still asleep, though now clutching the bed cover. At the door, he clicked off the light. He stood for a while, looking at her as if he longed to climb back in bed but was restraining the urge. At last, he walked over to the dresser, which was cluttered with tiny bottles and cosmetics. He wrote on a yellow notepad beside the phone that he'd be back by one o'clock, and then propped the notepad up against the phone. Her voice sounded, deliberate and clear.

"Is it that woman from the party?" she asked.

"What?" He turned around.

"Is that where you always go? That woman you were talking to at the party. Is she the one?"

"No," he said. "I'm not like that. I could never—"

"Okay." She rolled over, so her back faced him. A slight sound escaped her throat; she might have been crying.

"I have to pick up order forms. The book route is demanding more time than—"

"Okay," she said, almost in a whisper. "Okay. Just wash up before you get back into my bed."

He stared at her, his whole body tense, unmoving. When he spoke, his voice seemed so full of anguish that it might crack. "Don't break my heart," he said. "Not you. Please."

She didn't answer.

"Please," he said, still staring and motionless. "I'll be back right away. I'll rush like mad. I have to—" he began, but then quickly left the room. Walking down the hall, he softly said, "I'll be right back."

In the kitchen, he walked directly to a cabinet and took out two cans of tuna fish. He got a can opener from a drawer and left the kitchen. His pea coat hung from a hook in the hallway. Outside in the cold, he put on the coat and, in the same motion, slipped the cans of tuna and the opener into one of the deep pockets. Simultaneously, he buttoned up the coat, drove the station-wagon out into the road, and clicked off the radio. Then his expression went as blank as death, and he was only driving. He held the wheel with both hands. After a while, he passed into an underwater tunnel that moaned with the sound of car tires. He emerged from the tunnel and was greeted by orange cones and heavy machinery, abandoned road construction. The city was relatively quiet on this Sunday morning, moving in slow motion, groggy and just waking up. At last, when Ralph pulled up to a stoplight, his expression changed, not to take on life once again, but to set itself in a hard, brutal grimace, a block of bone, muscle, and cartilage thinly veiled beneath his skin. Suddenly, he drove through the red light and kept on driving with little regard for the laws of traffic, speeding through one intersection after another, turning without a signal. He came to a tight, cramped street, where the huddled buildings seemed to lean forward over the road, and the parked cars choked the passageway. He slowed down, but continued forward, until he found a spot where a large pile of heaped garbage bags had tumbled into the road; he gently plowed the station-wagon into the pile, and leaving the tail of his car protruding into the road, he shut the engine and got out. Although he walked briskly, and the air was fiercely cold, his face remained locked, but not exactly in irritation; rather, he seemed to be silently enduring a nasty pain. He walked several blocks and then turned down a side street. On the left was a long, windowless brick wall, the side or back of a building, along which a row of cars parked. On the other side was neither a curb nor sidewalk, so the doors simply opened up onto the street. The metal cellar doors and casement windows peeping over the edge of the road seemed to suggest that much of the life here was subterranean. Above him, several windows were sealed up with plywood, as if the residents inside—undoubtedly poor and very likely caught somewhere between struggle and defeat—

were gradually working their way down to the cellar, where lost and neglected people came to accept their own surrender. The building appeared to be a monument to living suicide, to those interred in life; and the cellar, most of all, seemed like a good place to end the heart-ache and the thousand natural shocks that flesh was heir to. Perhaps it was disillusionment with mankind, the crushing weight of discontent or of failure, or simply, in some cases, a tortured mind, that woke up a person's dormant capacity to succumb, as if anguish could fracture into pieces as numerous and light as snowflakes, float away, and dissolve, at the very moment a person laid down his head and yielded to sleep. Ralph entered the building through one of the doors and ascended a narrow staircase up to the second and then to the third floor. The hall was dimly lit, and little stubs of copper pipe stuck up from the floor where someone had apparently ripped out the baseboard heating. A person was walking down the hall. Ralph kept his gaze focused on the copper stubs, his face averted. The person, also with his head down, passed Ralph without acknowledgement and then bounded quickly and loudly down the steps. A radio was playing in one of the rooms. Ralph paused before one of the doors and glanced both ways down the empty corridor. He took out his keys and gently opened the door, letting the pale light from the hallway vaguely spread itself throughout the room, which was musty and poignant with the odor of disuse and trapped air. Ralph walked to the freestanding light. A figure stirred on top of the bed, but before Ralph could expose it to the light, it slipped to the floor and scurried under the bed. Ralph turned on the light. He then went back to the door, glanced up and down the hallway again, and locked the door. Moving quickly, without looking around to assess—or reassess—the setting, he put the two cans of tuna on the counter and opened them. He walked over to the bed that was pushed up against the cast iron radiator, and began to search the floor with his eyes. Still methodic, still with his face compacted into a hard knot, he dropped to his knees and briefly reached under the bed. Now with a green, plastic salad bowl in his hand, he rose to his feet again and walked back to the counter. He emptied the tuna into the bowl and set it on the floor beside the bed. He stepped back and crossed his arms at his chest. Motionlessly, he stared at the bottom of the bed. A dog leash, fastened to the radiator, trailed over the mattress and disappeared beneath the bed.

"Come on," Ralph muttered. "Come on."

Nothing moved.

"Come eat," he said, in a warmer tone. "Let me take the gag off. I know you don't like it. Come on, you bastard."

He continued to gaze. As rigid as wood or stone, he didn't say anything. Nothing happened. The muffled sound of the radio filtered in from another room; footfalls sounded in the hallway. Ralph unfolded his arms and let them hang at his sides. Then, all at once, he flung himself at the bed and pulled at the leash. The bed began to slide across the floor, as if the leash were also fastened underneath to the frame. Besides the sound of Ralph grunting and cursing, as well as the legs of the bed dragging across the floor, there was a faint but shrill voice— similar to the screechy cries of a scared rodent.

VIII

Kyle stood looking out the window in his living room, with his back toward a man who was sitting on the couch. The man was dressed in the dungarees and jacket of the refrigeration company. He held the cap in his lap. His gaze, which was soft and slow, continually drifted from the carpet before his feet, up to Kyle, then back to the floor again.

"I don't understand what's this all about," Kyle said, still looking out the window. "He knew I had my doctor's appointment this morning."

"I don't think that's the point. It wouldn't matter so much if you hadn't missed so many days lately," the man said. "You should've come in afterwards."

"Is that why you're here?"

"He didn't send me, if that's what you mean." The man was now fingering his cap. "I was worried that you might've gotten bad news today. That's all."

"No, my PSA is fine. The doctor says I'm in good shape."

"You've got it beat then. That's good." The man stood up and put his cap on, but he didn't advance.

"You've never got it beat. It could come back tomorrow. And then they'll want to take off some more of my cock."

The man grew still, uneasy, as if he didn't know if he should move or even look at anything.

Kyle was holding the curtain to the side. He didn't turn to face the man.

"About the other thing," the man began to say.

"What other thing?"

"Missing days at work."

"Ah hah," Kyle said, almost happily. "You are his messenger."

"I'm your friend. That's all."

"Tell him—"

"I'm not going to tell him anything," the man said. "I'm telling you."

Kyle suddenly let go of the curtain and turned around. He seemed half-startled, half-amused.

"The little bastard is passing by again. See," Kyle said, pulling the curtain aside. "There he goes."

The man stepped forward, but he didn't seem concerned with looking outside.

"I've got to get back to work," the man said.

"These kids keep riding their bikes past my house. Like I'm a freak show. They think I'm crazy."

"Nobody thinks anything."

"You weren't here when the police were poking around in my house and digging through my garbage. Half a dozen boys sat across the street watching, waiting for the men to carry out bodies or something. One of them, this little prick, told the police that I was all crazy and distraught when he shoveled my driveway that night." Kyle smiled, lowering the curtain again. "That was his word: 'distraught.' When do kids use a word like that? This little prick goes by my house all day long, like he's a detective or something, because he got to say that I was 'distraught' in front of the police."

"Anyone would've been distraught," the man said as he moved toward the front door.

Kyle nodded slowly, staring vaguely at the man's chest. He appeared to be contemplating the word anew.

"Maybe working again would be good for you," the man said. "It's better than staring out the window all day."

Still nodding, Kyle steadied his gaze upon the man's eyes.

"Okay," the man said. He opened the door and let in the cold air. "I'll see you Monday."

When the man departed, Kyle went to the window and watched him climb into his van and drive away. Long after the man had left, Kyle continued to stand at the window, with his palm resting flat upon the pane and his forearm holding the curtain aside. He stared blankly. He was dressed in a white tee-shirt and a pair of black sweatpants. His hair was a bit disheveled. Eventually, he lifted his hand from the glass, and as the curtain fell, he receded back into the house, taking slow steps. He seemed to be moving aimlessly, even as he entered the kitchen and began to fix himself a tall glass of cranberry juice and vodka. He didn't bother to stir it. He wandered from room to room, occasionally stopping at one object or another, such as a soup can filled with pens or a mess of sneakers in the hall closet. He would remain fixated for a while and then move on. He carried his drink with him, and at the instant he finished it, he happened to be back in the kitchen, as if the end of his listless tour of the house coincided exactly with the moment he needed to refill his glass. He lingered in the kitchen, leaning against the counter, until the dusk began to creep through the bay window. He moved again, and this time his wandering brought him to the upstairs bathroom. He set the glass on the back lid of the toilet and started to undress. Only when he was completely naked did his expression change; his eyes, which had been fixed in a bland, drowsy gaze, now became glazed. He seemed to be on the brink of crying, but once he stepped into the shower, if any tears were shed, they were lost in the water.

The shower appeared to revive him a little. He dressed himself in a pair of brown slacks and a button-down shirt, and after combing his hair, he even put a dab of cologne at the hollow of his throat and on the front of each wrist. He only had two sports coats in the bedroom closet, one black and the other a dark, murky brown, which he selected and hung over the edge of the crib. He checked his appearance in the full-length mirror on the closet door. Then he put on the sports coat and looked at himself again. He started toward the hallway, yet suddenly stopped and went back to the bathroom. He found his drink on the toilet. He stood in one spot in the bathroom until he finished the drink; lastly, he brushed his teeth.

Despite the cold, he left the house without an overcoat and walked toward a small detached garage at the end of the driveway. Firewood, covered with ice and snow, was stacked against the outside wall. A path worn by footsteps through the snow led to a side door. Kyle entered the garage and locked the door behind him. In the dark, he walked across an empty parking space, got into an old Honda Civic, started the car, and got out again. He placed a milkcrate in the empty parking spot, as if he intended to sit down, but he then just stood there. The dome light from the idling car cast low, broken shadows across the concrete floor and sent vague, diffuse light up into the ceiling. Kyle seemed frozen, confused, on the brink of tears again, as if by stepping upon the empty parking space he'd awoken something inside of himself that unnerved him. But whatever spell held him, he cast it off with a sudden lifting of his gaze and a tiny sniffle. Inside the car again, he pressed the garage door opener attached to the visor. As the door creaked and chugged its way up the tracks, the exhaust fumes dissipated into the crisp night air.

He drove along quiet suburban streets but soon entered the business section of a small town. Above the streetlights and buildings, the dark sky was full and depthless and blank. He parked beside the curb and then walked along the sidewalk. Most of the storefronts were shut down, but several people lingered under an awning up ahead. In the glow of greenish light, a thin girl was leaning against a man. She kept reaching for his cigarette, and he kept holding it out of her reach. Finally, she placed both of her palms on his chest, as if she'd been defeated and now surrendered herself to him. As Kyle approached them, he watched the couple with a subtle, averted gaze. He opened the door and slipped into the building as though he feared they might attack him. The people on the sidewalk, however, paid no attention to him.

Inside, the bar was shaped like a horseshoe, and tall, round tables lined the walls. People—a mostly younger crowd—cluttered together. Gray, hazy smoke floated above their heads. Although everyone appeared engaged with one another, the scene was like an elaborate pantomime as the loud music seemed to render them all mute and silly. Kyle looked for a stool at the bar, but quickly gave up and began to press his way across the room. He descended three steps into another room, which was quieter. People sat at tables littered with empty bottles and glasses. No sooner than Kyle found a seat at a corner table, a slight waitress, with her midriff exposed, came up and asked him what he would like to drink. He froze for a second, as if surprised that someone had spoken to him.

"Vodka and tonic," he said.

"House okay?"

"Sure." He smiled at her, but she left without looking at him.

A young man carrying a black bus box began to clear off Kyle's table.

"This yours?" he asked several times.

Still smiling, Kyle responded "No" each time and watched the young man as if he were the entertainment.

Shortly, the waitress brought him his drink and offered to start him a tab.

"Sure," he said.

He sat back, resting one arm on the table and the other on the wide chair rail. Although the room was open and square—completely exposed in a glance—oval security mirrors were perched in each corner of the ceiling. The floor was made of hardwood. On some evenings, the tables and chairs might have been carted away and the room used for dancing; or more likely, it had been used for dancing in the past, before the bar area had expanded and took over the space.

Sitting behind Kyle was a young man in a sweater with the sleeves pushed up. Occasionally, when he spoke to his friends, he leaned back in his chair and lightly bumped Kyle. This gesture apparently gave Kyle the excuse to glance at their table and grin. Across the table sat another young man and a girl who seemed too young to be in a bar. Her hand rested partly upon his forearm, a lover's subtle touch. She was the only one to notice Kyle's interest in their group. She smiled at him a few times, but then simply began to lower her eyes whenever she caught his gaze. By the time Kyle finished his second drink, he sat turned around in his seat, like a member of their table.

They appeared to be college students, perhaps studying philosophy, theology, or literature, because their conversation skirted rapidly over several related and bleak topics.

The young man in the sweater mentioned *The Book of Job*, and Kyle began to smile and nod, evidently appreciative of this new reference.

"At least, he had a shard of pottery to scratch his sores," the man said.

"Yes," Kyle said suddenly. "That's why his wife told him to curse God and die."

Everyone looked at him now.

"What's that?" the student asked.

"Because he probably had a boil on the tip of his cock. A woman needs to be fucked, you know."

"No doubt." The other young man, the boyfriend, raised his glass and drank, to toast Kyle's comment.

"And that's why the whole thing is hog shit," Kyle said, leaning his arm on their table.

"Watch it, chief," the first student said as he slid his chair away from Kyle. Even so, the young man seemed mildly amused.

"God told Satan, 'Do whatever you want; just don't kill him.' Right. See?" Kyle said. He focused his eyes mainly on the young girl. "So Satan put a boil on his cock, but he didn't neuter Job because later on Job was able to have another family. See. He had hope because he still had juice in his ball sack."

"Alright now." The young man in the sweater gently started to lift Kyle from the table by the shoulders of his sports coat. "You made your point."

"But do you get it?" Kyle asked quickly. "It wasn't a good test."

"I've read Hemingway too." The young man turned around, to dismiss Kyle.

"Fuck Hemingway," Kyle blurted.

"Relax, chief."

"What did I tell you?" the boyfriend said. "You can't talk religion." There was something pleasant in his smooth face. He had a sort of leisurely charm, a nonchalance that seemed well-adapted to making people feel comfortable.

Kyle suddenly glared at him and said, "It's not just talk; that's why."

"You're a well of wisdom," the boyfriend responded, which Kyle appeared to regard as an insult.

Nobody said anything for a moment.

But then the waitress returned, and Kyle turned back to his own table and ordered another drink.

"And give me their bill."

"Don't do that," the girl said, speaking for the first time; she was looking up at the waitress.

"Sure," Kyle said. He also addressed the waitress. "I got it."

"No, he doesn't," the girl said.

Without a word, the waitress walked away, obviously not caring one way or the other.

Kyle muttered something.

"Watch it, chief," the first young man said quickly.

Kyle sat and brooded. Although his glass was empty, save for the ice and a lemon wedge, he held it in both hands.

"He's right, though," the boyfriend said. "It's an existential problem. 'Repent,' Christ said when He was questioned about suffering, just as God told Job. The answer to the problem of pain is a call to action, a way of living, a practice—not just a bunch of talk."

"Talk, talk, talk," Kyle said into his glass.

"Words, words, words," the student responded in an English accent, and the girl giggled now, as if her lover were not only charming but clever and witty too.

Apparently bemused, Kyle looked at the group as though they were offensive and gross, a glistening knot of cartilage and skin.

"Go eat your white bread," Kyle said, and they laughed.

"It's past your curfew," he added.

"It's past your limit," the student responded. The girl was watching him; she seemed to adore the very sound of his voice.

Kyle's face contorted. If he at first loathed the group because they had shut him out, now it was plainly the girl's affection that further stirred up his disgust. Kyle turned his gaze from her to the smooth-faced young man.

"Go fuck your whore." He snarled.

Their laughter and grins ceased at once.

"Excuse me." The boyfriend started to get out of his seat as the girl clutched his arm. "You've got a problem."

"Stop," the girl said. "He's drunk."

The young man stared steadily at Kyle, who suddenly seemed very calm, as if he were now a mere observant and the situation had nothing at all to do with him.

"You've got a problem," the boyfriend repeated.

"Relax, chief," the other one said, even though Kyle was relaxed. In a quirky gesture, the young man rolled down the sleeves of his sweater and then pushed them back up again. He was the most agitated, unsettled; his friend stood rigidly poised before the table.

"Apologize, fuck face."

"Stop," the girl said softly, trying to soothe him. She gently tugged his arm.

Other people began to watch the commotion.

"Sure," Kyle said, looking down at his glass.

"Did you hear me?" the young man demanded.

"Sure. I was just—" Kyle began to say. "Why not repent?" His voice sounded meek and tired. He still didn't lift his head to meet their eyes. "I didn't mean anything. I was just thinking that you might like her bald cunt."

There was a brief moment when nobody reacted as Kyle sat all alone, dejected, and somber. If the boyfriend simply faded away, Kyle probably wouldn't have noticed or cared. But all at once, the young man leaped onto Kyle, knocking him to the hardwood floor and toppling Kyle's table and chair. The glasses crashed. People gasped and scuttled. At first, Kyle seemed lifeless, while the young man grappled and pummeled his limp body. "Fucker, fucker," the boyfriend kept repeating. Then a strange sound escaped from Kyle, as if he were some kind of deformed creature that was shocked and scared, and whose only recourse was to bellow. The young man stood up and staggered a few steps backwards. The incident had lasted only a few seconds, and the group of students was already gathering their things and heading away. Someone set the table and chair right, as the waitress squatted and began to pick up the broken pieces of glass and place them on her tray. Kyle remained curled up on the floor. The bottom of his sports coat was turned up over his head. Although people looked down at him, nobody touched him. He was whimpering.

IX

The apartment was lit by candles that were placed throughout the room: on the countertop, in the kitchen, and upon a pair of snack trays, which was a new addition to the scene. On the floor by the baseboard, a radio played techno dance music, its steady throb keeping the time and rhythm of a heartbeat. Despite the flickering shadows and the sound of music, the room seemed frozen. The moment was suspended, like a held breath, strained and ready to break. Ralph was sitting on the floor, with his forehead lowered to his knees and his arms wrapped around his shins. In the weak light, his bare flesh was ghastly, the color of ashes. His thin body appeared wasted. He didn't lift his head to look around, and he didn't move at all. Although the boy was standing—staring not so much at the man as beyond him, through him—the boy didn't move either. The chain, still fastened to the cast iron radiator, trailed across the floor, rose up the front of the boy's body, and ended at a black neck collar. One of the boy's stockings was pooled around his ankle, while the other stocking disappeared under the boy's red skirt. He stood with his hips cocked and one arm akimbo, as if he'd been posed. He was shirtless. His nipples were painted a bright, vibrant red; and the same shade of red, gaudy and perverse, was smeared all over his mouth. Yet, even when Ralph's body began to shake with tortured sobs, the boy still didn't move. His eyes remained as vacant as death.

X

The sunlight melted the snow a little, but by evening a cold, vivid darkness crept over the houses and streets, and froze the landscape all over again, turning the surface of the snow into a hard layer of ice, which reflected the next morning's sun so sharply that its blinding glare caused the few cars that were out to move slowly and the drivers to squint, while icicles dripped from gutters and windowsills, and long skins of ice dropped off of tree limbs like flayed bark, and trickles of water trailed down driveways to meet up with the more steady flow alongside the curbs: This was the sound of flaw as the rest of the world appeared suspended and hushed in an attitude of lethargy, and many houses seemed to cough up disease and silently create the gray sky out of chimney smoke. The blond haired boy named Ray and his friend climbed between the wooden rails of a fence and headed across a front lawn. They walked upon the icy surface with short, careful steps. They didn't have the shovels this time; there was no reason for them. Instead, Ray held a long stick, a makeshift staff he used for walking. The other boy was a pace behind him. They didn't talk. Before they came to Kyle's yard, they made a detour toward the road. Ray's staff tapped on the wet pavement. He was still in the lead. Both of the boys kept their gazes lowered to the ground, until they started to pass by Kyle's driveway. The tail end of the old Civic stuck out into the road, its engine softly idling. Despite the daylight and the glare upon the ice, the car's headlights were on, so the dark, slick driveway gleamed from their light. Ray and the other boy ceased walking. They still didn't look at one another or speak—even as Ray gave several light whacks to the car tire with his walking stick, as if testing the car for something. The other boy circled to the other side of the car, inspecting it. He peeped through its windows, although it was obvious that the car was empty. On the hood of the car was a wet, brown clump, which Ray first poked with his stick and then lifted into the air. It was Kyle's sports jacket. Both of the boys looked at the coat as though it were a strange artifact from a distant time. The other boy, still not speaking, sucked in air through his teeth, making a hissing noise, as if from disgust or brief, wincing pain. With wide eyes, he looked around rapidly and then dropped to his hands and knees, to check beneath the car. Ray shook the coat from the end of his stick. He stared up at the house, where nothing was moving.

"He's an odd bird," Ray said.

"Should we shut off the car?"

"I'm not touching anything." Ray continued to watch the house. "He's either dead or he's killed someone." Because he was squinting a little, he appeared as though he might have been smiling.

"Let's get someone."

"But he could be in there watching TV." Ray now turned toward the other boy. "Let's go check."

"You go check."

"We'll peek in the window."

"You go peek."

"Don't be a pussy," Ray said. "We'd look pretty stupid if we called the cops and he's in there jerking off."

"Let's go then."

"We'd look even worse if he had a heart attack and we didn't do anything."

The other boy turned his gaze away from Ray and up to the house. Then he looked at the idling car again; it was a bad omen. He put his hands in his jacket pockets, lowered his head, and started to walk away. Ray watched him for a moment, but Ray didn't follow after him or say anything. He stood silently, with his head slightly cocked, as though contemplating something profound and mysterious. When he began to walk up the driveway, he still held the staff, but he didn't place it on the ground. He rested it on his shoulder the way he had previously rested the shovel. He looked from side to side, perhaps expecting to find Kyle sprawled out on the ground. The shrubbery was caked with little beads of ice, and the ground was too hard to have been marked by footprints during the night or early morning. As Ray moved up the driveway, the sunlight caught the windows of the house at a new angle, making them burn black and yellow—but close up, on the walkway now, the windows again appeared still and somber. He cupped one hand upon the glass and peered into the family room. Nothing captured his attention or alarmed him. Everything was quiet, save for the ice falling from trees and the sound of trickling water. On either side of the front door were two slender, rectangular windows. Ray looked through one of these and then turned around to face the road. The other boy was now out of sight. Ray headed slowly back down the walkway. There was something hesitant in his step, as though he were thinking about something, possibly about whether or not he should walk around the house and look into the rest of the windows. Kyle easily could have been sitting at the kitchen table in his underwear, drinking coffee, and reading the morning newspaper. When Ray reached the driveway, he first glanced at the car and then looked down the length of the house. Although he carried the silly stick on his shoulder, he appeared somewhat sturdy and composed. For the first time, as if he'd never noticed it before, Ray stared at the detached garage. Its side door was standing open—at once conspicuous and normal—as perfectly concealed as any good trap. Ray left the driveway and walked on the frozen lawn, making a wide arc around the door and all the while trying, with a fixed gaze, to scan the interior of the garage. He eventually reached the back corner, and from there, he could see that the side and the back of the building were windowless. Gripping the stick more tightly, he crept alongside the ice-covered firewood that was stacked against the wall, and approached the doorway. When he came near the opening, he paused for a moment, and as if suddenly visited by a strange premonition, he slowly looked back over his shoulder. Then he glanced at the house again, which still appeared lifeless. He lowered the stick and vaguely probed the doorway in a way that suggested that he expected to trigger something to clamp down on the stick. When nothing happened, he leaned into the opening. He looked at an oil spot on the concrete floor, the cluttered shelves, and a mess of boxes and tools piled up against the back wall; a push-mower was partially buried. Ray stepped inside the garage. His eyes settled upon the turned-over milkcrate in the center of the parking space. His gaze was causal yet penetrating, as if he had discovered in the milkcrate not only a clue but also the last visible sign that the world had once moved. Another premonition seemed to have visited Ray because all at once his expression changed as something inside of him snapped open. He looked up. Yet Kyle's body wasn't hanging from the rafters—only the rope, the empty noose.

At last, everything in the boy that might have been called inspiration, precocity, or sturdiness abandoned him. He dropped the walking staff and fled down the slick driveway in a frenzied panic, like a spooked child, overwhelmed with terror.

XI

The world was in thaw and overcast with gray silence, as if a hard exterior had dissolved to reveal a soft, damp pulp. Ralph stood in his front lawn, his hands in the pockets of his open pea coat, his eyes fixed on the dark house. He stood for a long time, before he finally went inside and stood in the kitchen. All the cabinet doors were open; all the shelves were empty. The kitchen table was missing, the counter tops clear, and the walls barren. Although the blinds remained on the windows, there were no curtains. Ralph, now only in a white tee-shirt and jeans, stood before the sink and gripped its edge, as if he feared he was about to fall over or vomit. Eventually, he stepped away and shuffled into another emptied room. He muttered to himself, or maybe to someone else, possibly recalling words or composing them.

"First, you taught me love, and now you taught me heartache," he said several times, his voice no louder than a whisper, tender, and remorseful. "I feel like you died. This is death. Your leaving is death."

Abruptly, he sat down in the center of the family room, on the carpet, and stared blankly. All his past rigidity vanished, as if his bones were soft and his muscles were loose and gelatinous beneath his skin. As darkness began to creep into the house, he continued to sit. After a while, he slouched further and further, until he was lying curled up on the floor. It was nighttime when he finally got up. In the kitchen, he turned on the light, walked straight to the counter, and began to open the drawers. He seemed as though he expected to find something, but the drawers were empty, save for a plastic tray that separated utensils. He lifted a roll of paper towels from the wall and pulled out the wooden dowel.

Outside, a floodlight, which was attached to the corner of the house, came on and shone upon the driveway. The station-wagon sat beneath a canopy of barren tree limbs. The cellar windows then lit up along the base of the house, and shortly Ralph appeared from around the back of the house. He carried the wooden dowel like a hammer. Despite the cold, he still wore only the tee-shirt. He strode swiftly toward the car and beat the back door an abrupt blow with the wooden dowel. He stepped back, stared steadily at the car, as if challenging it somehow, and then struck it a second time. His breath hung gray in the air before his mouth. He began to pant, short, quick, halting breaths. He stooped and placed his free hand on his knee. Panting, he stared at the back of the station-wagon. The floodlight shone all around him, overexposing him in artificial light, his flesh washed to the same pallor as his tee-shirt. When he beat the back door again, the dowel splintered in his hand, but he didn't seem to notice; his attention was upon the car. Eventually, his breathing came under control, and he stood up straight, erect, with the rigidity of his other self. He took his car keys out of his pants pocket and stepped up to the back of the car. The keys remained in the lock as the hatch sprung open. He quickly pulled out a loose tire and let it drop to the ground, where it wobbled a few times, in a brief struggle with animation or life, and then collapsed all at once. The back of the car appeared empty, but Ralph pulled up the piece of floor panel that normally concealed the spare tire. No sooner, a bundle of blankets—bound in cords—began to flop as Ralph tugged it out of the tire compartment and let it drop onto the gravel driveway. He started to beat the moving mass with the dowel. The thing struggled all the more and began to screech. Ralph stepped back as the bundle twisted and flopped. Without a word, he watched the strange spectacle until the wrapped body eventually calmed down and the screeching ceased. Ralph was standing erect, composed, but his rigidity wasn't as solid as it was brittle, ready to snap. As soon as the bundle became still, Ralph approached it, stepping slowly, then squatting, and placing his hand gently upon it. Save for its small, quick breaths, the body remained motionless as Ralph touched it. Apparently, he was feeling for the head because when he came to it, he began to unravel the blanket until a clump of hair was exposed. Even though the boy wasn't moving, Ralph put his left hand upon the boy's head, to steady it, to keep it still, while he raised his other hand, wielding the dowel like a hammer. When he swung, in an attempt to bring the dowel down upon the boy's skull, the swift motion severed the already splintered rod, so Ralph was holding only a stub. His striking hand missed the back of the boy's head and smashed into gravel. Undaunted, as if he'd expected the dowel suddenly to break, Ralph stood up and dropped the stub. His hand was bleeding, but he didn't seem to notice or care. The boy wasn't moving; perhaps he was still waiting for the blow. Perhaps he wasn't waiting for anything. When Ralph went back to the car and took the tire iron out of the wheel compartment, as if he'd known all along where it was and that he would be using it at this precise moment—the boy, still mostly bundled, wormed and flopped his way beneath the car. Ralph—not looking at the boy, but at the back corner of the house, where the flood light shone sharp and white—reached down and grabbed the boy by the ankle, pulling him out from beneath the car, and dragging him along the gravel. All the while the boy screeched, but now the strange sound was almost mechanical, an involuntary reaction that had nothing to do with fear or pain, and Ralph—panting again, though he didn't move like a panting man, but rather as if he, too, were mechanical—placed his knee upon the bundled form, so the boy was face down in the driveway as Ralph raised the tire iron—not actually looking at the back of the boy's head, but at some indistinct space just above or beyond the boy's head—but then, all at once, Ralph's pants became deep and violent, so he was now gasping as his body began to tremble and his upraised hand became limp and dropped to his side. Ralph's body appeared to be revolting against itself. His gasping gave way to heaving and heaving, until he heaved dry and harsh, and he heaved again, his face strained and awful, the veins at his temples like deep fractures in his skull, and now this time when he heaved, something inside his stomach became unsettled, and with his heaving, something—black and stringy and rancid—bubbled out of this throat and landed upon the gravel. Even so, he continued to heave, although there was nothing left inside of him, not even bile.

XII

There were three boys now, coming down the center of the street, with Ray in the lead and another boy, who was fatter and shorter, walking a girl's bicycle with a pink frame and a white basket attached to the handlebars, and inside the basket sat a brown grocery bag, at which the third boy—the one who had abandoned Ray earlier—kept glancing, as though he feared the bag might fall out onto the pavement, and this boy was carrying a video camera strapped to his palm and aimed up the street, as the three of them walked, approaching a commotion of cars and a small pack of people standing on the sidewalk across from Kyle's house. The boys drifted from the center of the road to the sidewalk, although the fat, short boy walked along the curb, pushing the bike beside him. When they came to the nearest police car, Ray looked at it, and the boy with the camera followed Ray's gaze, so he was now filming the two policemen who stood near the back of the car. The boys stopped just behind the policemen and taped their backs. The two men didn't turn around and see the boys, apparently not realizing that they were there. One of the men was drinking a cup of coffee and looking up at the house.

"Men are the gory ones," he said. "Put a couple more years into the job and you'll see that I'm right."

The other man didn't say anything.

"Or you can read the research."

Kyle's car still protruded from the end of the driveway, although all the doors were now open and a man was poking around inside of it.

"Women like pills or poison, like they're fucking Cleopatra or someone. Dainty even in death." The man laughed, but the other officer silently continued to inspect the scene.

"After a little while, when the blood begins to settle and the skin turns black, no one stays dainty too long."

One police car had its lights flashing, but the siren was turned off. The front tire of the ambulance had ridden over the curb and was partially sucked into the wet soil of Kyle's lawn.

The man sipped his coffee; he seemed mildly amused.

"Women want to do it from the inside out; keep their image intact. Men," he said, and now he was actually smiling, as if entertained by his own wit, "they do it from the outside in. With guns or knives. And they always do at least one test cut. Practice wounds." He turned now, to address the other man. "One time, around last Christmas— Christmas is the season for this kind of shit, you know—this one fucker took his circular saw—" he said, but he abruptly stopped talking when he noticed the three boys standing directly behind him. His smile vanished, replaced by a sneer. The officer moved toward the boys, but they backed away.

"Come here," he snapped.

Ray already turned around and started running, while the boy with the camera kept pace beside him. The officer struck a stance as if he would spring out after them, but he simply watched them running away. He was still holding his cup of coffee. The two boys laughed as they ran. The fat boy was long gone, furiously peddling his bike far ahead in the distance.

"Did you see that cocksucker?" the officer said. "He had a camera on me."

But the other officer still didn't say anything. He stepped away from the back of the car. He moved slowly, as if nothing could possibly interest him, especially the other man or the boys. The brown bag was on the ground beside the curb; the man picked up the bag and without opening it, walked back and handed it to the first officer, who set his coffee down on the trunk of the car.

"What's this?" he asked.

"They dropped it."

The first officer looked into the bag and smiled.

"Those bastards," he said. Laughing, he pulled out several thick glossy magazines. On one cover, a skinny girl—with her head back, her skin pulled tightly over her ribcage, and her breasts rising up her chest, caught in motion, an action shot—was mounted upon a penis as thick as her own forearm. On another cover, a young girl grinned with a mixture of drunkenness and content as cum bubbled out of the corner of her mouth and dribbled down her chin. There were several other magazines, and the two men quickly began to shuffle through them.

Excited and greedy, one man pulled. "Give me that one."

"I like her."

The girl was on all fours.

"Daddy's princess."

The men laughed.

XIII

Small amid the towering buildings, the boy walked along a crowded sidewalk, and with every step, his wounded foot dragged upon the cement. Two women were reading a menu posted on a glass door. When the boy came up to them, he appeared to regard them as no more than cardboard cutouts because he began to shoulder his way between them. He made little grunting noises. One of the women instinctively hoisted her purse, like a football, under her arm.

"Hey, now," she said, looking down at him.

The boy didn't seem to hear her.

The two women stepped apart, to let him through. As soon as he passed them, the women turned their attention back to the menu.

The boy continued along the sidewalk. He was dressed in a set of navy green sweat clothes that were a little too big on him. Although his hair was neatly parted to the side, something in his hazel eyes made him appear unkempt, almost savage. He looked at the passing faces, with a broad gaze that simultaneously devoured and yet dismissed the faces. He walked up to a bakery. Wicker baskets of bread were displayed in the window. When the boy pulled the door open, a tiny bell tinkled. A young, dark haired girl looked down at him from behind the counter, apparently frustrated by the sight of him.

"Oh, God," she said.

"The man," the boy said fiercely, as if giving her a command.

"I don't know who you're talking about."

"The man." The boy turned his gaze from the young girl to a seating area where there were several tall, marble-topped tables and stools with black cushioned seats. A man with a gray beard lifted his head up from a book. A pair of adolescent students, both with backpacks, ceased talking and looked at the boy.

"The man," he demanded of the customers, but they simply watched him with vague interest.

"Why do you keep coming in here?" The girl had her hands flat on the countertop. "I just gave you a bagel a few minutes ago. I'm going to have to call someone if you don't stop coming in here and screaming like that."

"Hey," the boy said, "hey," as if the girl had turned away from him. "The man."

"I'm calling someone." She stepped back from the counter and lifted the phone from the wall. "See," she said. "You're going to get in trouble."

"Hey," the boy persisted, with rapid bursts. "Hey. Hey. The man!"

He then turned and walked briskly toward the door, putting his weight upon the heel of his wounded foot. Apparently oblivious to any threat, he yanked the door open. The bell tinkled once as he left the shop.

The man with the beard suddenly stood up.

"Call the police."

The young girl, as much fearful as confused, was still holding the phone, her eyes wide and her mouth partly open.

"Call them," the man barked at the girl.

He stepped away from his table and started toward the door. He paused, however, in midstride to explain. "His neck's all bruised." He then hurried out the door, but less than a minute later, he returned.

"He must've ran or something."

The girl was leaning over the counter, to get a better view of the door.

"I didn't see his neck," she said quickly. "I didn't know." Her bottom lip began to quiver, as if she might begin to cry. "I didn't—"

XIV

In a car lot bordered by a high metal fence, a man in beige coveralls was squatting beside the battered station-wagon. He placed his hand upon the front tire.

"And what do you think I want with it?" the man asked. He had a round face and a dark complexion.

Ralph took a pack of cigarettes out of the interior pocket of his suit jacket, brought the pack up to his mouth, tapped its bottom, and pulled out a cigarette with his lips. He put the pack away and then lit the cigarette with a silver lighter.

"Tires are all bald, the hoses are brittle, and it's burning oil something fierce," the man said.

"Yes," Ralph said, smoking his cigarette and staring out over the rows of cars. He had gauze and white surgical tape wrapped around his knuckles.

"This isn't worth anything," the man said.

"Well, how much will you give me for it?"

"It's not worth anything." The man stood up and patted the hood of the car, as if to prove his point.

"Five hundred," Ralph said.

"I'll give you a dollar to drive it out of here." The man smiled with his broad mouth and fleshy, burgundy lips.

"Five hundred." Ralph exhaled the cigarette smoke, apparently indifferent to the man's humor.

"You can't even get that from its parts. The only thing worth anything is inside the gas tank." The man chuckled now. "I don't mean to slight you," he said.

"Yes," Ralph said. "Well, how much do you think the gas is worth?" He wasn't looking at the man.

"About seventy-five dollars."

"All right then," Ralph said as he pulled a slip of paper out of his suit pocket, placed it upon the hood the car, and quickly signed it. "Two fifty." He handed the man the paper.

The man raised the paper and inspected it, as if checking for counterfeit money.

"I can take a crap and give you the title, if you want," the man said. He laughed at himself as he folded the title several times, until it was a small square, and stuck it in the breast pocket of his coveralls.

Ralph continued to smoke his cigarette, as if the man hadn't said anything at all.

The man revealed a clip of money from beneath his bib. He took out a hundred dollar bill and handed it to Ralph, who briefly glanced at it and then tucked it away in his pants pocket. He seemed to imagine that the transaction was over, and he merely stood there to finish his cigarette. The man, who continued to talk to Ralph, could have simply dissolved and drifted vaporously away. After Ralph smoked the cigarette down to the filter, he flicked the butt onto the loose gravel and started to walk away, without bothering to take leave of the man. Even so, the man came up beside him, as if he didn't realize that he'd been disregarded, and handed the yellow license plates to Ralph. The two men walked side-by-side across the car lot, the man talking all the while and occasionally pointing at one car or another with a screwdriver he had in his hand. He escorted Ralph up to the gate.

"It was a pleasure," the man said.

Only then did Ralph seem to acknowledge the man, by giving him a slight nod. Ralph walked along the fence, which ended at the corner of the block, and then he turned right, angling across the street. He stepped between two parked cars and continued along the sidewalk, still holding the plates, though now raising them up and looking at them, as if he'd just discovered that he was holding something. He was on a narrow side street, where the buildings were faceless, with neither curtains nor blinds in the windows. When he came upon a subway grate, he bent down and tried to slip the license plates through, but they wouldn't fit. He turned down a busier street. After a few paces, he suddenly stopped and headed back in the opposite direction. At the corner of the street, a drainage gutter was along the curb. Without losing stride, Ralph dropped the plates into the gutter, and then his bandaged hand rose up to his suit jacket and took out the pack of cigarettes again. Smoking the newly lit cigarette, he approached a cart on the corner, where a man in a bulky brown coat was selling hot pretzels. Ralph looked at the man intensely for a moment, and the man looked back at him with a puzzled expression, but before he could say anything, Ralph resumed walking. A little farther up, at another stand, Ralph bought a newspaper and a cup of coffee. With the paper tucked under his arm and the cigarette in his mouth, he descended the stairs into the subway.

XV

There was a girl this time, standing beside a tree behind Kyle's small detached garage and watching Ray as he walked up to the back of the house and then lifted himself up to peer into the bay window. He glanced at the girl. Before the back door, there was a slab of concrete, where a gas grill sat beneath a black tarp. He waved the girl over, and she left the cover of the tree and came across the lawn. She was slender, the openings of her short shirtsleeves flared a bit at her shoulders, and her sandy brown hair was pulled back from her face with a purple barrette. Ray looked at her as she inspected the house.

"There's no car in the driveway," Ray said. "That fat real estate lady hasn't even been here in almost a month. They'll never sell this place, especially that woman. She's a cow."

"Stop it, Ray," the girl said.

"It's true," he said. "Wait here. I'll let you in."

He walked alongside the house, and just on the other side of the air conditioner unit, he sat down on the grass and lightly tapped the bottom edge of a casement window with his heel. The hinges squealed, and they were so rusty that once the window was open, it didn't swing itself shut. Ray turned onto his stomach and slipped himself feet first through the narrow opening. Shortly after he disappeared, the window closed, from the inside.

The girl waited on the concrete slab. She stooped down and lifted up a ceramic flowerpot that was on the ground beside the door. When Ray opened the door and stuck his head out, he saw her standing there with the pot in both of her hands.

"What are you doing?" he asked.

"Looking for a key."

"I'm already inside." He smiled at her. "You're a goofy girl."

Putting the pot down, she said, *"You're a goofy girl."*

He held the door open, and she stepped past him. He followed her from the foyer, into the kitchen, where she took a seat at the table. He glanced out the bay window for a second, as a precaution perhaps, and then sat across from her. He kept his eyes upon her face as she looked about the kitchen as though it were a museum. When she met his eyes, she let her gaze linger a moment, before standing up and walking out of the kitchen. He followed her.

"You figure someone would sell the furniture," she said. "Have a house sale or something."

In the living room, she sat down on the couch. He stood for a moment, looking down at her, and then seated himself beside her. He put his feet on the coffee table, and she pushed them off.

"Don't be an ogre," she said. "Somebody's got to own this stuff."

"He had no family. They all left him without a word. I heard his wife took off with her lover and the kids," Ray responded. "As my dad said, 'Lonely people are a tragedy waiting to happen.'"

He stood up and walked over to the television.

"He's got some movies down here. We can watch something, as long as it's daylight."

"I don't feel like it," she said. She leaned forward, untied the laces of her sneakers, and slipped them off. When Ray returned to the couch, she said, "What does your dad know?"

"I don't know." Ray shrugged. "That's what he said."

"It takes more than one person to make a tragedy. Tell him that."

He smiled at her again, and she turned her head away.

"I'm not going to tell him anything," Ray said. He leaned back on the couch and moved a little closer to her, so his thigh touched her thigh.

"Let me kiss you again," he said, still staring at her.

"You are an ogre."

They sat silently, and after a while, she began to inspect her surroundings casually, as if Ray no longer sat beside her, touching her leg and looking at her face.

"It's like you're all coiled up inside," she said at last, not so much addressing him as speaking to the room itself. "And you're ready to spring on me."

"Let me kiss you," he said.

She turned her face toward him, and no sooner, he leaned in, pressed his mouth against hers, and let his hand glide up the bare flesh of her arm. She pulled her face away, but he kept his hand on her. She stared at his eyes, which were bright and eager.

"You're never satisfied," she said, a little breathless, and they kissed again. This time his hand slid up to her throat, where her fingers lightly touched his.

"You're like a puppy," she said. "All coiled up inside."

He smiled, his face close to hers. "I thought I was an ogre."

She held his hand more tightly against her throat, and as she leaned back, pulling him down on top of her, he brought his mouth first to her lips and then to her neck, pressing himself against her and searching her midriff with his hand until her shirt pulled loose and her naked stomach momentarily contracted and then eased beneath his touch, while her own hand, which had previously dangled over the side of the couch, now found its way onto his back, to feel him and hold him closer, and he seemed to want to burrow his face into her neck, as if all he wanted to know about the girl's body was her current offering: merely her stomach and neck because, without her permission, he didn't dare to explore any further, even though he was pressing against her and her hips were rising to meet him and both of her hands were pulling him down, and then he was beginning to take his cue from her motion, to follow her lead, so now his hands seemed at liberty to slip beneath her and touch her back, as though she'd asked him to venture, to hold her tightly and draw her up against him, allowing his hands, not to glide, but to move in clutches from her shoulder blades down to her hips, as if he somehow wanted to crush or devour her, and her hands were also moving, unabashed and tactful, as if she had never known fear or shame or anything else that might have held back her desire, clasped it down until it strained hard and furious against the seams, as if desire were something that she could regulate and control, rather than something that simmered and gathered strength, and thus she possessed liquid ease, in her torso and her limbs, all the while he rushed spastically forward, uncoiling in avid fits and bursts, even though she was showing him, perhaps by instinct, how a body moves and finds a rhythm within itself, her hands roaming without fear, her body yielding, arching and rising to meet him: the boy who labored above her with apparent and clumsy self-consciousness, which now—despite her flesh undulant, warm, and human beneath him—was beginning to fall away in flakes, leaving him all alone in his lust, because even though she was slender and soft, he seemed as if he needed to wreck himself against her, to bash himself to pieces, like a ship caught adrift, a captain-less vessel tossed against a rocky shore, pulled away by ebbing waters and then smashed again and again with the heaving of water, pulled away and then smashed, as if the only way to reach a deeper level within himself, to venture into mystery, was to become undone.

XVI

Water trickled in the dark, and farther away, beyond the arched opening, rain fell, and the wind, blowing across the face of the opening, filled the interior with a rushing sound, as if the entire edifice itself were moving and the collection of people inside, scattered and sprawled out upon the cement floor, were its passengers, but nothing was actually moving, save for the flicker of firelight and shadow against the back wall, while a woman's voice—somewhat harsh but jovial, originating not from any one of the dark forms in particular—wasn't something that really moved, though it possessed a strange kind of force or agency that seemed to give it a presence, perhaps simply because it was the only human sound rising intermittently from among the mute, motionless figures. "Little fucker," the voice sounded, "throw him another piece," and then paused, "he eats almost anything," as the rain fell and the wind rushed "probably ate his own toes" across the opening and the water trickled down the cement walls and the fire "throw him a raw piece this time" flickered against the back wall "a raw piece, damn it" the voice loud but then halting all at once in abrupt silence until softly, coaxingly "yes, yes, go on, you sweet-mouth fucker, go on, eat it" and then laughing.

XVII

There was one boy now. He leaned his head against the bus window and stared out at the edge of the road as it whipped along in a flickering procession of broken images whose only connection to one another was the fluidity of motion, as if the world were a thing that slid and darted past in an unbroken line; or perhaps the continuity was not exactly motion, but time, and the sliding was an illusion of the eye, so the world was actually stable, indivisible, and yet set into motion and set into time by whatever head leaned against the window and stared out at the passing landscape.

When the bus stopped and the doors opened, the boy stepped out onto the sidewalk. The bus rumbled for a moment and then started away, leaving behind the odor of its blue-gray exhaust. The day was clear, dry, and hot. The boy was dressed in a tee-shirt now; the legs of his navy green sweatpants had been cut off, to turn the pants into shorts. He walked without haste, his wounded foot moving at a pace slightly slower than his other foot. Now that his hair was cropped and a bright agility colored his hazel eyes, the boy's full, pouting lips, which had once given him a feminine quality, seemed to make him appear strangely angry. A dog barked at him, but unaffected, he walked on. The suburban streets were mostly peaceful. A few cars passed. In the distance, a lawn mower roared. The boy seemed to be governed by instinct as he selected avenues to turn down, continuing with his measured pace, not bothering to lift his head to look at street signs or houses. Eventually, he turned up the driveway to the yellow house where Kyle had once lived. The real estate sign leaned in the lawn, and the agent's brass lock-box was fastened to the front doorknob. The boy tried the knob, and finding it locked, he went around to the back of the house and also tried the back door. He crossed his arms and stood on the concrete slab for a while, staring up at the house. At first, he seemed almost rigid, but then he cocked his hips and lowered his head. He continued to stand, as if waiting for something. After a while, he walked around to the front of the house and tried the handle again. He didn't make any noise, not even to ring the bell or knock on the door. With his back to road, his hips cocked, and one thumb tucked under the waistband of his shorts, he stared up at the house for a long time. The boy didn't seem angry or scared; he didn't seem like anything at all.

PART FOUR:
SHADOW AND ACT

Although I had made an earnest effort to encounter life and tried to seduce whatever I could, from abstract flesh to abstraction in the flesh, from bovinity to probity, I was thwarted at every turn, as though all of society had conspired to keep me an isolated creature. People seemed indifferent to a person's particular obsession, whether lofty or depraved, as long as he stuck to himself. This was the modern revision to Christ's golden rule: Don't bother your neighbor. Everyone seemed hopelessly ignorant of the mental machinery of a certain kind of reclusive man; no matter if he were an academic, a pervert, or a poet, going inward was always a descent. Of course, many fine citizens—who are contently enmeshed in their ordinary lives and even shake their heads in confusion and disgust at the random madman presented in the press—would themselves turn into completely different animals if their attentions weren't so occupied with the average routines and customs of culture. Deprived of this external reference point, they would find themselves lacking definition. If they continued to look outward, they'd become susceptible to the first appealing figure or Führer that cared enough to remake them. However, if a man happened to look inward, even just for a glance, then the real devolution would begin, until finally one day he would be pulled out of his little hole and exposed to the bright lights, clicking cameras, and ordinary citizens shaking their heads in confusion and disgust.

In a bitter cold December, when the city's main concern was the surplus of homeless people freezing to death, I realized that society wasn't merely apathetic. Indifferent and devoid of the slightest bit of warmth, it seemed to have passively abandoned me. Yet I abruptly learned, on one harrowing day, that society actually possessed certain mechanisms to hasten a man's devolution. They didn't simply allow him to decay at his own pace; they dug him up just to throw lime on him.

It was a Tuesday morning, while I was pretending to be Marduk and chatting with several supposedly single Jews, when a phone call disrupted my connection to the Internet. The instant I heard the sound of the social worker's voice, I went numb and slipped into a defense mode: I adopted the equanimity of the conscientious and obliging citizen, and yet beneath this mask, I remained as alert as a spooked rabbit. Yes, I said. She wanted to know if I could come to the clinic that afternoon. Of course, sure, yes, I said. I even began to nod my head as I acquiesced, although the woman couldn't possibly have seen the gesture through the telephone line. There was trouble with the boy.

Months ago, when the boy had first met his social worker and doctors, his demeanor vacillated between extended stretches of stolid silence—less due to his distrust of the doctors than to his impulse to protect a secret or even a person—and stretches of tireless rants and tirades that were punctuated by flashes of grotesquely sexual knowledge and imagery. At other moments, however, he became a cheerful boy who lacked the faintest trace of depravity; during these calmer interludes, when he seemed most approachable, the doctors tried to advance their investigation. I imagine that this itself was surely a perverse scene because the boy would be sitting at the table, fiddling with the tongue of his sneaker, the tattered string to the hood of his sweat jacket, or whatever else was loosely attached to him, in a light blue aura of innocence, like an ordinary child; and then a full-grown adult, his size unsettlingly conspicuous in relation to the boy's slight frame, would cautiously sit down and try amicably to initiate an obscene conversation, asking questions that no healthy boy could possibly understand. From what I was told, the boy conveyed his responses, though fragmented, in a thoughtful and sweet tone, as if he were listing all the fun he'd had at school that day. He said that his father used to cut up his spaghetti into tiny bits, so he could eat it with a spoon. Also, he was afraid of the "bottle man" because he smelled of licorice and made bird noises. "Cunt-whore"—who was possibly more than one person, an amalgam in the boy's mind—was shaved clean; one of his legs was raw red below the knee, and his eyes would smile whenever he wanted a little spice or to make a cream pie. The fancy-dressed man in the dark room with the bugs sometimes used to cry, and he called the boy Missy. Although he often gave the boy small gifts, such as a can of soda or a box of colored markers, he also threatened that if the boy didn't stop ruining his home life, he'd make a necklace out of the boy's teeth. Other characters, all without proper names, appeared in the boy's story, but most likely only one or two people made several distinct reappearances in the boy's memory. Nevertheless, one thing was unmistakably clear: The boy trusted me. Apparently, he came to me when he was sick because I always made certain that we were even. I wasn't needy, consuming, or unfair. By some intuitive reflex unbeknownst to myself, I demanded that everything between us remain upfront and equal. If the balance was off in any way, it was because I was generous. With everyone else in his life, except for the shadowy image of a dimly remembered father, things were uneven in the other direction. In part, the originality of the boy's theory of scales seemed to throw doubt on any question of Stockholm syndrome. His allegiance to me was in earnest; I was a good man, not a captor. Yet, despite the boy's affection, I disclaimed him, telling the doctors and the police that I didn't really know the boy or what had happened to him. I had to wash my hands of him. I distrusted the investigators because I sensed that everything they told me about the boy's situation served as a roundabout way of trying to indict me; they were feeding me specific details to see what and when I would bite. Of course, I never let them suspect that I understood their insidious method, and rather than let them play me off of the boy, I acted like a vaguely curious bystander.

But then, after allegedly being cleared of suspicion and hearing nothing about the boy for several months, I sat at my desk and stared at the frozen screen of my computer: the suspended conversation between discontent people, the half sentence of a supposedly twenty-nine-year old marketing rep who went under the alias of Bonzo. He had been confessing, with a hint of self-pity, that he always came across as too cerebral, so he needed to be more open and free, to learn how to "live life through the fingertips." I sipped my hot tea and smiled, ready to point out his unintentional irony, with some clever comment about his typing skills—when the phone suddenly rang, severing me from Bonzo and the rest of the people in the chat room.

"Yes," I said. "Sure. I can come down this afternoon."

The social worker informed me that the boy was deteriorating, and she thought that maybe he would respond to me. For weeks, he hadn't said a single word, and each day he slipped more and more into a catatonic state, not so much by the clinical definition; it was simply a profound listlessness, a self-annihilation. He'd stopped eating, and he'd left the doctors no choice but to feed him intravenously. After several days in bed, hooked up to tubes, he'd decided to cease movement altogether, not even to relieve himself. Because he lacked certain traumatic symptoms, the social worker surmised that his condition was suicidal, not a cry for help, but a genuine disinterest in life.

When I hung up the phone, my immediate reaction was one of dread. With a simple phone call, on a random Tuesday, the problem of the boy thrust itself back into my life, and I was obliged to deal with it. As much as I wanted to tell the social worker that I had no interest in the subject—perhaps even affect a lazy yawn and apologize for finding the whole ordeal terribly boring, like a photo album of her cousin's wedding or a stack of back issues of a gardening magazine—I had to agree to visit her and the boy. I stood up violently from my desk and started stomping about the room, circling the coffee table and couch, making abrupt half-turns and new starts, and once or twice stabbing at the air with my fist, until my mixture of confusion and fear began to metamorphose into a different emotion. I was becoming angry. Yes, it was bad enough that I'd felt unwelcome in the world and had to seek refuge in my own cramped little room. Now, this tiny portion of security was being taken away from me too. I felt as though society had designated for me a lonely cage and, as soon as I submitted and agreed to lock myself in, the outside world decided to invade my space and root me out.

Of course, I would never reveal my unease to the social worker or anyone else. I would be as concerned, sincere, and helpful as needed. My appointment was a few hours away, giving me time to prepare both my attitude and my attire. After I ate my customary bowl of cereal—tiny, round, sweetened puffs—I hurriedly headed toward the bathroom, mildly reproaching myself for being J. C., the man who peed a lot. If I couldn't convince a few silly high school students that I was a serious writer, or Stephen that I possessed a dash of repose, or Lyle Tartles that I was an art aficionado, or Claudia Jones that I was harmless, then how was I supposed to convince the social worker that I was a compassionate citizen. Standing before the toilet, I thought about Claudia Jones again; she was divided up and categorized in my mind, a collection of parceled pieces. I continued to imagine her all the while I showered, brushed my teeth, wiped the steamy mirror with my underwear, and inspected my reflection. I could no longer see her distinctly; she became for me a jumble of images, which flitted, one by one, along the edges of my mind. The side of my head was a rich purple. Thankfully, most of the bruise was concealed beneath my hair. I didn't want the social worker to see my head and ask what had happened. I gingerly combed my hair, wiped the renewed steam away, and then touched my temple with a single, gentle fingertip.

I contemplated wearing the suit that I had worn at the bar with Stephen; the outfit now hung in a bag in the closet, freshly returned from the drycleaners, who'd hopefully removed from the fabric the stale odor of alcohol and cigarette smoke. But I couldn't wear a suit. It would have been too ostentatious, too out of place. I decided on a simple pair of slacks and a light gray button-down shirt, presentable but not too formal. The crowning accoutrement, of course, was my father's hat. It was an old-style felt hat with a snap button on the brim and six seams to the top point. Putting it on, I imagined myself dimly connected to a poor European immigrant of the 1930s or maybe to a migrant farmer. I liked it. Besides making me feel somewhat distinguished, like a man of eclectic tastes, the hat could be worn cocked at a slight angle and thus cover most of my bruise.

Wanting to give myself plenty of time to get to the appointment, I left my apartment as soon as I finished dressing. I knew what bus to take, but not how long I would have to wait for it. Bolting the door behind me, I hurried down the corridor, trying to scoot silently past Claudia's apartment, then out the front door and down the steps, keeping my head down, in case I accidentally saw my landlord. Out of fear of his rodent eyes, I focused my gaze on each square of the sidewalk for an entire block or two. My landlord and I had said all that needed to be said between us. He had offered me a simple, gentlemanly abolishment of my lease agreement. We never had to see each other again. He had even given me back my month and a half security deposit, so nothing would hold me back if an impulse to leave suddenly struck me one night. I didn't even have to bother saying goodbye. This was his solution to our altercation on the steps, a horrible, ugly scene that had occurred three days prior to the dreadful phone call.

II

Oblivious to how long I'd remained splayed and bleeding on the cold sidewalk, the instant I regained consciousness, I sat up and ranted at my landlord in a delirious panic. With my head throbbing, I was vaguely aware of him trying to tell me that an ambulance was on its way, but many of the roads had yet to be cleared of snow. I warned him not to touch me, and I called him a vile rat, among other things, as a few windows and doors began to open, allowing curious bodies to see what all the commotion was about. I wanted someone to come to my rescue because I was convinced that he had attacked me with a shovel and if not for the witnesses, he would have been dealing me a deathblow. But no one was helping me. The sight of blood on my palm and the crushing pain in my head drove me into the feverish pitch of hysterical frenzy. The louder I screamed that I had been struck down by this hateful creature, the louder the little man defended himself, bellowing that I was insane. He said that I'd fallen down the stairs all by myself. I said I would sue him and own the building. Hearing the sound of these words on my own lips, I was seized by a sudden flash of insight; I threatened that as soon as I owned the building and everything in it, I was going to throw him out on the street, so he could scurry back into the sewer with all the other vermin. Nobody watching us seemed to care, so we both shifted our focus, and rather than continue to address our audience, we insulted one another directly. We began to criticize the other's character and point out all the faults we could imagine. Still sitting on the sidewalk, in the process of getting up but not quite able to complete the act, I sensed that I was winning the verbal battle. There was more wit and flare to my abuse. At some point, I called him a loveless gnome, and this epithet must have pleased me because I began to tag it onto everything I said. When he called me gross, I grinned; he was so unimaginative that he had to use the same word for both my neighbor and me. All the while, people lingered in the windows and doorways. We were yelling at each other even after the ambulance arrived and a black woman with long, cool fingers began touching me. She tolerated us for a moment or two, but then she stood up and reprimanded us as though we were children, pointing her finger primarily at me, saying, "Mother of God. Mother of God," and whatever else she said I don't really remember. The rodent fell silent, moved back to the base of the steps, and began to glower. The woman touched me and spoke in a soothing voice. She smelt as though she'd been chewing a sprig of anisette. My delirium started to subside beneath this woman's gentleness. She didn't think anything was seriously wrong with me, but to play it safe, I ought to get x-rays, which, in the end, confirmed her initial diagnosis: Nothing was seriously wrong with me.

When I returned from the hospital a few hours later, I found my landlord waiting for me. He wanted us to come to an understanding. We acted composed and civil as we stood at the threshold of my apartment. I mostly listened and nodded as he presented his case. First of all, he didn't own a single brick or nail in the entire building. He managed things for a corporation in New Jersey, which was comprised of two Greek brothers who owned a small strip mall; roughly fifty acres of undeveloped land that, after failing a round of perc tests, only generated revenue from a gun club; and this apartment building. If I wanted the building, I'd have to sue the Greeks. Second, my landlord, who apparently wasn't my landlord after all, had warned me about the bag of salt. It was my fault that I'd tripped. Third, he gave me back my security deposit, so nothing would hinder me from leaving. Apparently, I didn't need to give him any notice. I could simply vanish, spontaneously combust, or fall victim to any sort of abduction or annihilation. I continued to nod. We stood silently for a moment, inspecting one another, not shaking hands to seal or confirm our potential pact, nor withdrawing to our separate little rooms. We both assumed that the other was waiting for something else to be added to the conversation. I slipped the money into my pocket. Part of me faintly realized that I could now give back some money to Morris the man; another part of me suspected that my landlord wanted my response right there on the spot. I was about to speak, maybe even concede to leaving, but then his face sagged, as if he were reluctantly about to yield, as if he were giving up. With a hint of a grimace and a small show of fidgeting, he informed me that Claudia Jones's website was possibly called "Choice Bits" or something similar. At the moment, I hadn't been thinking about the web address at all, yet I could now see what the man thought about me. In his little brain, "Choice Bits" was part of our negotiation; it was the reason I was holding out; it was my selling point, my weak spot. In response, I shrugged, as if I no longer had any interest or that perhaps all along my interest had been a sham. I thanked him for the money and closed myself in my apartment, where I remained undisturbed until the social worker requested my assistance with the boy. At the time, I never suspected how everything—"Choice Bits," my security deposit, the phone call— could possibly be connected, but I was on my way.

III

I arrived at the bus stop and concealed myself inside the glass enclosure. The metal bench was wet and frozen, so I stood back against the side wall and shivered. Remembering the day of the mist when I had sought shelter inside a different bus stop, I looked at the walls to see the posted flyers, imagining that I might find "Iago as

Id" or "Female Models Wanted." Besides the scrawl of graffiti, there was only a solitary sign, something handwritten in Spanish and referring to niños; someone named Marquita was offering her services as a babysitter. I had a strange, fleeting idea that even though I was childless, I could pay by the hour to have Marquita sit on my couch and watch television one night. Before the utter absurdity of this thought could check me, I plucked her phone number and stuck it in my pocket. I shrunk a little inside my coat as I remembered the black man on the motorcycle, Dr. Barnett, for I knew that the particular shape of his masculinity prevented him from ever entertaining the notion of paying for female company, sexual or otherwise. This was as likely as his putting a cowbell around his neck and skipping down Market Street in a thong. He was a man, composed of himself, and I was something else, something shapeless, a myriad of oozing parts.

After a while, a cold-bitten, watery-eyed woman joined me; she trailed behind her—attached by a purple mitten—a small, plump, excessively bundled creature, possibly a child, a dwarf, or a monkey, for only two black pupils peered out of a slit in a scarf that was wrapped around its fluffy-hooded head. When the bus came, the woman dragged the hobbling creature up the steps. As I started up behind her, I suddenly recalled one other incident during the misty day: Just before I had stepped inside the bus stop, I'd momentarily noticed a motionless figure standing against the building. Now, with some instinct or premonition arresting my stride on the bus steps, and with one hand holding the rail, I leaned out of the door and looked up the street. Everything appeared ordinary. Then I turned my head and searched in the opposite direction. Less than a block away, facing me, was a lone figure dressed in the same dark green baseball cap and corduroy jacket. I was immediately stunned. If not for the hydraulic hiss of the bus and the driver, ready to close the doors, giving the handle a brief, halting jerk—I might not have moved at all. But I stumbled up the steps and down the aisle. Once I was safely in my seat and the rumbling vehicle carried me away, my alarm began to settle down. In fact, I became amazingly calm, not because I convinced myself that the person on the street was a mere coincidence, but rather, deep down, I'd been conscious all along that he had been watching me. I'd been expecting it. Ever since the awful episode of the soiled boy, my body had been especially attuned to the threat of surveillance. Now, here it was at last, and perhaps by the clear spark of intuition or by some other sort of instant lucidity, I knew that it was not the watchful eye of the police, but the crazed glare of a slighted pervert.

The bus dropped me off a couple of blocks away from my destination and about an hour too early, so I had to find somewhere to wait. I started westward, in the direction I needed to go, suspecting that I might come across a place where I could sit down and drink a cup of coffee. The cold weather seemed to jab at the wound just above my temple, and the hat began to feel heavy upon my head, as though with every step a tourniquet tightened. I knew that W. McTeal was miles away, prowling about the vicinity of my home, waiting for my return. Yet I continued to look for him among the people on the sidewalk. Despite my alertness, I was somewhat blind, too preoccupied with W. McTeal and my imminent appointment, let alone with finding a coffee shop. I wasn't really taking notice of my surroundings. Even so, I started to sense that something unusual was happening in the road; a long row of cars was double-parked; and on the sidewalk, many people were simply standing in small groups, forcing me to walk around them. They seemed mute, hushed, almost secretive. One or two played the emissary, milling about from group to group, passing along some quiet communication. It was an oddly disjointed collection of people, dressed alike in dark, dreary clothes. Just when I began to wonder what these people were up to, they all appeared to respond to a mysterious signal that only they and maybe dogs could hear, for they began to move, to step off the sidewalk, and to get into cars. I stopped walking, as one by one, the engines turned and idled. From the tailpipes, puffs of gray exhaust tumbled onto the pavement and then drifted upward, thinning and fading. After a moment, the cars started forward, one after another, in formation, each shining its headlights on the rear of the car in front of it. I looked toward the head of the line, for the hearse, but the row had already rounded the corner up ahead. Although the somber faces behind the windows didn't turn and look at me, I sense that I was aligned with their grief and with the general sobriety of conspicuous mortality. I recalled that in older times, back when men wore black bands around their biceps, a person would show his respect for a funeral procession by stopping whatever he was doing, removing his hat, and quietly waiting until the last mourner was out of sight. Such customs must still exist, if not in the military then at least in small religious southern towns, where if not war then at least God served as a constant reminder of our vulgar fragility. When the final car turned the corner, I realized that despite the band cinching tightly around my skull, I'd forgotten to take off my hat.

The church was beside me, a monument of stonework, filled with stained glass, its spires reaching heavenward but tapering off to a point, possibly with a failing effort, a diminishing of faith, at which the architects of the Tower of Babel would have surely blushed and thought to themselves, Why not go higher? The building itself was set back at the end of a set of long, wide steps, as if the sidewalk, the road, all the other buildings, and thus the whole city block had been planned and erected around it. Lingering at the base of the steps, I looked up at a pair of large wooden doors. I felt a sort of instinctual and sudden revulsion, a physical reaction, as something inside my stomach turned loose and slimy. I took a deep breath and swallowed hard, confused by the abrupt change in me. Maybe the impression that the recent display of mortality had made upon me was now mixing with the aloofness of the ancient building and the frigid austerity of its masonry. Maybe my reaction had something to do with my appointment, the inflamed pervert, or the bits and pieces of my bovine neighbor. My disgust tasted as if it were bubbling up in response to something scatological, yet the church appeared hard and lifeless, unable to elicit the revulsion that I felt. I continued to stare at it. Although I was ordinarily indifferent to Christianity, dismissing it with a haughty wave of my hand, as most academics do, I now had an urge to mock it. I readily found the easy, common, and trite insults. I felt myself confronting the immensity, the absurd size, of the building. The whole towering edifice seemed disproportionate to the value I invested in it. By abstracting God from its history, I imagined that throughout the ages, many sexually troubled young men had looked toward the church; they hoped to discover their calling and thus to alleviate the pulse and anguish of their private lusts, yet these lonely men—who decided to commit themselves to self-denial, who were lured out of the cramped confines of their provincial homes, who were singly drawn from various parts of the land—soon found themselves assembled in a repressed and gaudy brotherhood, within the cold, quiet, stony chambers of the seminaries, amassed in their dormitories, congregated in bathrooms, and paired off secretly in darkened nooks; they were one body, sealed from the outside world for seven years, studying together to take their holy orders, finding release in one another, finding kindred pain, longing, and confusion, and finding sex—seven years of hushed and wicked pleasure—and so the supposedly sterile seminaries were hothouses in disguise, a secret club, which every season enticed new, troubled recruits who were hoping to extinguish their forbidden desire but soon discovered the welcoming arms and yielding bodies of their brothers in the Lord.

Inexplicably, my stomach was full of slime, and I spat on the steps.

What did I care about the sin, the sex, or the pretense. Yet I was angry. Although the building loomed above me, it seemed very far away, at an impossible distance, gloating in its own majesty, rather than condescending to the squat, shabby grime of low life—even though its stones, in fact, were less polished than they were weathered and soot-covered.

I spat again.

When I started to walk, I looked around, checking to see if anyone had seen my irreverence. I suspected that I wore my vehemence on my face and almost regretted no one was there to witness it. The intensity of my emotions was being wasted. Even so, not too far from the building, I began to feel silly. I was never that absurd fool who shook his fist at God; neither did I shake my fist at slugs or doorstops. The institution of religion, which was simply a manner of people, was a different issue. I couldn't blame it for not remedying the problems of the world because I knew that the failure of Christian charity—of its feeding of the hungry and of its clothing of the poor—was in direct proportion to my own failure to adhere, as though I'd imagined charity wasn't so much a product of footwork and sacrifice as it was a poof of smoke and a misty miracle.

I spat again, this time on a scrappy tree, planted to adorn the street but now choked and horribly displaced.

A couple was coming my way, the girl leaning against the boy. She was dressed in a heap of gray sweat clothes. He had a sweatband riding low across his forehead, covering his eyebrows; his black hair appeared to have exploded out of the top of his head, as if by a shotgun blast. She hugged his arm, snuggled it between her breasts. Her caramel skin appeared to glow with beauty, simply because she was happy to be on an afternoon stroll with her boyfriend in the bitter cold. Although they were young, and their affection toward one another seemed to contain something pure and innocent, I knew, of course, that they copulated as often as they had the opportunity to be alone, that she longed to take out his penis and adore it, and that she would work him dry in dirty adoration. She would grin filthily at his satisfaction. He would feign indifference, but that was part of his allure.

As we began to close the space between us, I wanted them to see the indignation on my face. Far away, on a distant street, a small dog began to yelp, faint but incessant. Somewhere in the back of my mind, my spirit was inexplicably emboldened by the notion of being on a mission: The boy needed me, and I was heading toward some heroic gesture. I felt more important than the young couple on the sidewalk. This feeling was similar to the sense of petty power that I had experienced when I was a gangly college student working as an usher in the local movie theatre. That job had lasted only a few weekends because I had found too much cynical joy in strolling up and down the aisle, then suddenly shining the beam of my flashlight on the faces of some young, cuddly couple, disrupting their warm, romantic mood.

As they walked, the boy said something to the girl, and she—all lovely and beautiful and devoted—smiled and held onto him, as though she lacked an ego of her own and only he, who was seemingly all grunts and stonework, was her abiding strength.

For some reason, I wanted to dismantle them, not with profundity or truth, but with disdain. I was leering, full of bile, ready for confrontation. I wished I had my flashlight. Perhaps if there was no ultimate happiness, then there should be no momentary happiness either.

The boy, however, had his eye on me. He was speaking to her, but looking at me. Before I could say anything, he cut me short.

"What are you looking at, poppy?"

And so we passed one another on the street, and only the dim shadow of my intended action fell across the happy couple. In another pace or two, I once again ceased to exist to them; they strolled onward in the aura of their own radiance, in love and impenetrable. As the sound of their footsteps gradually died, I continued to hear the crazy yapping of the dog. Now it sounded closer.

I consoled myself with the thought of the couple's insignificance. They were oblivious; they couldn't have known that not far away, laid out in a hospital bed, a tortured and emaciated boy waited for me. This portrait of the boy was displayed clearly before me, yet most of it was conjured out of my imagination because I'd never actually seen the boy in such a helpless condition, nor had I ever been to the building to which I was now heading. The social worker had given me the address over the phone, and I had surely passed the place numerous times during my tenure in the city, but I had no memory of a clinic being there. Perhaps it was inconspicuous, only a weathered shingle beside a thin door.

I looked at my watch; I had time to kill. My head ached with the cold, and I wanted to find a place to sit for a moment and drink a cup of coffee. I needed to recoup my thoughts, for my mind felt burdened by too many concerns. Chief among them was the strange and terrible McTeal, who seemed to be crouching in some darkened nook, biding his time, waiting to spring on me. There had to be a reasonable way to handle this threat, yet ever since I'd learned from Claudia Jones that I'd disturbed the pervert's fantasy world, I sensed myself delaying to come to any conclusions. Whenever this dilemma entered my mind, my thoughts would scramble around frantically, like startled mice in a cage, and then I would suddenly resolve to run away. Now that the actual crisis had manifested itself on the sidewalk, in a corduroy jacket and a green cap, I still had no viable solution. Perhaps I was planning to wait until he got closer, until he was finally hiding in my bedroom closet and listening for me to drift off to sleep. Although I was heading toward the boy, I would eventually have to go home, where it no longer seemed safe.

I passed an apartment with its windows lined with Christmas lights that were already turned on, shining and blinking in vibrant colors. Not only was it too early in the day for lights but also everything seemed too drab and cold for such a giddy display. Yet it subtly evoked a fresh train of thought, for I went rapidly from thinking of the imminent holiday season and all its trappings to Christmas carols; and then Claudia Jones was sitting on the milkcrate in the alley outside my window, humming "What Child Is This?" In the next instant, my image of her fragmented, and she was divided into all her particular parts, which randomly drifted along the edges of my mind—yet, before I was fully aware of what I was thinking, a small, hysterical yapping dog bounded out of a narrow side street and continued its frenzy on the sidewalk. A larger dog lingered slowly behind it. An imperceptible string seemed to connect the lowered nose of the larger dog to the tail end of the small one.

Alarmed, I stopped walking and fixed my attention on the animals. They were about ten paces in front of me.

The small dog, an indeterminable mixture of breeds, didn't seem to be barking randomly into the air, but actually at certain objects. It looked at the tire of a parked car and barked at it. Then the dog wheeled around and barked down the side street from which it had just emerged. Then it barked at the curb a few times. It turned and barked at the tire again. Its every movement was followed by the larger dog, some kind of gray-coated Husky which, bent at the waist, made awkward side steps and even circled around, always keeping its nose close to the other dog's tail. Both of them were without collars and seemingly disease-ridden, for the hair of the mutt was clumped and tangled, and its underbelly was especially dirty from apparently having trailed through slush; the Husky was missing patches of hair, and large black growths, shaped like cauliflower, blossomed from its joints.

At the curb was an old stone post with a metal hoop on top, to which older generations of men used to tether their horses. For some reason, the small dog focused on this post and unleashed a savagery of abrupt yaps. Because the dogs appeared absorbed for the moment,

I thought I had the opportunity to slip away unobserved. I wondered for an instant if I should retreat to the next street over or simply try to pass the dogs by crossing the road. Either way, my instinct was to get immediately out of their line of sight by stepping off the sidewalk and putting the row of parked cars between us.

The instant I took my eyes off the dogs and moved between the bumpers of two parked cars, the incessant yapping stopped. I stood in the road, beside the back fender of a car, completely unnerved by the sudden silence. I crouched down and looked through the windows, trying to locate the dogs. The tethering post was visible, but the beasts were no longer by it. I had no idea if my movement had distracted them or if it was something else and they were right now chasing after it. Afraid to budge in the slightest bit, I continued to look through the windows, but not seeing the stray dogs, I huddled closer to the car and decided to wait until I was certain that danger had passed. I wanted to hear the furious yapping again—but at great distance. I was half-hoping that some unfortunate pedestrian might casually wander upon the scene and fall prey to the full fury of the animals—for at least long enough for me to run away.

I waited, but everything was still.

My head throbbed with the pulse of blood as the flesh around my wound seemed to be spastically twitching. The car was champagne colored, and the gray breath that I was exhaling upon its fender made a faint patch of steam.

After a moment, once I began to collect myself and feel reasonably certain that the threat was over, I felt a slight pressure, barely perceptible, dimpling the back hem of my overcoat. All my muscles tensed. Then came the sound of nostrils inhaling, sniffing. The pressure became more real and tangible when a dog's nose pressed against me, as if the animal wanted to burrow its snout into the cleft between my thighs.

I shrieked like a ten-year-old girl.

Making a sudden dash to get away, I tumbled against the side of the car and landed on my back, on the wet, slushy pavement. For the brief instant I lay there, both dogs gathered around and continued to sniff me. I quickly scrambled to my feet and backed away from the dogs.

"Yah. Yah!" I screamed and made some kind of shooing gesture with my hands. "Yah. Yah!" I repeated, as if I were herding livestock, such as pigs.

The dogs were standing in the center of the road, with their heads slightly cocked, inspecting me with a strange befuddled gaze.

"Yah!" I screamed and retreated another step backward. I was cautious not to run or to show fear because I believed this would have brought them pouncing down upon me.

The scraggly mutt's ears perked up, and its wide black eyes blinked several times but remained fixed on me.

Still taking its cue from the small dog, the Husky didn't move until the mutt first advanced. Before I knew how to react, they both walked up and started sniffing me again. I stood frozen as their noses nuzzled and moved over my legs and feet. I feared that if I made any gesture, their interest would take a violent turn. While the large dog seemed particularly preoccupied with the back of my knee, the small one abandoned me, walked to where I had crouched beside the car, and peed on the spot with one quick, short burst. Then it started to bark at the champagne colored car. This aroused the Husky, which straightaway left me to commence sniffing the mutt's tail end.

I took a few steps backward and then slowly started to turn, to walk away, though still glancing over my shoulder to keep my eyes on them. The more distance I put between us, the faster I walked. I was beginning to feel more comfortable, and just as I started to take stock of my situation—in particular, that I had sprawled out on the fouled street and now the back of me was wet and dirty—all at once, the yapping ceased. I turned around to see the dogs trotting toward me.

"Yah. Yah!" I shouted.

I started to run, trusting that the distance between us gave me the chance to get away.

Without looking back, I ran, my heart thumping in my chest, my wound inflamed and twitching, the flat bottoms of my shoes clapping on the blacktop. Just behind me sounded a deep, solitary bark from the Husky. The horrible knowledge that the dogs were chasing me drove me to run faster. Fleeing wildly down the street, I recalled the sensation of pursuing my urban nymph, Celeste Wilcox, which was the last time I'd exerted myself, and how all the while I'd run after her, I'd dimly sensed in the back of my mind some obligation of a silly appointment. Soon, the Husky was running beside me. It circled around the front of me, only to reappear on my side again. The mutt kept pace, its tiny legs flickering at an incredible speed beneath its body, its head turned toward me, and the tip of its tongue hanging out of the corner of its mouth. When I slowed down to a walk, the dogs followed suit. My breathing was hard and painful. My face burned flush, and my underclothes were damp with perspiration. The dogs didn't appear to be affected at all.

I continued to walk, trying to ignore them, but they stayed with me. They occasionally moved in front of me, but always dropped back beside me again. I headed toward the curb, and then the three of us walked down the sidewalk together. When we passed people, they didn't take any special notice of us. I suspected that pedestrians would have been cautious, if not fearful, of the dogs, if the animals weren't walking so close to my heels. I briefly wished for my movie theatre flashlight again, not so much to signal my distress as to dazzle their vision, as if to say, "Can't you see what is going on here? Can't you see?" After a while, it seemed as though I were not so much leading the animals as I were a member of a motley pack.

Shortly, I came to the address that the social worker had given me, and it didn't appear to be a clinic at all. It was a narrow building. Drab yellow stucco covered the walls of the ground floor, but brick, painted the same ugly color, went up the rest of the way for several stories. There was a single storefront window that displayed, on a series of carpeted plateaus, foam heads with long necks. All the heads lacked mouths, noses, and ears, and had slight impressions where eyes should have been. Most of them were a dark, rich color: green, purple, and black. One, however, was a disturbing pink. For some reason, it faced the wall, adorned with long, straight turquoise hair. In fact, all the heads had hair.

"A wig shop," I said, looking down at the dogs, as if explaining to them.

Of course, this couldn't have been the place.

But then, I saw where I had to go. There was a glass door. When I looked through it, I was able to read a list of names with room numbers posted on the wall. A staircase led upward, not only to the offices of family counselors but also to a law firm and a specialist who fitted people with hearing devices. Although I was uncertain how the system worked, I suspected that the tree-shaped woman must have given up working for the state and joined a private practice. If this were the case, then she'd somehow retained her treatment of the boy, who was supposed to be government property.

Without bothering to look at my watch, I knew I had time before my appointment. I abandoned the idea of sitting down and drinking a cup of coffee. I needed to find somewhere to dry myself off and clean up. Yet, despite the wound on my head, my sweaty underwear, and my soiled overcoat, I felt somewhat carefree, a bit indifferent to how my appearance might be assessed by the social worker. The problem of the boy was somewhere beneath me. The woman would ask me a few questions; I would nod, express my sympathy, but ultimately go home and slip myself back into my uneventful life. The world was going to continue to rotate, and the same stars were going to dot the same night sky. It didn't matter if I lived the life that I'd thus far established or if I went out and started a new one. Of course, deep down, I knew all along that I was going to run away. The imminent threat of Claudia's private pervert was my catalyst. I had no reason ever to meet the man, let alone to confront him in a final showdown. I had nothing to prove to anyone, no score to settle, no relationship to salvage. The prospect of running away put me at ease. Not only were all my burdens going to be lifted from me, but also my future appointment with the social worker now seemed drained of significance. I had no reason to feel intimidation, anger, or anything else.

And so, it was settled: For yet another time in my life, I was going to fix my problems by fleeing from them. Although I tried to convince myself that this was the best solution, part of me knew that I was simply rationalizing.

Suddenly, I realized that I was walking alone. My fleeting membership among the stray dogs had ended; our pack had disbanded as quickly as it had been formed, lasting no more than a few moments. I turned around to see that they were across the street from the wig shop, rooting and pawing for something beneath a squat, blue mailbox.

I continued forward. My body was growing cold as my overcoat began to stiffen and freeze and perspiration chilled my flesh. I quickened my pace. My imminent appointment didn't unsettle me as much as before, yet I still remained curious about what to expect. It seemed like a silly place to set up a practice, for nobody who needed counseling would find comfort going up that dingy staircase, let alone passing all those heads.

"And if the family counseling doesn't work, at least there're lawyers—" I began to say, but abruptly stopped myself, conscious that I had spoken aloud, not even to a pair of dogs. I kept walking and finished the thought in my head: *Well, at least, it's pretty convenient to have lawyers nearby to handle the divorce.*

IV

I rounded the corner and started down a more congested street. The wind felt stronger here, more bitter, and everyone was walking briskly, with faces lowered. I was looking for a store, thinking that I could buy a change of clothes. Thankfully, I had the money from my security deposit on me because I had been cautious about leaving it unprotected in my apartment.

On an awning across the street, I read that somebody named Crowley had two stores side-by-side. One sold new and used CDs. Its front window was plastered over with images of rock stars in seductive poses. The door was covered in a mess of decals, stickers, and scribbled insignias or perhaps messages in the jargon of some particular subculture. I didn't spend any time trying to figure it out because I hurriedly entered Crowley's other store, which sold used and vintage clothing. Warmth and the odor of burning incense permeated the room. Slow instrumental jazz was playing softly. Racks of clothes lined the walls on either side, and above these racks were more racks. The upper ones were apparently reached, not by a step stool, but by tiny wooden chairs that were made for children. Near the back wall sat a low couch. A young couple was lounging there in an attitude of listless indifference, which implicitly conveyed to me that they weren't the salesclerks. The girl was dressed in worn corduroy pants, and reclined, spread-eagled, with one leg crossed over the young man's thigh. Neither of them paid any attention to me as I began looking through the clothes. Strangely, nothing was organized, not by size, make, or style, not even by gender. There were plenty of long, flimsy dresses and button-down shirts from a previous generation. Between a quilted flannel shirt and a denim dress with brass buttons down the side, hung a white nurse's outfit made of leather. At the exact moment I happened to have my hand on the garment, the girl muttered something to the boy and then giggled.

"Is there someone who could help me?" I asked. I felt cold and pressed for time.

"Customer," the girl called, turning her head toward an arched doorway that was partially obstructed by a stereo cabinet.

"I like the hat," the young man said as he straightened up and gently pushed the girl's leg off of his.

She whispered something to him, and he responded, "I don't think so."

"Thanks," I said.

Out of the backroom came a skinny woman in jeans and a hooded sweatshirt bearing the name Moravian. She smiled and walked up to me.

"Hi there," she said. "Did you find something?"

"No."

"Do you know what you're looking for?" She continued to smile and look at me kindly from behind a pair of black-rimmed glasses.

"Anything dry," I said.

"Oh no," she said and actually started to help me remove my overcoat. "You must be freezing."

"I have an important meeting to go to."

"What happened?" She draped my overcoat over the counter and then came behind me and took my sports coat off me.

"I fell down."

"Oh no," she said again.

I could feel her hand on my back, touching my gray shirt, then moving down to my legs.

"The bottoms of your trousers are frozen stiff. Literally frozen."

"I know."

"Poor thing."

"I didn't see anything formal."

"Don't worry; I'll set you up."

She threw my sports coat on the counter too, stepped in front of me, and looked at me carefully, sizing me up.

I watched her as she moved about the store, assembling an outfit for me. She dragged behind her a little chair that was missing chips of blue paint. Most of the garments she selected came from the upper racks. She would place one foot on the small seat and quickly slide the hangers along the bar. Her animation was at a pace anomalous to the mellow mood of the room. When she stretched, I was able to see not only two dimples on her back, just above the waistline of her jeans, but also that she had very small, indiscernible breasts. Occasionally, she turned to me and smiled.

I didn't notice that the music had stopped playing, until the young man got up from the couch, searched through the loose CDs on top of the stereo cabinet, and restarted the music.

The skinny woman came toward me with an armload of clothes.

"Try these," she said. "I got you several things to choose from."

"Don't you like his hat?" the young man asked her.

"I love his hat."

I noticed her eyes focus on my wound, but she didn't say anything about it.

"Come on," she said, and I followed her under the arched doorway, into the backroom.

I wasn't quite certain what to make of the room at first. It appeared to be a separate store altogether, with glass counters like those in a jewelry shop and shelves on the back wall stacked with various knickknacks. I gave it a cursory glance and continued behind the woman, mainly focusing on her.

"Over here's the bathroom," she said.

She clicked the light on for me with her elbow and deposited the clothes on a bench across from the toilet. Leaving, she pulled the door behind her, and although she'd left it slightly ajar, I didn't push it completely shut. I doubted, of course, that she would spy on me through the crevice, but, what's more, she had an aura of liberty that was contagious. Strangely, she made me feel relaxed enough not to mind the thin gap in the door.

The bathroom was more quaint and feminine than the rest of the store would have led me to believe. There was a shower stall beside the toilet, and an enormous mirror stretched the length of the wall above the basin. In the corner, on a tripod, burned a large three-wick candle. All the clothes the woman had selected for me were dark, solid colors. I stripped down to my tee-shirt, boxer shorts, and hat, and then I removed the hat and the tee-shirt. I stepped back and inspected myself in the mirror. The normal hue of my skin had become ashen; my flesh cold and clammy. Using a cloth hand towel, I patted myself down and rubbed dry some places on my body that needed to be rubbed dry. Afterwards, I dropped the towel upon my pile of discarded clothes, instead of returning it to the shower rod for reuse. I tried on all the clothes, except for a shirt with wide lapels. In the end, I dressed in a pair of gabardine pants and a black, shiny rayon shirt. I didn't look too bad. I leaned close to the mirror to inspect my wounded head. Apparently, the cold weather had given my skin such a pallor that the wound seemed less hideous and blended better with my overall drained complexion.

With my hat back on my head, I left all the other articles, including my own clothes, and stepped out of the bathroom.

The woman apparently wasn't waiting for me because I found myself alone in the backroom. I went up to one of the glass counters and saw a bunch of brightly colored pipes and silver lighters. Arranged on the shelf beyond it were hollow tubes sticking out of peculiar bulbous bases.

"You're looking pretty sharp," the woman said behind me.

"Thanks." I turned around to see her smiling at me.

"I found a jacket for you." She was holding a muddy green jacket with brown patches on the elbows.

"Thanks," I repeated and started toward her in the doorway. "It's just around the corner, but I'm running out of time."

"Well, try it on." Again, she helped me, standing behind me.

Once I had it on, she pulled lightly on the shoulders, checked the length of my sleeves, and ran her hand down my back twice, brushing the coat smooth.

"You're picture perfect."

"I left everything in the bathroom. Can I come back for my stuff. I'm just going around the corner."

"Sure," she said, moving out of the backroom. "Let it dry out. But we close in about an hour."

"I should be back by then. If not, you're open tomorrow, right?"

"No problem."

She went behind the counter that my coats were spread atop, drew out a calculator and a pad, and began figuring how much I owed her.

"I appreciate this," I said.

"What's the worst that can happen? You don't show up, and I sell your clothes."

"I'll be back."

"After tomorrow, they're going on the rack."

Because she was grinning, I couldn't tell if she was teasing me or not.

"Sounds fair," I said.

She told me the sum, which was more than I expected, but I paid it without hesitation. When she tore off the receipt, I waved it away, so she folded it in half and dropped it in a wicker pail.

"Are you Crowley?" I asked.

"No, my ex- was a whacky Zeppelin fan."

In response, I smiled, although her comment made no sense to me.

"He first wanted to call it the Boleskin House, but everyone would have thought we were a bar or something." She laughed.

"Crowley's is a good name," I said.

"A dabbler in sex, drugs, and magic," she said, which sounded like a bizarre way for her to describe her ex-, but I continued to smile.

I thanked her again, buttoning up the muddy green coat.

She came out from behind the counter to escort me to the door.

The girl on the couch said something to the young man, who answered by saying, "Not until Thursday." Then they both got up and disappeared into the backroom.

"What is that?" I asked, referring to the back store.

"Oh, just a little extra cash. There's a solid demand."

"What is it?"

Pausing before the front door, she looked at me, amused by my naïveté.

"A head shop."

Seeing that I made no reaction, she clarified: "Paraphernalia, you know, bongs, bowls, dug-outs, for smoking pot."

"Really?"

"Really," she mimicked, nodding her head. She pushed up her glasses and then made a gesture that led me to imagine for an instant that she was reaching out her hand to touch me, but instead she pushed open the door.

"Try to stay dry."

"Thanks."

I stepped out onto the sidewalk, glancing back at her briefly, before lowering my head and plunging into the cold. In the sudden absence of the incense, jazz, and warmth, and, of course, the soothing presence of the woman, the outside world seemed to be imbued with a starker kind of desolation. In the afterglow of Crowley's, I felt whatever concern I had for my appointment or for McTeal vanish. I was now about to go through the empty motions of a meaningless charade. I would enact my pantomime, nod where I was obliged to nod, and then—very soon—try to reemerge into life on a warmer, drowsier, more comfortable level.

V

Although the muddy green coat was bulky, it offered little protection from the cold, so I strode at a rapid pace, not bothering to turn my attention toward anything, until I came at last to the glass door, pushed it open, and stepped into the stale mustiness of the stairwell. The social worker's name wasn't listed on the wall, but I assumed she was one of the "Associates" of the family counselors on the second floor.

When I reached the top of the stairs, a corridor with a series of closed doors greeted me. The first few were unmarked, and I was slightly disturbed by the thought of having to knock on random doors. Then I saw one labeled as a restroom, with a symbol for handicapped people, although anyone in a wheelchair wasn't too likely ever to come up those steps. Near the end of the hall was the door I sought. I lightly knocked, perhaps just to signal my entrance, and opened the door.

An elderly woman, who had been concealed behind a formica counter, stood up and asked if she could help me.

"I'm Dr. Parker."

"Good. Good. Have a seat." With a pen, she pointed to a pair of black chairs in the corner. There was a small tree growing out of a wicker basket, and a coffee table with several magazines on top of it.

"It's going to be a few minutes," she said. "I'm sorry, but I'll let them know you're here."

As I started to remove my coat, the woman left through a doorway beside the counter. I placed the coat on one of the seats and sat down on the other. I attempted to act relaxed. Although I picked up a magazine and looked down at it, I didn't read a single word because I was thinking: *them, them.* Who else was I going to see in addition to the weary, tree-shaped social worker? The setting didn't seem right at all. I seriously doubted that somewhere in this building was a room with a boy who was wasting away on a bed. This wasn't the white ward of my imagination. *Them?*

Yet what did it matter if just the social worker and I were to play the game or if twenty other people had parts to perform and noises to mouth? Let them stuff themselves with a sense of their own importance at my expense. Because I was resolved to leave town, everything seemed harmless.

The old woman returned.

"A few minutes," she said and reclaimed her seat behind the counter, so we couldn't see one another. She began typing at a furious rate.

After a moment, I returned the magazine to the table and stood up.

"I'll be right back," I told the woman, whose typing didn't cease.

I left the room and headed down the corridor, toward the bathroom. Since it was apparently for both sexes, I knocked and waited for a reply, before opening the door. When I turned on the light, a fan clicked on. A single toilet was surrounded by metal rails bolted to the walls. As I urinated, I read a sign requesting that nothing but toilet paper was to be flushed—a message presumably directed at menstruating women. For some reason, it struck me as a symbol of something, perhaps the last vestige of the infamous female curse, out of which—I imagined—had sprung a whole alternative history of civilization: All the institutions and customs of man positioned their foundations around the bloody scene, which was at once loathsome and mysterious, in need of constant regulation and subversion, particularly during a time when wombs supposedly floated free and when dark, viscous humors, like transmission fluid or oils in a hydraulic pump, governed the functions of the body. Of course, maybe the sign actually symbolized nothing.

Now wasn't the time for such inane ideas.

Zippering up my gabardine pants, I began to think about Claudia Jones. All my previous notions about her had assumed a new shape after my discovery of "choice bits." She was no longer simply my bloated-tongued, idiotic neighbor who neglected her mail and hummed Christmas carols on a milkcrate in the alley outside my window. Neither was she any kind of sexual prospect for me—not the listless cow and certainly not the woman wrapped in the purple gauze of ennui, who moved in velvet shadows and waited to surround me with her touch. The real Claudia Jones was something more unsettling and uncanny.

Even though I had feigned indifference when my landlord gave me the title of Claudia's Internet site, the first thing I did when I entered my apartment was to boot up my computer and try to find the site. The quest was not as straightforward as I'd expected because my initial search mainly called up companies that manufactured or sold power drills, and also a Midwestern butcher who claimed to have not only the finest cuts of meat but also specialty items, such as tripe, polenta, and baccalà. I then added a single word to my search, which, obviously, was the word "porn." And this brought up pages and pages of web addresses. Uncertain where to begin, I clicked on the first one; red letters appeared on a black screen, asking if I knew the laws of my state and if I freely consented to visit the site and all the nasty things within. I agreed, scrolled down through a bunch of young women doing things that really, in essence, only the act of photography itself made perverted, and then exited the site, returning to my search page rather than following the links deeper into the world wide web. I entered a few more sites, only to find nothing regarding Claudia Jones. After a while, I narrowed my search even further, by including Claudia Jones's name. This merely directed me to more pornography sites, none of which seemed to have any relation to "choice bits," even though this was part of the search. I discovered that a certain starlet who had pioneered the adult industry, only to later repudiate it, was in one of her "classic" films either possessed or fucked by the devil, depending on how the preposition "in" was being used in the title. Another one of her groundbreaking films, called *Deep Throat*, made an apparent reference to the Watergate scandal, though in what manner I remained unsure because the site merely provided enough information to elicit a sale of the vintage movie. I didn't buy anything and proceeded with my quest. Eventually, I began to get a headache, and I went to bed, thinking that my landlord was lying or deluded. The search seemed impossible. I turned over and shut my eyes. Falling asleep was difficult, for the innumerable images of nameless people floated back up to the surface of my mind, taunting and exposed, yet remaining at an uncrossable, electronic distance. At last, I sank into sleep, and perhaps somewhere in my dreams, I was able to bridge the chasm because suddenly I was aroused out of my slumber. I lay in bed for a while, staring at the slashes of moonlight shining through my window blinds. I had no idea what time it was. I was alone and tired. I felt like a child of missed opportunity. Deceased hopes began to stir within me; old desires presented themselves like specters in the night. I wasn't longing for the past exactly, but rather for the feeling of possibility that had once motivated me. At one time in my life, I had tacitly believed that I'd find love and completion, and now here I was, a man grown gangly, quiet, and alone, with no one to call him back to a world of innocence and promises. I was steeped in a sense of my own repugnance, polluted by my own ineptitude, crushed by something I couldn't quite locate or define. I wanted a different life, where satisfaction wasn't so hard to come by. I wondered if this yearning was mine alone or if it belonged to the normal human heart. But other people always reminded me of mules with carrots dangling an inch before their mouths, so they would keep plodding on through life, never quite content, always thinking that the final reward was just one step in front of them. Yet, even if they somehow managed to get the carrot, they'd soon want another one because, in the end, nothing ever provided satisfaction. All the workings of man were products of his discontent. Perhaps this truth could be better understood once a person has spent hours before a computer screen, wasting his time, looking at images of anonymous people whom he could never touch or truly know. Of course, this was just one of many vacuous moments; and further still, in the chilly gloom of my bedroom, I was aware that I had to keep plodding on, looking toward a coveted carrot that I knew was just a mirage. Maybe it was this knowledge that separated me from other people—or at least from W. McTeal. He actually seemed to believe that Claudia Jones was a real thing that could be obtained. The only reason he had sent her pictures of himself, his "love letters," was that he wanted, if not exactly love, then at least some sort of connection to her. It was this that I had obstructed for him: the possession of Miss Jones.

As I left the bathroom and started back down the hall toward my impending appointment, I never considered turning and fleeing down the narrow staircase and into the street, even though I sensed that something was amiss. This place wasn't a clinic, which meant that there were most likely no beds, no nurses, and no boy starving himself to death. I should have been smart enough to leave, but I continued to play out the charade, not because of some latent fascination or curiosity or any other obscure motivation, but rather because part of me felt detached from these surroundings, as if they had nothing to do with me. Moreover, another part of me was somewhere else, occupied by Claudia Jones and W. McTeal.

I went back into the office and took my seat. Although the elderly woman was no longer typing, she still busied herself with something behind the counter. As I waited, I continued thinking about how I'd lain in bed and stared at the slashes of moonlight, unable to turn over because of my wounded head. The random mess of lurid images that had appeared on my computer screen had left a residue on my mind, making me feel drained. I wondered how W. McTeal felt about himself after he signed off the Internet, still devoid of human connection. This thought made me sit upright in bed; I had suspected earlier that I ought to have left "Jones" out of my search, but now I had a jolting hunch to incorporate W. McTeal. I got out of bed and went back online. Of course, my search included choice bits, Claudia, and porn, but it was the addition of two words that seemed to focus my quest. Still convinced that W. McTeal was a pseudonym, I typed in "wet clam," and by the thousands, web addresses appeared. Nevertheless, one of these had to be the prize. Whether or not I was wrong to assume that W. McTeal's name was an anagram didn't really matter because I felt lucky. I believed that I was onto something, and this burst of intuition was what compelled me to visit the sundry sites. I was able to gain access to so many bedrooms and intimate situations that all the normal and solid layers of the world seemed to have peeled back to reveal the dark, wet pulp of its underbelly. Here were your neighbors and friends, your aunts and cousins, your mothers and daughters—but without their social camouflage—in a carnival of bodies. Sometime during the bleary-eyed hours of the morning, I left behind my search results and followed a link deeper into the web because it promised twenty-four quality pictures of a "fat chick." She was an Asian girl with broad shoulders like a man's and a braid of black hair that she coiled around her neck. Obviously not Claudia Jones, the Asian chick nonetheless took me even deeper into the web because she listed several "friends' sites," all devoted to corpulent women. Even though none of these

sites had anything to do with Claudia Jones, I followed a link here
and another one there, until I found myself sitting in the middle of
a subterranean network of perverts who were all obsessed with large
women. Interestingly, the sites overlapped and borrowed from each
other. In one set of pictures, a girl named Brandy crammed herself
into a tiny bathroom, dressed in nothing but a white garter, and posed
atop a laundry basket. On another site, the same girl wore the same
garter and posed on the same basket, and the only difference was that
the pictures were larger and grainier and that the girl's name was now
Evelyn. There were hardcore fat chicks (both in couples and in groups),
softcore fat chicks, lesbian fat chicks, fat chicks with toys, fat chicks
with dicks, and all other manner of fetish—as if the fatness wasn't a
fetish in itself. Through some back avenue, I came upon a collection
of thumb-size pictures of a woman's breasts. A crooked, purple vein
arched out from a bulbous nipple in every picture. All of them seemed
to have been taken at different times. I found it bizarre that a single
page would contain nothing but images of these hideous sacs; even so,
on the bottom of the screen, I had the option of viewing more pages
of the same or of returning to the main menu. Because I'd come to the
site through some circuitous route, I decided to visit the main page.
The woman had completely categorized herself according to her body
parts; not only were there countless pictures of her breasts but also of
everything from her legs and feet to just her broad, creased, and creamy
stomach—everything, that is, below the neck. All the categories had
unique and sometimes vague titles, such as *Hills and Valleys, The Cleft
Peach, Red Wings,* and *The Balloon Knot,* as well as the names of several
different kinds of small birds, which apparently corresponded to
particular toys. Her favorite one seemed to be *The Canary* because it
was featured for seventeen pages. Although the woman never showed
her face, the menu also listed her personal journal, which was updated
nearly every day. She posted all her private thoughts, including stories

from her childhood and long, intricate fantasies. She had a whole collection of "unsent letters" to people she'd at one time loved or hated. The final item on the menu was simply miscellaneous pictures that either crossed categories or didn't quite fit anywhere; she called these her *Choice Bits*. Nonetheless, even before I noticed this section, I knew who I was looking at because something seemed familiar. Perhaps it was the gaudy fingernails; they were a recurring theme, dragging across the skin, dipping into folds and crevices, pulling things up, and spreading things apart.

"Dr. Parker."

"Yes," I said, rising out of my chair to greet the social worker with a handshake.

"Thank you so much for coming."

"It's no problem," I said. "I'd like to help wherever I can." Even though I sensed the words flowing easily out of my mouth, I felt somewhat displaced because despite the woman's polished presence, equanimity, and professional manner, I knew that all this was just a veneer. It was the part of herself that she presented to me, and it was through me that this burnished part found its definition and shine. I left my jacket on the chair, and she led me past the counter and held the door open for me. Walking beside her, I could smell her scent of baby powder, which faintly hinted at something more intimate. Of course, she had her own cleft peach and balloon knot, and perhaps she even played with small birds, and all her human connections were through some medium just as artificial and tenuous as a computer screen and a telephone line. She was talking to me, taking me toward an open door at the end of the hallway. I wanted to get this appointment over with as quickly as possible.

"What happened to the clinic?" I asked, referring to the place where we used to meet, back when the problem of the boy had been brand new.

"It's still there," she said.

Stepping into the room, I had a strong inclination that I wasn't going to see a white curtain, a bed, or even the boy. A desk was off in the corner, with a chair beside it and a small couch in front of it. The walls were lined with gray filing cabinets, which might have concealed a window or two, though I doubted the room had any windows at all. Two men were sitting on the small couch, and they both stood up at my entrance. The social worker directed me toward the seat beside her desk.

Both of the men greeted me, but neither extended his hand.

"How are you doing?" I asked.

"Oh, fine, fine," one of the men said, while the other one gave me a quick nod and sat back down.

"You know Dr. Ferguson, right?" the social worker asked as she moved behind the desk.

"No," I answered, looking at the man who was still standing. He was dressed in a dark suit but without a tie.

"I'm Bruce Ferguson," he said, as if this was supposed to clarify who he was and why he wished to meet me.

The other man wasn't introduced. As the rest of us took our seats, I could sense this man's eyes sizing me up. He had dark, almost purple skin and bloated cheeks, as if the turtleneck sweater he wore was choking him.

The only things on the desk were a letter tray and a laptop computer, which the social worker folded and moved to the other side of the desk, away from me. Through previous sessions with her, I was already accustomed to her style of having a clear, unobstructed view of me.

"So how have things been?" she asked.

"Good."

"And your work. No writer's block?"

"No, my book is coming along on schedule."

"Well, that's good," she said. She laced her fingers together and rested her forearms on the desk. Her usual mug of coffee was missing from the scene. "I see you've got a bruise."

"I fell down outside, hit my head on the sidewalk."

She winced for a second, as if her head were the one that had been wounded.

I wished I had something in front of me, such as a desk or a table, because I felt on display for the two men seated across from me. I became conscious of my arms lying along the armrests and of the balls of my thumbs gently tapping on the wood. I moved my hands to my lap and, like the social worker, laced my fingers together.

"Must have been quite a spill," Dr. Bruce Ferguson said, pointing cursorily at my head with his pinky finger.

"It hurt," I said, smiling.

"How's it now?" the social worker asked.

"It still hurts."

I felt myself smiling stupidly, which was my instinctive defense. When I used to be alone with the social worker, I hadn't minded her constant, warm gaze, but now in the company of these men, I had no hiding place. I was the object of observation; all I could do was smile.

"You've been apprised of the case," the nameless black man said. "You know the situation."

I couldn't tell if this was a question or an accusation.

"Yes," I said. "I hear the boy is not doing well." I turned toward the social worker. "You said so over the phone."

"It's very sad."

"Horrible," the black man added.

"Will he get better?" I asked.

"He's shutting down," the social worker said. "But I'm not his doctor."

"Is it psychosomatic?" I turned toward Bruce Ferguson, who raised his chin slightly when my eyes lighted upon him. I assumed he was the one caring for the boy's health.

"At this point, it doesn't seem to matter whether or not it's in his head. For him, it's still very real."

I nodded.

"Horrible," the black man repeated.

"Yes," I said, still keeping my eyes on Ferguson, who had a pleasant, amiable face.

"Is there anything that can be done for him?" I asked.

"We can set things right," the black man said.

"Hopefully." Ferguson turned toward the man. "I really hope so." He then returned his attention to me. "But as for the boy, I can't imagine anybody recovering fully from such an ordeal. Such trauma is overwhelming."

"He actually got worse under our treatment," the social worker said. "At one point, just before he stopped talking, he would merely grunt and breathe in quick, short breaths, almost like a panting dog. He would yell, 'The man,' over and over again, and when the doctor asked him, 'What man?' the boy pointed his finger at him and said, 'You are the man.' Of course, we thought we were close to something because the boy never mentioned his abuser unless we questioned him." The social worker unlaced her fingers and placed her fingertips on her chest. "'I'm not the man,'" she said, imitating the doctor. "But the boy insisted that he was. Later, when I was by myself with him, he did the same thing; he kept shouting, 'The man.' I remember taking his hand and asking, 'Who are you talking about, sweetheart?' The boy was delusional. Genuinely terrified. He pulled his hand away and pointed at me. 'You are the man.' It breaks my heart. He was actually scared of me."

I kept nodding my head. All this talk was building to something.

"And now he doesn't speak?" I asked.

"Not a word," the social worker said. Telling me this story seemed to have moved her; she no longer looked at me with peaceful eyes, but rather she bit her bottom lip and stared vaguely down at the desk, as if she were distracted and had forgotten that other people were in the room.

"I've only met the boy once," the black man said. His head, if not his entire body, appeared ready to pop, like a bloated tick.

"This is a different boy," I said.

"What's that?" the black man asked.

I looked around for an instant, wondering what I'd just said.

"How so?" the black man asked.

"Different," I said.

They were all looking at me, waiting for me to continue.

"The few times I met the boy, he was very alert," I explained. In fact, I always thought he was secretive and cunning, very distinct from the portrait they now painted for me.

"He was never healthy," the social worker said, pulling her chair closer to me. "Even when you were friendly with him, he was never a normal boy."

"I didn't—" I started to say, wanting not only to clarify my comment but also to qualify, if not defuse, her use of the word "friendly."

But the black man cut me off.

"Now, what do you mean by different?" he asked, and I felt myself losing to him, cowering a little because I couldn't look him in the eye.

"When I knew him, he was very alert."

"I don't know what you mean?" The black man, seemingly flabbergasted and confused, then looked at Dr. Ferguson, as if he could explain.

I thought that my comment was neither vague nor particularly relevant.

"When I knew him, he might have stolen cigarettes from—" I began.

"No," the social worker said. "He was outside your home, killing cats with a brick."

"I didn't know that."

"He was."

"That's horrible," I said.

"Yes," the black man said.

I still had no idea why they wanted to talk with me. Besides giving the boy a few dollars, I had done nothing more for him than call an ambulance. I imagined myself playing the older, charitable man to the poor, homeless Ragged Dick, but unlike that popular, dime-novel hero, the boy apparently didn't shine shoes or rescue drowning victims; he smashed small animals in a dirty alley.

"He was never right," the social worker said. "How could he be?"

I didn't say anything. I was curious about the boy's parents or guardians, where he'd slept at night, whether he'd been a bona fide prostitute with his own street corner and pimp or if he'd been held captive by some other method. It seemed impossible that he could have been entirely alone in the city. Nevertheless, caution prevented me from asking any question that could have been turned around on me. I was especially curious about the cats, but I checked my desire for the details.

Dr. Bruce Ferguson stuck his hand inside his jacket, paused for an instant, and asked, "I suppose you may be able to help us?"

"If I can."

He pulled out a few pictures and handed them to me.

"Who are these men?" he asked.

There were various photographs of two middle-age men, though none of them together. Both of the men looked caucasion, and both had a mop of hair that needed a more modern style. They mainly wore pocket-tees and tank-tops. One of the men had perpetual bags under his sleepy eyes and a stubby pug nose. The other man appeared as though he were always intentionally sucking in his cheeks. Not only their attire but also the sordid backgrounds in the pictures suggested that these men were poor and unkempt. Several shots featured the pug-nosed man astraddle a refrigerator that was lying on its side by a curb. The man seemed thrilled and boastful that he had just hunted and killed the appliance.

"I have no idea," I said, handing back the pictures.

"Coincidently, they both took a flight to London several days ago," the nameless man said, and I nodded, although I didn't quite understand the coincidence. "From there, we strongly surmise, they are headed to one of several locations in eastern Asia. You don't know these men."

Although the man's words sounded like an assertion, I answered, "No."

"You have any idea why they are traveling together and where they're headed."

"No," I said, and I used the brief, succeeding pause to turn away from the black man. As I watched Dr. Bruce Ferguson slip the photographs back into his pocket, I realized that he probably wasn't a medical or mental doctor.

Seeing me look at him, he asked, "Do you mind us asking you these questions?"

"No. I'd like to help where I can. Are these the men?"

"We can't say," the other man answered. He sat solidly in his seat, as heavy and immovable as a large black rock.

The social worker made some kind of movement at her desk, but I didn't turn to look at her. Just a few hours earlier, she had led me to believe that she needed my assistance with the boy, but now the obvious fact was that I was sitting in an airless office, across from two strange men. Although her deception was a simple move, it seemed unnecessary to me; perhaps the phone call had been impromptu, but most likely not.

"Tell me about Regina Ehman." The black man's eyes were unblinking; only his mouth appeared to move.

"I don't know anything. Is that a woman?"

"How about Kirk Shannon or Shannon Kirk?"

"I don't know."

"You never heard these names before?"

"No."

"I thought you wanted to help us."

"If I can."

"You're not acting like you want to help us."

I didn't respond as all of us sat silently for a moment.

"Is there anything you want to tell me?" Dr. Bruce Ferguson asked.

"Like what?"

"Are you a shifty man?" the black man abruptly asked, unveiling his hostility more fully. "I think you're a shifty, artful man."

"I don't know," I responded sheepishly.

"Only someone who is shifty would spend all his time in hiding. But I know you well. Believe me. I know your whole life story. You've been my special project these last few months. You're cautious. You've been very wary and quiet."

He seemed like so much contained energy that he was ready to burst all over me.

"Your special project?" I echoed, my voice small within me.

"Don't think for a second that you can eat or sleep without me knowing about it?"

"Why?"

"Why? Why did you give money to that boy? What was he doing in your home?"

"But—" I began to say; I had explained all this already. I looked toward the social worker, but she wasn't going to help me

"Are you going somewhere, Dr. Parker?" the black man asked.

"What?"

"You're leaving, aren't you?"

"What?"

"You got your security deposit back on the same day the other two birds flew to Asia. Were you planning on going with them?"

"I don't know those men?"

"Did something spook them or did they plan this trip on their own?"

"I don't— What?"

"You wanted to go with them."

"No."

"Come on now. An American with some cash, you can barter and trade in children over there. Are you sure?"

"You don't understand. Listen," I said.

My heart was pulsing in a spastic frenzy. Helpless, I looked at everyone in turn, and they all appeared casual and composed, as if my throbbing anxiety were insignificant to them.

"What's happening here?" I asked. "What is this?"

"Nothing," the black man responded. "We're simply talking. You're not in any trouble. We're just talking here."

"What did I do?"

"Nothing. You're a fine fellow. You're a peach. Keep telling yourself that, and maybe you'll be happy one day."

"All right now," Dr. Bruce Ferguson said as he began to get to his feet. He held out his hand for me to shake. "We've taken up enough of your time, Dr. Parker."

Standing up, I felt slight and flimsy, like something that had been overused.

"Yes, thank you." The social worker now stood, and she also shook my hand.

"I can go?" I asked, and then I looked down at the nameless man, who was apparently refusing to stand up or to shake my hand, because I disgusted him.

"When you eat and sleep," he said. "Remember that."

A thoughtful, concerned expression appeared on Dr. Bruce Ferguson's face.

"Relax a moment," he told me. "You look very frazzled."

"I don't understand any of this," I said, glancing briefly at the door beyond the man; I wanted to flee from the room. "I thought the investigation was over."

"We won't tell you when it's over," the black man said coolly from the couch.

Dr. Bruce Ferguson threw the man a brief look that seemed to communicate something, perhaps an instruction, reprimand, or plea.

"Go home and relax," the doctor said to me. "Maybe this is all a misunderstanding."

"Yes. Exactly."

The social worker stepped out from behind the desk, to escort me toward the door. Her manner seemed more reserved, as now all the pretenses of our previous discourses were finally torn away, and she wasn't quite certain how to conduct herself with me anymore. Since she had sacrificed my trust, her easiest posture was to fall in line behind these two men.

"Thank you for coming, Dr. Parker."

"Just one more thing." Dr. Bruce Ferguson was reaching into his suit jacket again. This time he pulled out folded papers. "These are for you."

I stepped forward and watched him place the papers across my upraised palm, and then I watched my fingers close over them as I anticipated some terrible words that were about to come out of this man's mouth. Somehow, holding the papers, having something to take home with me, wrecked my earlier notion that this appointment was going to be a charade with no lasting consequence. I now had an official document in my hand, making it all very real.

The nameless black man didn't turn around in his seat to watch my exit.

Clenching the papers against my thigh, I looked at the back of the seated man's head.

"You understand that it's part of the routine," Dr. Bruce Ferguson was saying. "We have to search your home again. Some things, mainly your computer, will be removed from your premises."

Although the social worker was standing beside me, she was looking down at the base of one the gray filing cabinets. She appeared somewhat embarrassed and uncomfortable, as if she didn't belong in the room.

"Hopefully," Dr. Bruce Ferguson said, "this is a misunderstanding. You can go home now and relax, though my men should be there right now."

For some inexplicable reason, I thanked the man.

I stepped past the social worker and into the hallway. My body felt disproportionately large as the walls and ceiling seemed to swell and press in on me. When I entered the reception area, the secretary's mouth moved and emitted a sound, to which I responded with the sound of my own voice. I picked up my muddy green coat from the chair and left the room, with my dying sound lingering behind in the room and the corridor now leaning in on me. Feeling constricted and smothered, I descended the narrow staircase, pushed open the glass door, and stood on the sidewalk, in the cold rawness of twilight, sensing in the air that another storm was coming. Although I could see people walking along the sidewalk and hear cars traveling on nearby streets, the city seemed devoid of human life. Behind the wig shop's window, the heads were shaped against the interior darkness of the closed store, their distinct colors dissolved into the colors of silhouette, their lack of features effaced by the failing light. I hurried away from the building, trying to distance myself from the place, from the people within it, and from the appointment, which now loomed stark, definitive, and irrevocable—despite the progress of time. My mind shuffled and reshuffled the details and the words, in an attempt to manage the meaning of the conversation. My life was permanently damaged. Although I had told myself that I no longer cared about Morris the man, his quaint little sister, and all the other people in my social circle, I now dreaded the idea that for the past few months, behind my back, the investigation had most likely wormed its way under their flesh and turned their hearts to stone against me. I wasn't quite certain where I was walking, only that I couldn't go home, not to my ransacked apartment, not to the possible ambush that the pervert had waiting for me. I felt as though I had been rooted out into the open, and the air was aswarm with pestilence. I was vulnerable and exposed. The thousands of pieces of Claudia Jones were still fresh on my computer, let alone my winding search through a carnival of bodies.

VI

I found myself standing under Crowley's awning. My encounter with the skinny woman seemed to have happened a long time ago, and although I was already beginning to forget her face and the sound of her voice, something within me was being lured back to her, and this had nothing to do with the clothes that I'd left behind. In fact, I didn't want them back. At the moment, I preferred the vintage outfit, which to some degree protected me from the madman who wasn't looking for a man in gabardine pants and a putrid, bulky coat with patches on the sleeves. Uncertain what I actually expected from the woman or what I was going to say to her, I tried to pull the door open, but it was locked. Even so, I knew she was somewhere inside. Not only was a light burning in the backroom, but also the music was playing. I knocked on the glass, waited a moment, and knocked again. Because I was now standing still, rather than walking, I noticed that the evening seemed to have grown darker and colder, making the streetlights appear somewhat puny and ridiculous against the expanse of barren sky. After a moment of waiting alone on the sidewalk, I had a strange sensation that the sky itself was in the act of settling upon the world, in an attempt to suffocate it.

When I knocked on the door again, I peered into the store and saw the lighted doorway that led into the headshop. The skinny woman emerged and stood in the arch. I couldn't tell what she was doing, until I saw her squat and I realized that the music ceased. I knocked again. Just as a new song began to play, the woman straightened up and started toward me. When she came to the door, she stopped, crossed her arms, and faced me. Although I knew that she was looking at me, I couldn't read her expression in the dusky light. Her glasses obscured her eyes. For an instant, I thought she was going to leave me outside, to simply watch me from the other side of the glass. However, shaking her head, she reached forward with a key in her hand and unbolted the door.

"What a poor creature," she said, holding the door open. "You're shivering."

"Thanks, Ms. Crowley." I stepped inside, forgetting that Crowley was just the name of the store. "I'm sorry to bother—"

"Call me that again, and I'll put you back out."

"I'm sorry. Really. I'm—"

"Relax. I'm just teasing you. Come in," she said and took hold of my sleeve. "Come on. I have your things. Let me lower the radio."

I stood beside the counter. The racks of clothes loomed dark and still, and the empty couch seemed abandoned to the shadows. She stood in the lighted doorway, bent down, and lowered the volume of the music. She came toward me again.

"What's the matter?" she asked, her voice soft and mollifying, her eyes tenderly searching my face. "Relax. You look like you're going to—"

"What?" I asked.

"You look upset."

"I'm fine."

"Good."

She then retreated into the backroom, from which I could smell the burning incense, the jasmine.

She called to me:

"They're not quite dry yet."

I stepped up to the doorway. My clothes were hanging from the back of the bathroom door, and she was feeling the hem of my pants.

"You want to take them like this?" she called again, even though I was only a few paces behind her.

"Not really."

She turned and looked at me.

The possible impropriety of following her into the backroom never occurred to me, and neither did she seem to care. Rather, she had such a look of concern on her face that I suspected my expression revealed my frayed emotions.

"Do you want to sit down and warm up a bit?"

Walking past me, she motioned to a set of stools at the end of one of the glass display cases.

"I was just drinking a glass of wine. Sit down."

Behind the counter was a little cart on wheels, which had a coffee maker on top and glasses and mugs on a lower shelf.

"You know, I was waiting for you," she said. "I told myself that

I would give you twenty minutes." She brought two glasses to the counter; one was partly full.

"Pinot grigio." She showed me the bottle. "I love pinot grigio. Santa Margherita is the best."

As she filled both of the glasses to the rim, I took a seat.

"You put the idea in my head. You had that slip of paper in your pocket with that name on it. That sounds good, I said, so I had my niece watch the store while I went out and bought myself a bottle." She handed me the glass and continued talking. "Oh, I'm sorry. I emptied your pockets. I don't know why; I was afraid something might get ruined."

"That's okay," I said.

She set the bottle of white wine beside my elbow on the counter and walked back around. With the hood of the sweatshirt gathered behind her head, I couldn't tell the length of her blonde hair.

"You know, I gave you twenty minutes, but then I was sitting here, drinking a glass or two of wine, listening to the music, and reading that book you had. I don't really read books. I had no idea that people write like that. That's good writing, right? When people say a book is great, that's what they mean, right?"

She took the novel of out her purse, which was on the floor by the doorway, brought it over to me, and then picked up her glass of wine.

"I was going to take it home," she said.

"Keep it."

"Really?"

"Sure," I said. "That's the best writing can get. That's what they mean by great writing."

She smiled as if I'd just complimented her.

"I like that part about kissing his mother. What a poor kid. He fell into that ditch with the rat in it."

"I remember."

"I knew you were smart when I first saw you, a person who reads hard books. You've got that kind of distant look, like you're watching everything." She was standing in front of the counter, scanning the back cover of the book as she spoke. Her voice lowered a little, becoming almost apologetic. "Not now, though. Now, you look like somebody passed away or something."

"No," I said. "Nothing as sad as that."

"Well, that's good." She continued to inspect the book, turning it over in her hands, as if she'd never seen it before. After a moment, she set the book on the counter. When she took a sip of wine, she peeped at me over the rim of the glass.

"Don't make much of me; that's just the way I am," she said.

"Sure," I responded, although I didn't know what she meant.

"The wine is good though."

"Yes," I said and tasted the wine for the first time.

She pointed to the cart behind the counter and said, "I would have offered you coffee, if I was drinking coffee."

"I like the wine."

"Me too," she said, with a complicitous, little smile. "Margherita knows what she's doing. Strange thing that you had that name in your pocket."

I discerned in her tone that she was fishing around for explanations, perhaps not so much about the name in my pocket but about why I had looked upset. Although she seemed to be somewhat quirky, a little too friendly, the woman exuded such a sense of comfort and simplicity that I almost felt obliged to talk. Of course, I was still cautious enough not to become too beguiled by her voice, her smile, and her eyes. I wasn't going to reveal to her that officious men, at that very moment, were rifling through my belongings, looking for evidence of a moral cripple, nor was I going to explain that a pervert was circling around me, closing in, waiting for the opportunity to dive in upon his prey.

"Do you know who Margaretta is?" I asked.

"No."

"She's Martin Luther's mom."

"Really?"

Although the woman didn't seem to know who I was talking about, I continued my babble, perhaps out of nervousness. "She used to believe that gnomes and elves lived in the woods outside her house, and they would steal eggs from her."

"Really?" The woman put her hand on her stomach.

"Chicken eggs," I clarified.

"Well, she may have been a nut, but she makes good wine." She raised her glass to her lips but then set it on the counter without taking a drink as something else apparently caught her attention.

"Do you know what?" she asked. "Speaking of elves and gnomes."

She moved behind me and walked around to the other side of the display case. When she reached up toward a shelf that contained the tubes and other contraptions, I was able to see a slight sliver of pale flesh just beneath her naval. She took down a shiny brown figure that appeared to be made of polished glass.

"This is the wizard," she said, placing the thing before me. It was a sculpture of a long-bearded man; he was standing beside a tree that had several limbs cut off. A hole was in one of the stumps, and the trunk, which went straight up along the wizard's back and reached higher than the fold of his drooping hat, also had a hole at the top.

"People use this to smoke?" I asked.

"Only serious people." She smiled. "Or maybe people with friends. He's been on the shelf for a while. I sell a lot more bats."

"Bats?"

I partly imagined that she was going to pull down some leathery winged creature to accompany the wizard on the counter.

However, she pointed through the top of the glass case to a row of little metal cigarettes displayed on a green felt mat.

"A bat," she said. "A one-hitter. A dug-out."

"Those are bats?" I asked.

She smiled at me, as if I were a young, unworldly boy. "They don't write about stuff like that in your books?"

"None that I've read."

"Everyone buys them, which is kind of sad. If you're going to smoke, I think you should do it with a group, you know. These are made for people to smoke by themselves."

"And that's sad?"

"Yeah. Smoking is supposed to bring people together. But these here." She tapped on the glass. "They remind me that people are lonely and they want to get high alone. Isn't that sad?"

"I suppose. Why do you sell them then?"

She shrugged, looking at me, smiling slightly.

"Don't mind me; that's just the way I am," she said for a second time, and I still had no idea what she meant by this expression. I suspected that it was simply meaningless padding to her conversation.

"You look better," she said. "More calm."

"I'm fine."

"A glass of wine is good for the nerves. I hope it wasn't serious, whatever was bothering you before."

"Nothing really." I looked away from her, down the length of the glass counter. "I like the smell in here; it makes the place feel warmer."

I knew she was still looking at me.

"You don't have to tell me," she said after a moment.

"It's nothing," I said. "I just lost my home, that's all. I have to move."

"Not out of the city, right?"

"I don't know. At least, out of my apartment."

"You have no place to stay?"

"I'm not officially out. All my things are there, but I can't really go back anymore."

"I'm sorry," she said, her voice filled with sympathy. She leaned nearer and patted the back of my hand. "I understand."

Her fingertips left a trace of warmth upon my skin.

"It's a rough situation," she said. "When I divorced my ex-, it was hard. I didn't realize how much I'd grown with him until afterwards, but then, you know, I knew I made the right decision. Deep down, it didn't feel right staying with him."

Her gaze settled on my eyes, reading me. My countenance must have been so pathetic that it evidently confirmed for her whatever suspicions she had about me, and to some extent, she had guessed correctly: I was a man with a broken heart.

"We were supposed to operate a horse clinic together," she said, "but instead, we ended up in the city. All this time goes by, and I gradually started thinking. I was just sitting there, you know, and I had no idea where I was." She turned her head and glanced around the room, as if it pained her. "Fifteen years, and I'm still sitting here."

She laughed, and she briefly touched my hand again.

"Isn't that funny? I actually argued for this place, and I paid some short, overweight lawyer, with hair growing in his ears, to make sure I got this place. Don't mind me. I'm sorry. Are you okay?"

"I'm fine. Like you said, it was the right decision. I know that."

"That's good." She scooped up the wizard and returned him to the shelf.

Watching her, I felt invigorated. Here was a woman who perceived me in a way that was far different from how I perceived myself. This woman actually assumed that I was someone who had been living with another person, that I had been able to stir up love in another's heart, and, in short, that I moved in the arena of normal human relationships.

"I'm sorry," she said as she corked the bottle and slipped it somewhere beneath the counter.

"It's okay."

"I didn't know. I feel like a fool."

"Why?" I got off the stool.

Oddly, this woman's meaning eluded me again, and I had a sudden suspicion that it was my fault that I didn't completely understand her. If her gestures and words had a further implication, my brain was probably too stunted and sterilized to apprehend it. Her language was part of society's regular discourse, but I moved on a different, perhaps more subterranean, level.

She began to bustle about, preparing to close the store for the evening. Watching her made me feel guilty for some reason. I drank a large swallow of wine.

"I don't know why you feel like I fool," I said.

"Was it a hard breakup?"

"No. It was the easiest thing in the world."

"What about for her?"

"It was even easier."

She was standing by the door, stooped over her purse, in the process of putting away the novel, when she lifted her head and smiled at me.

"You're just trying to make me feel better."

"Well, you made me feel better," I said, beginning to sense what was going on.

Still smiling, she straightened up and pointed to my clothes hanging on the bathroom door.

"Are you going to come back for those tomorrow?"

"Unless you think they're worth something."

"No," she said, "but I'll buy your hat."

"I'll have to think about that."

"Oh," she said, and her expression suddenly became more serious. Gesturing to my head with her eyes, she asked, "She didn't—?"

"No," I said. "I tripped over a bag of salt." I touched my temple with my finger. "A sidewalk did this to me."

"You fall down a lot, I suppose. You don't have to rush," she added as I took another big gulp of wine.

"No, I'm ready." I set my glass on the counter beside hers, which she'd already emptied.

I walked past her in the doorway, while she reached down and shut off the music. Then, behind me, she clicked off the light, and the room with the used and vintage clothes fell abruptly into deeper shadows. I went and stood by the front door. The darkness outside in the street had a hint of blue, like the color of exhaust fumes. The skinny woman was attending to something behind the counter, and I had to wait for her because she had locked us in. Although the keys hung from the lock, I didn't think it was appropriate for me to touch them. I could faintly see the woman getting herself into a long coat.

Something in the woman had an unusual effect on me. She made me feel stronger. Maybe it was her casual manner, as well as her assumption that I was a better man than I actually was, that made me sense my ego vaguely shaping itself around her image of me, conforming to her perception. Apparently, she had waited for me to return from my appointment because she had wanted to see me again. I didn't know what I had done to provoke her interest. Perhaps when I had purchased the clothes, she had noticed the wad of cash that my landlord had given to me. Perhaps she had interpreted my request to leave my wet clothes behind as a signal of my interest in her.

"Listen," I said, even though I couldn't see her, for she was lost again somewhere in the shadows of the store. "I was about to get myself some dinner. Would you—?"

"Oh," she immediately said, stepping out into the open. "I don't know if that would be too smart. You're just getting out of something."

"It's not like that. I'm already out. I've been out for a long time."

"It puts me in a bad position."

"No, it doesn't. It's just dinner."

"I don't know." She came toward me, buttoning up the front of her coat. "Where would you want to go?"

"Wherever you want. Someplace where we can sit down."

"My niece was just telling me about this Thai place. She said the tilapia was really good."

"Let's go there," I said, even though I'd never eaten Thai food nor had any idea what tilapia was.

She opened the door, and together we stepped out into the cold.

She locked up, and then holding the keys in her gloved hand, she pointed.

"My car is over here."

I followed her across the street, which was fouled with gray slush and ice.

She had a little black car, a two-door Volkswagen, with a top that could apparently be removed in warmer weather.

Once inside the car, she said very sincerely, "I'm a good listener."

"Thanks," I said, not really certain how I was supposed to respond.

Strange, tiny ceramic figurines, perhaps effigies of eastern gods, were lined up along the dashboard, and because they didn't slide off, I suspected that they had been glued down.

At a stoplight, she glanced at me and then looked forward again with a slight smile on her face.

She began talking and asking me questions, perhaps to gloss over any awkwardness. The unmistakable fact, which we both surely understood, was not so much that we were two strangers but that we both had some visceral need that compelled us to steer our way closer toward one another. The more the woman talked, the more I began to realize, to glean from her words, that our maneuvering had certain rules. Apparently, if I was on the rebound from a recent relationship, then neither of us could expect much of our going out to dinner, nothing beyond her ability to offer me a sympathetic ear. Yet, even though this seemed to be our guidelines, there also existed a lower, more implicit set of guidelines, because the woman's explanation of her role as listener sounded almost obligatory, a pretense that we both recognized as a pretense, but was nonetheless necessary for the woman to say, in case, at some further point in our acquaintance, things turned sour; then the woman would have the advantage to remind me that she had established our situation from the very beginning, not merely as tentative words, but as the fixed order of things. She could retreat to that higher ground and deny that there was ever a deeper impulse. The woman might not have been completely conscious of this, but I understood that she was trying to keep a balance between taking a risk on me and simultaneously protecting herself from me.

Her name was Vanessa Somerset.

VII

She was in the process of telling me that she normally wore a different pair of glasses, but she had accidentally crushed them under a pot of spaghetti sauce, so now she had to wear an older pair that not only were the wrong prescription but also left sore, red impressions on the bridge of her nose.

Suddenly, she pulled the car over to the curb. She opened the door and got out, so I got out too, stood on the sidewalk, and waited for her to walk around.

"And I can't wear contacts," she said. "They bother my eyes."

"Really," I said, borrowing her word.

We entered a liquor store, which greeted us at the door with a blast of hot air and the twangy-voiced noise of a woman singing "Silent Night."

I followed Vanessa briskly down one aisle that shelved wine both in the gallon and in the box, and then down another aisle in which bottles were displayed in reclining crates.

"I think the restaurant is BYOB," she said. "How about a chardonnay?" She plucked a bottle out of a crate and showed it to me.

"That's fine," I said.

At first, I simply looked at it, but because she continued to hold it out, I took the bottle out of her hand. I understood that I was supposed to pay.

In line before us at the counter was an insufferable, globular animal with a tuft of hair growing out of the back of her thick neck. She was buying lottery tickets, and she apparently had such a precise regimen that the young clerk behind the counter was following her dictate with a bit of anxiety over messing up and setting the woman into a angry frenzy. After the woman bought the lottery tickets, she asked for three packs of slim menthol cigarettes, and when the clerk pulled out a different kind—perhaps ultra thin or menthol green instead of menthol blue—the squat, crotchety animal turned around and gave me a look that expressed her frustration in having to deal with people as stupid as this one. When she and the clerk settled the dilemma of the cigarettes, she asked for her bottle of cognac to be rung up separately from the beer and cigarettes because her boyfriend had only given her a twenty-dollar bill, as if this somehow explained why she needed two receipts.

While my disgust mounted—for I was unfortunately imagining the man who would act as this creature's boyfriend, wallow in her squalor, and no doubt top her sweaty body—Vanessa had a placid smile on her face as she read the label of a discounted bottle of wine displayed by the counter.

"This looks good," she said. "BYOB is actually cheaper; you don't have to pay by the glass."

"Is that good wine?"

"I've never had it."

"We might as well try it."

She set the second bottle on the counter, just as the creature moved away and a new song began to play. Hearing "What Child Is This?" and watching the slow, waddling woman, I had a sudden remembrance of Claudia Jones. Yet all I could recall of her were the categorized parts of her body, which were regrettably cached and filed on my confiscated computer. I had so many things to worry about that I knew going out to dinner was a mistake, but I had no idea what else I was supposed to be doing. Right now, I was with Vanessa Somerset, and perhaps now that I was with her, I could efface every moment that preceded her entry into my life. Perhaps I was already beginning to reinvent myself on a warmer, cozier level. This, of course, meant that I needed to kill my past by severing all my connections to the previous drudgery of my life. I could start afresh with just the money in my pocket.

When the clerk rang up my order, and I reached into my pocket to pull out my cash, I noticed that Vanessa was occupied reading the labels on discounted bottles of wine; she didn't appear curious about my little stash of money nor the total on the register.

Back outside, the first few flakes of snow were falling. Vanessa turned her face upward, as if she could somehow gauge the weather by inspecting the sky.

The Thai restaurant was only another couple of blocks down the • road. In the window, purple tubes of light spelled out the name of the place in a winding script. A bench, now coated with ice and frost, was on the sidewalk, where patrons could presumably wait for their tables, in different weather of course. I held the door open for Vanessa.

"It smells good," she said.

Since it was a weeknight, we had no problem getting prompt service. A little girl, dressed all in black, stood patiently behind us as we hung up our coats, and then she led us to a table next to the wall.

When Vanessa sat down, I wondered if I should have pulled out her chair for her or if that form of courtesy was long dead. Even so, I knew that I ought to let her order first. As Vanessa studied the menu, another little girl came up to the table. She was dressed in the same black attire, and her straight dark hair was pulled back in a simple ponytail. Interestingly, all the staff appeared as if they actually were from Thailand or at least of that descent. I suspected that the girls probably weren't as young as they looked.

Our waitress asked which bottle of wine we would like to open first, and I said that we wanted to try both of them. The girl smiled as if I had said something witty. After she opened the two bottles, she asked Vanessa which one would she like to start off with.

"I'll have the chardonnay."

When the girl poured, she twisted her wrist, slowly rolling the bottle, so there wouldn't be a drip.

"I'll have the same," I said, and the girl repeated the operation with me.

Vanessa ordered a seaweed salad with pine nuts and also, from the special menu, pan-seared tilapia. I ordered some type of Mediterranean chicken that came in a brown curry sauce with chunks of avocado and onion. Even though I knew this was ethnic food, I was beginning to doubt—between the seaweed, the chicken, and the curry—if I could point to Thailand on a map.

After declaring the wine delicious and the fish perfect, Vanessa asked where I planned on staying the night.

"A friend's house, I suppose," I said, though I had no friend. "Or maybe I'll see about renting a room."

"You don't want to wait too long," she said. "You might be stranded."

"I'm not worried," I said.

She smiled at me. Perhaps she imagined a note of confidence in my voice. Truthfully, however, I hadn't yet considered where I intended to spend the night. I realized that I might have been stalling, as if deep down I secretly wanted the time to run out, so I would've been forced to accept no other option but to go back home in a mood of insincere reluctance.

Throughout the dinner, I learned that in addition to being an only child, Vanessa Somerset was a change-of-life baby. Thus, in her adolescence, she felt isolated and detached from her parents. She always picked shitty boyfriends, ones who were older and controlling. She married at a young age, but not for love, because she was too giddy and immature to know what love was. She just wanted the comfort of a man, as well as the opportunity to allow her ego to flake away and dissolve into the presence of her husband. For the most part, he treated her well, but she began to see that he had less strength than she'd first imagined. He was unmotivated, and he believed that the interval between weekends was merely wasted time and that true life happened on his couch with a couple of stoned drinking buddies. Eventually, she began to recognize that she was shriveling up. There was no horse farm or any other kind of dream for the future. Yet she didn't bear the man any ill will; in fact, she earnestly loved his family. Her niece, the girl with the corduroy pants, often helped out in the clothing shop. According to Vanessa, the girl remained convinced that her uncle had lost the best thing he ever had going for him, namely Aunt Vanessa.

"Was he controlling too?" I asked.

"In some ways." A slight smile turned the corner of one side of her mouth.

"He was nice, though?"

"Most of the time." She was smiling fully now, as if guilty of something. "Here," she then said, holding out a forkful of fish. "You've got to taste this before I eat it all."

As the fork advanced toward my face, my first instinct was to turn away, but I checked myself, opened my mouth, and allowed her to feed me. No sooner had I swallowed the morsel than Vanessa began to laugh.

"It's not poison," she said.

"It's good stuff," I mumbled, curious if she'd realized that my initial reaction wasn't due to the fish itself but to the intimacy of Vanessa's utensil entering my mouth.

She then stuck her fork into my bowl of brown sauce and came out with a chunk of chicken. She ate it in two bites and said matter-of-factly, "Mine's better," as if declaring herself the winner of some contest.

"That fish is horrible," I rebutted.

"That fall must have really damaged your head."

Apparently amused by herself, she sat up straight in her chair, looked down at her plate, and continued to eat.

I merely watched her.

When she reached for her wine, she lifted her eyes and looked at me. Her simple gesture awoke in me a singular sensation: I felt myself pulled toward her, as if she had just somehow made herself prettier and this glance of hers, silent and suggestive, was merely a brief glimpse at possible pleasures, an indication that she possessed the ability to become, at will, even more alluring. Looking at her, I realized that her expression of happy contentment, which almost bordered on smugness, had less to do with her witticism about my head than with her own sense of charming me. If there were a competition, Vanessa Somerset was winning.

"Tell me about your broken heart," she said.

"There's nothing to say."

"Now, that's not fair; I told you about my marriage. Besides, you've been kicked out of your home. There's got to be a story there."

"I can go back," I said. "She's not even there anymore. But, by now, it's just a matter of principle."

As I spoke, she studied my face. Her eyes suggested to me that she accepted my explanation, even though I had no idea what principle I could possibly be invoking. The trite phrase simply sounded appropriate for the moment.

"Are any of her things still there?" Vanessa asked.

"She took some stuff, most stuff actually. But that's part of the reason I think it's better to stay away for now."

"I guess when you're just dating, even if it lasts several years, you can't really call in a lawyer or judge to say whose things are whose."

"Exactly," I said. "Still, I'm not one to quibble over material things. She can have it all."

"There's nothing you want?"

I thought about the question, considering it as though I were actually placed in such a situation. The only thing I seemed to have a vague attachment to, which I might have wanted to take with me on my flight, was my marble-covered notebook full of bad poems. Of course, its rightful place was in the garbage can, but I didn't spend any time trying to figure out my irrational affection for the book. But then again, the poem "Footprints" was displayed in a gilded frame in my living room, and my father's final letter to me was folded in thirds and concealed behind the back panel. And maybe, I just remembered, my mother had sent me a Christmas card, which never failed to contain money. I needed to check the mail.

"Just some stuff from work," I answered.

Rather than take the opportunity to ask me what I did for a living, Vanessa continued with the topic of my phantom lover.

"How did you meet her?"

"Our paths crossed," I said obliquely, wishing that I could somehow avoid lying to this woman.

Vanessa refilled both of our wine glasses, and then she crossed her utensils on her plate, evidently to indicate to the little, dark-haired waitress that the place setting could be cleared away.

"That's not a good answer," Vanessa said.

"She's an artist," I responded, conjuring up one of the fantasies I had woven around Celeste Wilcox, my urban nymph. "I liked her artwork, so I contacted her, thinking that I might commission her to do a piece."

I had several versions of this story in my head because back when I had discovered the gallery and still clung to the prospect of meeting the artist, my brain had sputtered out a collection of possible encounters with the woman. I usually played the model, patiently posed, while she inspected me over the top of her canvas. Yet something in my posture wasn't quite right, so she had to come out from behind her easel to adjust my limbs and turn my head slightly. Wanting my inner thigh to catch the light better, she touched me, stepped back to assess the alteration, and came forward to fine-tune the position of my leg. Again she squatted and put her hands on my leg. Then she found the need to take hold of my hips like a steering wheel. With a slight hint of annoyance in her voice, she said, "I can't paint you if you're going to be aroused like this," and for the sake of her artwork, she had "to take care" of the situation for me.

"What kind of art?" Vanessa asked.

"Pretty sophisticated stuff," I answered, and when I saw Vanessa's face imperceptibly sag, I knew that she was comparing herself to Celeste Wilcox. While my ex-lover was talented and smart, Vanessa lacked formal education and had wasted years of her life trying to melt into a man.

"But she didn't have the heart," I added. "She had the head to be an artist, but she lacked passion and other stuff, if that makes sense."

"Sure," Vanessa answered.

Wordlessly, the waitress came to our table, topped off our wineglasses, once again cautious of the drip, and then absconded with our dirty plates.

"Do you want to split a Crème Brulee with me?" Vanessa asked.

"Sure," I said.

When the waitress returned, Vanessa placed her order, turned down an offer for coffee, and requested two spoons. At this, the girl smiled as if Vanessa were suggesting more than she'd actually said.

"She's cute," Vanessa said as the girl headed away.

I agreed, though something about the girl unsettled me, if not quite her indeterminate age and origin, then perhaps the obsequiousness with which she waited on us, as though the girl weren't so much performing a job in order to make money as she were acquiescing to her prescribed station in life.

Vanessa wanted to know the details of my relationship and breakup. Although confiding in her created a level of intimacy, it also seemed to open a gap between us. Every word I spoke felt laced with significance, like evidence in a trial that had the potential to go either way. Vanessa appeared to be measuring my words, but how she arranged and assessed them in her mind was a mystery to me.

Finally, the desert came. Vanessa perked up in her chair and smiled at me.

In a little ceramic petri dish was something like warm, creamy cheesecake that was burnt on top. I watched as Vanessa cracked the charred surface, took a dab of cream on the tip of her spoon, and slipped it in her mouth. When she noticed my attention, she looked at me in a way that seemed to give my eyes permission to linger on her.

All the while, we were still talking about my ex-lover.

"Was she pretty?"

"Yes," I said.

"What does she look like?"

"She's an Italian girl with pale skin and dark eyes. She is dainty, almost fragile, as if she could easily be crushed by anything."

"And you love her?"

"No, not anymore. But I thought I did. I wanted to protect her, to gather her up in my arms, and keep her safe."

"And she loves you?"

"I don't know how she feels now, but at one time, she used to say that I was the only person in the whole world who had ever loved her."

"I'm sorry," Vanessa said, and she reached across the table and squeezed my hand.

"Don't be," I said. "It feels like ages ago."

Feeling Vanessa's hand on mine somehow enabled me to see a level deeper into her expression, which was only in part sympathetic and warm, for at a lower frequency, barely perceptible, quivered something imploring, naked, and raw. I had left her dangling alone for a moment, on the cusp of my words, and I felt the urge to draw her back to me.

"I have no relationship," I said. "I have nothing to go to, and it's a good thing."

"What happened to you guys?"

"Fate, of course." I tried to sound cheerful. "When love goes wrong, fate is always the culprit."

"And when love goes right?"

"That might be fate too, but in that case, we don't like to give her any credit. We say it's all our own doing; we attribute it to our own truthfulness and trust and commitment."

"Yeah, but some people credit destiny." Vanessa had a slight smile on her face, which I now suspected to be a constant aspect of her countenance that had less to do with me than with habit. She removed her hand from mine, to push up her glasses and then pick up her spoon.

"That's just how they explain it to other people," I said. "When they are together, there are no dreamy illusions; they expect, even demand, honesty and fidelity and all that stuff. They know that they are the ones giving themselves. They're the ones taking all the risks and stuff, not destiny."

"Your cheeks are getting red," Vanessa said.

"It's the wine," I said, conscious that I inexplicably kept using the word "stuff."

"Me too," she said. "It's starting to catch up with me."

Later, when the bill came, Vanessa once again seemed to have no interest in the cost. I over-tipped the waitress, who without bothering to count the money thanked me sweetly. I had an idea that even if I'd given her nothing at all, she would have acted in the same manner.

When we stood up from the table, Vanessa touched my shoulder, brought her face closer to me, and said that she'd be back in a minute. I watched her steer her way between the tables and chairs, which were mostly unoccupied, and disappear around a corner.

Three of the little dark-haired girls in their black attire were gathered by the hostess station near the front door. Most likely, they were ordinary young American women, but I imbued them with a disconcerting servility. Of course, I wouldn't have been disturbed by them, or even have given them so much notice, if I hadn't recently seen a picture of a goofy man astraddle a refrigerator. I imagined that with a simple plane ticket he was able to enter a region of the world where he could have all the slavish attention of these quaint creatures directed upon his lusts. The images of the two men, stupid and sloven, resurfaced in my mind, and they disgusted me.

Vanessa returned, and as we walked together, somewhere between our table and the coat rack, she momentarily took hold of my arm.

Back outside, the snow came down in a swift slant, the flakes small and quiet.

Just as I opened the car door to get in, Vanessa said to me over the snow-covered roof, "It's not too crazy, us going out like this on the spur of the moment." Then her head disappeared behind her side of the car.

I got in, closed the door, and said, "No."

"It's no crazier than Internet dating."

"It's not crazy at all."

With the thin layer of snow coating the windows, we seemed to have hidden ourselves within a pale, fragile enclave.

Vanessa started the car, and the wipers cleared the front window.

"Are you okay to drive?" I asked.

"Probably not." She smiled as the car started forward. "I'll go slow."

Although I didn't know where we were heading, I didn't bother to ask. I knew that eventually, before the night was over, I would end up back in my apartment. Perhaps in the morning, once I had collected my thoughts and calmly assessed my dilemma, I would run away. Vanessa was holding the steering wheel in both hands and staring forward. All the other windows were still covered with snow. Something in the silence prompted me to reach out cautiously toward her, but my hand only crossed half the distance and came to rest on the console. I wasn't certain whether she noticed my gesture, even though she turned her head and glanced at me, seeming to smile not exactly at me but simply at the idea of my presence. I knew that I was getting prepared to leave behind my old life, but I didn't know to what extent, or if at all, Vanessa Somerset would constitute any part of my new self. I wasn't sure what I felt about her. On the one hand, she seemed so desperate that she readily allowed herself to find something strong and valuable in me, regardless if it actually existed or not; this made her somewhat transparent and flimsy. Yet, for all I knew, her openness was a natural part of every romantic relationship. There's a fine distinction between need and neediness, and I had yet to discern which held sway over Vanessa. Nevertheless, on the other hand, I was a desperate man.

"Did you want to do anything else?" she asked. "I know it's a weekday."

"It's not too late."

"We can go someplace and talk. Get a cup of coffee."

She drove me to a place that from the outside I never would have guessed was a coffee shop. The front door was thick, black, and wooden, with a metal hoop for a doorknob. Although books lined the walls, they apparently remained unused, for the dim light wasn't suitable for reading. A chunky, young girl in a scarf and a brown, form-fitting sweater stood behind the dingy counter. Vanessa ordered some type of frothy, vanilla-flavored gourmet coffee with a chocolate biscotti on the side, and for the sake of convenience, I ordered the same thing.

"If you pay now, you can have a seat, and I'll bring it to your table," the girl said.

"Sounds like a plan," Vanessa said, and then to me, she added, "I've got it this time."

For the two cookies and the coffee, the bill was thirteen dollars and change. Vanessa gave the girl seventeen dollars: two fives and seven singles. She flashed the girl a smile, slipped her arm under mine, and directed me into the seating area, which was primarily occupied by high school or college students. I suspected that they took themselves for bohemians, radicals, and artists.

A hollow-cheeked boy with a disheveled mop of brown hair nonchalantly pointed one of his lanky fingers at my head and complimented my hat.

Vanessa thanked him on my behalf and released my arm when we came to a vacant table in the center of the room. I sat down. To my right, less than a yard away, a girl sat cross-legged on her chair. On my other side, a boy, who was apparently excited, had one knee on his seat and was leaning across the table. He accused another boy of possessing only opinions. This boy sat with his arms crossed and his shins pushing against the edge of the table. He retorted that not everything is an opinion. Strangely, the table between them, in addition to their debate, appeared to be contested ground.

"Even that," the first boy shot back. "What you've just said, you see, that's an opinion too."

"It's my opinion that not everything is an opinion."

"Yes."

"So, you're saying that it's a fact that everything is an opinion."

"I never said it was a fact. Don't put words in my mouth."

Although Vanessa looked at the pair of boys as though they were performing magic tricks, I had to turn away before their stupidity made me dizzy.

Between the drabness of the walls, the water-stained panels in the ceiling, and the faint, stale mustiness permeating the air, I had a sense that the general attitude of the clientele emitted a palpable influence, like a contagion. This grunge appeared symptomatic of their belief that in order to be intelligent and deep, a person needed to look beyond appearances and refuse to be held captive by the sensibilities of the larger society. Surely, mental freedom might entail a spirit of repudiation, but such a spirit in itself wasn't a guarantee of any poignancy, save for their own funk.

Vanessa leaned across the table, as if to tell me a secret, so I bent down nearer to her.

"As soon as they're old enough to drink, none of them will be here. They'll go to bars instead."

"Probably," I said.

In the intimacy of leaning in toward one another over the table, Vanessa looked steadily at me, searching me. Because she gave me no indication that she would turn away, I felt somewhat obliged to keep my eyes on her—so both of us became fixed—and even though we appeared to be in an interlude of keen, probing consideration, I felt a little silly and uncomfortable. Perhaps normal people felt inclined to break the awkwardness of such moments with a kiss. Our spell, however, was broken by the chunky girl setting a tray on our table.

The gourmet coffee was as sweet as a milkshake, the long cookie as hard as bone. In fact, the only way to eat the biscotti was to let it soften in the creamy froth.

Vanessa began telling me anecdotes from her life. When she was a young girl, during an Easter egg hunt, she found a dead cat in a window well. Before this tale properly concluded, it segued into another story in which she and her "then-husband-at-the-time," as she called him, were vacationing in Kentucky, to attend a horse show. They set up their tent in the far corner of a campsite, away from all the trailers. Every morning, an emaciated dog came up to the metal fence, and she fed it hotdogs through the diamond-shaped links. Without the fence, the animal probably would have starved because it was too savage to approach otherwise. Vanessa suspected that other campers complained about the dog because one morning it stopped showing up.

"Maybe it died," I said.

Vanessa shook her head. "My ex- heard people talking about it. It was put down."

I nodded thoughtfully, although I had no idea what the point of the story was. Perhaps Vanessa believed that conversation of any sort, regardless of the subject, was what united two people. After all, *communication* was the mantra of all the relationship gurus on the daytime talk shows. This might have been true, but still I had trouble keeping an interest in Vanessa's stories. She started telling me about hoof and mouth disease, the West Nile virus, or some other kind of equine pestilence. A veterinarian walked through contaminated feces and carried the disease on the soles of his boots to healthy horses in a different stable fifty miles away.

Beside me, the two boys were working themselves to the idea that if opinions are a form of knowledge, then—following the same route as certainty and truth—opinions also didn't exist.

"Then what's in my head?" one boy asked.

"I don't know. Reactions, maybe."

"Reactions to what?"

"Impressions."

"But then, who, or what, is doing the reacting?"

Although their topic was slightly more interesting than Vanessa's, they often seemed baffled by their own reasoning. Whatever ground they gained on one point, they lost on another. Leaping vast stretches of time and excluding many thinkers and whole schools of thought, they traveled from Plato to Hume at the speed of language, and the combined acumen of both boys afforded them at best a cursory understanding of these two philosophers. One of the boys not only continually misquoted the author of *The Book of Hebrews* as saying, "Knowledge is the certainty of things unseen," but also wrongly attributed the phrase to Peter.

I had a desire to write down the titles of a few books that might have helped them, or maybe to turn to them and explain some rudimentary ideas, giving them a stable starting point, such as that the line analogy and the allegory of the cave, when taken together, reveal the inverted correspondence between Platonic epistemology and ontology, thereby elevating opinions above a multitude of raw actions and the formless, mute shadows cast by effigies on a stone wall. These were the obvious and basic terms that I believed the boys woefully lacked, the most banal and traditional kind of topological imagination, against which our more contemporary, rhizomatically-inclined sophists rail. I felt I could quickly sketch the whole schema on a napkin for them. As Vanessa spoke, I continued to look at her and nod; meanwhile, I casually fished in my pocket for a pen and something to write on. When my hand touched the folded papers—the official dictum that granted men I didn't know the authority to root through my belongings and my home—I felt anew the urge to run away. All the while I had been eating Mediterranean chicken and drinking chardonnay, strange men were dissecting my computer, following my virtual path over hills and valleys, and descending below the conspicuous level of playmates and pornstars, into the carnal pulp of the world's subterrain. These men were not exactly thinking my thoughts after me or even pursuing the course of my mouse clicks, but sterilely uncovering the slow, cheerless delineation of my darkening descent.

Vanessa was in mid-sentence when I pulled out the folded sheets of paper and set them on the table. She appeared curious for a moment, as if she expected me to do something amusing or at least explain the papers.

"Okay," she said, smiling at me.

Suddenly, I wanted to tell her about the boy, my bovine neighbor, and all the other reasons why I was afraid to return home, which had nothing at all to do with an ex-lover. I was a charlatan. I felt uneasy cultivating any further Vanessa's false impression that I knew how to conduct myself, not just on the normal level of human affairs, but also as a lover.

"What's that?" she asked about the papers.

"Just cleaning out my pockets," I said. "Are you ready to go? I feel misplaced in here."

"Sure." She stood up from the table and began re-buttoning her coat.

"That's sad about the dog," I said, just to show her that I'd been listening.

She didn't say anything as she took her gloves out of her pocket and put them back on.

"Do you want to hear a funny story about dogs?" I asked.

"Sure," she said, and as she came around the table, I offered her my arm, which she casually accepted.

I began the story in the coffee shop, and outside on the sidewalk, as the snow lighted upon her shoulders and hair, I described for her the scrappy little mutt that incessantly yapped at everything. We slowed our pace, as if to prolong the moment, but eventually we reached the car. The snow had coated the windshield again, and now when we sealed ourselves inside, Vanessa turned the engine but left the car idling and the wipers off. I made the story vivid and even imitated the deep, solitary bark of the Husky. All the while I spoke, Vanessa looked at me and smiled. The wine seemed to have slowed her down a little and put a touch of giddiness in her voice. Whenever something amused her, she grabbed my wrist, and she especially liked how the little dog's legs fluttered rapidly beneath its dirty belly as it ran. I skipped the part about the social worker's dreadful office. Getting a bit caught up in the tale, I concluded by saying, "They led me right up to the door of your store. The hounds of destiny."

"You're a liar," she said.

"No."

"Then, at least, you're an idiot."

"Maybe."

She looked at me with a mixture of happiness and feigned disapproval, and then her expression dissolved into something else as her smile faded and the luster of her eyes deepened beneath a more somber mood.

"You're an idiot," she repeated, and she turned away from me, but I knew she wasn't actually insulting me because a low and sensuous note played within the sound of her voice.

The wipers came on, and the car started forward. We sat in silence. The pale darkness within the car seemed to be rendered fragile by the crisp air. I was uncertain where we were heading, but after a few moments, Vanessa asked where I lived, so she could take me home. I told her the address, and she continued in silence, making no reference to my renting a room or staying with a friend. Occasionally, I looked over at her as she kept her eyes on the fouled road. Without a word, she took one of her gloved hands from the steering wheel and calmly, without even a glance in my direction, placed her hand gently over the back of my hand, so our forearms rested side-by-side along the console.

She turned down my narrow street and drove slowly between the lanes of snow-covered cars. I had her pull over in front of the alley beside my building. I noticed that although the snow hadn't accumulated too much, my landlord had recently cleared off the steps. The car idled, and the wipers came on intermittently. Vanessa continued to hold my hand.

"You're a good guy," she told me. "Thanks for the book and everything."

"I'm glad you went out with me."

"I'm going to read that book, you know. And then we can talk about it."

"Good."

"Don't forget I still have your clothes."

With her eyes fixed on me, she slipped back into silence for a moment, waiting, as if she wanted to tell me something or to hear me speak. But I had nothing to say. Her fingers tightened slightly around my hand, and again I sensed that she was offering me permission, not merely to look at her, but to accept her yielding. Despite our privacy within the car, the simple distance between our seats, and her face turned toward me with a subtle mixture of pleading and surrender—I remained frozen, unable to lean close to her and give her the hug or kiss that she wanted. The moment seemed to be straining to the breaking point. I was about to say something, anything to offer us a release from one another, when Vanessa moved toward me, simultaneously raising my hand to the hollow of her throat and placing her lips, softly and slowly, on the side of my mouth. Afterwards, her face briefly lingered near to me, her breath trembling warmly upon my cheek, my fingers pressing lightly against her neck. But then she reclined back into her seat and released my hand.

"It's nice to be with a gentleman for once," she said.

"Thank you for the cookie," I stupidly responded.

Yet, rather than regard me as a schoolboy or an idiot, she smiled as though I were teasing or flirting with her.

"I'll see you tomorrow," she said, which was my cue to get out of the car.

VIII

And then I was standing in the cold, with the snow slanting in on me. Even though I was on the sidewalk in front of my building, I was somewhat disoriented as I watched the red taillights of her car fading into the distance. My blood pulsed hot, and my body felt tuned to some taut and quivering cord. I didn't even have a moment to collect myself, to allow my excitement to settle down, for I was still in the afterglow of Vanessa's presence, heading toward the front door of my building, when I had a terrible sensation that with each step I took, I was getting closer to my prison, and what was worse was the premonition that once again I would be on display for a hostile world. I was returning to the life I wanted to abandon. And even this meshing of my emotions—my simultaneous thrill and dread—didn't have time to quiet down, for I was mounting the concrete steps, and then in the process of opening the door, when I looked into the building and saw on the staircase to my right a pair of descending legs and a hand on the banister.

Moving backward, I gently pulled the door shut again, retreated down the front steps, and stood on the sidewalk. I gazed up at the building, afraid to go inside. Although I didn't know who was coming down the steps, my intuition warned me that I needed to hide before the person could emerge from the front door and look down at me upon the sidewalk. I briskly started away, thinking that maybe I would duck down the alley. I was only a few paces away when from behind me came the sound of the front door opening and then closing. I didn't turn around to look. With the person possibly walking behind me, I could no longer veer into the alley without drawing attention to myself. Keeping my head down, I started to cross the street. As I stepped between the parked cars, I glanced over to see that the person headed in the opposite direction.

And still I didn't have time to collect myself or to ease the strain of my excitement. Even though the person was putting distance between us, my heart beat with a new terror. Suddenly, at the unmistakable sight of the corduroy jacket and the green baseball cap, I became aware that McTeal had been hiding in my building, waiting for me to come home. He surely must have seen me from behind when he'd stepped out the front door; he must have given me at least a cursory glance. Thus, Vanessa Somerset's vintage clothes had saved me for the time being.

The man had a slow, lumbering gait like a pregnant woman's.

Although he had been obsessed with Claudia Jones long before I'd ever offended him, I didn't suspect at the moment that a part of his freakish behavior might have been to prowl around her building and slobber on her doorstep. Preoccupied by my own safety, I was gripped by the idea that he wanted me. By luck or contrivance, he had managed to get past the inner door and most likely lingered in the hallway or on the staircase, somehow avoiding contact with anyone who might have questioned his presence.

He was waddling away, heading into the snowy evening, but he would be back.

My building loomed beside me. Even though the lighted windows speckled its face, the building appeared as dark, cold, and impenetrable as a single block of stone. This was no longer my home, especially now that it had been violated not only by the investigators but also by McTeal.

As I stood for a moment watching him, I began to feel my anxiety start to subside. Being able to look at him, without him seeing me in return, seemed to give me an unexpected advantage.

Up ahead, he passed under a streetlight, where the illumination made the falling snow appear whiter and denser. Curious whether he was going to turn the corner, I walked forward a few paces, and then a few paces more, until I was standing by the other side of my building. McTeal continued straight. Only an inch or two of snow coated the sidewalk, and as I started forward, I looked down at McTeal's footprints. Not quite certain what I was doing, I hurried a little in fear that McTeal would get too far away and I would no longer be able to see him. For months, I had been the one under scrutiny, but suddenly, by a bit of chance, the roles had shifted. While I might have been homeless, at least now nobody would be able to find me and put me under surveillance again. Following McTeal gave me a strange sense of freedom and control that I'd never had before.

When he crossed the street and headed down a side road, he left my field of vision. Yet I quickened my stride. He had small shoes with smooth bottoms, and his heels pressed all the way to the cement, while the tips of his toes left almost no impression at all. I reached the crossroad and peered in the direction that McTeal had gone, but I couldn't see him. In the street, where the passing cars had disturbed the snow, I couldn't see his footprints. Even so, on the opposite sidewalk, they reappeared. I followed them up to the next block, and the strange, waddling man came back into view.

I didn't know how far or where McTeal would lead me. For some reason, I suspected that he was headed toward a dark, dirty room, where he spent all his time festering in his own perverse delusions, abandoning himself to the lure of his fantasies. Perhaps he had peeled away sections of wallpaper, broken holes in the sheetrock, and scrawled his thoughts with a clumsy black marker, his personal graffiti: *I have several children I'm training to be killers. Wait till they grow up,* or maybe something as indiscernible as *Hi. I'm Mr. Williams. I live in this hole,* with a crooked arrow pointing to a small jagged orifice, knee high, in the sheetrock. Of course, McTeal's home might have been nothing this deranged, and more like that of an ordinary man, with potpourri in a little glass bowl in the bathroom, a fine collection of DVDs beneath the television, and a wife sitting at the kitchen table and cutting up a grilled cheese sandwich for their young daughter. This latter scenario was more unsettling.

McTeal waddled on.

I kept a safe distance behind him, but he never once looked over his shoulder. I was nervous but thrilled. The biting cold made me conscious of my wound again, for my temple began to throb. The muddy green jacket might have disguised me a little, but it provided poor insulation from the weather. I began to think about Vanessa Somerset; even though she had deluded herself into liking me, she began to settle warmly inside of me. I wanted to see her again. Perhaps she hadn't deceived herself in the slightest bit. After all, Vanessa was a grown woman with a string of past relationships, heartaches, and lusts, so undoubtedly she was old enough to know what she wanted, and experienced enough to know how to maneuver her way around me. Perhaps I was the one who was transparent and deluded because I was oblivious to the extent to which she'd charmed me. Noticing the loops of tiny colored lights in a window, I briefly imagined myself buying Vanessa a Christmas present.

McTeal turned a corner and stepped out of sight.

I hurried forward. I had a new idea that maybe I would discover the man in a little pigpen of debauchery, and I could turn him over to Dr. Ferguson and the intense black man. Somehow, by sacrificing McTeal, I would be rewarded. I wasn't looking to be a hero, but simply to be granted immunity. At the moment, as I strode toward the corner on this quiet, snowy evening, I neglected to consider that the authorities would wonder how I knew about McTeal in the first place. I would have been tying myself to the pervert.

When I came to the end of the block, I was standing in the full glare of a streetlight, so I approached the corner slowly and peeped around the edge of a wet brick building. Besides a woman in a purple overcoat who was fishing in the trunk of her car, nobody else was in view. I looked down and saw McTeal's footprints. Cautiously, I surveyed the area, fearing that maybe he'd known all along that I was following him and he was now crouched behind a car or in a doorway, ready to spring out and bludgeon me over the head. I tracked the footprints for roughly twenty yards, at which point they sharply turned and ceased at a large closed door.

I stepped back and looked up, wondering which window belonged to McTeal; at any moment, he would turn on the light.

"Get the door, sweetie."

The woman in the purple coat was stepping toward me, carrying several plastic grocery bags in each hand.

Without saying anything, I turned the handle and pushed the door open.

Stinking of cigarette smoke, the woman shuffled past me into the building.

"Merry Christmas," she said.

"You too," I responded, a little off-guard by her cheerfulness.

The woman bypassed the staircase and continued down the hall, walking dead center on the matted runner, heel to toe, as if she were on a tightrope and using the bags for balance.

The warmth of the building compelled me to step inside.

I had no idea what I was doing, and I figured that I had lost track of McTeal. Even so, I stood in the corridor, thinking that the instant I went back outside, I wouldn't know where to go. Although I hadn't seen the interior of any of the apartments, the building seemed nicer than where I lived.

The woman set down her bags, dug her hand beneath the collar of her coat, and pulled a strap over her head, from which dangled a set of keys, like some gaudy amulet.

I stepped aside in case she looked over and saw me lingering by the door. I heard the jangle of her keys, the sound of her bags being lifted, one by one, and dropped onto the floor of her apartment, and at last the shutting of her door. When I looked back down the hallway, I saw that her boots had left little clumps of snow on the runner.

Because McTeal was wearing flat-bottom shoes, he apparently didn't leave a trail of snow for me to follow.

The staircase not only went upward but also turned and descended into a brightly lit basement. I bent down and touched one of the steps leading to the second floor. A spot on the coarse, gray carpet was damp, presumably from McTeal. The steps creaked as I started upward. Most likely, I was only going to arrive at an empty corridor, as well as the pointless option of continuing on to the third floor, yet I wanted to follow McTeal until the trail ran completely dry. Part of me recognized the absurdity of my entire pursuit, but somehow by making this offensive move, by taking a little control, I was ridding myself of the threat of McTeal to some minor degree. I felt as though I were somehow pinning him down, fixing him in a little box, and limiting his strength. Of course, I wasn't fully disarming him, but merely dulling his weapon. Perhaps seeing the man's home would simply make him more human.

At the top of the flight of stairs, I wondered if I should continue upward or retreat. Save for a fire extinguisher attached to the wall and a pair of little black boots on the floor beside a door, the hallway was empty.

I looked up the staircase leading toward the next floor, the succession of steps seemingly ending at a white wall.

My chase appeared over.

As I turned to go back downstairs, I saw that less than ten feet from me, a door suddenly opened wide, and without pausing an instance to see who was about to emerge, I wheeled around and mounted the steps toward the third floor. There, midway on the staircase, I gripped the railing, crouched down, and listened.

The door closed.

Realizing that I would have been discovered already if the person were heading upward, I started back down the steps. I stooped and peeped into the corridor. The little boots and the fire extinguisher were still there, but nothing else

It appeared to be a false alarm; my chase was over.

Even so, when I turned the corner of the staircase, ready to leave the building and venture back out into the cold night, there was my madman again, waddling down the steps, this time carrying a plump navy blue sack over his shoulder and holding in his other hand a bulky red container with a blue cap.

I froze on the steps and watched him. He reached the bottom and lumbered out of sight.

I waited, listening for him to leave the building, but I couldn't tell where he'd gone, save for the obvious fact that he was going to do his laundry. I remembered from the photographs, his "love letters," that he used to change his sheets all the time, causing me to speculate, in that elaborate character study that I'd been compelled to destroy, why he changed them so often, what did he do off camera to make them so dirty?

Now that I knew where the man lived, there was no reason to follow him any further, merely to spy on him sitting on a bench and separating his whites from his colored clothes.

One day, from a safe distance, perhaps when McTeal was just beginning to forget about taking his revenge on a man who had inadvertently intercepted his love letters, I might send him a brief note in the post or maybe even slip it under his door. I could rewrite our whole conflict, making myself the victor:

Dear Fruitcake:

Consider this: The whole time I knew who you were and where you lived. Now has come the moment for me to alleviate your fears and disabuse you of your misconceptions. I never spoiled your campaign to woo my bloated neighbor; she disliked you of her own accord. I never burned your insipid little photos, nor considered them anything but loathsome. But I did make copies of them. As you read this note, everyone dear in your life—from your employer to your mother—is opening up a manila envelope, marked "Photos. Do Not Bend."

I walked over to the door to McTeal's apartment, to get the room number: twenty-two, which was easy to remember: the second door on the second floor. Although I had a pen, I didn't have anything to write on; otherwise, I might have crafted him a little note on the spot. However, it was probably better to wait a while. The surprise of hearing from me would be more disarming once he'd stopped thinking about me. I had a vague idea that I could pull a similar kind of joke on my landlord.

Standing before the door, I looked down the hallway to make sure no one was watching, and then I leaned my head closer to the door, still curious if McTeal was a family man or if he at least had a roommate. Yet, before my ear reached the surface, the brim of my hat knocked against it, causing my hat to tumble to the floor behind me. I instantly looked around again, but nobody was there. Moving slowly, more like a thief than a trespasser, I pressed my ear to the door. Everything was silent.

An impulse seized me, but before I acted on it, I put the hat back on my head, walked to the top of the stairs, and looked down to make sure that I was alone.

Back in front of McTeal's apartment, I took hold of the doorknob, and to my horror, it turned. As the door inched inward, I peeped around the edge and saw the lighted interior of the man's home. Before I fully registered the spartan décor of the place, I looked around for any signs of life. The main living area was apparently vacant, and although someone could have been in another room, I had a sense that McTeal lived alone. The walls contained no pictures or bookshelves. The few pieces of furniture were mismatched, undoubtedly acquired at various times, at different locations, from department stores and garage sales to the attics of relatives and the basements of friends. Even though there was wall-to-wall beige carpeting, between the couch and the television was an area rug with a maroon and black floral design. Here was another clue that he was a lonely bachelor, for I imagined that the sensibility necessary to place that rug on the carpet seemed to obliterate the likelihood of a woman's touch. The room felt colder than the hallway because a sliding glass door on the far wall was slightly open. If the man were in any way vile or obscene, nobody would have been able to discern it from the room.

Interestingly, I didn't see a computer station, which meant that one of the darkened rooms to the right was where he squandered his time and called up the lurid images of Claudia Jones, where he pined and lusted, where he slobbered, ached, and groaned. Perhaps, if guests ever visited him, he closed the door to that particular room, and as they sat on his couch, placed their drinks on his coffee table, and made their usual polite talk, they had no idea that they were sitting in the middle of a façade. In the main living area, everything looked nondescript and normal, if not almost barren.

McTeal was doing his laundry, and by the size of the sack, he probably had about two loads.

Glancing back into the empty hallway, I stepped into the apartment and closed the door.

My heart began to race like mad, but I was only going to take a quick look around and then run off, perhaps leave a note magnetted to his refrigerator, something to indicate that I had won our little battle, something unsigned and unsettling:

Dear Fruitcake: I have peed in select corners of your home.

On his coffee table were several blank postcards, all featuring the Grand Canyon, as well as a glass ashtray with one snuffed cigarette butt. Once I saw the ashtray, I became aware of the odor of smoke. And when I saw a cat box that contained dark clumps of litter and a tiny, disgusting plastic shovel, such as might belong in a sandbox or on the beach, I detected an acrid fecal smell too. The sliding door must have been open to let in some fresh air or perhaps to allow the cat free passage in and out.

The long blinds were pulled to the right, and leaning against the glass was a hollow metal rod, as if McTeal had taken a hacksaw and cut a mop handle. Holding the battered rod in my hand, I looked out through door and saw the falling snow gathering on the railing of a small balcony. A single lawn chair was covered with snow, and beside it was a five-gallon bucket, which might at one time have contained plaster or paint, but now probably functioned as a table. Beyond the balcony, a small courtyard was surrounded on three sides by the backs of buildings, and by a low brick wall on the other. Some of the balconies and windows were decorated with Christmas lights. In the courtyard, the snow-topped trees, shrubbery, and a pair of benches were visible in the arcs of light cast by lamps that lined the blanketed walkways. McTeal apparently had a healthier and more peaceful view from his balcony than I had into the gritty alley outside my window.

Still holding the piece of handle, I walked toward the dining area. Newspapers were spread over a tabletop. McTeal must have recently built, repaired, or dismantled something because several hand tools remained on the table. The hammer had a smooth wooden handle, with two nails driven into the top of it and bent over to keep the head from coming off. I looked around to see what McTeal was working on, when I noticed the cat watching me from beneath the couch. I put the hammer down, picked up a pair of needle-nose pliers, and then returned that too. The cat, with only its fluffy orange head sticking out, continued to study me. Its eyes were two pieces of black glass set into a puff of fur. I didn't know if I had spooked the animal to hide beneath the couch or if that was its normal refuge.

Less than a minute, I told myself. I kept time in my head.

As I started toward the two darkened doorways, I imagined that another living and cowering creature might also be present in the room, alert and tense and suspicious. Once again, I was seized by the sudden awareness that I had no idea what I was doing, and this knowledge seemed to come from outside of myself, as if I were watching a lanky man in a muddy green coat and a silly hat as he stepped cautiously across a span of carpet in a strange room, wielding a section of mop handle like a weapon, approaching the private rooms of a man he didn't know. And before I began to comprehend my motive, let alone judge what kind of person I was, I found myself standing beside one of the doorways, first peeking around the edge of the doorframe, and then reaching my hand inside and sliding it up the cool wall. And before I even knew that I felt the light switch, an abrupt glare exposed the room; the tiled walls and floor glinted, white and blue. And even though I was looking at a completely vacant bathroom with nobody in the tub and nobody on the toilet, I hadn't fully reckoned with the possibility of finding a person, not just with what I would do but also with how the person would react to me suddenly flipping on the light—and this was probably because I never really believed in the first place that anyone was in the apartment. No one could have been there, not because reason or evidence demanded that this was the case, but rather because I implicitly understood that McTeal was alone in the world, with no friends or relatives to give him furniture or to talk politely in his living room over a cup of coffee: He was too inept or twisted to have made any sustainable human connection. Still, I raised the cut handle as I approached the second doorway, which I already knew—before I even reached my hand into the gloom and turned on the light—was going to be an empty bedroom. The bed sat square and tight without a single crease in the covers, without a headboard, as though it belonged in a barracks or a hospital. The nightstands on either side of it were polished, clear, and seemingly unused. Just as in McTeal's photographs, in his "love letters," the wall above the bed was barren. In fact, all the walls were barren. I expected to find a tripod set up and directed toward the familiar scene; however, what I discovered was a coffee can on the edge of a dresser directly across from the foot of the bed. The only thing on the dresser was the can, upside down, as though the plastic lid served as a coaster protecting the wooden surface from scratches. Atop the can was perched a tiny gold-colored camera.

Maybe two minutes now, I told myself.

Although I didn't think of it at the time, the ultimate thing—the thing that would have unnerved and baffled McTeal more than any note slipped under his door or posted on his refrigerator—would have been to take a picture, one which would have revealed myself not explicitly, such as a full body shot or a portrait of my grinning face, but rather tangentially, from an angle that would somehow simultaneously provoke his fear and his curiosity. He would realize that I figured him out and defeated him. No matter what the photograph depicted—a close-up of my head-wound, the brim of my hat, one glimmering cat eye, the hooked claw of his hammer—the image would've indicated far less than it would've suggested, provoking McTeal's soggy mind to work out the details.

Yet I wasn't thinking any of this as I looked at the bare walls and the sparse furniture, which could have belonged to any man who hadn't taken the time or the opportunity to live among his own things, in his own home, and thus leave an impression of himself or a trace of his personality. McTeal's apartment wasn't a pigpen of debauchery, a home for a loving family, or even a façade to mask his private perversion. It was simply devoid of character.

Because I didn't see a computer station, I suspected that either he had a portable laptop or else he visited libraries or computer labs at some college.

Of course, I was overlooking the most obvious reason that the apartment appeared unused. Stooping down to peek under the bed, I wasn't really thinking yet. Instead, I stood up and moved toward the closet, still holding the cut handle and still imagining that if I continued with my search, I would find something. But I never reached the closet or opened its door because I was feeling the object in my hand and dimly considering that it might be as old as the building itself, older than McTeal, when I realized that the handle didn't belong to McTeal at all. He was just renting it because it came with the apartment. When the sliding glass door was shut, the handle fitted into the track, so the door couldn't be opened from the outside. And yet I still didn't fully comprehend the significance of the things I saw. Just as I was shutting off the light and exiting the bedroom, a part of me was beginning to surmise that McTeal was merely a tenant, which meant that he had as much connection to his home as I had to mine. Crossing the span of carpet again, moving swiftly now, I wanted to leave the handle where I'd found it and to get out of the apartment. At the moment, I wasn't so much thinking it as I was sensing it, namely that McTeal was in transition. He was in the process of moving, and he was several steps ahead of me because he had already packed and taken away most of his things. His home wasn't actually bare by design or neglect, but because he was clearing it out. I was squatting down to lean the handle back up against the glass door, feeling the cold air blow in, and wondering why McTeal was preparing to take flight, when all at once I arrived at the idea. McTeal was on the brink of action. I understood that he was moving, but I didn't have the chance to ask the question: *Why? What are you about to do, fruitcake?*—when I heard an unmistakable sound behind me: The front door opened.

Without looking around, I crouched down between the back of an easy chair and the sliding door. I hadn't yet returned the handle, so it was still in my hand, being pressed into the carpet as I leaned my weight upon my palm. My hiding place was horrible; at any moment, McTeal could have casually walked around his apartment and discovered me. Afraid to move, I strained to hear the sound of his laundry bag being flung to the floor or the clear thumps of receding footsteps into the kitchen or bathroom. Yet all I could discern was the indistinct sound of McTeal shuffling his body across the carpet, as if he didn't actually walk but rather spread himself out in several directions at once, like something heavy and gelatinous. At last, when the bulk of him seemed to settle in one indeterminable spot, I could hear the internal motions of his body, which weren't quite breathing and not quite gurgling, but the sound of some viscous liquid being drawn up to the top of a hollow tube and then released back down, drawn and released. Then he was moving again. My muscles tightened in terror, and listening, I became conscious of the sound of my own breathing. Although I was afraid to risk peeking around the side of the chair, I noticed that McTeal was reflected in the black pane of the sliding glass door—not in distinct contours—but as some translucent and boundless form. He was close by, perhaps as near as the coffee table, and he was doing something, moving vaguely, almost shimmering, as his reflection, the dark pane, and even the shapes in the night beyond the glass, bled into one another. As I waited, my heart pulsing in my breast, my wound twitching and tender, I began to focus on a single idea, which kept repeating in my head, silently commanding McTeal as if by telepathy: *Go to the bathroom; go to the bathroom; go to the bathroom.* In response came the small grating rasp and the momentary hiss of a lighter being struck. The flame was a brief orange gash in the dark reflection. McTeal grunted, and he coughed one time, almost like the cough of a small child. Instantly, I smelled the cigarette smoke, and before I had a chance to anticipate the next second, to prepare myself, McTeal emerged right beside me. His feet were in beige slippers; his thigh, naked and hairy, swelled upward to a pair of white underwear that was apparently at least a size too small; and a large tee-shirt draped over his firm, rotund stomach. He held the burning cigarette up to his mouth, stepped closer to the glass door, and looked out over the balcony and into the night. Suddenly, the door slid open, and the cold air rush in around McTeal. He drew on the cigarette and then extended his arm beyond the threshold to tap his ashes onto the snowy floor of the balcony. All he had to do was slightly turn his head and look down over his left shoulder, for I was only an arm's length away. I didn't even have a moment to consider how I would react if he saw me because all at once his body began to move: a slight involuntary motion, the contraction of his chest and the tightening of his throat, in that brief instant just before a cough—but it might as well have been the explosion of a pistol—because startled and terrified, I lunged at him, pushing him out onto the balcony, where he simultaneously coughed and stumbled against the railing. As he quickly gathered himself, wheeling back around, I pulled the door closed and dropped the handle into the track. No sooner, McTeal threw himself up against the glass door, his chest smacking hard against it, almost as if he were a bird in flight that didn't see its passage was obstructed.

Staggering back against the easy chair, I watched the bizarre and furious spectacle. Nothing in McTeal's expression indicated that he was alarmed or afraid; he was simply angry. I could see the pocks in his face clearly now as his jaw appeared distended and his eyes turned to fierce slits behind his glasses.

He hissed, "I'm going to kill you."

Without the door between us, I never would have been able to get this close, face-to-face, with the lunatic.

He kept wrapping the butt of his palm savagely against the glass. The entire door shook, as if ready to explode.

And he kept hissing, "I'm going to kill you."

But I already knew that, so there was nothing for me to do but to leave him on the balcony. There was no way I could safely release him. I backed away, keeping my eyes on him, as he stood framed against the dark night with the snow falling around him. His ferocious expression didn't change or soften by the slightest degree, not even when he must have realized—in the instant I started to turn my head away—that I was going to run out the front door.

PART FIVE:

GOATS AND MONKEYS

The exact details no longer mattered, for not only was the plotting out of certain points in my life an arbitrary and fantastic construction, but also no one point was definitively linked to any other point, for each was a cause ad infinitum and an effect ad infinitum, within a larger system of constant flux, a web of contingency, governed by attraction and repulsion, push and pull, a sad and pointless bumping together of parts. Of course, looking at my life in a grander, metaphysical—or perhaps macrophysical—context provided me another way of sighing and slouching over in resignation. From a more grounded perspective, I was tired and confused, and I didn't want to bother with thinking any longer. More precisely, a naked old man—his arms covered by the dark purple splotches of long ago tattoos, his belly flabby and pasty—made a grunting noise as he reached down to towel off his inner thighs and scrotum, and while witnessing this horrible spectacle, I had no idea what I was doing or how I had managed to make the sort of choices that brought me to this particular circumstance. Another old man at least had the decency to wear a pair of thin, yellowing briefs.

"We should've spent ten minutes in the sauna," he said. "It loosens you good."

"Don't blame me," the naked one replied. "You do what you want to do."

"You got the appointment, not me."

"Drive yourself next time."

"Who's stuffing the barrel now?"

Although this question completely eluded me, both men laughed.

"Crazy bastard," the naked man said.

His pale penis looked like a soggy, uncooked chicken neck drooping from a puff of gray hair.

I turned away from the men. Unfortunately, before they had emerged from the showers and stationed their slow, wet bodies beside me, I had already committed myself to a locker by hanging up my muddy green coat and shelving my shoes. Since I'd been caught in the process of disrobing, I now stalled, poking around in my locker, searching my pockets, and delaying my nudity, but the men showed no sign of urgency. The one in the yellow briefs, which at one time had probably been white, sat down on the bench, uncapped a green can, and began to spray each of his feet in turn. The other man, still nude, bent over a duffle bag and rifled through an exorbitant arsenal of beauty supplies, before finally selecting his deodorant. He eventually revealed a pair of crisp, white underwear and a tee-shirt, but rather than put them on, he set the garments on the bench and began combing his hair.

I soon realized, after inspecting all my pockets twice, that I had no choice but to strip out of my clothes.

Thankfully, the men disregarded me. The one in the yellow briefs was explaining different cuts of beef, from chuck steaks to filet mignon, which evidently intrigued the naked man.

Once all my clothes were stored in the locker and a towel was wrapped about my waist, I headed toward the showers. Even though my back was to the old men, I sensed a momentary pause in their conversation and imagined them simultaneously lifting their heads and eyeing me, as though I offered them a bit of droll amusement. My suspicion was confirmed the moment I passed through the swinging wooden door and stepped onto the cold tile floor: Both men chuckled.

Of course, this could have been a reaction to my exaggerated poking around in my pockets or my silly display of painful modesty, but I felt the deeper sting of their ridicule. Despite the pale loose flesh that was draped over their deteriorated meat, packed with clumps of pudge, and held up by their brittle, rickety frames, like an overburdened coat-rack—I became fretfully conscious of my own body, as though my shrunken chest and slumped shoulders were innately humorous, even to old men.

On my left were two doors, one glass and one wooden, that led to a steam room and a sauna. Across from them stretched a long counter with several sinks, where men customarily lathered, groomed, and preened themselves. The shower room was up ahead. Although I heard no water spewing from the showerheads, I averted my eyes in fear of seeing anyone.

I silently cursed the old men, holding against them their freedom to come to the gym at eleven o'clock in the morning, on a weekday, when ordinary people were busy with life, as though the old men were slighting the rest of society and failing to respect their own decrepitude and inevitable fate. The old fools ought to have been in bed. What was additionally offensive was that the door had not even swung closed behind me before they'd begun to chuckle because they didn't care whether or not I heard them. Instead of being enfeebled by their old age, stricken and humbled by a constant awareness of their tenuous mortality, they were emboldened. They no longer concerned themselves with civility, not simply because they'd lived long enough to stop worrying about what other people might think, but also because they no longer had any stake in society—similar to a pair of rutting high school boys, limited by the milky flush of testosterone over their spongy brains.

But then I saw myself reflected in the mirror above the long counter. Although my body might have given the two men plenty of reasons to laugh, the true cause sat atop my head: I had forgotten to take off my hat.

Continuing forward, I saw a series of hooks mounted to the tile wall near the entrance to the shower. The floor was wet, a small pool gathered about one of the drains. There were no stalls or partitions, just one common room with all the showerheads jutting out with a fierce, cold formality, such as in a hospital ward or a torture chamber.

I placed my hat upon one of the hooks, and turning my eyes to the floor, I removed the towel and hung it up also.

Naked, I stepped across the threshold into the vacant communal shower. The tiled walls were the color of peach pulp, and the dark floor glinted like the raw side of a kiwi's skin. I selected a spot in the corner, moving somewhat slowly and warily, as though I were afraid to make any noise—but the water exploded out of the showerhead, the sound amplified by the starkness of the room.

I showered facing the wall. Even though I dispensed a long pink coil of shampoo into my palm and lathered myself all over, I felt as though I couldn't get completely clean. A thin film of grime coated my skin. Perhaps some contaminant lurked in the public water—or perhaps it was just in my head. After all, a long time seemed to have passed since I'd last bathed, and in the interval, random forces had evidently conspired to defile me. By a volition other than my own, I had fallen on my back in a slushy street, been chased by dogs, sweated beneath my clothes, put vintage hand-me-downs over my clammy body, suffered through a police investigation, dined in disguise with Vanessa Somerset, followed a perverted creature back to its den, and escaped only by locking it out on a cold balcony. And then I had wandered the nighttime, all the while forsaken, miserable, and homeless. Despite finally having the opportunity to run away, I had continued to linger in the city. Rather than flee to a bus station and keep on traveling until I was safe from everything that threatened me, I had roamed the streets like some lost or abandoned pet, some slush-bellied mongrel. In an all-night diner, I had taken a long time eating a potato pancake. Afterwards, brandishing my identification card, I'd entered the college library, stowed myself inside a cubicle, and fallen asleep atop a musty book. Although I'd found some relief in my dreams and allowed myself to play in the garden of my memory—where I could nurture my private flowers and pluck my weeds—I wasn't aware at the time, or perhaps I simply lacked the comfortable distance from which to speculate, how this gesture of mental retreat was merely the precursor to a more definitive action: my final escape.

But the pitiful irony, of course, was that I hadn't done anything wrong; I had nothing for which to reproach myself: not the ruined boy on my bathroom floor, the lurid pictures on my computer, the frothing madman behind the sliding glass door, and especially not Vanessa Somerset. On one level, perhaps my sense of innocence accounted for my delayed getaway, but surely the main cause—if I could be honest with myself—was my loneliness. Throughout the night, a heavy smothering feeling had gradually crept upon me, transforming by degrees the desperate and divorced Vanessa Somerset into a viable option for love. How could I forget that she'd treated me like a man or how she'd softly, willingly, kissed me? She seemed to be the reward at the end of a long series of blunders. Not long ago, I had committed myself to pursuing risky choices, to venturing not just out of my apartment but also beyond the imaginary barriers I'd erected around myself, and to making a concerted effort upon the playing field of men. I'd vowed that I was no longer going to repeat all the mistakes that, regardless of my intentions, always led me back to solitude. After I had tried to step out into the world, and after all my stumbling and abortive advances, in bookstores, bars, and art galleries, which had left me stewing in my own lethargy and funk, Vanessa Somerset had emerged by luck. Dogs had chased me toward her, and she'd received me. Now she was expecting to see me again, and no excuse but my own cowardice could have explained avoiding her.

I lathered and rinsed myself a second time. Despite the fierceness of the water, I still felt the residue on my skin. Perhaps I was unaccustomed to something in the gym's water, such as calcium or salt, or the lack thereof. When I began to consider seeing Vanessa again, and how I would be in the same clothes from the day before, and that I had no deodorant for my body or comb for my hair, I felt a compulsion to prepare myself for her as best as I could—so if my first ablution was to cleanse my body, the second one seemed to have Vanessa as its goal.

When I left the shower, my feet smacking on the tile, I discovered that the two old men hadn't left the locker room. Fortunately, they were both dressed now, one in gray trousers and a button-down shirt, and the other in a red sweat-suit. They were still bickering about quitting the gym early and skipping their customary sauna because one of them had an appointment with his lawyer. The details weren't important, something about an escrow account and a contractor's lien. Feeling less self-conscious about my public nudity, I dropped my towel in front of the two men and got dressed. After slipping on my coat, I ran my fingers through my hair, and holding my hat in my hand, I started away from the men. They seemed as though they would go on talking long after I was gone, even though they were supposedly hurrying away on business.

In the weight room, the metal plates struck and clattered as several men occupied themselves either with grunting and huffing upon the benches or else strutting about the machines, tottering forward with their broad chests, one shoulder and then the other, rocking themselves into slow mobility.

Further on was the dull murmuring of motors as the belts of a pair of dueling treadmills whisked round and round, thumped upon by the thumping footfalls of two lumbering, middle-aged women, bent over and supported by the rails.

A row of bikes sat unused, their plastic stirrups looped beneath their pedals.

One wall was all mirrors, and another was windows, offering a view of a drab parking deck that seemed to be rendered heavier and more compact by the gray weather.

On my way to the exit, I had to pass a counter, behind which a boy was folding towels. When he had admitted me earlier, he had been overfriendly, and not only his alacrity but also his sculpted black hair and the rolled-up sleeves of his tee-shirt had bothered me a little.

He wasn't going to let me walk past him unmolested.

"Done already?" he asked, smiling.

"I only used the shower," I said, deciding to be honest.

His smile waned, as though he were disappointed.

"Use the rest of the gym. Enjoy yourself," he said.

"No, thank you."

"You need to try the facilities. Did you see the nautilus machines?"

"I saw them."

"Did you try them?"

"I saw them," I repeated. "Thank you." I started moving toward the exit.

"Hopefully, you'll spend more time with us next time. Remember that your trial membership only lasts for—"

"Okay," I said and cut him off by stepping outside.

Windless and unmoving, the cold issued itself all about me and blanketed everything in sight with a gloomy silence, such as might have pervaded the gutted interior of an abandoned cathedral. The vaulted sky was as gray and unadorned as flat, gray stone, and the dark, damp sides of the buildings were tall, drab walls. No echo could have sounded here, and no puny voice could have survived the suffocation, and even now, it is difficult for me to say whether I was coloring the urban landscape with my mood or whether I had been the one who had suffered a long, general smearing of my consciousness from the world without.

Compelled by my solitude, I headed down the sidewalk, trying to settle on my reasonable options. I didn't want to be swayed in the wrong direction by my emotions. If I simply disappeared, then the social worker, Dr. Ferguson, and the black man, who reminded me of a blood-bloated tick, would have assumed that I'd fled the continent and joined up with two perverts to play in the Orient, where parents and other beloved family members sold the favors of their children for food. But I wasn't one of these perverted men. I was just a reclusive scholar who possessed neither a strong allegiance to what he studied nor the literary ability to assemble and convey a lifetime of random gleanings. Nothing in my character would have prompted me to behave like those two men in the photographs, not to sit victoriously astraddle a discarded refrigerator and certainly not to prey upon the children of a ruined country. Even so, as much as I didn't want to do anything that would have further incriminated me, the authorities already regarded me as a suspect; otherwise, they wouldn't have searched my apartment. Now they had my computer with its cache of Claudia Jones's choice bits. What everyone thought of me was beyond repair, so perhaps I shouldn't have cared if my sudden disappearance caused them any further disturbance or alarm. In fact, it was their false suspicions that gave me the best reasons to leave at once. But then again, I couldn't forget W. McTeal. He was an excellent reason in himself. Even though I had locked him out on his balcony and thus beaten him at the game of ambush, I knew that I couldn't preen down the street as a proud champion. I doubted that I was responsible for the frozen corpse of that strange, solitary man because if his fury hadn't smashed the glass door, then his screams had surely startled his neighbors, and if neither his fury nor his screams had rescued him, then the snow covered ground, just a story beneath his balcony, had broken his fall. I half-wished that he'd contorted his ankle, popped his knee, or shattered both of his thighbones. Any of these injuries was better than a soft, harmless landing, which would have allowed him to hunt me again, but with additional rage and revenge to add to his usual state of lunacy. I was convinced that he was planning something devious and that I— not Claudia Jones or somebody else—was his primary object. While I had been out with Vanessa, he'd lain in wait at my apartment building. Moreover, from the look of his home, he was evidently in the process of moving, as though he'd already plotted his escape route. Although I remembered his table with newspapers spread atop it, the pair of pliers, and the hammer with the bent nails that kept the head from flying off, I had no way of guessing what was being constructed or destroyed.

Perhaps it was no use even to bother guessing.

Now that I was showered, I needed deodorant and maybe a fresh set of clothes, so I could present myself to Vanessa. Walking forward with my head lowered against the cold and my hands thrust into the pockets of the muddy-green jacket, I began to make mental calculations, trying to figure out how much money I had spent, how much I had left, and how much would be required in order to set myself up anew. Not only did I have to eat, but I also needed a ticket out of the city and at least a month's worth of rent. Once I was situated in a new apartment, in another place, I would have to find a job. Because I could no longer rely on Morris the man, I needed to sustain myself until my next paycheck from a job I had yet to procure. Thankfully, the cost of living was exorbitant in the city, which meant my returned security deposit would go further elsewhere, particularly in the outskirts of a rural town. A part of me had a secret wish that Vanessa Somerset would accompany me and we could pool together our resources and start our lives afresh in a warm, cozy room, scented by candles.

An old man with a crooked spine was on the sidewalk, sprinkling salt on a patch of ice. He cocked his head to look at me and then smiled, stretching his mouth into a long slit, his lips the same ashen color as his flesh.

"Watch your step," he said.

"Thanks," I responded, lowering my eyes from his bulbous, carbuncled nose to the slick sidewalk.

"The weather's a bitch."

"Yes," I said.

He threw a handful of salt before my feet.

"Thanks," I said again, still with my eyes averted. "Is there a pharmacy or supermarket around here?"

"Two blocks that way, make a right. Then three more down."

I sensed him pointing as he spoke, so I stole a glance at him, hesitant about getting another glimpse of his ugly nose.

He was looking off down the street.

"It's on the left. You can't miss it," he said, and when he started to raise his chin and turn his head back toward me, I saw a wattle of loose skin, cinched in his neck collar, begin to pull out and stretch like a deflated balloon.

"I appreciate it," I said, my feet crunching on the sidewalk as I stepped away.

"Happy holidays," the man said.

"Thanks. You too."

His kind words started me thinking about my mother and how every year around this time she would mail me a present, usually a card with money in it. She had her own way of celebrating the holidays. With a few old biddies from her church—mostly widows and spinsters—she would take a tropical vacation, at sun-baked resorts or aboard Caribbean cruises. The ritual was a nice way for the ladies to stave off the loneliness of the season. My mother had decided to join the group when I had made my formal repudiation of all things religious, which included the gelatinous cranberry sauce and lumpy mashed potatoes that each year decked my wizened aunt's dining room table, surrounded by several plump cousins and any recent additions that currently occupied their lives, from plump girlfriends and pregnant wives to wailing cherubs and small, toddling creatures plumping—plop—onto their bottoms. Any day now, my mother was going to call my apartment to inform me of the details of her imminent vacation and try to fish out of me any hopeful developments in my life. As far as she knew, I was still attempting to regain my social status by allowing Morris the man to help me reestablish myself. Although she was generally acquainted with the events that had driven me to take a new apartment in the first place, she knew nothing about the boy or what had followed his intrusion into my life, and she would have been surprised to learn that I was quitting my apartment so soon—unless, of course, Dr. Ferguson and the black man had questioned her about me. I had no reason to doubt the thoroughness of their investigation, but fretting over it now seemed pointless, not only because I was going to leave it all behind but also because the details no longer seemed to matter. I still hadn't decided whether I was going to contact my mother after I'd moved away or whether I was going to sever myself completely from the past. After all, I believed that I understood the real reason behind my mother's annual sojourn; it wasn't just to fight loneliness but rather to drown out her memories. She was still haunted by her previous life, and so for her, all the festive carols, the twinkling lights, and the holiday cheer wasn't so much the commemoration of a religious event as it was anniversary of my father's death. My father's letter remained hidden in the picture frame. I had carried it with me for so many years—back when the author of "Footprints" had still remained anonymous—that I now experienced an unexpected sense of remorse at the idea of leaving it behind. Moreover, the possibility of anyone else ever reading the letter was a little unsettling. If the quaint poem in the gilded frame could survive the grubby claws of my landlord, then it might eventually end up on a shelf in a novelty shop or in a cardboard box at a sidewalk sale, with a little, round sticker on the glass, pricing it at seventy-five cents. From there, it would change hands, and if fortune, chance, or the random flux of events heaved and humped in a certain way, then maybe the frame would remain intact, placed upon someone's end table or mounted to a kitchen wall. But ages from now, the poem might fail to stir up the proper religious affections, and the owner of the frame could possibly be moved to exchange the poem for something more sentimental and personal, such as a snapshot of her dog stretched out long, supine, and white-bellied in the grass. And then, in pieces upon her coffee table, the pretty picture frame would un-house its secret, the fading letters slanting across the stiff, yellowed sheet of paper: *Don't try to understand because I don't even understand it myself. Don't even bother mourning. Just be as happy as you can.* Of course, the picture of the dog sunning itself would still go inside the frame, but meanwhile, my father's letter would get passed around a circle of friends, relatives, and casual acquaintances, from fellow employees in the cafeteria to neighbors in the hall. What an intriguing little note; what a mystery, they would say, but the poor child with hair as filthy as a rat's nest, hopefully he grew up as happy as he could and died peacefully in his sleep at a ripe old age, survived by many loved ones who all smile warmly at his memory.

Although I had a sudden desire to have the letter back in my possession, I warned myself about the possible threats lurking around my apartment. Now, to some degree, I was in hiding, and it was best to stick to my original plan.

Inside the pharmacy, I found the deodorant right away, yet I roamed the brightly lit aisles, not looking for anything in particular. Rummaging through an array of candy on a table by the front counter, some type of squat creature sidled back and forth, all bundled up with the hood of its coat nearly cinched closed at its face. I walked up one aisle and then down another, and the globule remained stooped over the table, obstructing my passageway with its broad, high bottom.

"Excuse me," I said.

The creature gathered its body closer to the table, but there was little room to pass. Rather than try to squeeze by and risk rubbing up against the bloated thing, I retreated back down the aisle.

"That's okay," I said.

Glancing over my shoulder, I suddenly felt vaguely uneasy about the body, as though its shape were in some way advising me to be on guard.

On a shelf at face height was underwear, white cotton briefs and tee-shirts wrapped in clear plastic. Thinking that I ought to put on a fresh pair of briefs, I selected a three-pack, which was the smallest quantity. I could stuff the other two in my pocket.

The bloated thing lingered at the end of the aisle, poking around boxes of candy with its gloved hand.

And then, all at once, my unfocused suspicion turned into a distinct, palpable fear. I imagined that the black man was spying on me; although I couldn't see his face, I trusted that he was following through with his promise to know when I ate or slept. Because he was investigating a crime with an international scope, he was certainly more than a typical policeman. Thus, I imbued him with all the wily and sophisticated techniques of a covert portion of the government. And now that I thought about it, neither he nor Dr. Ferguson had told me what agency they worked for. Somehow this lack of definiteness seemed to extend their power into a more mysterious, less ethical realm.

With my two items, I walked around and came back down a farther aisle. As I passed a long display of cards for all occasions, from birth to death, I began to rationalize that the bloated body was simply a fat, ordinary citizen. Even so, when I approached the cash register, I kept my purchase guarded from his view. I didn't need him speculating about my underwear or creating a special file for all things that occurred—or didn't occur—beneath my beltline. Despite my awareness of the corpulent creature in my periphery, I didn't give in to the temptation to turn my head and take a fuller look. However, when I exited the store, I glanced back through the glass door and noticed that the body had moved away from the candy and was now browsing among the cosmetics, holding a little brown tube in its gloved hand. As I headed down the sidewalk, I was confident that my alarm had been raised, not by the black man, but by some white woman.

A little later, I found myself in a fast food restaurant, in a cramped bathroom stall. Because the floor had been fouled by many wet shoes, and the rim of the toilet was flecked with urine and sprinkled with a few curly hairs, what should have been a simple operation of putting on a fresh pair of underwear was now hindered by my fear of touching anything. As I contorted and struggled in the stall, I accused myself of being an unusual man, one who lacked a proper regard for his own appearance, because most people, especially women, had regular dressing habits implicitly governed by a principle of self-respect. For some reason, I recalled, from a hundred years ago, the pretty, gimpy girl named Gerty MacDowell whose chief care, among all the dainty particulars of her attire, was her undies, and how on the summer day when she'd worn her blue pair for luck, she'd inadvertently ushered in the modern world, before limping away. Perhaps I was exaggerating a little the historical significance of her dinky set of blue panties with the pretty stitchery and ribbons, but it was difficult for me to imagine that she or any other girl, from any generation, would ever find herself leaning her shoulder against the scratched and graffiti-scrawled wall of a narrow bathroom stall, awkwardly using one arm to hold up her disrobed gabardine pants, and with the help of her other hand, trying to step into a pair of briefs without brushing them along the floor or hooking them with her foot—all the while, just on the other side of the partition, someone flatulently strained and plunked, between his groans, several small, hard balls into the toilet water. When I finally righted myself, and was holding the tab of my zipper between my thumb and forefinger, I decided to take the opportunity to relieve myself. As I urinated, I began to think about the discrete parts of Claudia Jones, wondering if even she, with all the luridness of her commodified and fragmented flesh, possessed enough control over her own life to keep herself from ever being forced to sleep, shower, and dress in public places. Vanessa Somerset probably wouldn't have suspected that I was such a desultory man. After I left the bathroom and purchased a cup of coffee, I went back outside, vowing to myself that I would never again be so negligent of my own wellbeing. I wanted to rekindle in my breast that feeling of strength and normalcy that Vanessa had sparked the previous night.

Even though the social worker's dreadful office above the wig shop was nearby Crowley's pair of stores, I decided to visit Vanessa at that very moment, while I still had the nerve. Rather than spend more money on a new outfit, I would go as I was. Once I got there, I could put on my own clothes: the slacks, the light gray button-down shirt, the sports jacket, and the charcoal colored overcoat.

Thus, around noon on a bitter cold Wednesday in December, I took the sort of courageous action that I supposed would have been respected by the joyriding, helmet-less black man on the motorcycle. By the time I got near the bottom of my coffee, I was half-hoping to see him burst thunderously out of a side street and, with his front wheel skimming along the pavement and spewing slush in all directions, race out of sight and sound, like some indefatigable hero from Camelot to cowboy, riding ever and so long into the dustless, meridian farewell.

With my hat slanted across my brow, a stick of deodorant in one pocket, some new underwear in the other, and a paper coffee cup in hand, I set out to encounter a new life. I was headed toward Crowley's, and if a pair of dogs barked at me this time, I was ready to bark back at them. Cars parked along the street were still covered in a layer of snow from the previous night, snow capped the railings and window ledges, and out of the mouths of gutters snaked tendrils of ice.

Although I ordinarily lack both pluck and resolve, I sensed that Vanessa Somerset was having a strange influence over me, as if the warm glow of last night's kiss hadn't faded just yet—even though, somewhere in the back of my mind, I dimly feared that it eventually would, and then the timid toad in me would reemerge and leap back into its cesspool. But meanwhile, I needed to plod on because I imagined that if I could keep plodding and allow the momentum of this newly found masculinity to carry me forward, then I might be able to break out of my prolonged moratorium in adolescence and, thus, finally mature into another stage of life, not just on a warm, cozier level, but as a full-blown adult.

Of course, this wasn't the first time I had these thoughts; in fact, on the very day I had followed my landlord down the corridor and watched him knock two times, hard, on Claudia Jones's door, I had told myself that all I needed was packed in my single suitcase and that my new apartment was going to be my new chance at life. I was going to set my sails toward a western exile, like some lone seaman aboard his meager skiff, and if neither a mermaid, a fish, a seabird, nor a barnacle would give me a hand, I'd man my rod alone, tend my sails, and without regrets, attempt to gaff whatever might suit my pleasure. However, before I even had enough time to plot my course, let alone push off from the dock, the boy had slimed his way into my apartment, staining my couch and spewing and slathering himself upon my bathroom floor.

Even so, I wasn't disheartened by my awareness that the vitality that now motivated me was, in fact, closely fashioned after similar episodes in my life. I was running away and starting over, just as I had done before, but simple logic dictated that hope needed to repeat itself for at least one last time in order for the final rebirth to have a permanent existence. Seeing Crowley's awning up ahead, I continued forward, imagining for an instant that if I were to look back, I'd behold a sidewalk strewn with a series of miscarriages and the aborted carcasses of my past.

When I came closer to the pair of side-by-side doors, with the myriad of stickers on the glass, I began to feel a greater intimacy with Vanessa, for she also seemed to be a person who had failed to progress and had been living trapped in a single moment for fifteen years. As I reached my hand out for the door, I suddenly realized that maybe part of the legal settlement of her divorce had kept her ex-husband nearby, in the other half of Crowley's, where he could nurse his affection for popular music and watch over his ex-wife. Just as it had taken her a long time to admit that her marriage had been stifling the best parts of herself, maybe she was now prepared to have a similar revelation about the clothing store—and another drastic escape was possibly at hand.

I stepped into the store's warmth and its odor of incense, which rescued me from the cold and seemed to welcome me as well. This time the couch was empty, and the music was turned so low that it was just a whispering sound in the background. I moved past the racks of clothes and stepped up to the counter. Yesterday's trash was still in the wicker basket, my folded receipt still on top. I leaned across the counter and tossed in my empty coffee cup.

When I turned, Vanessa was standing in the archway to the backroom. The book I had given her was closed upon her finger. In her other hand, she held her black-rimmed glasses, and smiling, she pointed at me with the arm of her glasses.

"I was just thinking about you," she said.

She came toward me and opened the book upon the counter.

"I read this paragraph a couple of times," she said, pressing the book flat with the heel of her palm.

"What's that?" I asked, looking to where her finger now guided me to the lines. She'd apparently read a good portion of the book, and thoughtfully, because many pages were earmarked.

Recognizing the passage at once, I said, "He's watching her in the water."

"Yeah, but what's she doing in the water? At first, I thought she was going to bathe or swim, but she's got her clothes on."

"She's going to the bathroom," I said.

Vanessa tapped me on the shoulder with the back of her hand.

"That's what I thought," she said. "But he's a stupid kid. He acts like he's watching some type of miracle."

"It inspires him to write a poem," I said.

"There's nothing inspirational about that."

Vanessa was looking steadily at me, as though she were fully willing to absorb whatever I said.

"Remember he recently decided not to be a priest," I explained, looking back at the book. "And he's given up on God, so when he sees something very earthy, very bodily, he's moved by it. It's the sort of thing that Christianity ignores."

"I've got to think about it." She lifted the book close to her face. "But right now, I'm not buying it. If he was a gentleman, he would've given her some privacy. Poor girl." Vanessa slid her finger halfway down the page and read aloud. "'Long, long she suffered his gaze.' What a jerk. Let her pee in peace."

She abruptly closed the book, put it on the counter, and pushed it beside the cash register.

"To me, he doesn't understand girls," she added.

"I think you're right," I said, which made Vanessa smile.

Just then the door opened, and a young woman in a ski jacket entered the store. Her cheeks were red from the cold, and she briskly wiped her boots on the front mat.

"Hi," she said. "Tell me you got a baby doll dress."

"I think I might," Vanessa replied, stepping away from me.

"From the sixties?"

"Let's look."

Vanessa led the young woman over to a rack of clothes where they began inspecting one garment after another. All the while, Vanessa addressed the young woman more as a friend than as a customer. Evidently, one of the woman's co-workers was having a Christmas party, and everyone in her department was invited. But rather than have a traditional party, the co-worker wanted to throw a retro-bash. There were going to be lava lamps and mood rings and lots of Janis Joplin and Bob Dylan. The whole time the young woman spoke, Vanessa smiled, as though she were also going to the party. Occasionally, she glanced over to me, but to show her that I was comfortable waiting, I took the book and went and sat on the low brown couch, which I now realized lacked legs. I rested my shin upon my opposite knee and looked down at the book opened upon my raised thigh, yet I didn't read anything. Vanessa herself seemed exceedingly kind. The attention she gave to the young woman—from helping her off with her ski jacket to listening to her story and showing her various articles—made Vanessa appear miraculous to me. Today, I was able to see her more clearly; the bulky Moravian sweatshirt had been replaced by more elegant clothes. A pair of gray slacks, perhaps soft cotton, elongated the length of her legs and flared slightly above her black shoes, and her simple top was also black, with its neck scooped low and its sleeves stopping short of her wrists; it clung close to her lean body, seeming to broaden her shoulders and flatten her stomach, leaving no confusion about her breasts, which were mild swells, barely more than just two conspicuous nipples. And her blonde hair, which had once been concealed by the hood of her sweatshirt, now trailed down between the points of her shoulder blades. Every time she smiled, I was gently thrilled, for her mouth appeared more sensual, glistening from a touch of lip-gloss.

Just as I had considered preparing myself for her, she'd obviously wanted to look good for me.

Eventually, the young woman took several items into the bathroom in the backroom, and Vanessa stood in the archway and waited.

"Isn't she cute?"

"Yes," I answered, even though the woman had round, pasty cheeks with red splotches on them.

"I bet she takes the green one. It will go with her eyes," Vanessa said, looking off into the backroom. After a moment, she turned toward me and asked, "Don't you have to work today?"

"I set my own schedule," I said, aware that this was the first time she'd expressed an interest in what I did to support myself. "I'm on leave from the college to do research for a book."

"You work for a college?" she asked. "That seems like you. My ex-has a lot of school, but he never went far enough." She shrugged and smiled. "Thus, no horse clinic."

"It's hard," I said, and seeing an opportunity to plant a seed in her head, I added, "But I'm not tied to the college. I can work from anywhere I want."

"Not me," she said and then disappeared into the backroom to answer her customer's call for assistance.

True to Vanessa's prediction, the young woman ended up purchasing the green dress, in addition to a pair of high white boots and a matching scarf. At the register, the young woman, apparently inspired by the paraphernalia on display in back, told an anecdote about a time in high school when someone had punctured a hole in the side of an empty beer can and created a make-shift marijuana bowl.

"Necessity is a mother," Vanessa said.

"Lucky his pot was in plastic because he'd dropped it in the toilet along with his papers."

"Poor kid," Vanessa said.

"You're about half right." The young woman laughed. "He was my boyfriend at the time."

"Poor girl," Vanessa corrected and patted the young woman's shoulder.

"I'm recovered."

The young woman was still laughing when she finally exited the store, and Vanessa upgraded her from cute to adorable.

She leaned in the archway again.

"You came earlier than I expected," she said. "I'd just sent my niece to the drycleaners with your clothes. I wanted to surprise you."

"Thank you," I said. "That's nice of you."

Vanessa bent down and inspected my head.

"It looks worse than yesterday."

"It hurts less," I said.

"I don't know when your clothes will be ready. They said sometime today, but it'll probably be at least a couple of hours." She straightened up and returned to her spot in the archway. She looked at me for a moment without saying anything, which made me conscious of being in the outfit she had sold me the day before.

Lacking an adequate explanation, I rose awkwardly to my feet.

"I need to thank your niece," I said. "I suppose I can pick up my clothes myself."

"Sure." Vanessa nodded. "But you need to wait for Connie to come back with your stub."

"No problem." I briefly looked back down at the couch, not quite certain if she intended for me to take a seat again.

With a slight smirk upon her glistening lips, Vanessa watched me, as though my momentary confusion amused her.

"Or you could come back at closing time," she said, rescuing me.

"Sure," I said, nodding now myself, wondering whether this was my signal to leave or if I was supposed to stay a little longer. After all, we'd hardly talked.

But she rescued me again.

"My niece and her boyfriend are having dinner at my place tonight, if you want to join us. I have a big piece of salmon in the refrigerator that I need to cook. I'd planned on cooking it last night," she said, and her allusion to our impromptu date put a suggestive smile on her face.

"Sure," I said again, still nodding.

Despite my earlier confidence, I felt myself growing flushed and ready to stammer, but Vanessa seemed to ease me gently out the door by placing me in charge of picking up some wine and warning me not to work too hard on my book today. Also, she advised me that Connie preferred something sweet, such as a white zinfandel or a blush.

"She's old enough to drink?" I asked.

"If she's old enough to have a boyfriend," Vanessa replied, and this casual euphemism for her niece's sexual maturity lingered in my mind as I headed back outside along the sidewalk. Although I had no precise destination, I avoided going anywhere near the social worker's dreadful office. As long as I remained as unobserved as possible, the exact details of that afternoon didn't matter. I ate lunch, which was two more potato pancakes and another cup of coffee, wandered briefly about the regal busts and sculptures of a Rodin exhibit, checked the timetables for my imminent departure, and, of course, purchased several bottles of wine. Meanwhile, dark clouds grew denser over the city, and big snowflakes, like the ashes of a burnt building, began to blow through the streets. As twilight gave way to evening, and the wind increased, swirling gusts of snow became visible from streetlight to streetlight. Higher up, however, above the tops of buildings, the sky was utter darkness, devoid of both snow and motion. I plunged forward, on route back to Crowley's store. Only now did I wish for a little more time, thinking that perhaps a brief visit to a bar for just one quick drink would give me another boost of confidence. But I kept walking. Although I'd had several hours to contemplate my own motivation—let alone to prepare an explanation for where I'd spent the previous night and why I hadn't changed clothes—I had no idea what I was doing. All I knew was that somewhere between the tilapia in a Thai restaurant and the salmon in her refrigerator, I'd decided to take a risk on Vanessa Somerset. Yet, in that interval, none of my actions appeared to be the result of careful contemplation or a full assessment of the possible consequences. In short, I was simply responding. Vanessa had asked me on a second date, and I obeyed without question, like a dog catching wind of a distant scent and trotting after it.

By the time I returned, the interior of Crowley's music store was dark, and a metal gate obstructed its glass door. Vanessa's side was also closed, for only the backroom was lighted. Hugging the brown bag full of wine bottles, I hurriedly entered, escaping the cold.

Connie's boyfriend was sitting on the counter, while Connie faced him, standing between his open legs.

"You're back," she said happily.

"Hello," I said, and imitating the manners of the young woman with the red cheeks, I briskly wiped my feet on the mat.

The boyfriend mutely greeted me with a nod.

"Hold on," Connie instructed me. Then, as sprightly as a child, she sprung away from the counter and disappeared into the headshop.

Left alone with the boyfriend, I nodded back at him, flashed a brief smile, and absently began to look around.

Although I could hear Vanessa and Connie talking in the other room, I couldn't completely discern their words above the music, the slow, aching procession of a single plaintive guitar.

I sensed that the boyfriend still had his eyes on me. When I ventured a glance at him, he finally spoke:

"So you're the fourth wheel tonight."

"I suppose."

He scratched under his chin with one lazy finger. Even though he continued to look at me, he didn't seem as if he had anything else to say.

I wiped my feet again before stepping forward between the motionless racks of shadowy clothes. I intended to poke my head into the backroom, not simply to say hello to Vanessa but also to rescue myself from the boyfriend's discomfiting lassitude. But Connie reappeared in the archway. She now had a white knit ski-cap atop her head. She was proudly holding aloft a broad black bag that was the length of her entire body.

"What did you get me?" she asked, referring to the paper bag in my arms.

"White zinfandel and blush."

"Two for me." She turned toward her boyfriend and nodded her head, smiling, as though I'd just impressed her.

"What about me?" he asked.

"I got pinot grigio for your aunt, a chardonnay, and a riesling. The clerk said that's sweet."

Feigning disappointment, the boyfriend said, "Nothing for a man."

Connie slapped his knee.

"There'll be nothing for you," she told him, and her tone seemed to imply a threat, as though she were coercing him to be respectful.

He apparently understood what was at stake because he sat up straight and grinned at her.

"You'd crack first," he responded. "You're worse than me."

Laughing, she smacked his knee again and said, "Shut-up."

Unmoved, he continued to look at her. "I know you," he said. "You'll crack before the cock crows."

"We'll see about that."

Shaking her head and smiling, she approached me with the long dry-cleaning bag.

"I'll trade you," she said, and as she made the exchange with me, gathering the bag of wine into her arms, I noticed that she had a dry warm scent that reminded me of slow-smoldering pine cones.

Just then, Vanessa emerged from the backroom. She was dressed in the same coat and gloves from the day before.

Depositing the wine onto her boyfriend's lap, Connie told Vanessa, "He's being horrible."

"What did he do?" Vanessa asked, looking at me.

"I don't know," I answered.

"See," the boyfriend said and grinned at me approvingly.

"Don't take his side," Connie said.

"I was—" I began to say, but Vanessa came toward me and in one quick motion, gave me a peck on the lips and grabbed the awkward dry-cleaning bag out of my hands.

"You came back," she said, echoing Connie's initial greeting to me.

"Sure," I said, confused not only about the young lovers' happy quarrel but also about the general amazement over my return.

In the process of bundling themselves up and getting prepared to close down the store, they conversed about various topics that had nothing to do with me. However, Vanessa did briefly suggest that Connie's boyfriend could learn how to behave himself properly by my example.

In the car, the young couple shared the small backseat, sitting close together in order to make room for my dry-cleaning and the wine. Meanwhile, for the entirety of the ride, Connie's head, rounded in the white knit hat, continually poked itself up between Vanessa and me, while the two of them talked about the shop. Vanessa expressed concern over a boxful of beige capris that were all brand new but defective: The buttons were too small for their holes. She thought it would be worth the effort to replace all the buttons, so she could get a better value.

"What do you think?" she asked me.

"It makes sense," I responded, even though I didn't know exactly how much work would be involved because I had only a dim idea what a capri was.

Up ahead, in the beams of the headlights, the white dots of snow appeared spontaneously out of the darkness and rushed toward our vehicle. Vanessa's row of odd statuettes was still mounted to the dashboard.

Connie expressed her giddy astonishment over how many adult women have never learned how to dress: They squeeze into outfits that are too small, hide in baggy clothes, and generally have no sense of what best flatters their body type.

She happily blathered on for a few minutes without interruption, seemingly in possession of copious examples, if necessary.

"Why walk around with your ass looking like mashed potatoes?" she asked rhetorically, just as Vanessa pulled the car up beside the curb.

When I got out of the car and followed them hurriedly across the street, where the falling snow was swept along in gusts, I realized that we weren't too far from my apartment. I was about to remark this to Vanessa, but she was no doubt already acquainted with the fact.

She took my arm as we mounted the snow covered steps. Then, upon the landing, she released me in order to unlock the front door. Connie was hugging my dry-cleaning, the bag folded over her forearms. Her boyfriend was carrying four loose bottles of wine.

"You're missing one," I said.

"The bag ripped in the car."

Inside the building, we ascended to the second floor, to a small platform with two doors. The staircase was dimly lit by one weak fixture, which housed dead insects, drying up under its glass plate. The walls were plaster, cracked here and there along the edges of the lath.

Nevertheless, despite the dreariness immediately outside of Vanessa's apartment, once she opened the door, I was greeted by the cozy warmth and the vanilla incense that pervaded her home.

The floors were dark, polished wood, with an area rug beneath the dining room table and another under the coffee table in the living room. These two rooms were distinguished by a simple change in décor. On the left was the clean delicacy of a liquor cabinet with bottles, stacked tumblers, and long-stemmed glasses; the china hutch with bone-white plates and teacups displayed behind glass doors; the oval, wooden tabletop with a glass bowl, filled with cashews, in the center. On the right side of the apartment, everything seemed deep, dark, and lush—from the couch rounding the far corner, the single easy chair with an end table beside it, the folded afghans, and the portly pillows to the wooden coffee table and a set of matching floor cabinets that were topped with black lace, an arrangement of picture frames, and various knickknacks, some of which were similar to the effigies on her dashboard. But none of these details mattered as much as the general mood of comforting relief that their totality conveyed.

We all hung up our coats in a closet beside the front door and took off our wet shoes. Connie was apparently such a regular guest that she, along with Vanessa, had her own pair of slippers keeping warm beside the radiator.

Vanessa immediately began to delegate chores to everyone. The boyfriend was in charge of setting the table, while Connie was assigned to kitchen duty, beginning with the washing of lettuce. My task was simple: Vanessa pointed me down the hall, saying, "The bathroom is that way, if you want to get changed."

On my way to the open door at the end of the hall, I glanced into another room, attracted by the darkened shape of Vanessa's bed centered against the wall. The rest of the furniture faded into shadows.

Inside the bathroom, I was once again reminded of the delicacy and care that females devote to their own bodies, for the back ledge of the bathtub contained a variety of bottles, and from a shelf suction-cupped to the glass wall of the shower door dangled a selection of brushes. A small basket of fanned and folded wash clothes and a glass bowl of colored marbles adorned the top of the toilet tank. Also, although the broad, shiny counter around the basin was mostly clear, displaying nothing more than a bar of soap and several toothbrushes brass-ringed around a plastic cup, both the vanity and the lower cabinet were packed inside with a multitude of beauty supplies. I had difficulty imagining that Vanessa used or needed so many lotions, creams, powders, and perfumes, especially since I could recall only two items stored beneath the sink in my own apartment: black shoe polish and bug spray.

With my dry-cleaning bag hooked on the shower door, I began to disrobe, and then, with the gabardine pants and rayon shirt rolled up on the counter, I leaned closer to the mirror to inspect my head wound, which bloomed stark and grotesque from my temple, disappearing beneath a swath of black hair and the inner band of my hat. I started to step back in order to get a fuller view of my body, but the sound of music from the other room startled me into motion.

I shortly left the bathroom, once again glancing beyond the threshold of Vanessa's room to the square, thick bed sitting immobile and plump, beyond the reach of the hall light, in the quiet gloom.

The table was set, and the salmon, garnished with parsley and garlic, was already in the oven. Connie and her boyfriend had absconded into the corner of the couch. A long-stemmed wineglass was upon the coffee table, while Connie, sitting with her legs crossed, balanced a second glass upon her knee. About the living room candles burned vanilla and warm.

Vanessa inspected me from the kitchen doorway. Her whole face, from her glasses to her mouth, appeared to twinkle with amusement.

"You're more daring than I first thought," she said.

"Why's that?" I asked.

"You're standing in my dining room. I don't know." She shrugged her shoulders and smiled. "It's a nice surprise." She turned back into the kitchen, saying, "I poured you some chardonnay." When she faced me again, she extended the glass toward me.

"Thank you," I said. "I like your apartment."

Looking briefly around, she quaintly shrugged again. "I keep it cozy."

She directed me to take a seat at the dining room table and then called for the happy couple to join us, saying that we could get started on the salad and corn; the fish would be done in a minute.

I sat alone for a moment with my back toward the liquor cabinet.

When Vanessa excused herself down the hall, I turned to watch her walk away, her dark clothing shaping the length of her trim and elegant body.

"Look at you," Connie said as she and her boyfriend sat down across from me. "You dress up nice."

"Thank you," I said, although I was beginning to find it strange that my smallest gestures—from standing in the dining room to wearing my own clothes—somehow provoked mild astonishment.

"You too," I added, which made Connie laugh.

Her boyfriend began scooping corn into his plate, but rather than commence eating, he rested his chin in his palm and stared blankly at the table.

Connie snapped out her napkin and laid it across her lap. She started to talk, and I couldn't determine if she were at the beginning or middle of a story, but she was saying something about a handicap ramp at the entrance to her college and how some boy had accidentally thrown his cell phone into the garbage.

Vanessa briskly passed the table, carrying a yellow plastic shopping bag and the sports jacket and overcoat, which I had left hanging in the bathroom.

"I'll put these things in the closet," she said.

"You can have your clothes back," I said.

"No way." She laughed. "It took me almost a year to sell that ugly jacket. It's yours now." Passing again, heading toward the kitchen, she said, "Eat, eat."

"I'm trying to teach him some manners," Connie said, to which her boyfriend made no response at all.

As the three of us waited at the table, I remembered my hat, and suspecting that politeness called for me to remove it, I set it upon my lap.

In Connie's story, the boy with the lost cell phone was trying to prevent a chunky, little girl from discarding a purple, slushy drink into the trash. Then the girl's mother appeared, lumbering up the handicap ramp, with a diapered infant saddled upon her broad hip.

While I was listening to Connie, trying to look interested, though her tale sounded like the pointless rambling of an excited child— Vanessa brought the steamy loaf of salmon to the table. Using a spatula, she served me the first slice and then wordlessly divvied up the rest of it. Before she took her seat beside me, she casually reached into my lap and relieved me of my hat, placing it upon a bottleneck on the cabinet behind me.

I hoped that her presence would rescue me from Connie's story; however, her boyfriend stirred himself out of his daze, just long enough to ask her, "Well, what happened?"

Apparently, the trashcan was enclosed in a metal bin, and when the cell phone was at last retrieved with the help of a custodian, it was half-submerged in a container of coleslaw. Strangely, the mother cheered in joyful vindication and demanded that the hapless boy apologize to her chunky daughter, who still held the cup of purple slush. Just as I began to suspect that this story was being told for my sake—as though I needed to be entertained—the boy's fouled cell phone began to ring, and Connie laughed at her own telling of the tale.

As the dinner progressed, I learned that Connie was a freshman taking nine credits at a junior college where I had once taught a single course many years ago at an adjunct's rate. I was familiar with the name of one of Connie's hoary professors, whose wife—long before I'd actually met the man—had begun a slow emotional deterioration, ending up in a bed-bound depression. According to the hushed and clipped gossip around the department photocopier and in the lounge, my former colleague—baffled, frustrated, and sad—had seemed to melt away in commiseration for his wife, never fully understanding the putrefaction of her nerves, that is, not until long after she'd finally hanged herself in the basement with a wire clothes hanger. Prior to her problems, she had undergone an innocent hysterectomy, and the doctors back then had failed to recognize how this surgery was connected to her psychological collapse. I always suspected that it was the old man's personal tragedy that made him a brilliant teacher, for by the time I'd met him, he was already accustomed to living without his wife, avoiding all forms of sociability, and burying his face into book after book.

"He knows everything under the sun," Connie said.

"Yes," I said, deciding to keep the details of his history to myself.

"What are you studying?" I then asked Connie.

"Physical therapy," she answered enthusiastically, but then added, "I think."

Her boyfriend worked part-time in a factory with large spools of very fine wire, but he wasn't exactly certain what the wire was used for—perhaps in medical equipment, aviation, or telecommunication. Regardless, the boyfriend's ignorance didn't seem to bother him.

Later, under the lowered lights, as we moved from the chardonnay to the zinfandel, and from the dining room table to the couch, none of the particular points of our conversation was significant to me, for I was growing more and more preoccupied by the idea of my departure, and the longer the evening stretched out, the less likely seemed the possibility of Vanessa accompanying me. I had trouble finding the appropriate moment to even hint at the subject.

Connie and her boyfriend were ensconced in their corner of the couch, her forearm resting along his thigh and her head against his shoulder.

I sat upright at the other end, with my knees butting against the coffee table.

Meanwhile, the music had stopped, and Vanessa was squatting in front of the stereo system. In the momentary silence, we heard the wind blow hard against the window. Vanessa looked back over her shoulder and smiled.

"Maybe we'll get snowbound," she said.

Once again, my ineptitude revealed itself, for rather than welcome the suggestion of being trapped together and perhaps finding some soft nook in which to snuggle the night away, I felt the urge to leave before it got too late.

"I have to go," I flatly stated.

"Oh," Vanessa said, straightening up, her smile now replaced by a mixture of subdued concern and curiosity.

"Not yet," I said quickly, bumbling. "I just—"

"Well, drink your wine." She turned back toward the stereo, and as the music resumed, she bent down to sniff one of the candles.

Connie nestled more fully into her boyfriend, so her elbow slipped from his thigh, down onto the couch cushion between his legs, and her arm rested along his crotch.

I looked away. On the end table beside me leaned a solitary picture frame, in which a plump toddler, dressed in pink, was sitting upright on a white carpet. She had a round head, and her small, dark eyes were pinched into slits between her fleshy brow and her round, dimpled cheeks. Despite the child's giddy expression, she seemed to possess an underlying vacancy, as if at any moment her eyes could become unmoored and drift about in their sockets.

"That's my angel," Vanessa said, sitting beside me on the couch.

"She looks happy," I said.

"Yeah," Vanessa said, the word seeming to slide out of her, as though she were easing herself into a place as comfortable as a warm bath. "She always knew how to cheer me up. She was a happy baby."

Rather than respond, I looked at the picture again and attempted to smile at it, as if I could appreciate Vanessa's memory of the child. Vanessa's use of the past tense explained to me what I didn't need to ask.

After a moment, she rescued me again from awkwardness by breaking the silence with a simple explanation: "She had Down's."

"What's her name?" I asked.

"Janis."

"That's a pretty name."

"That was your mom's name too," Connie said.

Vanessa nodded. She lifted my drink from the coffee table and handed it to me.

"Let's put in a movie," the boyfriend then suggested, which was the first thing he'd said that I actually liked, for talking about the dead child made me uncomfortable. He added, "We still got that rental from the other night."

Vanessa was looking at me, trying to read my expression. Without turning toward the happy couple, she said, "You guys watch it." She stood up, and holding my hand, she led me up from the couch.

"We don't have to watch it," Connie quickly stated.

"Don't be silly," Vanessa said.

The boyfriend leaned forward, forcing Connie to lift herself off of him, as he refilled their two wineglasses.

"You're spending the night?" Vanessa asked him.

"I'm already snowbound."

Escorting me toward the dining area, Vanessa spoke directly into my ear: "More like fogbound."

"I heard that," he said, and his tone suggested that he was neither offended nor amused, but, as always, simply unmoved.

Vanessa's mouth was at my ear again, her words rolling velvety and warm from her glistening lips: "The next time I'll whisper."

While we sat at the dining room table, with our own bottle of wine between us, the movie sounded in the background and the happy couple stretched themselves out together on the couch, washed in the soft blue light from the television screen, their bodies concealed beneath an afghan. Vanessa began telling me a story about how when she was a little girl her father had taken her to see the birth of a pony. Despite the gore, she had been giddy with excitement and thrilled by the beauty of the event. I nodded, watching her as she spoke, her lips shaping the words, her jaw moving, and the ligaments of her bare throat, ever so easy, stretching and relaxing with the sound of her voice. I listened somewhat dreamily—amid the shifting radiance cast by the television screen and the candlelight swaying in the undulant gloom—to some sensuous strand of Vanessa's vitality lolling me to a lower rhythm of life.

Even after her voice ceased and her mouth settled into a mildly coquettish grin, I continued to watch her.

"Tell me something personal," she said. "I just told you about my father."

"He seems like a good man," I said.

Vanessa smiled at my comment. "Now you," she persisted.

"My father ruined himself with discontent," I said. "So I don't really have any good stories about him."

"Then tell me a bad one," she said sincerely, almost as if she were asking permission to collect me in her arms and protect me.

"From his phone bill," I began, looking briefly at the wineglass, then back up to her waiting gaze, "I learned that out of the blue he called a few people he'd gone to school with or worked with, and even a couple of his old girl friends, and he just told them all that he was sorry. For what, I don't know exactly. He apologized for things most of these people had forgotten about. Also, he sold all the tools and equipment in the garage in order to pay off his credit card debt. Sometime around dawn, because he'd set his alarm clock to get up really early, he spread a bunch of cardboard on the kitchen floor, so he wouldn't make a mess, and he lay down and shot himself in the head—but it took him quite a few days to die. In the meantime, he was a crippled madman, always at the heightened pitch of terror. That's my worst story."

Vanessa reached across the table to hold my hand.

"I'm sorry I made you tell me that," she said.

"It's okay."

"You don't think I'm rude?"

"No."

"I've never met anyone without at least one sad story to tell. It's good to remember that. It keeps you more patient and kind, I think."

"You're very kind," I said.

Vanessa's fingers tightened upon my hand.

"Finish your wine, and I'll take you home." She turned in her seat to glance back into the living room. "Besides, I think they'd be happy to get some privacy."

"I feel bad about having you drive me. I can walk. It's not far," I said because I had no intention of going back to my apartment, despite my father's letter and the possibility that my mother had sent me a present in the mail. I had already checked the train schedule and planned my escape route, figuring that I could sleep throughout the night as I traveled.

"You can't walk in this weather," Vanessa said.

"I feel bad about you driving," I said again, not to mention that my apartment was in the wrong direction.

"I can't blame you for the snow. It's been a bad season."

I nodded, deciding not to refuse her offer a third time. I'd just have a longer walk. As we drank our wine, I knew that there was no way I could ask this woman to come with me. After all, we had just met, and she was still trying to get to know me. Nevertheless, for two consecutive nights, in the middle of the week in a cold December, Vanessa Somerset was the closest I'd ever come to a real relationship. That's my best story.

"We talked about too many sad things tonight," she said. "Next time, we'll focus on the positive stuff."

"Sounds like a good plan."

She swallowed the last of her wine and got to her feet. Together, we put on our shoes and coats and then bid the happy couple goodbye. Seeing Connie sprawled atop her boyfriend, I now understood that he had been right: She would crack before the cock crowed.

So Vanessa and I left her apartment, abandoning the warm gurgle of her radiators; the crisp delicacy of glass and polished wood; the thin, gray-black streams of smoke twisting out of the gutted hulls of vanilla candles; the lingering smell of garlic slices over the baked pink fish; the recumbent lovers on the couch; the senseless, exuberant chatter emitted from the television speakers; and further on, in a darker room, the high, plump mattress, the clean, white linen, and the nighttime promise of comfort and sleep.

But none of these details mattered: our descent down the dingy staircase; the rush of wintry weather at the opening of the front door; the brisk, lighthearted sound that burred from Vanessa's lips; her arm slipping through mine, upon the first snowy step; her shoulder leaning against me as we crossed the street; and her separation from me in order to clear the back window with a swipe of her forearm, before she scrambled into the car.

And then, as the engine turned and the windshield wipers arced through the snow, she spoke again: "Next time, I'll make you tell me a good story, so get prepared. Start planning ahead."

"Okay," I said.

Slowly rolling forward, the car's tires crunched over the fresh snow, while the falling flakes eased silently through the beams of the headlights.

"But you know what they say," Vanessa said. "Whatever doesn't kill us only makes us stronger."

"And the opposite?" I asked.

"What's the opposite?" She glanced at me, smiling, as though she anticipated a joke.

"Whatever doesn't sustain us only makes us weaker."

"That sounds reasonable." She laughed, perhaps because she had been ready to laugh.

As she slowed the car to a stop at a traffic light, the loose wine bottle rolled along the back floorboard, bumping against the bottom of Vanessa's seat.

"What's that?" she asked, so I reached between our seats and found the bottle, which made her as happy as if I'd just pulled a rabbit out of a hat.

"Imagine that," she said. "That's yours. You take it home."

"You can have it. I bought it for you. It's the Santa Margherita."

Looking at me, Vanessa pushed up her glasses with her thumb.

"And gnomes and elves steal her eggs," she said. "What made her believe that?"

"Superstition."

"I think you drank too much wine." She turned her head back toward the road as the car started forward again. Then nodding, she added, "Me too."

When she approached my narrow street, she announced the turn, by saying, "Left turn."

I looked out the window at the sidewalk that I'd traversed numerous times and had hoped never to traverse again, at the faces of buildings— some of their windows lighted, some dark, some decorated in the holiday spirit with Christmas trees blinking behind the panes—then at a street light reaching its arm above the road, at the falling snow passing through its dim yellow glow, and finally, at last, at the alley beside my building into which the snow coated strip faded from silver to blue into the dark.

"We're here," Vanessa said.

"Yes," I nodded, feeling a portion of my vitality shrivel up a little, just at the sight of my old home. I wanted her to drive us away.

As promptly as always, my landlord had already cleared off the sidewalk and steps.

"Guess what I just realized," Vanessa said, killing the headlights and leaning her left forearm on the steering wheel. "I've got your hat at my place."

But I was distracted by the world outside my window as a tinge of apprehension tightened my nerves.

"I'll keep it for you," she added. "I won't sell it."

Her expression became more serious, and her gloved hand slowly rose and arrested itself in the air, as if she'd intended to touch my face.

"I hate that bruise," she said. "I bet I could make it look better with a little makeup."

I tapped one finger on the glass. "It was those steps."

"Enough falling down. That's my new rule for you." She smiled at me, her raised hand now lowering to my arm. "I hope you enjoyed coming over. I'm sorry if Connie is such a chatterbox."

"She was fine."

"I'm not much of a fan of her boyfriend sleeping over all of the time. I know her mother wouldn't like it. Besides, the walls are pretty thin."

I nodded, remembering the bawdy pun of Connie cracking before the cock crowed.

Vanessa removed her hand from my arm. She turned her eyes away from my face and for a moment fixed them on the dashboard.

"Sometimes I feel like I'm intruding in my own home. I got to start making some rules. For one, nothing in the bathroom or on the couch."

"That's not too bad," I said. "I always feel like an intruder."

She brightened a little and looked at me again, as though I'd intended my comment to amuse her.

"I thought you were going to tell me that they're young and I ought to expect it," she said.

"No," I said.

"Well, you're not an intruder," she said. "You seem very connected."

Even though I nodded, I felt an urge to disabuse her of her misconception. Yet we fell silent for an instant, suspended and paused, with her eyes searching my face. She touched my arm again.

"It's kind of stupid to talk in the car," she said. "We'll freeze. It's too cold to sit here."

"I agree with you," I responded, mildly surprised by Vanessa's gentle but abrupt turn in the conversation. However, I wasn't offended. Perhaps parting with her now would have been for the best. I had a long walk ahead of me. But her next action revealed to me that what she'd implied was far different from what I'd heard: Rather than bid me goodbye for the evening, she turned off the engine and opened her door. Evidently, I'd just invited her into my apartment.

"Don't forget your wine," she said.

And while my brain suddenly scrambled in a panic to reclaim and correct the previous moment, I found myself getting out into the snow and watching Vanessa walk around the front of the car and step up onto the sidewalk, where I was standing and, as she undoubtedly assumed, waiting for her. Once again, she slipped her arm under mine, so I could escort her. I can't say which one of us shut my car door, but it shook loose a gray, slushy clump from the wheel-well, and as a sheet of snow began to creep from the roof onto the windshield, I felt Vanessa tug me gently into motion by the forearm.

"I'll protect you on the stairs," she said.

"Thank you," I replied, though my mind was now rushing ahead of us, past the mail gathered on the floor, then into the corridor with the dust smoldering on the radiators, and farther ahead, into my apartment, where unknown men on official business had recently poked and rummaged. I was afraid not only of what we might find but also of what monster might be waiting for us.

Yet I managed my keys well enough to let us into the building, and as we moved through the hall, Vanessa was saying something about not interrupting the young lovers, and then laughing about how I'd just left my clothes in her car; I was always forgetting my things. Approaching my apartment door, I was strangely eager about hurrying inside, in fear of lingering vulnerably in the hall. But Vanessa didn't seem to notice my agitation, for she was still laughing as my door swung open, and the part of my mind that had rushed ahead and feverishly searched all the rooms to make sure everything was in order, now sped back around to greet us at the door.

When I turned on the light, nothing scurried away to hide or leaped out to bludgeon me.

In fact, despite the decades that had seemed to elapse since the previous day, everything appeared unchanged.

Even so, I remained alert with apprehension. I crept forward, slowly surveying the items in the room.

Although Vanessa continued to talk happily, her voice sounded thin and meaningless. I was aware of her stepping around me and slipping off her coat, her movements as swift and nonchalant as always, yet now like a shadow skirting past my shoulder.

She was asking me something, and I wanted to turn and give her my attention, but my eyes were still searching for some sign that my home had been investigated.

"Sure," I responded because Vanessa wanted a bottle opener.

As I started toward the kitchen, I realized—calmly, almost as a matter-of-fact—that the little illuminated clock on the VCR was nearly three hours behind. Then, in the kitchen, I noticed that the teapot was on the front burner of the stove, rather than the back right one, and all the chairs were pushed in around the table.

When I returned to the main room, Vanessa was sitting on the couch, peeling the seal off of the bottle top.

"You have a guy's apartment," she said.

I set two glasses on the coffee table and handed her the opener.

Looking briefly around, she added, "It could use a female's touch."

"I've got no style," I confessed, which made her smile, as though I were flirting with her.

"Your ex- didn't leave anything behind."

"I cleaned out every trace of her," I said.

As she held the bottle in her lap and twisted the corkscrew, she kept her head up and her eyes on me, her black-rimmed glasses perched midway down her nose. The cork popped free. Still without looking at her hands, she set down the bottle opener, with the cork impaled upon it, and picked up a glass.

"You going to take off your coat?" she asked.

I turned aside and began to unfasten the buttons, conscious of her gaze. Rather than hang up my overcoat, I draped it over the back of a chair, where Vanessa had deposited her things.

Just then, I noticed that although my monitor and all my computer accessories remained on the desk against the wall, the computer itself was missing.

"Are you okay?" she asked.

"Yes," I said, my voice faltering a little. "I'm just a bit anxious about moving out of here."

"Yeah, I remember you mentioning that. Here."She held up a glass of wine. "You're not moving tonight. Try to relax," she added, sliding over to make room for me.

"I'd like to go tonight," I said, sitting down.

"Well, don't run away on me. Let me know where you go."

"Would you come with me?" I abruptly asked.

"I might visit you as long as you don't move too far away." She laughed and sipped her wine.

"Do you like your clothing store?"

"I like that it's mine. Besides, I've got to do something."

She shifted slightly, moving herself closer to me.

"I think a person needs to make a major change occasionally," I said.

"Me too."

Even though I discerned something mildly insipid and sluggish in her smile, I felt an urge to persuade her to flee with me. I suspected that she might have been using the wine—both this night and night before—to take the edge off the awkwardness. Perhaps in the future, if she felt more comfortable with me, she would drink less.

"Sometimes, a person needs to lift herself up and head in a new direction," I ventured. "Otherwise, you might find yourself caught in a rut or repeating the same mistakes over again."

"Absolutely," she said, eager to nod, her knee now bumping against my leg. "You can't live life without an occasional risk."

"That's what I'm doing now," I said, referring to my imminent flight from the city and all the horrors it contained. But, of course, she didn't know about my problems, so she most likely assumed that I was talking about our budding relationship, which, for her, was the occasional risk.

"That's good," she said.

Her knee steadily touched my thigh.

"But you always make the same mistakes," she said. "You think that you're heading in the opposite direction, but you end up in the same pile of shit that you just left behind." As I watched her nod her head in agreement with her own observation, I imagined that she was remembering some particular occurrence in her own life.

"Not always," I said.

"Well, you've got to hope."

"So, risks are bad?" I asked.

"No, you've got to take them." She slid closer and leaned against my arm.

We slipped into a moment of silence and drank our wine. While I was somewhat alarmed by Vanessa's unexpected intimacy, she simply seemed to be relaxing against me, with her head resting upon my shoulder. After a while, I thought she might fall asleep. From my seat on the couch, I began to inspect my apartment. The remote control was on top of the television, instead of beside the couch where I ordinarily kept it. Nothing else seemed disturbed, even though I suspected that all my drawers and cabinets had been opened. I wondered about the nightstand that had once carefully concealed behind its back panel, in a secret crevice, my character study and the bizarre photographs of W. McTeal exposing his hard, bare, rotund belly and his sleepy penis, in attitudes that often appeared confused or indifferent, and in pregnant postures mostly of full-frontal birth or penetrable submission, knees on the mattress and ass to the camera. But I had burned everything, so even if the investigators had discovered my hiding place, they could've scarcely guessed what it'd once housed.

Several paces from the front door, the religious poem "Footprints" was still framed upon the wall, with my father's letter safely inside.

From my seat, I quietly searched everything a second time

As Vanessa breathed, I felt her body gently press against me and then ease, press and ease, her rhythm so constant and soothing that I imagined myself—perhaps somewhere in the future, in a different city, in a different room, and on a different couch—being able to fall asleep next to her. Just as I began to wonder if she were awake, she raised her glass to her lips.

In the silence, I could hear the sounds of the building. The floor overhead creaked beneath someone's footsteps, a television played through the wall, and the wind gathering in the alley outside my window found its passage obstructed and, thus, moaned its way up the walls, into the cracks and hollows of the stonework. But these details didn't matter.

Vanessa reached forward to get the wine bottle from the coffee table and refill our glasses. She then settled against me again.

As the silence ensued, I sensed it beginning to change, so it was no longer just silence—but something like peace. And for the first time in my adult life, I had a momentary glimmer of what it meant to be ordinary. For so many years, the burden of anxiety, relentless introspection, and disengagement from the world had governed my behavior and rendered me a social cripple. But now, next to Vanessa, I saw the possibility of ease and comfort. The question, of course, was could I ever light vanilla candles on my own or take a long bath or smoke a cigar on a summer night, without feeling self-conscious, as though I were being watched and judged, with the verdict always coming back the same: *You are not permitted to enjoy simple pleasures because your solitude is your condemnation, and your own body is the source of your discomfort, and, thus, you are sentenced to loneliness and absurdity; until the day you die, your every attempt at satisfaction, never mind love, will only heap upon you further reasons for guilt and shame.*

But now, Vanessa Somerset was quietly leaning against me, without any urgency, awkwardness, or compulsion to speak. Outside, the snow could smother all the parked cars in high drifts and bury my narrow street, and the night could extend itself hour by hour. Meanwhile, Vanessa wouldn't care. She was a grown woman, comfortable with herself and responsible for her choices. Remembering her little Janis in the picture frame, I tried to imagine the trials and sorrows that Vanessa had endured. She was a strong, tender woman. Her divorce now presented itself in a new light, for the death of the child, let alone its infirmities, had surely strained the marriage. For both her and her husband, it must have been difficult to keep on loving in the wake of lost hopes and under the grim constraints of crippled life.

Sip by sip, we drank our wine, and now that my attention was no longer diverted by looking for signs of the investigation, I grew more conscious of the living creature beside me. The top of her head touched my neck, and her blonde hair gave off a faint trace of coconut. Her right arm was caught between our bodies; the fingertips of her trapped hand played gently, though almost immobile, upon my thigh. In her other hand, she held the wineglass near her chest. Her slender forearm, lightly downed, appeared out of the black sleeve; a blue vein forked upon the back of her hand and faded at the ridge of her knuckles. Below the hollow of her throat, where the low collar of her top bordered her flesh, was a thin white line, slightly sunken, in her skin, apparently an old scar.

"What's this?" I asked, and I saw my hand rising above the swell of her breast and my index finger extending toward the mark.

Vanessa briefly rubbed the spot with her thumb.

"I was canoeing with my brother in a lake. When we came back to the dock, he got out first. He took both of the oars, and for a joke, he gave the canoe a shove. I remember his foot coming up and pushing the side of the canoe. I got scared. I don't know why. I guess I thought it was a mean thing to do, because he was standing there and laughing when I started to drift away from the dock. So I jumped out."

Vanessa rubbed her chest again.

"Or I fell out. The metal point of the canoe got me here."

"Was it bad?" I asked.

"He wouldn't sit with me on the school bus either," she added, and it took me a moment to see the connection between her thoughts.

Vanessa pulled her legs up onto the couch, her bent knees hanging over the edge, the weight of her body resting more fully against me, and the fingers of her trapped hand now holding onto my thigh.

While her body appeared to shed every hint of tension and to dissolve itself further into comfort, I felt my muscles tighten, so I was sitting bolt upright and rigid, with my blood—heated by her soft proximity—starting to rush and pulse in my every extremity. Even though she must have noticed my excitement, she remained unfazed, as though she were already long acquainted with the wild palpitations of my heart.

After she finished her wine, she held the glass beneath her chin.

Looking down over her forehead, I could see her dark lashes flick once and then rest for a while. Yet, from my position above her, I wasn't certain if her eyes were shut, although I imagined that I saw a thin glimmer of one of her pupils reflected in the inner lens of her glasses.

While we sat wordlessly together, each passing moment did nothing to ease my nerves. Rather than become accustomed to her touch, rather than let go of my mind and allow myself to enjoy the intimacy, I felt my body grow more knotted and hard, as though the tenderness of this woman was causing a mass of calcified nubs to sprout up under my skin. And the more conscious I became, the less likely seemed the possibility of yielding.

She stirred, as if just to take one deeper breath, and when she resettled, with a soft exhale—I was able to feel, through the fabric of my shirt, the emerald stud of her earring pressed against my shoulder.

At last, I broke away by reaching for the wine bottle and pouring the remainder into our glasses.

"We've kicked it," she said somewhat dreamily.

"That's the last bottle."

"Perhaps that's for the best." A contented, happy tone played through her words, even when she straightened up and added, "I've got to pee."

At the moment, little did I know that these would be the last words I'd ever hear from Vanessa Somerset.

She set her glass on the coffee table, pushed herself up from the couch, and ran her hands down her thighs to smooth out her gray slacks.

I gestured to the short hall that led to the bathroom, and then I watched her as she walked away. She wobbled a little, not so much as if she were intoxicated, but as if she hadn't used her legs for a very long time. In the darkened archway, she placed her palm on the wall and glanced into my bedroom, pausing for an instant, before stepping into the bathroom. The light suddenly exposed the hall, but then the door shut.

When I stood up, I felt wobbly myself. Looking vaguely at the VCR clock that was three hours behind, I tried to calculate how many glasses of wine I'd drunk. I carried our refuse to the kitchen sink, once again noting all the minor details that were out of place, from the teapot and the chairs to the remote control. But regardless of what the investigators found and how they wanted to use it against me, nothing really mattered now.

I sat down again and waited for Vanessa to return. Leaning my head back against the couch, I closed my eyes and listened for noises: the bathroom faucet spraying water into the sink, the toilet flushing, Vanessa's body rejecting food and alcohol in a gush of regurgitation. But I heard none of these sounds.

Gliding my tongue over my teeth, I found a tiny sprig of parsley that had once adorned the salmon. With the tip of my tongue, I worked the parsley free and swallowed it.

I remembered that maybe a present from my mother was waiting for me in my mailbox; I could've surely used the money.

My mind wandered for a moment back to Vanessa as her absence stretched itself out longer than I would have expected. But let the woman take her time, I concluded.

I then tried to remember some thought I had earlier in the day, sometime before or after I'd encountered the two old men in the gym locker room—but my memory wasn't working well, and so I was left with only an inexplicable desire for potato pancakes, though I'd eaten them earlier in the day and I wasn't hungry in the least.

I couldn't hear Vanessa, but I suspected that she was sick. I didn't want to be responsible for her, and I even started to regret spending so much time with her—unless, of course, she'd end up running away with me and, thus, make all my risky efforts and tender moments worthwhile. She was a beautiful woman who treated me like a man, but I wasn't certain how to handle her.

With my eyes closed, I saw her in the aisle of her clothing store as she stepped one foot onto the little chair and reached into the rack of hanging garments, her body long and slender and clean.

Despite her dead child, her divorce, and her fifteen-year moratorium, she remained cheerful and kind, believing that the brutish events of her own life were a general experience, and because no one was free from pain, everyone was entitled to be treated with patience. Unfortunately, I had trouble ascribing to Vanessa's view of life, for most people tend to suffer their griefs by themselves, store up in their hearts a mound of private anguishes and petty gripes, and come to believe that they are alone in the world, with only their own thoughts and emotions to serve as faithful, lifelong companions. Convinced that they could never be truly known, that the complex weavings of their past experiences could never be adequately shared, and that the tiny associations that join one thought to the next in their minds could never be fully communicated—they find themselves ever disconnected, even to those they love the most. They go through life only partially revealed. Vanessa was being naïve. If heartache does anything, it grants people a special status in their own hearts, a personal perspective on reality that is shaped by a lifetime of scarring, with many of the wounds broadened and deepened by the imagination.

But maybe this was a point that Vanessa would've willingly conceded, and to which, all the same, she would have responded: Yes, be patient with people.

Eventually, I opened my eyes and got to my feet. A little groggy but still concerned, I shuffled myself around the couch and toward the darkened hall. The bathroom door was open, and the light inside was off. I briefly expected to find Vanessa sprawled out on the white, tiled floor. But even in the gloom, I could see that the room was empty. The floor mats were missing, which meant the investigators had taken more than just my computer. At that very moment, they were probably examining one of the light blue follicles under a microscope or else shaking my crumbs out of the mat. But none of this mattered.

My discovery of Vanessa's absence was quick to awaken my mind. I abruptly turned around and looked back into the living room, thinking that she—or perhaps someone else—was now behind me. I took a cautious, creeping step to the edge of the hall, ventured my head out of the shadow, and scanned the room from left to right. Unless she was in the kitchen or crouched in some corner, she wasn't there, although her coat was still draped over the chair.

Maybe, I thought, and as a new idea began to shape itself slowly in my mind, I found myself inching back the other way—but not to reexamine the barren bathroom floor or even the shower. *Maybe*, I thought again, but before the idea could expand any further, I saw its stark conclusion all at once. Vanessa Somerset lay face down, her body stretched to full length, upon my bed.

I stepped to the threshold, my every nerve piqued to attention, straining through the darkness and reaching the prone form of the woman, which didn't seem to move, even though her breaths were steady and deep. One of her black boots rested against a leg of the bed, and while the other wasn't anywhere in view, both heels of her black-stockinged feet pointed toward me. Her head, without the support of a pillow, was turned on its side, her face concealed by her hair. Her right arm clung close to her body, but the left stuck straight out across the mattress, the bedcovers pulled up around her fist, as though she'd been recently clawing at the bed.

"Vanessa," I said, and finding her unresponsive, I said it several more times, the volume of my voice gradually rising from a whisper to the clear level of speech.

Fixed in the doorway, my body riveted by a mixture of alarm and bewilderment, I stood for several moments as my eyes, perhaps the only things in motion, probed the pale darkness.

At last, as if my words had just then reached Vanessa, she stirred, and with a sigh of deep comfort, she rolled onto her back, yanking half the bedcovers over top of herself, so nothing but a solitary hand remained exposed.

"Vanessa," I said more loudly, hoping to penetrate her drunken slumber.

The mound, folded up in the covers, didn't move. On the other side of the bed, the white sheet appeared smooth and undisturbed, as though the empty space was reserved for me.

But I remained paralyzed on the spot, even though I could have easily crawled into bed beside the woman, who might have expected, or even wanted, me to join her. She had kept her clothes on, so perhaps all she was looking for was a good night's rest, and in her current condition, she lacked any reservation about sharing the bed.

However, I didn't want to presume anything, so I retreated a step, thinking that I could sleep on the couch. In a gesture that I would like to believe was an act of courtesy, I took hold of the doorknob and carefully drew the door toward myself, without a single creak or squeal from the hinges. I left it slightly ajar, so that a person's hand could hardly pass through the gap.

When I returned to the living room, my tension started to subside.

I looked down at the couch. On the bottom side of one of the cushions remained a dark-rimmed stain that no amount of scrubbing could fully remove. Remembering the boy again and all the horrors he'd suffered, I knew that the investigators wouldn't cease until they'd satisfied their hunger for justice. The morning, I suspected, would bring them to my door, unless, of course, the bits and pieces of Claudia Jones—along with all the female flesh that was strewn across my virtual path on route to the gross woman, cached together in lurid heaps in the recesses of my computer—would instantly inflame the suspicions of the authorities and bring them pounding on my door at any moment, before the cock had a chance to crow.

I might have been imagining the worst, but then again, even if I could swear my innocence with relentless fervor and constancy, the law was in the hands of fallible men and women, who in their eagerness to settle a terrible crime might contort reason and pervert evidence in order to satisfy their outraged morality, at the expense of my name and freedom. I saw that a crisis was gathering itself around me, and if the woman in my bed wasn't going to accompany me, then I was forced to leave her.

I would like to say that I simply slipped on my sports jacket and overcoat, knotted the strings of my shoes, and headed out into the wintry night—a fugitive at large but hopefully, in time, forgotten, a name blotted from the annals of humanity. I would like to say that the sleeping woman had a peaceful evening, and though mildly confused by my unexplained disappearance, she was able to resume her life and enjoy all the pleasures of friendship, fortune, and health. In fact, I would like to have never written a word, with no actions to vindicate and no conscience to relieve. But I have been honest thus far, and in the end, maybe none of this matters.

One last look around strengthened my impression that I was trespassing in another man's home, and if its appearance revealed something of the nature of the man, then his existence was probably as stark, random, and drab as were his mismatched furnishings.

Buttoning my coat up to my chin, and wary of making any sound that would disturb the sleeping woman, I crossed the room toward my desk. The top drawer—which, despite living alone, I kept ritually locked—didn't yield to my pull as I'd at first feared it would. I felt a moment of relief as I sought in my pocket for the small key on my key-ring. Yet, after I opened the drawer, I dropped all of my keys inside, having no further need of them. Suddenly dazed and unthinking, I shut the drawer again. My dread was immediate because in addition to a few items I didn't care about, the marble-covered notebook was missing; my thoughts in choppy verse had been discovered. The image of the black man's bloated body pulled up before a large desk, a coffee mug near his meaty hand, and the notebook opened beneath a lamplight, made me cringe—not so much because I could see him angling me into the corners of some standard profile, fitting the pieces of me into his readymade portrait of a madman or pervert, but more so because I felt embarrassed, as though the blunt reality of his body and the humorless severity of his mind would brook no nonsense and deem my literary labors silly.

"Goodbye," I whispered, barely above a breath, as I threw a final glance toward the short darkened hall that led to spoiled possibilities. "Goodbye."

I lifted "Footprints" from the wall and found that it fit best in one of the inner pockets of my overcoat. Clicking off the light, I entered the hall and pulled closed the locked door. I passed the gross woman's apartment, where ages ago I'd stood pining in my dishevelment and discontent, but now I didn't even raise my head. I had read her online journal, a mess of fragments and compound sentences, and I knew that she was a curt, disgruntled creature—whose father, before she was even born, had vanished in Europe or Canada to escape enlistment in a war he didn't believe in and a family he didn't want—and whose mother had wrecked herself on other men, the best of which couldn't keep his dirty boots off the coffee table nor learn to shut the bathroom door. But these sparse details in her journal appeared as fleeting moments in an otherwise bawdy fantasy world, which her fans, one in particular, adored.

Before I made it to the end of the corridor, I realized I'd made a mistake: The key to my mailbox was now in my desk drawer, so if my mother had sent me money, it was irretrievable.

Wishing I had my hat, I stepped into the cold, and pausing for a moment on the landing, I heard the heavy door latch itself closed behind me. The snow hadn't eased up at all. As I remembered something in the news, a report about the aged and the homeless freezing to death, I started down the steps. I had a long walk ahead of me, and I hoped that other people were as diligent as my landlord in shoveling the sidewalk.

And I wasn't even thinking about W. McTeal, when I thought, *No, it couldn't be.*

But a fresh set of footprints on the sidewalk ascended the stairs, loitered about the door, and since it was locked, came back down, pausing for an indeterminable moment to gaze up at the building, in the very spot where I presently stood.

No, I thought again as I peered up and down the length of the quiet street, as far as the darkness would permit me. But all was motionless beneath a layer of snow.

And looking down at my feet, I wasn't even thinking about following the tracks because I was cold and I needed to move and I had no way of telling if my intuition was correct. But from the clear impressions in the snow, I was able to conjure up the waddling figure of the strange man—and the tracks, even though I had no intention of pursuing their course, turned sharply to the left and bid my eyes to follow them into the alley beside my building.

And there he was, in all his absurdity, in the same baseball cap and in the same corduroy jacket that came down to his knees. He was directly beneath the window where the boy had used to receive petty errands from me.

Alarmed, I ducked out of view behind the corner of the building and waited a moment, feeling my heart racing in my chest. But I knew he hadn't seen me because his back was turned. I wondered if I should circle around the building or simply lower my head and walk in casual strides across the entrance of the alley.

But first, I needed to peek at him again.

Apparently, he had taken the milkcrate—upon which the gross woman had used to sit and hum and watch her clothes drying on a pair of lines—and he had placed it beneath my window.

Still with his back to me, the shadowy figure was fidgeting with something near his waist, and then pulling his hand out from the interior of his jacket, he revealed what appeared to be a hammer. Although the darkness prevented me from descrying the crooked nails driven into the top of it, I suspected it was the very tool I'd seen on his kitchen table. He almost seemed to brandish it for an instant above his head, as though it were some glorious and primitive weapon.

Then, in a gesture that was much sprightlier than I'd imagined the man capable of, he stepped up onto the milkcrate and scrambled the upper part of his body through the window. And before I could fully register what was happening, I watched his legs kick out once, with a tiny jerk, and then slither themselves through the opening. He was gone.

I stood for a second, aghast and terror-stricken.

The cold air bit at my face.

And not yet, not until I plunged my hands into my pockets and started across the opening to the alley, did I envision him walking silently through my living room. I had no idea if my apartment was new to him or if he had frequented it a thousand times before. Perhaps it was just as much his as mine. And I wasn't even thinking yet, not until I increased my pace and reached the end of the block, that a woman was sleeping in my bed. In my surprise, I had forgotten about Vanessa Somerset. I abruptly stopped in the slushy crosswalk and looked in the direction I'd just come. But there was no going back now. There was nothing I could do.

As my brain played out the various scenarios that were possibly being enacted in my old home, I continued forward. I had to gaze down at the fouled sidewalk. In some scenes, the madman realized his mistake and crept away without making a sound, but in others, the hammer fell before he knew what was beneath the covers, and still more, in other scenes, he peeled back the covers first—and since these were the worst, I tried not to allow myself to imagine them.

I walked for a long time, but eventually, not far from the bright early hours of the morning, I approached the subway that would take me to the train station. Fretful over the weather, I hoped that everything was still on schedule. I stepped off the sidewalk and began to descend the staircase. Halfway down, a crumpled pile of rags was heaped against the wall, and if not for the solitary hand that reached out of the mound and held onto the metal railing, I wouldn't have known that I was passing at least one, if not two, human beings. Yellow bulbs glowed against the wet walls, but even so, it looked darker at the bottom. Shortly, commuters would be crowding along the passage in their morning rush. *My God*, I thought, but I went down nonetheless, aching with every step.

THE END

Michael James Rizza has an MA in creative writing from Temple University in Philadelphia and a PhD in American Literature from the University of South Carolina. He has published academic articles on Don DeLillo, Milan Kundera, Harold Frederic, and Adrienne Rich. His short fiction has recently appeared in *A Clean, Well-Lighted Place*, *Switchback*, and *Curbside Splendor*. He has won various awards for his writing, including a fellowship from the New Jersey Council on the Arts and the Starcherone Prize for Innovative Fiction. His current projects are a book about the theories of Fredric Jameson, Jean Baudrillard, and Michel Foucault, and a novel tentatively titled *Domestic Men's Fiction*. He teaches at Kean University. He lives in New Jersey with his wife Robin and their son Wilder, who was named after a character in DeLillo's *White Noise*. He welcomes you to visit his website: **mjrizza.com**.

Also Available from Starcherone Books

Starcherone Books, Inc., exists to stimulate public interest in works of innovative prose fiction and nurture an understanding of the art of fiction writing by publishing, disseminating, and affording the public opportunities to hear readings of innovative works. In addition to encouraging the development of authors and their audiences, Starcherone seeks to educate the public in small press publishing and encourage the growth of other small presses. We are an independently operated imprint of Dzanc Books, with new titles distributed through Consortium Distribution and Open Road Media. Visit us online at www.starcherone.com and on Facebook. Our address for correspondence is Starcherone Books, PO Box 303, Buffalo, NY 14201. Starcherone Books is a signatory to the Book Industry Treatise on Responsible Paper Use and uses post-consumer recycled fiber paper in our books.